THE GHOST OF YOU AND ME

Part three of the Behind Blue Eyes Trilogy

By

Joanna Lambert

Visit us online at www.authorsonline.co.uk

An Authors OnLine Book

Text Copyright © Joanna Lambert 2010

Cover design by Klubovy and James Fitt ©

All rights reserved. No part of this publication may be reproduced, stored in a retrieval system, or transmitted in any form or by any means, electronic, mechanical, photocopy, recording or otherwise, without prior written permission of the copyright owner. Nor can it be circulated in any form of binding or cover other than that in which it is published and without similar condition including this condition being imposed on a subsequent purchaser.

British Library Cataloguing Publication Data.
A catalogue record for this book is available from the British Library

ISBN 978-07552-1260-6

Authors OnLine Ltd
19 The Cinques
Gamlingay, Sandy
Bedfordshire SG19 3NU
England

This book is also available in e-book format, details of which are available at
www.authorsonline.co.uk

ACKNOWLEGEMENTS

As this is the last part of the trilogy there are many to thank for their help on this writing journey.

My husband Steve for his love and support. James at Authors on Line for his patience in translating my typed script into printable format. Barbara and Judy for their friendship, kind words and encouragement. Elaine Hensel in Germany who provided much appreciated professional assistance and guidance.

And last but not least, in memory of Ziggy, my beautiful ginger cat, who loved to curl up on my desk and keep me company during my writing sessions. Sadly he recently lost his battle with diabetes. A much loved, special boy fondly remembered and sadly missed.

ABOUT THE AUTHOR

Joanna Lambert lives in a village on the outskirts of Bath with her husband, Ruby the Mini and a large collection of Radley handbags

BY THE SAME AUTHOR

When Tomorrow Comes
Love, Lies and Promises

CHARACTER LIST

MERIDAN CROSS

Willowbrook Farm
Richard Evas, Peggy Evas (1st wife) d. 1966
Mary Evas (formerly O'Farrell) m. 1967, Niall O'Farrell, her son

Little Court Manor
Laura Kendrick
Ted Williams, her gardener, Ettie Williams, her housekeeper

Saddlers End
Nelson Miller
Rowan, his eldest son, Ash, his youngest son

Village Shop
Margaret Sylvester
Rachel, her daughter

The Somerset Arms
Tom Bennett, publican, Lily Bennett, his wife

Moredon Mill
John Tucker, Mill Owner, Sylvia, his wife

Joe 'Doggie' Barker, Odd Job Man & Poacher
Reverend Farr, Vicar at All Hallows Church, Meridan Cross
Peter Merrick, the Evas's family solicitor
Dr Beckwith, the local GP

ABBOTSBRIDGE

Liam Carpenter, Architect
Melissa (Mel) his wife, Richard Evas's daughter
Mac Wilson, Senior Architect in Liam's practice

Nick Kendrick (Mel's son) married to Jenny
Jenny (formerly Taylor) his wife
Christopher, their small son

Bob Macayne, Co-owner of Taylor Macayne Construction
Andy, his son

Ella (Mel's daughter) Andy's wife, Lucy, their baby daughter
Dora Catt, Bob's Housekeeper, Bert Jessop, Bob's Gardener
Helen Baxter, Andy and Ella's Housekeeper

Jack Taylor, Co-owner of Taylor Macayne Construction
Betty, his wife
Mick, their son divorced from Nina (formerly Harrison)

Tad Benedict, Night Club and Hotel Owner
Faye, his wife
Matt, their son

Ron Harrison, Carpenter with Taylor Macayne
Elsie, his wife
Elaine Lester, eldest daughter, Barry Lester, her husband
Ryan, their small son
Nina, youngest daughter - now divorced from Mick Taylor

**Miles Anderson, Abbotsbridge Council Planning Chair, Landowner
and Wealthy Local Businessman**
Alex Nicholson, Wealthy Local Businessman

Martin Templeman & Gavin Briggs Howe
Owners of Mirage Holdings Development Company
Gracie Templeman & Selina Briggs-Howe, their wives

Bill Matthews, Bob's Solicitor
Charles Fitzallen, Taylor Macayne's solicitor
Marcus Goddard, Ella's Solicitor
Tony Rutherford, Accountant

Matt's Band - The Attitude
Baz Young, Jeff Turner, Paul Fussell, Todd Graham, Steve 'Paddy' Patrick
Sonny Scott, the Band's Manager

KINGSFORD

David Llewellyn, owner of The Bridge Hotel
Cheryl, his wife
Isobel (Issy) Llewellyn, their daughter

1972

ONE

Wednesday 2ⁿᵈ August

Mel Carpenter emerged from the changing room in Christiana's Boutique, stretched out her arms and gave a theatrical twirl.

'Well, what do you think?'

Her husband, seated on the velvet chair by the mirror smiled and nodded. 'Lovely!' He said, gazing at the blue sequinned shimmer as his wife walked towards him.

'Is that all you can say Liam?' She pulled up sharply. '*Lovely?* This is the most spectacular dress I have ever seen! Don't you realise how important Saturday is going to be for me?'

Liam Carpenter stroked his beard thoughtfully and studied his wife for a moment. He had been following her around Abbotsbridge all morning, looking for a suitable dress for the opening of the new Civic Hall, which was due to take place this coming Saturday. She was fussy, her requirements precise and she had already reduced at least three shop assistants to tears. With great effort he summoned up his most enthusiastic smile.

'Of course I do! And yes, I agree, this is *the* dress!' He clasped his hands together dramatically as he turned to Marianne O'Donnell, Christiana's owner. 'Doesn't she look simply sensational Marianne?'

Marianne nodded in silent agreement as she watched Mel move this way and that. She wanted to smile; Mel Carpenter's vanity and self-obsession completely blinded her to the fact that her husband's comments had been mocking rather than admiring.

'Look Liam, look how the beading catches the light.' Mel said swaying rhythmically before moving over to the full length mirror where she stood admiring herself and running distracted fingers through her blonde hair. 'And the little jacket is divine - I just love the high collar! This dress,' she said, hand on hip as she exposed her leg through the thigh high split on the left side of the skirt, 'is *exactly* what I've been looking for. After all, as wife of the architect who has designed the new Civic Hall - and the new shopping precinct of course - it is essential I create the right impression. I must have it.'

'How much is the dress Mel?' Liam asked, his gaze scanning her from head to foot once more.

'I hope you're not quibbling about price, Liam.'

'No.' He shook his head. 'I just asked a simple question, that's all.'

'I haven't a clue. Does it really matter anyway?' She looked at him with a condescending smile. 'I don't hear you arguing about the bills you pay to that expensive American care home your father lives in. I love this dress and I want it. Just remember I'm your wife darling - you need to keep me happy too,' she blew him a kiss and twirled again gracefully in front of the mirror before making her way back to the changing room.

Liam gave a heavy sigh and pulled his cheque book from his inside jacket pocket. 'So, what *is* the damage?' He gave Marianne a resigned look.

'Actually, I'm not sure.' Pushing her cascade of heavy black hair back off her face, she moved over to the counter where she began checking through a list of consignment notes. 'Sorry,' she looked up apologetically at Liam, 'it's part of a new delivery, only came in yesterday afternoon; I hadn't got round to pricing up yet.'

Liam waited quietly, knowing the bill he was about to be presented with would probably equal half of what he paid one of his draughtsmen in a month. But then, Mel did everything to excess; only the very best would do. There was a time when he enjoyed spending money on her; now all he saw was a spoilt woman who thought only of herself. It wasn't an attractive picture but it was too late for regrets and far too late for change. He was stuck with the monster he had spent years creating; now it was all about damage limitation.

A ripple of disturbance entered his thoughts as Marianne handed him a sliver of folded paper. 'I thought the blow would be softer this way.' she said quietly.

He took it from her, opened it up and whistled. 'As much as that?'

'I'm afraid so.'

With a sigh of acceptance he opened his cheque book, found his pen and began to write.

Later, with her purchase carefully wrapped in tissue paper and gently placed in one of Christiana's distinctive silver and turquoise carriers, Mel left, Liam trailing in her wake. En route to the nearest shoe shop for another expensive cheque book moment Marianne decided as she watched the pair of them cross the street. She may be one of my best customers, she thought, but she's a complete bitch - poor

Liam! Here was a gifted man, a brilliant architect who had designed the town's new shopping precinct and Civic Hall and all Mel could think about was herself.

The phone rang. She turned away from the window, back to the counter where she picked up the receiver. 'Christiana's, good morning.' She smiled as she recognised the voice. 'Good morning! Yes, yes the new consignment has arrived. Came in yesterday. I've sorted out a few really lovely styles for you to see that I think she'll love. Two fifteen? Yes, that's fine, I'll see you then.'

Replacing the receiver she pushed through the beaded curtain into the rear of the shop where she kept her stock. Sheathed in protective polythene, the three dresses hung on the end of one of the tubular rails. Marianne studied them for a moment then went back to the main rail. Her fingers skimmed through the garments hanging there. Finding what she was looking for she checked the size and added it to the other selected items, a sly smile on her face.

Later that afternoon she watched a very satisfied customer walk away from her shop carrying his purchase. Of course she had not influenced his decision in any way; the only act she had been guilty of was adding the dress to the collection for his approval. But she knew as soon as he saw it he would say he just had to have it. Oh they were going to notice Mel Carpenter on Saturday night, all right; but the main reason would be because of the dress her customer had just purchased not the one Mel was going to be wearing.

Saturday 5th August

'Smile please!'

'Do we have to do this Mick?' Issy Llewellyn gave an impatient groan and frowned.

'You know Mick always records special events for posterity, Issy.' Jenny Kendrick laughed, tossing her dark hair off her face. 'Strike a pose everyone!' She tilted her head back and gave a radiant smile, her arm sneaking around her husband Nick's waist.

'Can you squeeze up a bit?' Mick peered into the view finder. 'No, this isn't working.' He waved an impatient hand at them all. 'Can I have the men standing and the ladies kneeling in front of them please?'

'But I'll crease my dress!' Issy complained as she sank to the carpet.

'You'll be fine, pull your skirt out like this.' Ella Macayne, whose house they had gathered in for drinks, knelt down beside Issy, adjusting her green satin dress, 'Stop fussing Issy,' she whispered, 'this is only going to take a second.'

'Not the way Mick takes photos!' Issy argued. 'We could be here for hours!'

Mick pushed his sandy hair out of his eyes and looked at them all through his viewfinder again. He had to admit that this gathering of twenty-somethings made a glamorous group. There was Jenny, his small dark haired sister and her tall blond husband Nick Kendrick who taught at one of the most prestigious private schools in Abbotsbridge. Next to her Ella, Nick's sister and Jenny's partner in their recruitment business, One Plus One. She was the one who had it all; looks, brains and a good head for business. He remembered the first time he had met her all those years ago when she had been at school with Jenny and Issy. She had her sights on becoming a vet then. But, after being reunited with her long-time absent mother Mel and moving to Abbotsbridge, those dreams had been well and truly turned on their head. For social climbing Mel had a totally different future planned for Ella; one which eventually saw her married to Andy Macayne, son of Mick's father's business partner Bob. Andy, who had inherited his Italian mother's dark good looks, was a work shy waster with an eye for a pretty face. Sadly marriage to Ella, a real beauty with her mass of long, dark curling hair and soft grey eyes had in no way curbed his reputation as a womaniser. After all, hadn't he been the one responsible for Mick's own break up with his wife Nina? There had been a lot of anger at the time, but Mick realised with hindsight that marrying Andy's ex-girlfriend had been a very big mistake; a moment of pure unrivalled madness on his part. It had taken a long time for things to settle down, but now they had and everyone had moved on. He was in another relationship and with the arrival of their baby Lucy, Ella and Andy's marriage appeared calmer and more stable.

'Come on Mick! What are you doing? My legs are going to sleep!' The complaining voice woke him from his daydream. He smiled at the last member of the group; blonde, blue eyed Issy Llewellyn; his little Welsh dragon. Function Manager for her parents' hotel and cordon bleu cook - her beef stroganoff was the stuff of legend. After years of suffering Issy's sharp tongue, and being made to feel like an idiot, his divorce from Nina had unexpectedly thrown them together. Of course, it was still on a very platonic footing, but he was working hard to change all that. However, with someone as feisty as Issy there wasn't much option other than to take things at a steady pace. He'd known her long enough to realise the softly, softly approach was definitely the way to go if he was hoping to get results.

Smiling he gave the thumbs up.

'Thank God, I'm in agony!' Issy grumbled.

'Right! Nearly there! Hold it!' Mick set the camera to automatic and rushed across the room to join the group. The six individuals stood there in a frozen tableau; the flash exploded over them and with a collective sigh they all relaxed.

'Right, everyone take a seat and I'll get some drinks organised.' Ella disappeared into the kitchen, returning moments later with a tray of glasses and a bottle of champagne.

'We should really have invited Liam.' Andy said as he took the bottle from her and despatched the cork with healthy pop. 'After all it is his evening.'

'Don't forget your father and Jack Taylor.' Ella replied, watching her husband pour the golden foaming liquid into each of the glasses. 'Liam may have designed the Civic Hall, but they built it. Anyway, if Liam had been invited here, think about it, he'd have had my mother in tow.'

'Ah yes, your mother,' Andy looked at her thoughtfully as he handed out glasses to the others, 'perhaps not then.'

'Definitely not.' Ella smiled. 'We don't want to sour the evening before it starts do we?' She raised her glass. 'Come on everyone - to absent friends - Bob, Jack and my stepfather Liam Carpenter - a wonderful man and a remarkable talent!'

TWO

Saturday 5th August

Nina Taylor sat in front of her dressing table mirror putting the finishing touches to her make up. She gazed at her reflection in the glass as she applied her lipstick. Blotting her mouth with tissue she smiled; she was really looking forward to the coming evening. Re-capping the lipstick she returned it to her make up bag then stopped for a moment to gaze at the third finger of her left hand and the three carat diamond which sparkled there. 'Mrs Alex Nicholson,' she said out loud. 'I'm going to be Mrs Alex Nicholson!'

Nina had worked for Alex since January. She had emerged from her divorce from Mick minus the monthly allowance she had insisted she had been entitled to. Instead there had been a generous one off payment, but unfortunately it meant in order to sustain the lifestyle she enjoyed and had grown used to, she would have to work. Landing the job as Alex Nicholson's Personal Assistant had been real coup, not only for the money he was paying, but also because being single he required someone to accompany him on both work and social functions. Nina was ambitious. Growing up on the Parkway Council Estate she had seen first hand how young women, including her older sister Elaine, ended up pregnant, married and then tied into a wretched hand to mouth existence that saw them old before their time. She was determined this was not going to happen to her. Her plan was to find a rich husband and escape her working class roots. With her long thick tawny hair, green eyes with a slightly exotic slant and a body which someone once told her was made for sex, she was fully aware that men found her attractive. And it was a weapon she did not hesitate to use in her mission to fulfil her dream.

Nina had set her sights on Andy Macayne with his Mediterranean good looks and a father who owned half of Abbotsbridge. Andy came with a reputation where women were concerned; his girlfriends, mostly nice middle class girls from good homes, never stayed long. But Nina became the exception, holding his interest with what he described as the most amazing sex he'd ever had. A year later she was dreaming of engagement rings and wedding bells, confident she had him just where she wanted him   But when Ella Kendrick arrived in town, astonishingly

Andy's interests took a sudden shift in another direction. Eventually Nina decided to cut her losses and turned her attention to Mick Taylor. Mick, who was Andy's close friend, had always been infatuated with her. He asked her out and proposed in less than a fortnight. She accepted, hoping it would be just the thing to bring Andy running back to her. When it didn't, there seemed little option other than to marry Mick. For a while she convinced herself that second best wasn't that bad. But she soon discovered she had married a committed workaholic who was rarely at home. By that time Andy was married to Ella and had found out monogamy wasn't all it was cracked up to be either. Discovering their joint unhappiness, it was only natural that everything should start up again. And that's how it had been for the last three years. An on-off relationship driven by sex which had come to a dramatic halt after Andy's father Bob had discovered them together. But where one door closed another opened. Whoever would have thought Alex had any thoughts about her at all other than work. His proposal had come completely out of the blue and she had grabbed it with both hands. Mid forties, with film star looks, Alex was divorced and loaded. This really was the big prize and there was no way she was going to lose it. She could quite easily leave Andy behind now. In the time they were together, if there was one thing she had discovered, it was that when push came to shove he would always look after number one. 'Now I have something better.' she said to her reflection in the mirror, 'something wonderful and fantastic!'

The sound of a car engine in the street below drew her from the dressing table to the window. Alex's grey Aston Martin pulled up outside. She watched him as he got out, leaned back into the car and pulled out a large silver and turquoise box. She smiled realising that it must be the special dress he'd bought her for the opening of the Civic Hall this evening. Giving herself a final spray of perfume and loosening the top of her silk robe to reveal a tempting glimpse of cleavage, she ran to the door to let him in.

'Well, another excellent job.' Dressed in dinner jacket and bow tie, local entrepreneur Tad Benedict, gazed around the foyer of the new Civic Hall, an approving smile on his handsome features.

'Are you referring to the efforts of Citizen Macayne?' At his side, dressed in her favourite turquoise, his petite wife Faye laughed as she handed their coats to the cloakroom attendant.

'No, I'm talking about Liam Carpenter.' Tad gazed down at her, his light brown eyes alight with admiration. 'Bob Macayne may have built this lot but the Master Genius created it from his imagination.'

Tad gazed around the foyer where they were both standing. Liam was an exceptional architect and he had very high regard for someone who could design such a beautiful building - from the pale wood of the doors and floors, giving it a Scandinavian feel to the main feature wall at the far end in beige brick with the council's crest set in its centre. They moved on, down circular steps with polished chrome railings which led into the main function room, at the far end of which stood a large stage set with heavy gold velvet curtains. A five piece band was playing and around the edge of the room tables of six had been set with starched white tablecloths and gleaming cutlery, each table centre set with a small bowl of bright flowers.

'This must have cost a packet.' Tad whistled, taking two glasses of wine from a black uniformed waiter, his gaze drawn to the rich pale wood of the high ceiling which continued the Nordic theme.

Faye laughed as she took one of the glasses from him. 'Miles Anderson did well out of the deal I expect.'

'What do you mean?' Tad frowned as they found their table and sat down.

'Rumour has it he made sure Bob got the building contract for this and of course then Liam automatically got the design.'

'I thought it was done with sealed bids.'

'So it may have been, but remember Bob only clinched the deal because he built the multi-storey for nothing. Generous of him don't you think?'

'What are you driving at Faye?'

'No one does something for nothing Tad.' Faye leaned her auburn head closer to her husband and whispered. 'Especially Bob. You can bet Miles must have got something in return.'

Noticing a shimmering movement to his left, Tad looked towards the top of the steps where Mel Carpenter, dressed in a brilliant blue full length beaded evening dress with matching jacket now stood appraising the room and its occupants, Liam and Bob on either side of her.

'Well, you do surprise me.' He said. 'I thought at least Liam was straight.'

'Oh Liam is totally honest.' Faye said watching as Bob and Mel left Liam behind and came onto the dance floor together. 'That's half his trouble. He doesn't see what's going on under his nose,' she gave Bob and Mel a hard stare, 'or behind his back.'

'Are you saying they're having...'

Faye nodded. 'So rumour has it.'

'You and your rumours!' Tad laughed.

'They were seen checking out of the Ragbourne Grove Hotel together a few weeks ago. At the time Liam was in the States visiting his father.'

'Could have been a pure coincidence.' Tad said watching as they danced past.

'Cozying up to each other with an overnight bag each?' She laughed. 'I don't think so!'

The Aston Martin glided easily into the car park, coming to rest in its gentle, thoroughbred way in a convenient parking space. Nina sighed and smiled. It was going to be a great evening, she just knew it. Beside her, Alex Nicholson looked at her in the darkness and ran a hand slowly down her thigh; she could see he was smiling.

Her little pre-arrival diversion to say thank you for the dress had confirmed to her once again how good Alex was in bed. Of course she knew he was crazy about her; even more so since they had slept together. But she knew she could never feel the same about him. Only Andy had ever managed to make her feel that way and on reflection she decided, perhaps that was dangerous, for it had weakened her and made her dependent. No, it was far safer to lock passion away, to be happy instead with a man you liked who was capable of good sex - and had money, of course. And there was so much of that wasn't there? Far more than the Macaynes. Oh yes, things really were going well for her.

Alex leaned over and kissed her. He smelt of expensive cologne. All of a sudden she felt a great need to be alone with him again, making love to him, teasing him with her body, making him gasp and moan and beg for more. For whilst he might be in command of what happened in the boardroom, she knew almost certainly that she held the power in the bedroom. Having such dominance was highly addictive and like any other addict she knew when she was with Alex she would always be looking for a regular fix.

'Do we really have to be here tonight?' She whispered, as her hand stroked his face. 'You know I just want to be alone with you.'

He broke away and looked at her seriously. 'I know darling. But tonight is important; there are people I need to meet with.' He straightened his bow tie in the rear view mirror. 'It's only a few hours then you can have my undivided attention, I promise.' He kissed her lingeringly on the lips. 'Now come along or we'll be late.'

Sitting at their table waiting for drinks to arrive, Ella, Issy and Jenny were busy watching the activity on the dance floor.

'Where *did* your mother get that dress?' Issy asked, watching as Mel came onto the dance floor on the arm of Bob Macayne.

'Christiana's I think.' Ella said, frowning as her mother gave an expert twirl and clasped herself dramatically to Bob, revealing a large expanse of thigh in the process.

'Marianne should be banned from selling things like that to women over forty.' Issy said with a slow shake of her head. 'Showing all that flesh is totally disgusting.'

'You're right Iz.' Jenny's quiet little voice chirped up. 'She looks like an emaciated turkey covered in blue tinfoil.'

'Jenny!' Issy turned in mock horror at her outburst and they all began to laugh.

Mel, tight in Bob's embrace, moved across the floor to a fox-trot, unaware of the disparaging comments flying around at the other end of the room. As they manoeuvred between the other dancers she smiled. To be expertly guided around the dance floor in this way was ecstasy, she became as one with Bob; it was a blending of bodies, their rhythm fluid, almost sexual. She lost all sense of direction on occasions like this, relying on him for guidance. Closing her eyes for a moment she let her feet do all the work, following his in a familiar pattern of movement as they whisked around. Then without warning they came to a jarring halt and she opened her eyes to find they were standing near the carpeted steps up to the foyer. She looked up at Bob; saw the cold anger in his face.

'What the hell is she doing here?'

Mel followed his gaze to where a solitary woman was taking off her wrap, her long, thick tawny hair gleaming in the light. Mel watched her, her eyes drawn to the silk wrap as it slipped from her shoulders and then to the garment she was wearing beneath it. A deep blue jacket and matching dress with a split up the left thigh.

Unaware of such close scrutiny, Nina Taylor turned and began to walk towards them, looking down into the depths of her evening bag as she tucked the cloakroom ticket safely inside it.

'Oh my God, she's wearing exactly the same dress as me!' Mel put her hand to her face as she looked first at herself and then at the approaching Nina. 'Why didn't Marianne tell me there was more than one? And what made her sell it to *her* of all people?'

Nina snapped her small silver evening bag shut. She had reached the top of the stairs which led down to the main function room with its tables set around the room. Alex had told her they were going to be seated with the Briggs-Howes and the Templemans, two of Abbotsbridge's wealthiest couples. She was pleased with the arrangements, eager to get to know this new clique of people who once she was married to Alex, would become her friends . However, as she looked up she unexpectedly found her path blocked by Bob Macayne and Mel Carpenter.

'It's invitations only tonight.' Bob loomed over her. After breaking up her affair with his son last March he had issued her with a warning that in future he didn't want to see her anywhere Andy was likely to be. The consequences of disobeying him, he had told her, would be that her father and brother-in-law would be kicked straight out of his employment and into the dole queue. Six months had gone by without a sign of her, but now here she was, on one of the most important nights of his career, eyeing him with an arrogant smirk on her face.

'I have an invitation.' She said haughtily, pulling the card from her bag and handing it to him.

Bob gave it a cursory glance. 'I don't see your name anywhere.'

'I'm the *and partner.*'

'Is there a problem Bob?' Alex appeared by her side his eyes dancing with amusement at the sight of both women wearing the same dress. 'Nina is my guest. In fact slightly more than a guest. Darling show them.' He turned a benevolent smile in her direction. Nina held out her left hand obligingly.

'We are engaged to be married.'

Bob handed the card back to him, looking as if he was about to explode.

Alex pocketed the card and let his gaze scan Mel for a moment.

'Good evening Mrs Carpenter.' He gave her a formal bow.

'Lovely to see you Alex.' She gave him one of her most charming smiles.

'Good to see you both too.' He said, his gaze suddenly drawn to the other side of the room. 'Ah, I think I see Martin and Gracie Templeman. Sorry,' he turned back to Bob and Mel, 'can't stop; maybe we can catch you both later.' And giving Bob's shoulder a friendly squeeze he quickly ushered a smiling Nina away.

Mel watched them cross the floor to a warm greeting of handshakes and hugs. She looked at Bob, her expression venomous. 'Engaged, to that tart? Has he lost his mind?'

'He's got to be joking!' Mick Taylor looked at the other occupants of the table with total disbelief as the applause rang around the room. The evening had started with Miles and Alex both on stage to welcome everyone. Then Bob, Jack and Liam were asked to join them on stage where they were presented with sets of Waterford Crystal as a mark of appreciation from the Council for the designing and building the Webster Centre as the Civic Hall was to be called. They both left the stage to a rapturous applause and as this died away, Alex Nicholson stood triumphantly in the spotlight, Nina by his side. His arm around her, he announced their engagement. The applause returned, this time polite and muted.

'And now Ladies and Gentlemen,' Miles swooped on the microphone immediately, aware of the atmosphere and eager to move things on. 'What better way to continue the evening than to ask Alex and his bride-to-be to re-start the dancing.' He gave them a warm smile and nodded to the band, which immediately launched into *Hello Young Lovers*.

Out on the dance floor Nina Taylor in a blur of blue sparkle whirled around in the tight embrace of Alex Nicholson, leading the other dancers who had followed them onto the floor. Nina was in her element, putting on a show for everyone, loving the attention she was getting. Ballroom dancing lessons had certainly paid off.

'What does she think she looks like?' Mick said with a sigh and a shake of his head.

'She's wearing my mother's dress too, God I bet that's gone down well.' Nick began to laugh.

Only Andy remained silent, unable to take his eyes off her. He hadn't seen her since the day his father had discovered them in bed together at the Highcrest Motel and in the time since then his mind had partially obliterated the memory of her. He had looked back on that period of his life as something he had fallen into accidentally because of circumstances with Ella; thought of it as behind him - over. But now watching the twist and turn of her body against Alex's and the way the dress moulded itself to her curves, he realised it was anything but. As he sat there totally under her spell he knew that he no longer cared about Ella or his marriage. Nina was the woman he wanted. The one he should have hung on to right from the start, whether his father agreed or not. And as he watched her he decided that marrying Alex Nicholson was the last thing he was going to let her do.

'Wow! Just look at Fred and Ginger out there.'

A laughing Issy, returning from the cloakroom with Ella and Jenny, sat herself down beside Mick.

'You missed the news.' Nick said with a smile. 'They've just announced their engagement.'

'What?' The three girls chorused together.

'She didn't waste much time did she?' Jenny shook her head.

'Well she's really hit the jackpot this time.' Issy said watching them thoughtfully. 'Alex Nicholson is absolutely loaded!'

'And look at that dress!' Ella settled herself next to Andy with a laugh. 'I bet that's really ruined my mother's evening!'

'One can only hope.' Nick replied. 'Right, who's for another drink?' He asked, pausing to count the nods around the table before signalling to a passing waiter.

'Same again everyone? OK, vodka and tonics for the two girls there, three pints for us men and an orange for Jen.'

'Orange?' Mick looked at his sister in amazement as the waiter left. 'What's the matter with you? You never drink orange.'

'Yes she did.' Issy looked at Jenny. 'All the time when she was pregnant.'

'Pregnant?' Echoed Mick.

'You're not!' Ella said disbelievingly.

'I might be.' A radiant smile broke over Jenny's face as she looked up adoringly at Nick.

'Actually we were going to invite you all round for supper in the week and break the news officially,' Nick said, squeezing Jenny's hand, 'but, it looks as though we've been rumbled. Yes, Jen's pregnant, baby number two should be with us in February.'

Nina was not in the best of moods. The evening had started well, with plenty of champagne, which relaxed her, enabling her to flirt with Alex's developer friends Gavin Briggs-Howe and Martin Templeman. She also found blonde outgoing Gracie Templeman and the quieter more sophisticated brunette Selina Briggs-Howe pleasant enough company. They were in business together, importing wine and delicatessen from Europe and she listened with interest to the stories of their trips together. They were off to Bruges next month to buy Belgian chocolate and even suggested she might like to accompany them. Alex seemed pleased with her. She was good for business, his lucky mascot he called her as he wheeled her around the floor. And the dress! It had been worth every penny Alex had spent on it, and she reflected, it looked much better on her than an old leg of mutton like Mel Carpenter.

However, towards the end of the evening discussion around the table had centred on business and the men had disappeared, summoned by Miles Anderson to some private room in the building. Nina felt put out; to talk business at the table was one thing, but to abandon their partners at a public function like this was annoying. Left to chat with Gracie and Selina, everything had been fine for a while, but then the husbands of a couple of their friends arrived at the table and whisked them both away for a dance. Left alone she began to feel bored and irritable. She caught sight of Mick dancing by, partnering Issy Llewellyn. They looked so happy, laughing together, Mick watching Issy with his adoring Labrador eyes.   Two pathetic losers she thought, tipping back her wine; two nothings in the great plan of things; a discarded husband and a frosty virgin. Two jokes.

Deep in conversation as they moved around the room, they eventually passed close to her table again. Mick whispered something to Issy who turned for a moment to look in her direction. Then they were gone, both laughing as they danced away. Empty glass in hand, Nina watched them, infuriated at the thought that they might have been laughing at her. She made a note to add them to her unfinished business list.

The band was playing the last waltz, the end of the evening imminent.

'Well, what a night!' Faye looked over Tad's shoulder as they moved slowly around the floor. 'Who ever would have thought that Nina Taylor would turn up wearing the same dress as Mel! And engaged to Alex! Whatever can he be thinking of?'

'Not to mention all that closeted secrecy in the River Room with Miles and his cronies.' Tad added. 'What's that all about eh?'

'Some new project I expect. And Jenny and Nick having another baby in February. I'm so pleased.' Faye gave a happy sigh. 'That little boy of hers is adorable; I hope the next one's a girl.'

Tad surveyed the room with a satisfied smile. 'Yep! All in all, I'd say we've had quite an interesting evening wouldn't you?'

'I agree.' Faye smiled up at him. 'And there was me thinking it would be one of those deadly boring nights out with the great and good falling all over themselves to pat each other on the back. Hey, it looks as if the ex-Mrs Taylor's ready for bed.' She nodded to the far corner where Nina was stifling a yawn as she sat beside Gracie and Selina who were deep in conversation.

The band finished to loud applause and Tad and Faye returned to their table; Faye finding her bag and retrieving the cloakroom tickets from her purse. Saying goodnight to people they knew, they collected their coats and made their way towards the main doors

The night was clear, the moon a bright sphere sharing an inky black sky filled with stars as they joined groups of people drifting out to the car park. Doors banged, headlights flared, engines fired and one by one cars nosed out of the car park.

Nick and Jenny emerged through the main doors with Mick and Issy and stood chatting for a moment before they moved off in different directions to their cars.

Shortly afterwards Mel appeared, a little unsteady on her feet as Liam helped her down the steps.

'Looks like he's got his hands full there.' Tad said with a laugh as he unlocked his BMW. 'Come on, let's go home.'

With his arm around Issy's shoulder, Mick walked slowly through the car park, making for his Triumph Stag. They had left the others behind, waiting for Bob, Jack and Andy who had been pulled into the meeting with Miles. Mick was glad he hadn't been included. Right now all he wanted was to be alone with Issy.

He looked down at her, aware that all the difficulties there had been in extracting himself from Nina had been made so much easier by her support and fighting spirit. He knew without her he would have fallen apart. As they reached the car he gave her a hug and gently kissed the top of her blonde head.

'What was all that about?' She stopped, looking up at him in astonishment.

'For being one of the most amazing women I know.'

'Mick Taylor, is that the drink talking or just your usual nonsense?' The tone was one he was used to from her, but tonight there was a teasing look in her eyes as she spoke.

'Neither, just shut up and kiss me.' He said, grabbing her by the shoulders in a moment of totally uncharacteristic rashness. As he bent his head towards hers, a familiar voice intruded into the moment and broke the spell.

'Hello! Can you help?'

'Oh God!' Mick groaned at the sound of the voice behind him. Letting go of Issy he swung around to see Nina coming quickly towards them, her dress reflecting off the car park lighting.

As she reached them, slightly out of breath, she looked relieved.

'Oh Mick, I'm so glad it's you.' She said in a breathless girlish voice, totally ignoring Issy. 'I'm totally lost. I can't find Alex's car. I've looked everywhere.'

'It's over there, by the river.' Mick pointed out into the darkness. 'It's the only Aston Martin in the car park, can't see how you missed it.'

'An Aston Martin, is that what it is?' She said innocently. 'I had no idea.' She gave a silly giggle. 'I just knew it was big and expensive.'

Not taking his eyes off her, Mick felt in his pocket for his keys, eager to get Issy and himself into the car. He knew Nina too well; behind the silly scatterbrain act he sensed something else lurking. Something unpleasant.

'Well,' Nina gave a syrupy smile and moved closer, placing herself between them. Turning her back on Issy, she ran a finger down one of the lapels of Mick's jacket. 'How's life treating you then Mick? Do you miss me?'

'Like a hole in the head.' He pushed her hand away.

'Oh you're just saying that for the benefit of Fanny Craddock here.' She turned, giving Issy a quick glance.

'No I'm not Nina, I'm deadly serious. My life has never been better.'

She sighed and moved away. 'Oh well...' Taking a few steps forward she stopped and turned.

'Mick.'

'What now?' He gave an impatient sigh

'Would you walk me to the car? Only it's not very well lit over by the river and it's a bit scary.'

Mick sighed and closed his eyes. Anything, he thought, anything to get rid of her. Finding his keys he tossed them to Issy. 'Here, I won't be a minute.'

'You're not serious.' Issy, who had remained silent during the whole of Mick's conversation with Nina suddenly found her voice.

'I'll only be a moment. You get in the car; lock the doors if it makes you feel safer. I won't be long.'

Issy's face twisted with annoyance as she opened the car door and slid into the passenger seat. Mick gave her an uneasy smile, knowing Nina had well and truly ruined his evening.

'Come on!' He said sharply. 'This way.'

Nina took a few tentative steps forward before the girly voice surfaced again. 'It's very dark Mick, I'm a bit scared of tripping up.'

'Don't give me that Nina; you came down here as sure footed as Nijinsky just now. Just get going!'

He gave her a slight nudge in the back and she moved off, still complaining.

'But Mick, I can't really see properly, please, just hold my hand would you?'

'No.'

'I think you're being very unreasonable...oooh!'

Mick saw her fall against a parked car and stood watching her while she righted herself.

'Ouch! Ooh I can't put any weight on my foot. I think I've broken my ankle.'

'Don't be ridiculous!'

'Well you feel it then if you don't believe me!'

Irritably he squatted by her and felt her ankle, he heard her wince.

'Ooh, you know I'd quite forgotten what a gentle touch you had.' She said breathlessly.

'You've probably twisted it that's all.' He said abruptly, getting to his feet. 'Come on I haven't all night.' As he took her by the arm to help her along, he felt her arm snake around his waist.

'That's better.' She tucked her head into his shoulder and they moved slowly off together.

Soon the Alex's car was visible and he let go of her arm.

'Thank you, you're so kind Mick.' She simpered. 'That's what I remember about you most, you know; your kindness.'

'Just go Nina!'

'Oh Mick, you're being so hard, but admit it, you do still have a soft spot for me, don't you?'

Mick gave an irritable sigh.

'I think you do you know and I'll prove it to you.'

Injured ankle quite forgotten she threw her arms around his neck and kissed him on the mouth. He tore her hands away and pushed her from him, but not before the headlights of a passing car had caught them. He groaned. Issy would have seen everything.

He stood there, watching her as she walked away laughing, knowing any thought of a romantic ending to the evening with Issy was now almost certainly in ruins.

Nina walked purposefully towards the Aston Martin laughing quietly to herself. What a wonderful night it had been. First she'd been queen of the evening, enjoying centre stage with the announcement of her engagement. Then an enjoyable evening with Alex and his friends followed by the opportunity to settle a few scores. First Bob and Mel and now her ex-husband and his girlfriend. How fortunate that she had been right behind them when she came out of the Civic Hall. Of course it wasn't that difficult to cause upset between a couple like Mick and Issy. He was so gullible and she was so distrustful - those two character traits alone would make for massive fireworks. She laughed, knowing almost certainly that Issy would be giving him hell now.

She checked her watch. 1.20. She wondered whether Alex had finished the meeting which had pulled several business men into one of the small conference rooms with Miles Anderson. Miles, she knew, was a man who made things happen. He was extremely wealthy, had great influence on the council but he also had powerful friends all over the area. The fact that he specifically wanted to see Alex meant something very important was being discussed.

The car stood alone in a corner of the car park by the perimeter wall of the Civic Hall. She found the keys Alex had given her and inserted them into the door. As she swung it open she was aware of someone behind her. She spun round, stifling a scream.

'You!'

'Yes me!' Issy replied. 'I think it's about time you and I had a little chat.'

'What could we possibly have to chat about? Mick? And the fact that he's a complete pushover?' She gave a smug grin. 'As you no doubt saw he's still can't resist me.'

'What I saw,' Issy replied coolly, 'was pathetic. You just can't leave it can you Nina? You can't bear to think that someone doesn't want you any more, so you try to spoil things. First Ella, now me.'

'Ella?' Nina screwed up her face in a frown. 'I really don't know what you're talking about.'

'Oh don't come the innocent with me. Alex might be able to dress you up and pass you off as a lady, but there are some things clothes and perfume will never disguise.'

'Meaning?'

'Being the unscrupulous tart you are.'

'Don't you dare speak to me like that, I happen to love Alex!'

'Really?'

'Yes, I do. He's been the only person in my life since Mick divorced me.'

'Obviously maths wasn't your strong point at school. I make it two.'

'Pardon?'

'Andy Macayne.'

'What are you talking about?'

'March this year when Ella was rushed to Abbotsbridge Maternity.' Issy continued. 'The baby was on the way but no one could find Andy. No one had a clue where he had gone. But Bob found him didn't he? He was at the Highcrest Motel in bed with you.'

'Where did that rubbish come from?' Nina gave a derisory snort.

'From Bob actually.'

'He told you?' There was wariness in her eyes.

'Indirectly. You see I was sent down to the waiting room to let them know Lucy had been born and I just happened to walk in on a conversation I shouldn't really have heard.'

'So, I was screwing Andy.' Nina smiled unpleasantly, 'Big deal! I'm going to marry Alex now. Even bigger deal! Funny old world isn't it?' All at once the smile faded and her eyes narrowed. 'A word of warning.' She said leaning forward, bringing her face close to Issy's. 'I should think twice if I were you about going to Alex with this. The damage you might do to me, should he ever decide to believe you, is nothing in comparison to what you will do to Ella. She's your best friend, someone you care about a lot, right? So the last thing you want to do is hurt her and break up that happy little family of hers. If I were you I'd just forget we ever had this conversation. That way no one gets hurt and we can all live happily ever after. Ah here's Alex.' She said, her hard expression changing to a pleasant smile. 'The meeting must be over. Just like our conversation.' With an arrogant smirk she swung herself easily into the passenger seat, closing the door behind her as the tall figure of Alex Nicholson appeared out of the darkness. He climbed in behind the wheel and started the engine. Alone under the car park floodlights, feeling angry and frustrated, Issy watched the Aston Martin leave.

Mick appeared almost immediately out of the darkness, his face full of worry. 'I've been looking for you everywhere. Are you OK?'

She nodded bleakly as he came and put his arms around her.

'I thought you'd left me.'

'No.' Issy said calmly. 'I wanted a word, with *her*.' She nodded in the direction of the departing car. 'Not that it did much good!' She added bitterly. 'There's no justice in the world Mick, there really isn't!'

THREE

Sunday 6th August

Nina opened her eyes and stared upwards, watching as strands of sunlight filtered through the pale curtains and danced along the ceiling. With a smile she reached out for Alex, frowning as she found the bed empty. She rolled over and sat up, watching as the door opened and he appeared carrying a small tray of coffee.

'I intercepted Alice, got her to rustle us up some coffee before breakfast.' He said, setting the elegant silver tray down beside the bed.

She watched him as he poured out two cups of hot black coffee and added cream and sugar.

'Here we are.' He handed her one, smiling.

'Thank you.' She took it from him and watched as he hung up his dressing gown and joined her back in bed.

'So,' He said, picking up his cup, 'today's the big day! Lunch at Leigh Manor to toast one million pounds worth of investment in the North Somerset Marina project.'

'One million pounds, that's an absolute fortune Alex.'

'It is, but it will work miracles. The coast between Watchet and Minehead has been crying out for something like this for some time. Good old Miles, he's got a great nose for these sorts of business opportunities. Take the Manor, overgrown and derelict; he bought it for a song and has completely transformed it.'

'Yes, I'm really looking forward to seeing it. They say it's very beautiful.'

'It is. Miles has spent a fortune on it; nothing else to spend his money on.' He gave her an indulgent smile. 'Unlike me.'

'But you inherited Hope House and all the wonderful things in it from your father. Everything was here from the start. That's why you can afford to spoil me.' She laughed and then all at once her face became serious. 'Did you really mean what you said last night?'

'What was that? Something in my sleep?' He was teasing her now. 'A man can't be held to anything he says when he's not properly conscious you know.'

'No, when we were making love. You said I was the most wonderful woman you had ever met and that you were going to shower me with gifts.'

'Did I?' He made a silly face. 'Really?'

'Yes, you did.' She gave him a playful punch. 'You said you would buy me a red Ferrari. And a villa for us in Spain so we could jet away and relax when we felt like it. And that you wanted to make me a partner in the business.

'What a memory for detail you have! Did I really say all that?'

'Yes, and do you know which of those I like best?'

'Well,' he put his cup down and looked at her thoughtfully, 'I would say the Ferrari. No one else in Abbotsbridge has one, not a red one anyway.'

'Mmm,' she smiled at him, 'I do like that, but not as much as I like being a partner in your company. Everyone will know I'm not just a wife. I shall be a business woman, just like Ella Macayne.' She lifted her head haughtily. 'Better, actually.'

'Ella where's my blue shirt?'

'In the airing cupboard.'

'I've already looked there, I can't see it.'

Ella made a face and got up from the dressing table. She was about to put on her make up when Andy's call for help drew her out of the bedroom and onto the landing.

As she approached the large walk in airing cupboard he emerged, holding a pale blue shirt on a hanger.

'It's OK, I've found it...'

Ella gave a sigh, went back to the dressing table and set about applying a light foundation to her face.

'I don't know what I'd do without you,' Andy grinned, struggling with the button at the neck of the shirt as he joined her, 'there's a lot to be said for having a wife at home.'

'Yes, well enjoy it while you can,' Ella said, watching him in the mirror, 'it won't be for much longer.'

'Meaning?' His fingers, hovered at his cuff buttons as he stood there, frowning at her.

'Meaning,' she swung round to look across at him, 'that I'm needed back at the Agency. Jenny's pregnant again and Joan's family have decided to share the responsibility of their elderly mother. They don't want her going in a home. So Joan will be taking three months off, which means I shall be going back part time to cover.'

'And when is all this happening?'

'I don't know, in three or four week's time.'

'I see.' He stared at the floor thoughtfully and then raised his head to look at her, anger in his face. 'Did it not cross your mind that you should consult me first?'

'No, not at all.' Ella shook her head, her eyes full of innocent amazement. 'This house has run very well without me before, and no doubt it will again.' She smiled. 'Helen's coming back.'

'Well, it seems you've taken care of everything!' There was a sarcastic edge to his voice. 'I thought you'd finished with work Ella! You told me you'd finished with work!'

'No, I said I was taking a break Andy.' She gave an exasperated sigh as she slid grey-blue shadow across her lids. 'Look I was intending to take a year off, but circumstances have changed. I'm going to do eighteen hours a week, that's all. I'll start when Joan leaves, then by the time she comes back Jenny will be ready to go on maternity leave. Half time, is that really so bad? It still leaves plenty of time for me to be with Lucy.'

'Ella,' He said, moving over to the open wardrobe and choosing a tie from the selection hanging there. 'I'm sure if you can get someone to run this house then you could just as easily get someone to run the business so you could stay home with Lucy.'

'No Andy, I couldn't.' She lay down her eye shadow brush and looked at him. 'It's my business we're talking about and giving a stranger the kind of control I have defeats the object. I might just as well sell up.'

He sat down on the bed only feet away from her, frowning with concentration as his fingers worked the tie into a knot. When he had finished he looked up. 'Well why don't you? It might just be the right solution.'

'Who for Andy? Me? Or a husband who obviously wants to keep his wife at home, dependent on him.'

'Don't be stupid!' He stood up and walked over to the mirror, watching her in its reflection as he straightened the tie and turned down his shirt collar. 'Since when have you been dependent on anyone? You're not exactly strapped for cash are you? And you've a large inheritance kicking in next year; you'll have more money than you know what to do with then - and even less reason to work.'

'On the contrary,' she shook her head, 'I think I'll have even more reason. I need to feel there's more to life than shopping and lunching. I don't want to end up like my mother; I want to feel I've accomplished something. My business fulfils that need; I would have thought that being in business yourself you would have understood that!'

He watched her pick up her lipstick and cover her mouth in frosty pink.

'Well I'm sorry Ella I don't. I'd kill for the chance to give up work. I hate it! I think women are bloody lucky staying at home. Anyway a mother's place is with her children.'

'Children?' She turned, pushing the cover back on her lipstick with a loud click. 'We have one child Andy.'

'At the moment.' He replied. 'But I was thinking maybe we ought to try for another baby in the New Year. Lucy needs a brother or sister. It wouldn't be fair to rear her as an only child. With a baby to see to and a toddler running round, you won't have time for life in the office.' He tilted his head, all benevolence. 'Take my advice Ella, sell now. I can find you a buyer who'll give you an excellent price. Then you'll be able to relax and enjoy your domestic bliss.'

She turned to face the mirror again, picking up a string of creamy pearls from the dressing table and securing them around her neck, wishing for all the world they were a rope she could throttle him with. As she clipped on matching pearl earrings she caught him watching her, a small, self-satisfied smile on his face.

'I'm sorry my darling,' he said with a shake of his head, 'but you have to face facts. Men are in charge, women stay home. It's the way of the world.'

With a final look at her reflection, Ella got up and walked over to where he stood pulling on his jacket. Her hands reached up automatically to smooth out his lapels.

'Maybe that happens in your world Andy,' she whispered as she brushed her lips briefly against his cheek, 'but it certainly doesn't in mine.'

'Look at this; it was brilliant sunshine half an hour ago.' Miles Anderson, glass in hand, waved disappointedly towards the rain lacing the French windows. In conversation with Liam, he was in his drawing room where his lunch guests had assembled and were now busy chatting.

'Never mind,' the ever optimistic Liam responded, 'it'll take more than a shower to dampen our spirits. You know the more I think about the Somerset Marina project, the more excited I become. I was involved in a similar project in Australia many years ago. It's going to completely revolutionise the north Somerset coast and it will bring in much needed jobs. If there are any dissenting voices, take it from me, they won't be there for long.'

'I agree,' Miles nodded, 'and I think we ought to take a trip out there as soon as possible. I really need you to get a feel for the place before you put your ideas on paper.'

'That's a good idea - give my secretary a call, I'm sure she'll be able to find a suitable slot in my diary.'

'Gentlemen!' Mel slid between the two men with a smile. 'Not talking boring old shop I hope?'

'Now would we do such a thing Mel!' Miles looked at Liam in mock horror. 'Actually, I was just telling Liam how lucky he is to have such a glamorous wife. You always look so stunning. Look at you today, darling; emerald green is definitely your colour.'

'You really are an old flatterer Miles!' Mel's blue eyes flashed appreciatively as she brought her glass to her lips.

Miles laughed and checked his watch. 'If you'll both excuse me I'll just see how the lunch preparations are going. Catch up with you later Liam.' He patted his shoulder.

'Good old Miles, ever the diplomat.' Mel said as she watched him leave the room. 'Now what have you two really been discussing?'

'Oh,' Liam looked at her and smiled, 'I was just getting enthusiastic about the project that was all. Remember Kookaburra Falls?'

'I do, it was a wonderful job. I detest boats, but when I saw that marina I actually wished we owned one.'

Liam laughed. 'Only so you could tell everyone your husband had designed the place.'

'Of course.' Mellowed by the wine, Mel looped her arm affectionately in his.

Across the room Ella sat with Issy and Betty Taylor on a semi circular cream couch. Directly opposite them were Gracie Templeman and Selina Briggs-Howe, heads drawn together discussing holiday plans for Grenada, while Ella, Issy and Betty were talking about Jenny's new baby, their partners drawn into a huddle by the window with Bob Macayne.

'It was such a wonderful surprise!' Betty was saying, her plump face glowing with pleasure, 'I know Christopher will just love having a new brother or sister.'

'Yes,' Ella agreed, laughing, 'when I took Lucy round to Jen's today he was so excited. He kept leaning into the carry cot trying to kiss her.'

Betty patted Ella's knee affectionately. 'I bet that's got you thinking hasn't it? About number two? Oh dear, what am I saying? Being a little bit premature aren't I?'

'Just a bit.' Ella smiled, remembering her earlier conversation with Andy. 'Perhaps in a year or two though.'

'It's a beautiful house isn't it? Very traditional.' Issy said gazing admiringly around the room with its heavy oil paintings and huge inglenook fireplace fronted by a massive fresh flower display. 'Can't say I'd go much on the dusting though.'

'If you lived here that would be your last consideration,' Ella replied, her eyes on the door, which had just opened, 'Miles has a full time staff to look after this place. You could just relax and play lady of the manor.'

'And here's someone who'll soon be doing just that!' Betty said with a knowing look at both girls. There was no mistaking the anger in the older woman's voice as Miles entered the room followed by Alex Nicholson. Nina at his side, wearing a yellow silk dress, gazed at all those assembled in the room, then followed Alex, deliberately ignoring everyone she passed with the exception of the Templemans and the Briggs-Howes.

'Stuck up little madam!' Whispered Betty, as Miles poured the two new arrivals a drink, 'I knew she'd be awful when she married Mick. But now she's going to be completely insufferable.'

Ella watched as Nina wheeled out the charm, lacing arms with Miles, leaning towards him provocatively as she tilted the glass to her lips.

Pouring himself another drink, Miles guided his new arrivals back towards the couches. 'Perhaps you'd like to join the ladies, Nina.' He indicated a space at the side of Selina and Gracie.

'Actually, I'm not much for women's chat Miles.' Nina replied. 'I'm far more interested in what you men are up to. After all Alex is going to give me a partnership in Nicholson's once we're married. So I need to learn all I can about business from the experts. After you,' she waved a hand towards the window where Bob and the others were congregated. Miles shook his head irritably and shot Alex an icy look.

'Nina.' Alex's hand came firmly down on her shoulder, 'I really think maybe on this occasion...'

Miles' housekeeper Madeline saved the day, walking into the room to announce lunch was ready.

'Ladies and gentlemen,' Miles gave a sigh of relief and smiled. 'Lunch is served. Perhaps you would be good enough to follow me through to the dining room.'

'Well, that was wonderful Miles.' Jack Taylor dabbed his mouth with his serviette as the meal reached its conclusion and coffee was poured. 'My compliments to Anton, he's done it again.'

'Thank you Jack.' Miles nodded appreciatively before taking his attention back to the occupants of his lunch table. He had spent the last hour and a half watching everyone with great interest. He had arranged the seating carefully; this was to be an enjoyable event and he wanted to minimise the discomfort amongst this group of people, a few of whom were setting aside personal differences to sit together for lunch. Tactically he had completely split couples up, seating everyone in a man-woman sequence around the long mahogany table. He saw the key problem areas as Mel and Nina, both the kind of women who attracted trouble. Mel for her outspokenness and Nina for her inability to leave men alone. He was still trying to understand what kind of madness had possessed his good friend to choose a woman like her for his wife. It had the potential for big trouble and suddenly made him realise that being gay perhaps made life far less complicated.

And so they had taken their places and the meal had opened up some interesting situations. Ella Macayne, who he had previously only known by sight, proved to be an intelligent, entertaining young woman with a lot of business savvy, while her blonde friend Issy talked mostly about expanding her business into mobile catering for company lunches and office functions.

As he listened to his immediate dinner companions chatting, his eyes had been watching the rest of the guests. Bob was now keen to purchase wine from Gracie and Selina, Martin knew Betty Taylor's cousin and Mel and Alex appeared to be getting on extremely well. Then he noticed Andy, his gaze continually straying across the table, first to Alex then to Nina.

Miles had deliberately seated Nina at the end of the table, deciding she couldn't get into much trouble with two men as harmless as Gavin and Liam, but the whole thing appeared to have backfired. Gavin and Liam seemed to be engrossed in conversation across the table to the exclusion of Nina, and it was evident from her expression and the way she was constantly lifting her glass for a refill from

Hendricks his butler, that things were not to her liking. Andy Macayne too had seemed to have been broodingly quiet; equally bored it seemed by the company of Selina and Gracie. As he watched these two human beings totally isolated and removed from the general enjoyment and conversation which was going on at the table, he saw Andy look up suddenly, his eyes meeting Nina's only for the briefest of seconds, but there was no mistaking the ripple which passed between them. Aware of the rumours he had heard about the two of them, it made him feel even more concerned for his old friend.

Coffee over, he suggested a walk in the gardens. The rain had cleared away, the sun returning its warmth to the late afternoon. Paths were drying, puddles shrinking. The small group trouped behind him as he showed them the vast sweep of lawns with their statues and fountains. Beyond this was the kitchen garden swathed in its high walls of red brick and the stables where his beautiful thoroughbred horses were kept. And last but not least, the maze, where he assured them, everyone got lost.

Faced with high walls of sculpted green, the majority seemed eager to take up the challenge and disappeared into its depth. He called after them that he was returning to the house and if he didn't see them all back there in half an hour he would send someone to rescue them. With an amused grin at Liam and the Taylors, who had decided to opt out and head for the sun terrace, he walked back to the house, to say a proper thanks to his chef Anton for the wonderful lunch he had prepared.

Andy felt as if he had been wandering aimlessly in the maze for ever. He had deliberately lost Ella, still angry with her for her pig-headed insistence on returning to work - a conversation that had resumed in the car and caused him to become so wound up that he nearly collided with a tractor in the narrow country lanes on their way here. After that everything had got progressively worse. At lunch, to his relief, he had been placed away from her, between Gracie Templeman and Selina Briggs-Howe, but then found to his horror that they were two more career women, talking of nothing but their deli import business and 'hops' across the Channel.

He heaved a sigh of relief when Miles had suggested a tour of the gardens to help walk their lunch off. Here was an ideal opportunity to get away completely, to be by himself after such a traumatic few hours. He had let Ella go on ahead of him with the others and once in the maze had taken a left to her right, ensuring he could at last be by himself. And now he wandered aimlessly; haunted by depressing thoughts. Had he ever really loved her? Of course not. He had been obsessed with the desire to have her, to deprive Matt Benedict of the one woman he wanted. That had coincided with his father putting a strangle hold on him to settle down, dangling a Directorship in his new house building company as the irresistible carrot. And what better choice than Ella? As his father had said, she was an attractive, well educated girl, just the right type to run his home, play hostess to his business colleagues and eventually become mother to his children. He was keen to please his father and even keener to have half of Taylor Macayne Residential for himself. And so he had eventually agreed to his father's demands, thinking maybe he was talking sense, that it was time for a change.

He remembered the night he proposed, sitting on the quayside in that small Cornish fishing village among the lobster pots. How vulnerable she looked, so young and naive. Seeing her then he thought he would have no trouble moulding her into the wife he wanted. It had seemed so easy at the time to plan for his future. To have it all. Of course, looking back he knew exactly where he had gone wrong, it was helping her open her business that had started them on the journey to where they were now. How could he have been so stupid to think it was just a hobby she would tire of once their first child came along? Instead it had become her obsession; she lived and breathed One Plus One. It was everything to her, even more perhaps than him. And it was the power and independence it had given that had changed her. Turned her into the wilful wife who always had to have the last word. The wife he now felt he was gradually losing control over.

The green walls suddenly widened into a small open area, a miniature fountain set in its middle circled by two smooth stone benches. He sat himself down on one, still deep in thought. So what was left? Sex? No, even that had become mechanical and infrequent. Since Lucy's birth his expectations that things would get back to the way they were in Italy had not been fulfilled. And now Nina had entered the picture again, disrupting his life, filling his mind with madness.

Immersed in his thoughts, the unexpected touch on his shoulder took him by surprise. Looking up he saw her standing over him. He closed his eyes and opened them again, sure he was dreaming.

'I'm lost.' Nina said settling herself next to him, very real and smelling of expensive perfume. 'Looks as if you are too.'

'In more ways than one.' He said with a heavy sigh.

'Not wife problems again Andy.'

'It's no joke.'

'Want to talk about it?'

'No! Talking about it just makes me feel angrier.' He looked at her with his familiar little boy smile. 'Anyway I wouldn't want to bore you.'

'You'd never do that Andy.' She smiled graciously. 'I can truly say hand on heart that if anything, life with you was never ever dull.'

'Thank you. Such compliments, I'm flattered.' He returned her smile, noticing the way she was playing with the solitaire on her finger.

'Nina, about Alex.' He blurted out suddenly. 'You can't marry him, you know.'

'Why not?'

'Because he's nearly old enough to be your father. Besides...'

'What Andy?' She frowned, confused.

'I could give you much more than he could.'

'Don't be silly!' She laughed. 'He's far richer than you are.'

'Who's talking about money?' He said leaning towards her, his hand reaching for her breast through the silk of her dress, his mouth seeking hers.

Alex had no idea how he had become parted from Nina, only that she had disappeared around a corner and was now nowhere to be seen. He had wandered around calling her name, but there had been no response. He was sure she was playing with him and walked carefully along, peering around each bend just in case she was hiding there, waiting to jump out on him. He stood quietly for a moment, to see whether it was possible to identify any part of the garden or house from where he was standing. A building or a tree would give him some idea of whether he was going in the right direction, but all he could see was hedge and blue sky.

A few paces on he came to a cross roads. He halted at the edge of the small clearing, looking left, right and straight on, wondering which direction to choose. As he shook his head, totally confused he was aware of the murmur of voices close by. He cocked his head and listened. A man and a woman, talking softly together, through the hedge to the left of where he was standing. He closed his eyes and smiled. Company at last. Maybe a team effort would get them all back to the entrance.

He moved forward, turning to his immediate left. Suddenly the voices stopped and he was aware only of birdsong and the rays of the sun warming his back. Whoever had been there had obviously now moved off. Quickening his pace, he hurried after them; they couldn't be that far away surely? He rounded the bend in the evergreen corridor and stopped abruptly, stunned by the scene he had come upon. Two people on a bench entwined in each others arms. So it was all true after all. Those rumours he had overheard concerning the break up of her first marriage. The ones he had put down to empty, spiteful gossip. They really had been involved with each other. But what was worse was the fact that despite her engagement to him, it still appeared to be going on. The pain of the betrayal he was witnessing was intense, almost as bad as when his first wife Sylvie had walked out. So, Nina was only interested in his money after all, just as the rest had been; and he had been foolish enough to think despite her love of material things, she was different.

Standing there trying to suppress his rage, his initial instinct was to march right up to them and pull them apart - create a scene and finish with her there and then. But that was too easy and besides it would only set off a chain reaction, dragging other innocent parties into the affair and causing an embarrassing incident for his old friend and host Miles. No, he concluded as he turned and walked away, Nina was worthy of a far more spectacular punishment for her duplicity and he knew exactly what that was going to be.

'I think we've been along here already. Look at this small hole here,' Issy pointed to a break in the hedge, 'I'm sure I've seen this before.'

'We can't have Iz. Or can we?' Mick shook his head and grinned. 'Do you think we should start shouting for help?'

'No, come on, I refuse to give up.' She checked her watch. 'We've still got ten minutes; let's see what's around the next bend.' Grabbing his hand she hurried him along the green corridor. As they turned the corner they came face to face with Ella sitting alone on an ornate stone bench tucked into a small recess in the wall of the maze.

'Don't tell me, you're lost too!' Mick said joining Issy as she down beside her.

'I'm afraid so.' She looked at both of them. 'You haven't seen Andy have you? I went off ahead and when I turned round he'd disappeared.'

They both shook their heads.

'We thought about calling for help, but I don't think anyone will be about until the half hour is up.' Issy laughed. I think Miles means to teach us all a lesson.'

'Well,' Ella got to her feet, 'I've been thinking about the route while I've been here and I remember when we entered the maze the sun was in front of us. So theoretically if we keep it at our backs we have a good chance of finding our way out.'

'Sounds plausible.' Mick looked at Issy and they both nodded.

'Right!' Ella said, clambering up onto the bench. 'Let's find the direction of the sun then we can be off. Oh my God!' She stood there silently for a moment peering over the top of the hedge.

'Ella, what is it?' Issy asked impatiently, tugging at her skirt. 'What can you see?'

'Something I wish I hadn't.' She said stepping down, holding her hand to her face.

Frowning, Issy climbed onto the seat and parted the evergreen. Below, the maze widened out into a small circle and there was an empty stone bench similar to the one she was standing on. 'There's no one there,' she said, jumping down, 'Ella what was it?'

'They were together on the bench.' Ella stared at her. 'He had her in his arms. He was kissing her and his hands were everywhere. It was disgusting!'

Issy looked at Mick, who gave a puzzled shrug. 'Who did you see Ella? Was it...' she hesitated for a moment. 'It wasn't Andy was it?'

'Andy?' Ella replied, shaking her head. 'No. Right family though; it was his father - with my mother.'

Wednesday 9th August

With Lucy in her arms Ella watched from the bedroom window as Andy's Mercedes pulled away from outside the house. Why was he being so difficult? What was it that made him so determined she should not return to work? Surely part time wasn't going to disrupt their lives that much. Helen, who had been working for the agency on short term assignments, was more than happy to return and take up responsibility for Lucy and the house. It wasn't as if she was leaving her home and daughter in the hands of a complete stranger. Attempts to discuss the problem, however, had now collapsed and their lives together had become frustrated and bad tempered bouts of arguing. There had been threats too, silly statements that burst out in moments of temper, about what he could and would do if she didn't change her mind. Things she knew he didn't really mean; the bottom line was that having her at home, Andy had lapsed into an old fashioned view of marriage, probably aided and abetted by his father. He saw himself as the main provider and now things were about to change she knew he probably felt threatened.

'Silly, silly Daddy!' She said pressing her face against Lucy's as the car finally disappeared out into the road. 'Why doesn't he understand that Mummy has a life too?'

He had now moved himself into one of the spare rooms declaring he would not be back until she saw things his way. Andy, she concluded, despite his arguments to the contrary, was nothing but a closet chauvinist. Ah well, once Helen returned he was bound to calm down. He liked her and enjoyed her cooking. Give him a month and he'll be admitting I was right she told herself confidently.

'Come along darling,' she said, stroking the dark downy hair of her daughter, 'let's sort you out some breakfast.'

She carried Lucy down the stairs into the kitchen, placing her carefully in her high chair before moving to the cupboard to find a jar of baby food. The trouble with Andy, she thought as she removed the lid, is that sometimes he's just a little too much like his father.

Bob. Standing at the kitchen window spooning the contents of the jar into a small dish, she stopped for a moment as Bob Macayne's image floated into view, locked in a tight embrace with her mother on the bench in Miles' garden. The circle of grey-black hair, the coal black eyes, the cleft in his chin; every inch the plunderer. Is that what attracted her mother to him she wondered? The excitement of being with a hard, dangerous man who always took what he wanted. But did he really want her? Surely not. After all, who in their right mind would want a spoilt, vain creature like her mother? There must be some hidden agenda, she decided, but exactly what at this moment in time she could not imagine.

Andy's first port of call that morning was to see Charles Fitzallyn, the company's solicitor, to update himself on the progress of the contracts on the last plot at the Bracken Down site. He sat for nearly an hour in Charles' cluttered office and listened without much attention to the current state of play as he had every last minute legal detail explained to him. He smiled and nodded, feigning interest. How could he possibly concentrate on work, when his home life was in such turmoil and all he could think about day and night was Nina?

That night he lay in bed, unable to sleep, running the scene over and over in his mind yet again. He just couldn't help himself, she was so close. How could anyone resist those magnificent breasts and the softness of her lips. Everything had been going so well too, she was certainly up for it; it was just like old times. Unfortunately, when he started talking about seeing her again - about buying a place so they could meet in private - she suddenly sat bolt upright, her eyes cold and hard.

'Do you know,' she said quietly, 'listening to you talking like that, I realise all I am to you is a good lay isn't it Andy? Someone to have a bit of fun with when life isn't as good as it could be at home. Sad isn't it that once all I ever wanted was to be with you; to be your wife. But you're only ever interested in what you can't have. Twice we've been involved since your marriage to Ella and now here we are again! You want me back. But this time it's because I'm involved with someone else. And you think that by just laying on the old charm I'll play your games with you. But that's not going to happen. I have Alex now so I don't need to be your other woman any more!'

No woman had ever spoken to him like that, he realised as he watched her walk away. He knew then it was no use - he had to have her and if the only way to do that was to be free and single, there was only one answer to the problem. He'd just have to rid himself of a wife he now knew he no longer wanted.

Sunday 27th August

Ella opened the door to a smiling Nick.
'Hello, I've left Jen and Christopher in the car. Are you ready?'
'Yes, I am, but Andy's disappeared. Come in a minute.'
'Well, where is he?' Nick asked, stepping into the hall.
'I have no idea.' She shrugged. 'Picks his moment doesn't he?'
'Have you two been rowing?'
'Nick, life with Andy is just one long row at the moment.' Ella replied shutting the door. 'I tiptoe round him, but it still makes no difference, he's always spoiling for a fight. Anything and everything has the potential to set him off these days.'
'Did you have a row this morning?'
'Strangely no, he was missing when I woke up. I phoned Bob; he thought he might have gone out to one of the sites, but I've tried all the office numbers he gave me and there's no reply.' She raised her hand in frustration. 'He's simply disappeared.'
'So what are you going to do? We can't have Lucy's christening without her father being present but having said that, Reverend Farr can't hold up proceedings indefinitely.'
Ella checked her watch and gave an impatient sigh.
'I'll go up and get Lucy. We'll give him ten minutes. If he's not back by then, we'll just have to leave without him.'
'Nina will you *please* let me in.'

Nina stood in the communal hallway, watching Andy silhouetted against the frosted glass of the front door, his fingers pushing up the horizontal flap of the letter box, dark eyes peering in at her.

'Andy please go away, there's nothing more to discuss. I meant everything I said to you last Sunday.'

'I know you did, and you've every right to be angry.' He said calmly. 'But I've come to tell you I'm different now, Nina. I've spent all week thinking about what you said to me. You were right you know, I was a spoilt brat, always wanting what was just out of reach; never satisfied. But I realise now what was really right for me was there all along but I was too blind to see it. You Nina, you were always the one and I let you down. I should have stood up to my father and I didn't. But I'm determined to change. To be the man you want.'

'Sorry Andy,' she looked calmly at the letterbox, 'I don't believe you. Anyway I have the man I want - Alex and I'm going to marry him next week.'

'No you're not, I won't let you. You belong to me.'

'No I don't.'

'Nina. I'm going to divorce Ella....'

'Is that right?' Nina laughed. 'Told your father have you? Give me a break Andy!'

'It's none of his business...'

'Ooh, brave words.' She was laughing again, enjoying the pantomime which was going on outside the front door.

'It's true, I *will* do it!' He protested indignantly. 'Please, Nina, let me in, we have to talk about our future.'

'We have no future Andy. Go away.'

'If you don't come out I'm going to stay here until you do!' He shouted back.

'Damn!' Nina looked at her watch, realising that Alex was due to collect her in just under an hour's time for Sunday lunch at his Golf Club. The last thing she wanted was him finding Andy camped on her doorstep shouting words of undying love through the letter box. She thought for a moment, wondering what she could do to get rid of him. Then it came to her.

'Shame about your husband not being able to get here today.' Reverend Farr smiled indulgently at Ella. 'The christening service lost something without him I fear.'

'Yes, it did.' She smiled lamely, glad that Bob Macayne had come forward to support her story that he had unfortunately been called away to an emergency.

In a corner of the terrace at Little Court where the celebratory christening tea was taking place, Mel sat with Bob. 'So where exactly has Andy got to?' She asked, sipping her glass of champagne.

'I have no idea.' Bob said grimly. 'I made up that story about him being called away to an emergency to help Ella out. Don't worry, I'll give him a damn good talking to when I do find him. How dare he do this! It's totally unacceptable!'

Mel turned her attention across the room, watching her father as he circled the large table, helping himself to food. She thought he looked pale and had lost weight. She ought to try and have another little chat with him. She remembered the visit to Willowbrook with Bob last year when she had hoped to try to persuade him to sell Fox Cottage and part of Hundred Acre Wood to Bob. It was an essential area of land for access for the currently very much under wraps luxury holiday complex Miles had planned with Martin and Gavin's company Mirage Holdings. With this in his possession Bob would make huge financial gains when he eventually sold it to Miles. And once the ink had dried on the contract she could finalise her plans to leave Liam and get her new life with Bob underway. Unfortunately what she thought of as a fairly simple task had gone badly wrong, ending with her and her father having heated exchanges.

Now as he crossed over to one of the empty tables and sat down she considered her strategy. Scanning the scattering of guests she found her stepmother Mary deep in conversation with Laura Kendrick and Liam. Perhaps it was time to seize the moment.

'Bob.' She looked at him and then nodded towards her father. 'Shall I?'

'All right,' He said quietly. 'But for heaven's sake think before you speak this time.'

'I will,' she turned and smiled at him as she got to her feet, 'I promise.'

'Dad,' she hovered uncertainly in front of the table, her hand on the back of one of the chairs, 'Mind if I sit down with you for a minute?'

'It's a free country.' He shrugged indifferently. 'I suppose you've come to talk to me about…what did you call it? Ah yes, scaling down.'

'No, actually I came to apologise.' Her face softened as she pulled out the chair and sat down. 'I was very presumptuous; after all it's your land - your home, not mine.'

'Nice of you to realise that.' He said bluntly, resting his half eaten sandwich on the plate as he studied her quietly. 'You look as if you're planning to stay. Was there anything else?'

'Yes,' she hesitated, 'I also wanted to tell you that I'm concerned. Those tablets, the small blue ones. The ones you took the day we visited the farm. They're heart pills aren't they? And that means you're not well.' She shook her head. 'Dad, why didn't you say?'

'It's nothing to worry about. As long as I keep taking them I'll be fine.' He said stubbornly.

'But farming's a hard life and even with the tablets, you're not getting any younger are you? If you continue like this goodness knows what might happen!'

He picked up his sandwich again and took a bite, nodding gently as he chewed slowly. 'Very clever Mel,' he said as he finished it and picked up another sandwich, 'very clever.'

'What are you talking about?'

'The new caring approach.' Richard continued with his sandwich. 'Well let me tell you something.' He leant across the table with a pleasant smile. 'It won't work. You'll just have be patient and wait for your inheritance.'

'*My* inheritance?'

'Well you're my daughter aren't you? I've no one else to leave it to.'

Mel gave a self satisfied smile, barely able to conceal her elation. The old goat had actually said the words she had been waiting to hear. Willowbrook was indeed going to be hers.

He stopped to look at her for a moment. 'Got big plans for it have you, when I'm gone?'

'Oh yes, Dad,' she smiled. 'As a matter of fact I have.'

'I hope you're not planning to do anything to upset the locals Mel.' His voice intruded gruffly into her thoughts.

'Upset the locals? Me? Of course not Dad.'

Andy peered through the letter box wondering where Nina had taken herself off to. One moment she had been standing in the hall arguing with him, the next she had disappeared up the stairs and out of sight.

'Nina!' He called out but there was no reply, just an eerie silence in the long narrow hallway.

He got to his feet and grabbing the brass knocker began banging it against the highly polished surface of the front door. Suddenly he heard the sound of a window being opened. He looked up and saw her head appear over the ledge above him.

'Nina! Come back down here at once!'

'Or what Andy?'

'I'll kick the door down.'

'Not a good move. The caretaker's large, bad-tempered and lives in the basement flat.'

'Look, all I want is for us to talk.' He said irritably, his patience exhausted. 'Is that so unreasonable?'

'I guess not.' She said after a moment's thought, 'OK, but I want you to stand right back from the door till I come down.'

'Why?'

'Just do it. Please?'

He sighed impatiently, took a step backwards and looked up at her.

'A bit farther, can't see you properly.'

'Nina, what is this!'

'Do it!'

He took a step sideways and slipped, twisting his foot.

'Ouch!' He went down on one knee, clutching his ankle. It was as he looked up to complain that the water hit him. He squatted there, spluttering and shaking his head, trying to clear his vision with the back of his hand.

'What the hell did you do that for?' He screamed up at her.

'Because you haven't listened to a word I've said!' She said leaning angrily out of the window. 'I don't want you Andy, not now, not ever. Is that clear? Just go away!'

She withdrew her head and he heard the window slam shut. It was at that precise moment he remembered the christening.

Tuesday 29th August

Eager for news of Andy after the Bank Holiday, Jenny told Trudi she would be in late that morning and had gone straight round to Chelwood Lodge to see Ella.

'Well,' she said, as she followed Ella through to the kitchen, 'exactly where did Andy get to on Sunday?'

'I have no idea.' Ella shrugged as she tripped the switch on the already warm kettle, pulled two mugs from the rack and retrieved the coffee jar from the cupboard.

'But surely he had some explanation.'

'Nothing that was remotely believable.'

'Well, what *did* he say?'

'That he'd had a tip off about some land at East Holbrook, about ten miles away and got up very early to go to look at it. He got talking to a couple of the locals, suddenly realised the time and headed back to Abbotsbridge but on the way he had a puncture.'

'What?' Jenny eyes widened with astonishment.

'Oh it gets even better!' Ella said, pouring hot water onto the coffee and reaching for the milk jug. 'While he was changing the tyre there was a downpour and he got soaked.' Ella saw Jenny's puzzled frown. 'I know, we had cloudless skies on Sunday, but I suppose he had to have some explanation for the wet clothes he left in the laundry bin.'

'Amazing!' Jenny took the steaming mug of coffee offered. 'What do you think really happened?'

'Oh, I think Andy set the whole thing up on purpose, just to get back at me for wanting to return to work.' Mug in hand, Ella leaned her back against the sink and smiled thoughtfully. 'The christening was another sore point. He wasn't very keen on Rachel as a godmother either. Said it Bryony Knight or Annabel Tate would have been as he put it, more suitable.'

'Is he usually this petty?'

'At the moment, yes. He really has a strop on about my return to work. He's already threatened to wreck the business if I go back. But I'm not going to be bullied, Jen. I'm sure given a few weeks he'll get used to the idea. It's only half time for goodness sake.'

'Has Bob caught up with him yet?'

'Yes.'

'And?'

'The usual. A lecture and a slap on the wrist.'

'Typical,' Jenny shook her head, 'Bob blusters but at the end of the day no matter how badly Andy behaves he always seems to get away with it.'

'Yes,' Ella gave a tired shrug, 'he certainly has a charmed life.'

'Ella, why do you put up with this?' Jenny looked at her sadly. 'It's so unfair.'

'I know, but I knew this marriage would never be easy and now there's even more reason not to give up. Andy adores Lucy and when he's with her I can see how it could be. You know I'm not a quitter Jen,' she gave a hopeful smile. 'And right now I'm pinning all my hopes on our daughter. I think she just might be the key to turning him into the man we all want him to be.'

'Andy's here to see you.' Marion hovered in the doorway of Bob Macayne's office. 'He says he knows you're busy but it won't take long.'

'How am I fixed for time?' Bob asked, pre-occupied with the transfer of files from his desk to his briefcase.

'You've got fifteen minutes.'

'Tell him I'll give him ten and send him in.'

Marion stood to one side, watching with an indulgent smile Andy walked past her, dark suited and business-like, briefcase in hand.

'Dad,' He settled himself down easily on one of the leather couches, pulling the briefcase onto his lap. 'Thanks for seeing me, I won't hold you up.' He said flipping open the locks on the case.

Bob looked at his son and laughed.

'What's all this about?' He said watching as a buff envelope appeared.

'I want you to look at this. Take your time.' Andy handed the envelope to him. 'Let me know what you think. I call back in a few days time.'

'What is it?'

'I've been to see Charles. I got him to draw up a transfer of some properties from you to me.'

'Properties? Which properties?'

'The ones Ella runs her businesses from.'

'Any particular reason?' Bob pulled out the document and flicked through it briefly.

'Oh I just thought it would be a good idea to have them in my care. Makes things, how shall we say - tidier.'

'Having a spot of bother?' Bob looked at him, understanding.

'Nothing I can't handle once the leases are in my possession.' He saw his father's expression and knew an explanation was expected. 'She's planning to go back to work.'

'When?'

'Beginning of September.' He said angrily. 'Helen's going to look after Lucy and the house. Ella's arranged everything without even discussing it with me!'

Bob crossed to where Andy sat and settled himself beside him. 'Well,' he said pulling his fountain pen from his breast pocket and opening the transfer document once more, 'we'd better put a stop to this nonsense once and for all hadn't we?'

FOUR

Saturday 1st September

So it was here at last, her big day. Nina threw back the covers, slid out of bed and crossed to the window, pushing back the curtains. Outside the window the morning was bright, blue sky with white clouds and warm early autumn sunshine. She glanced at her bedside clock. 8.30. In three hours she would be Mrs Alex Nicholson; the thought was totally exhilarating.

In the bathroom she slipped out of her night-dress and showered, letting the warm needles of water invigorate her skin. Today was the beginning of a new life; she would be joining the ranks of the Abbotsbridge élite and she was determined make the transition with as much style as she could.

To this end she had planned the whole wedding meticulously, making sure everything was just right. Alex, in his normal indulging way, had allowed her to control every aspect; the outfits, the guest list, the reception. He was, he said, only there to pick up the bill and arrange the honeymoon - a month in the States, coast to coast, all the cities and sights. She had spent a fortune on new clothes to take with her and couldn't wait to board the plane at Heathrow later this afternoon.

She towelled herself dry and carefully rubbed Chanel body lotion into her skin as her mind ran over the details; vases of cream roses to decorate the Registry Office; the guest list - close friends for the ceremony and two hundred guests afterwards at the Ragbourne Grove. She had deliberately excluded undesirables like the Taylors, the Benedicts and the Carpenters - and of course her own family. She had decided maybe today was an appropriate time to close the door on them completely. She had not seen her parents or her sister for almost eight months. They had disowned her since the divorce, appalled by her behaviour and what her mother had called the shame she had brought on an ordinary decent hardworking family like theirs. That was a joke for a start she thought cynically, what with Elaine's husband yo-yoing in and out of prison all the time.

She felt quite honoured that Alex had persuaded Miles to give her away. He was arriving in his black Rolls Royce at 11.00 to pick her up. She had specified dove grey suits for the men while for her own outfit, she had decided on a white long skirted suit and wide brimmed hat just like Mick Jagger's wife Bianca had worn at her wedding last year. Of course because Alex was such a local celebrity, the press were bound to be there to take all the details and ask them to pose for pictures. The thought of being in all the papers excited her. Let them all see, she thought. I've made it. I've really made it!

After a snatched breakfast of cereal and coffee she stood waiting at the window for Sammy from Headlines to arrive to style her hair. Today, she reflected, she could start her new life with Alex knowing that she had tied up all the loose ends in her old one. She had put Bob Macayne in his place, shaken Mick and Issy up a bit and sorted out Andy once and for all. After the drenching he'd had the other Sunday he should hopefully have got the message, but just to make sure she had invited both him and Ella to the wedding so he could see he really was history. As Sammy's TR4 pulled up to the kerb below she left the window and went downstairs to let him in, eager to begin the journey towards her new life.

Across town Andy and Ella were in the middle of breakfast and a row.

'You couldn't wait to dump her on Jenny again, could you?'

'It's not like that and you know it. The invitation said adults only. Helen's not back from holiday until the weekend and Jenny offered to have Lucy for me and said she'd come over early to collect her.'

Andy gave Ella a scornful look and bit into his toast.

'Honestly Andy,' Ella said irritably, getting to her feet and beginning to clear the breakfast things, 'there was nothing wrong with Jenny's timing. Nine thirty was fine; it leaves us one and a half hours to get ready for the wedding.'

'And of course,' He gave a sarcastic sniff, 'you'll need every minute of that!'

'What's that supposed to mean?'

'Well, you're bound to have some sort of clothes crisis. Bloody wardrobe full of clothes and you always take ages to get ready!'

'Ah but not this time. I knew I'd come in for criticism, so I decided on my outfit yesterday.'

'Wonders will never cease!' He pushed his plate to the centre of the table and picked up his coffee cup, watching her as she began to pick up the remaining breakfast clutter, returning marmalade to the cupboard and butter to the fridge.

'You know Ella I look at you sometimes and I think to myself, how the hell does she manage to run a profitable business?' He gave a bitter laugh. 'How does she make an *executive decision* that concerns her *vast* business empire when it takes her at least half hour each morning to decide what she's going to put on her bloody back?'

Ella ignored his jibes, turning towards the sink, filling the bowl, squirting in a good measure of Fairy Liquid and pulling on pink rubber gloves. Here we go again she thought, sniping and snapping. Well he could rant all he wanted, she was going back to work and that was that. And contrary to his pronouncements, it wouldn't bring the catastrophic changes to their lives he envisaged; in fact it would not make a shred of difference. Because she would make sure it didn't.

'Ah now you're sulking.' He said quietly coming up behind her, sliding his cup and saucer along the draining board, his voice soft and taunting in her ear.

'I am not.' She said staring out of the kitchen window as she lifted the last plate from the water to the draining board, her face a peaceful mask. 'I just wish we could find some compromise. Why do we have to fight like this all the time?'

'Because you won't see sense, you just don't see how damaging your actions are, do you? For me, for Lucy and for our marriage.'

'Oh stop being a drama queen Andy, we don't know until I've tried it.' She pulled off her gloves and began to wipe up, stacking everything neatly on the worktop.

'I don't want you to *try it* as you put it; I want you here at home.' He said leaning against the draining board with his back to the window, watching her.

'You're behaving like a Victorian father.'

'And you're behaving like a spoilt child.'

'I'm not, I'm a sensible adult.'

'That's a matter of opinion.'

'Andy, please!' She put down the tea towel and closed the gap between them. 'Just give me a month to prove my case. Surely that's fair.'

'No.' He shook his head, moving away from her. 'No way Ella.'

'Look,' she said, putting the crockery away with a tired sigh, realising she was getting nowhere. 'I really think we should call a truce for the day. We're going to a wedding, don't let's drag our differences there and spoil someone else's day.'

'Wedding! What a farce!' He exploded. 'She must be crazy; he's nearly old enough to be her father!'

Ella looked at him curiously, standing behind one of the kitchen chairs, grasping the back of it tightly, the whites of his knuckles clearly visible. She could almost reach out and touch his tenseness. Why had mention of the wedding triggered even more anger?

'Andy, what is it? What's upset you? It's not just me you're mad with, there something else isn't there?'

'Don't be stupid, of course there isn't!' He reacted angrily, releasing the chair and turning quickly towards the door. 'Don't try and shift the blame Ella. You're the cause of my upset - you! Now I'm going to take a shower.' He waved an impatient hand at her as he left the room. 'Heaven forbid I should be the one accused of making us late for this fiasco!'

The Rolls Royce containing Miles Anderson and Nina made an elegant sweep into Bridge Street. Miles looked out of the window, bored with the constant chatter of his companion. This woman had the IQ of a shop window dummy, how could Alex be so foolish? He was mad about her, of course; crazily in love and all Miles could see with her track record was big trouble. The Town Hall loomed ahead with a small crowd littering its steps. Dixon, Miles' chauffeur pulled up neatly to the kerb and slid out quickly to open the back door for his employer. Miles got out and pulling on his top hat, walked around the car and opened the near side door, extending an arm to Nina who emerged elegantly clutching her bouquet of pink roses. She smiled benevolently at those gathered to watch her.

'Stuck up bitch.' She heard one woman grumble. 'Too grand for her family now, thinks she's really something doesn't she? I can remember when she used to wander the streets of Parkway with a snotty nose and no knickers.'

'It's the no knickers that have got her where she is today.' Another woman said, her comment causing collective coarse laughter.

Nina didn't even bother looking at them. She raised her head and walked past them all. Let them say what they wanted. Who cared anyway? They were irrelevant little people now, beneath her contempt. She tightened her hold on Miles' arm and climbed the steps to the main doors of the Town Hall shutting out the malicious stares of her mother's neighbours.

Once inside they climbed the elegant flight of stone steps to the first floor where the Registry Office was situated. In the waiting room the small select group of guests were assembled chatting animatedly. Selina was the first to look up and see Nina. She smiled and got to her feet, kissing her on the cheek as she reached her.

'You look lovely darling,' she said squeezing Nina's hands warmly, 'now all we need is the groom.'

'Isn't he here?' Miles raised a surprised eyebrow and consulted his watch. 'Cutting it a bit fine, isn't he?'

'Traffic I expect.' Selina replied. 'You know what a bottle neck Abbotsbridge can be at times.'

As they spoke the Registrar, a tall grey haired man in a blue suit, appeared.

'Are we ready to go in?' He cast a curious eye over the assembled crowd.

'No groom yet.' Miles said with a smile. 'Delayed in traffic we think.'

'I can only give you another five minutes I'm afraid.' The Registrar said checking his watch before disappearing.

'What's going on?'

Ella, who had been resting with her eyes closed in the airless Registry Office waiting room, opened them immediately at the sound of Gracie Templeman's curious whisper.

'Alex is late.' Selina hissed, as she sat down. 'Traffic we think.'

Ella leaned forward and unsnapped her handbag to look for a mirror, noticing Nina for the first time. Standing beside Miles she was clutching her bouquet tightly, a tense expression on her face. Pulling out her compact Ella checked her hair. Satisfied, she snapped it shut and pushed it back into the bag. As she secured its clasp she shot a sideways glance at Andy. He sat beside her, his legs pushed out in front of him, hands in his jacket pocket staring at the ceiling a look of boredom on his face. He sighed, crossed his legs and pushed his hands deeper into his pockets. He wasn't enjoying this at all she thought. Of course, none of their crowd was here, there was no one to chat to; they were mostly Alex's friends and business colleagues. And, of course, Andy only ever came alive when he was centre stage.

The Registrar was hovering again, checking his watch. Miles looked serious, Nina anxious.

'What's happening now?' Gracie whispered to Selina.

'I'll just go and find out.' Selina said, getting up.

'I'll have to move you into the main chamber,' the Registrar was saying, 'there's another wedding at eleven fifty and the guests will begin arriving soon.'

Miles nodded and moved over to talk to everyone.

'Would you all like to come through please?' He beckoned. One by one everybody got to their feet and followed him down the corridor.

The chamber was high-ceilinged and decorated in pale blue and gold, with matching chairs. The room was warm from sunshine which flooded in through a large sash window. Miles showed Nina to one of the seats facing the Registrar's table.

'I'll just go and check with Alex's housekeeper.' He said. 'I won't be long.'

The small wedding party settled itself down, a low murmur of conversation filling the room.

'What's keeping him?' Andy hissed irritably.

'Oh he'll be here soon; he's probably forgotten to set his alarm.' Martin Templeman said with a laugh.

'But Alex is never late darling,' Gracie said in a hushed whisper, 'he's the most punctual person I know.'

'I hope nothing's happened to him.' Selina added anxiously.

As Miles crossed the black and white tiled floor of the foyer towards the telephone booths he heard someone call his name. Turning he saw his chauffer hurrying towards him.

'What is it Dixon?'

'A messenger Mr Anderson. Asked me to let you have this.' He handed him a long white envelope. 'Said it was urgent.'

Miles took the envelope and ripped it open, pulling out its contents. He ran his gaze slowly over the two sheets of pale green paper.

'Not bad news I hope, Sir?

Miles refolded the letter and tucked it back into the envelope. 'Not for me Dixon.' He said as he turned back towards the stairs.

Nina could hear the next wedding party arriving down the corridor. They were a noisy group; one woman had a particularly loud laugh which surfaced continuously and had become exceptionally irritating. She turned to look at the gathering behind her, most of them giving her encouraging smiles. She could feel

Andy's eyes on her but couldn't look at him. She imagined how amused he must be at her discomfort after the things she had said to him the other Sunday. But where *was* Alex? What was the delay? Had he got cold feet? She pushed the thought from her mind. Of course not, he was besotted with her. There must be some rational explanation.

All of a sudden Miles was at her side, whispering in her ear, pulling her from the chair. She followed him blindly, aware of the curious faces of everyone in the room.

'Is there somewhere private I can take the bride?' He asked the Registrar.

'What is it?' Nina was aware of the panic in her voice. 'What's happened?'

Miles put a calming hand on her shoulder but she brushed it off.

'Tell me, tell me now! I don't want you dragging me off into some room. You can tell me here. He's had a terrible accident on the way here, hasn't he? Is it bad? He's not dead is he?' She felt herself slipping into hysteria.

'I think this is something we should discuss privately.' Miles said diplomatically.

'No, I want to know now!'

'In front of all these people?'

'Yes.' Nina was insistent.

'As you wish.' Miles gave a great heave of his shoulders. 'While I was downstairs just now...'

'Miles, please!' She snapped, abrasive with impatience.

'Alex won't be coming. He's cancelled the wedding.' He said simply, his hands clasped neatly in front of him.

'Miles, that isn't funny!' She glared at him. 'Tell me what's wrong!'

'As I said, he's cancelled the wedding.' He leaned his head towards her and whispered. 'Nina I think we need to speak about this somewhere a little more private.'

'Why should I speak to you? It's nothing to do with you! Take me to see him now!' Aware of the fact that all eyes in the room were on her, she took a deep breath, 'I'm sorry.' She said quietly, 'but I'm sure whatever is wrong we can sort it out once I see him.'

'He's not here, he left early this morning for New York.'

'America? But we're supposed to be going there on honeymoon. He showed me the tickets. What's happened? Has he taken someone else with him?'

'No, he's quite alone.'

'There is someone else isn't there Miles?' Panic seized her again. 'Another woman.'

Miles shook his head solemnly. 'There is no one else Nina.'

'Why then? What reason?'

Miles looked around the room, then at the Registrar. 'I really think it best if everyone leaves, then I'll discuss it with you.'

Nina shook her head. 'Oh no, I appreciate your loyalty; that you want to save your old friend from any embarrassment. But I think everyone has a right to know why they've been dragged here today for nothing. Come on, tell us all!'

'I can't do this; I refuse to take the responsibility.' Miles shook his head. 'Here,' he took the envelope from his pocket and handed it to her.

Nina slowly opened the letter and began to read, scanning back and forth across the familiar sweep of Alex's writing.

'No!' She wailed, pushing her fingers to her lips. She looked up at Miles, aware that she was shaking.

'Now,' He said, 'do you still want to tell everyone?'

Nina felt she was in freefall with the ground coming up to meet her and braced herself for the cold, hard impact. She looked around the room at the faces; curious, wanting to know what had happened. These were people who had once welcomed her into their social clique with open arms, but not any more. Alex had rejected her and because of that so would they when they discovered the sordid details contained in the sheets of paper she held in her hand.

She raised her eyes to look at the assembled guests. Once this was out it would prove an amusing topic of conversation over lunch at the Rotunda or during Sunday's round of golf. She suddenly felt small and inadequate, her dreams in tatters, a have not amongst the haves. It was time to leave, to toss the letter away, leaving them to scrabble over it like dogs over a morsel. Time to find a small dark corner and scream. Brushing Miles aside she headed for the door, screwing up the letter into a ball and throwing it to the floor as she went.

The room erupted with excited voices as people got to their feet and crowded around Miles, demanding an explanation. The Registrar appealed for calm and Miles carefully fielded questions, instructing all the guests to head for the Ragbourne Grove where lunch courtesy of Alex, was waiting. In all the confusion it was only Ella who noticed that the discarded letter had rolled right next to the leg of her chair. Carefully she leaned over and retrieved it.

'You don't want to read that!' Andy tried to snatch it from her hands but she deliberately avoided him.

'Why? Does it have something to do with you?' She asked accusingly, holding the crumpled ball out of his reach. 'Is this the reason for all that bad temper this morning? What have you been up to Andy?'

'Nothing! You're being ridiculous!'

He watched her as she began to pull the letter apart, smoothing it out over her knees. As she lifted it to read he grabbed it and quickly stuffed it into his pocket.

'Andy!'

'Ella,' He said firmly, getting to his feet, 'I will not have you getting any ghoulish pleasure out of other people's misery. There's a free lunch at the Ragbourne Grove going begging, I suggest we join the others.'

Hauling her roughly to her feet he pushed her towards the doorway and hurried her along the corridor and down the stairs to catch up with the rest of the abortive wedding party. As they reached the entrance a solitary figure stood waiting in the tiled foyer.

'Sorry for keeping you waiting.' Andy smiled apologetically as they joined Miles.

'She doesn't know does she?' Miles said looking at Ella with cold pale eyes. 'Hasn't got a clue what you've been up to.'

'Me?' Andy looked at him then gave Ella a puzzled shrug.

'Yes *you,* you rotten little bastard!' Grabbing him by the collar and propelling him to the edge of the room, Miles pushed him down onto one of the nearby velvet covered benches. 'All this is down to you isn't it? You're not satisfied with the woman you're married to, so you have to mess around with somebody else's. Alex Nicholson is an honourable man, worth ten of you; he didn't deserve this!'

'Miles, will you let go of me!' Andy said struggling against the strong grip of the older man. 'Honestly I don't know what you're talking about.'

'Oh yes you do,' Miles smiled maliciously, 'and you're going to tell your wife everything or I'll break your neck.'

'Break it then!' Andy said defiantly. 'There's no way I'm going to lie to my wife.'

'You bloody little hypocrite!' Miles shook him angrily, pushing his face into the the seat.

'Miles, please,' Ella tugged at his arm, 'you're hurting him.'

'Hurting him? I feel like killing him for what he's done today. To Alex and to you!' Miles' pale eyes softened as they looked up at her. 'You don't deserve this either Ella!'

'I think there's been some awful mistake.' Ella said in a quiet voice. 'Please Miles, just let him go will you?'

'Oh Ella!' Miles gave a despairing sigh. 'How can you be so loyal to this?' He shook Andy viciously. 'If only you'd been able to read Alex's letter then maybe you'd understand why I'm so angry.'

'It's in his pocket.'

'What?'

'The letter,' she stepped forward and slipped her hand into Andy's pocket, 'It's here.'

FIVE

Saturday 1st September

In the back garden of their house in Tennyson Avenue Jenny sat cross legged on a tartan rug, blowing bubbles energetically through a small metal hoop while Christopher, squealing with excitement toddled unsteadily around her trying unsuccessfully to catch each burst in his chubby fingers before they were eventually carried across the lawn by the warm afternoon breeze. Eventually he grew tired of the game and settled beside his mother, snuggling into her lap and gazing up into her face with his thumb firmly embedded in his small mouth.

'Poor tired little man,' she smiled down at him, smoothing his fair hair across his forehead with her fingers. 'I think it's time for your afternoon nap, don't you?' Christopher continued to watch her silently, sucking noisily on his right thumb as his eyes grew heavy.

'Come on then darling.' She got to her feet, scooped him up into her arms and began walking towards the house. She had almost reached the French windows when Nick appeared.

'What is it?' She said, noting the serious expression on his face.

'Ella's here.'

'Already?' She checked her watch and frowned. 'I didn't think they'd be back till well after four. Here,' she offered him the small sleepy toddler, 'can you take his lordship. I'll just go and fetch Lucy.'

Nick retrieved his small son, cradling him gently in his arms. 'Jen,' he looked at her uncomfortably,' I think it would be best if you left Lucy for now. Come and talk to Ella first will you?'

'Why, what's the matter?' Jenny looked at him warily.

Miles Anderson appeared in the doorway beside Nick.

'I'm sorry for the intrusion Jenny,' he said gently, looking at Nick, 'but under the circumstances I thought this was the best place to bring her.'

'What circumstances? What are you talking about?' Jenny frowned.

'The wedding has been called off.' Miles said calmly. 'Alex has gone to America on his own. He left Nina a letter. Did you know she'd been seeing your brother-in-law? That she's been involved with him while she's been with Alex? And, Andy tells me that it goes back beyond that. To last year when Ella was pregnant.'

Jenny looked horrified. 'Oh God, poor Ella, where is she?'

'In the kitchen.' Nick said quietly, stepping aside to let his wife through.

Nina, with a large glass of brandy, had curled herself up in the corner of one of her settees watching athletics from White City on BBC2. She wasn't really interested in what was going on, it was movement, an interaction of sorts with other human beings; the sound of the commentator making the room a little less lonely. In a dramatic gesture she had hurled her wedding finery into a skip at the back of the flats, wanting to be rid of anything which would remind her of such a humiliating day. Once she had done this and was back behind the privacy of her front door, she finally let the misery she felt take her over completely. Curling herself up in a corner of the settee, she began to sob, unable to believe that the most wonderful day of her life had turned into such a nightmare. Of course it had been a crazy and dangerous thing to do, letting Andy touch her again, but she had needed to let that happen in order to put an end to his constant pestering once and for all. It was just her bad luck that Alex had caught them at the wrong moment.

She closed her eyes, remembering the words he'd written. Black ink on green paper. A cold letter full of pain and anger from a man betrayed by the woman he loved. She knew him well enough to realise that the dream of fast cars, a home in the sun and a foot in his business was now never going to happen. That any explanation she gave him, even if it was the truth, would be too late. He was beyond listening to anything she had to say.

Wrapped in her dressing gown she now sought consolation in alcohol. She took a large swallow of brandy; it burned her throat and made her cough. Stubbornly she drained the glass, reaching for the bottle again, hating everyone and everything. Her life was well and truly wrecked, no Alex, no job. Nothing. So at this moment getting drunk seemed the best way of coping with it all.

Engulfed in her misery, she was suddenly aware of something above the sound of the TV, something which broke its way persistently into the alcoholic fog which swam around her brain. Puzzled, she pushed herself off the couch and went across to turn down the volume. Silence immediately invaded the room. It must have been her imagination she thought tiredly and leaned forward to turn up the volume on the set once more. Then she heard it again; the long determined ring of the doorbell - someone demanding that she let them in. Could it be Alex? Her heart pounded. Had she been wrong? Had he come back to give her a second chance? Abandoning her drink, she rushed out of her flat, down the stairs to the front door and threw it open.

But it wasn't Alex who stood there; it was Andy looking quite pathetic, a bruise circling his swollen left eye.

'What do you want?'

'I came to see if you were all right.' He said weakly, seeing her severe expression.

'I'll survive.' She said resentfully. 'Who gave you the black eye?'

'Miles.' He said gingerly fingering his face. 'First violent poof I've ever come across. It bloody well hurts.'

'Dear, dear.' She shrugged uncaringly. 'I thought for a moment Ella might have punched you.' she gave a mirthless laugh. 'Although knowing you I don't suppose she has any idea does she? No doubt you've managed to wriggle out of it again with some excuse, like you always do.'

'Not this time.' He pulled a face. 'Miles showed her the letter.'

'Did he?' She said, feeling a small shred of satisfaction. 'Well, looks like you've got yourself a bit of a problem then doesn't it?'

'I'm going to divorce her.'

'If she doesn't divorce you first. Not that either of you will have a say about anything once your father hears about this. He'll have you back together in no time.'

'No he won't! I won't let him.'

'Big brave words!' She looked at him contemptuously.

'It's the truth; I want to be with you.'

'Please, don't start that again.' She closed her eyes and held onto the door, tired of arguing. At this moment all she wanted was to blot out the world; to be alone. 'Look, I'm really not in the mood for this.' she raised her eyes to look at him again, her voice flat.

'Nina, nothing's changed since the other day. I meant what I said. I love you and I want to be with you - always.'

'Please...' She gave a tired sigh. 'Just go away Andy!'

'No! I won't!' He said stubbornly, prising her hands from the door and pushing her back inside. 'It's always been you, don't you see? No matter how many times we're parted, something always brings us back to each other. We're meant to be. Please, give me a chance to prove how much I love you!'

She looked at him in amazement as he stood there, tears beginning to trickle down his face. He's never showed any emotion for anything or anyone in his life. He must really mean it! And if that's true - she hesitated. I just got lucky; very lucky.

Eyes misting with her own carefully choreographed tears, she closed the gap between them. 'Oh Andy!' she said and pulled him into her arms.

Jenny sat beside Ella, watching her pale, drawn face with concern as she sipped her coffee. They had been like this ever since Miles' departure with Nick twenty minutes ago to find Bob Macayne. Piece by piece Ella had unravelled the events of the day.

'So what happened after you'd read the letter?'

'I did everything Grandma brought me up not to do,' Ella replied, 'I just went crazy, shouting at him and punching him. Then he slapped my face. Said afterwards he did it because I was hysterical and he was trying to calm me down. Miles obviously thought differently and punched him. Knocked him onto the floor. I think it was just the excuse he'd been waiting for really. He was so angry.' She paused for a moment to finish off her coffee, clasping the cup and saucer in her lap as she continued. 'Then Miles hauled him to his feet and shook him, told him what a nasty little rat he was and how he didn't deserve me.'

'He is! And he doesn't!' Jenny agreed indignantly.

'When Miles eventually let go of him he just stood there holding his face and looking at me. He said perhaps now was a good time to get everything out into the open. He said he was sorry; that he had tried really hard to make things work, but somehow he had never been able to let go of Nina. He blamed One Plus One for a lot of our problems, but he also pointed the finger at his father and my mother for in his words, pushing him into a marriage of convenience.' Ella put her hands to her face and shook her head. 'I don't know what to believe any more Jen.'

'He's lying Ella!' Jenny reacted angrily. 'I remember the night he arrived at the pub in Portmeryn and proposed; I was certainly convinced his intentions were genuine.'

Ella looked beyond Jenny towards the window and the blue Jaguar which had just pulled up outside. 'Well we won't have to wait much longer for the truth. Bob's arrived, let's hear what he has to say.'

Tuesday 5th September

'Well?'

Bob Macayne stood in front of the fireplace, hands clasped behind him, a severe expression on his face as he looked at his pale faced son standing there, a rich purple bruise circling his left eye.

'Sorry Dad.' Andy said, shifting uncomfortably from one foot to the other.

'Sorry!' Bob's voice filled the room, loud and angry as he paced back and forth. 'Do you realise that the North Somerset Marina project is now in crisis? Alex has put everything on hold until he returns from the States and that includes his contribution towards the funding, which is crucial to get the whole bloody thing moving!' He stopped and glared at Andy. 'On top of that I've had to lie to Ella about why you married her. What possessed you to open your mouth like that? And last but not least there's Mel, when she finds out about all this I dread to think what she'll do. And why am I facing all this unwanted turmoil and hassle in my life? Because you can't keep away from that little whore.'

'She's not a whore,' Andy objected, 'a whore will go with anyone for money.'

'I agree, they do; and from where I'm standing sex and money have always been Nina's main motivators.' Bob moved across the room to pour himself a drink, 'Look at the men she's been involved with - you, Mick Taylor, Rich Tate and now Alex. Common denominator? Money. She's a gold digger, trying to pull herself out of the Parkway Estate swamp.' he returned the stopper to the decanter. 'Nothing more, nothing less.'

Andy stared silently at his father's savage expression, knowing he would have to steer a careful path. He knew that in this sort of mood he would have to play a waiting game, convince his father that women were very firmly off the agenda for the moment. He would throw himself into his job, become a workaholic like Mick and persuade his father that he had changed. Because looking at Bob's expression right now he knew that getting him to accept Nina was something for the future - the very distant future.

'So,' Bob walked over to the window, glass in hand and stared out across the lawn. 'What's happening with Ella? Have you spoken to her since Monday?'

'Briefly,' Andy replied with a shrug, 'It's over Dad. Finished. She's currently looking for a solicitor and I've an appointment with Bill Matthews tomorrow.'

'Pity,' Bob turned to look at him, 'I was rather hoping there was something that could be done, if only for Lucy's sake.'

Andy shook his head, his expression serious. 'It's too late. There are too many flaws in our relationship. Ella will never trust me again, not after this, and I'm not so sure I want to continue living with a mad career woman. It's as simple as that.'

Bob shook his head and raised his hands in a despairing gesture.

'Dad, I know it's upsetting,' Andy's tone was firm. 'But I think it's the right decision for both of us.' He looked at his watch. 'Look I'm sorry but I'm going to have to go. Someone's coming to look over Plot 8 at three; they're very keen – I'm hopeful of a sale.' he crossed the room and gave his father a hug. 'Work's all I have left now Dad, I need to make a success of something, I seem to have made a mess of everything else. Can I catch you later this week? Perhaps we could do dinner at the Rotunda on Friday night. My treat - as an apology for all the trouble I've caused?'

Bob nodded and stepped back, noticing the determination in his son's face as he left the room. He felt a small stab of pride. It seemed Andy, in the middle of such a personal crisis, had found salvation in the strangest of places; work. Although divorce now sadly seemed inevitable, one positive thing seemed to have come out of all the negativity. It looked as though Andy was at last on the road to becoming a responsible adult.

Returning to his desk, he thought of the fallout he was going to have to try and contain. It certainly was a real mess and this time there wouldn't be any quick fix solution. Coaxing Alex back into the project would take a huge amount of delicate negotiation on his part and then there was Mel. He shuddered inwardly at the thought of trying to pacify her outrage. She had been the one who had started all this, madly keen to get Andy and Ella together, convinced they would make a perfect match, but now that dream was over. Distraction - that was the name of the game. Now what would cause her to forget all this, to push it into the background? He remembered a conversation which had taken place some time ago. With this in mind he picked up the phone and began to dial.

Wednesday 6th September

'Ella it's me, what on earth's going on?'

Ella took the receiver away from her ear and made a face at Jenny, annoyed that her mother should be ringing her at the office and interrupting their shared lunch. For a moment she was tempted to cut her off, but thought better of it.

'Sorry Mother,' she lifted the receiver to her ear once more. 'It's a bad line. What did you say?'

'I said, what is going on?'

'Nothing, its 1.05 and I'm sitting here with a sandwich.' She swung round in her chair to look out of the window. 'It's raining outside and, yes, the dustmen have just arrived to empty the bins. Oh and thank you for the card and the earrings. Liam said he chose them. They're really lovely.'

'Ella, please, do not be facetious. You know exactly what I mean. Why have you left Andy?'

'Andy doesn't want me any more.' Ella said lightly. 'He wants to be with Nina.'

'Oh for goodness sake, don't be so silly! Some men occasionally stray. It's a fact of life.'

'Is it? And exactly what constitutes *occasionally* Mother? On and off ever since we got married *and* all through my pregnancy?'

'What?' Came the choked reply.

'To be fair, he tells me all this isn't really his fault. All he ever wanted was Nina but he was persuaded to marry me instead. By you and his father. I was the right sort of girl apparently. The right looks, the right background. *A suitable match*, isn't that the term? Mother! Are you still there?'

'Yes! Yes of course I am!' Tetchiness was evident in Mel's voice now, accompanied by a slight tremor of panic.

'Well, say something please!'

'Like what Ella?'

'Were you or were you not involved in arranging my marriage of convenience?'

'I did have lots to tell you,' Mel's voice boomeranged back, full of indignation. 'However if you're going to bully me like this, I don't think I want to talk to you any more. Goodbye!'

'What's the verdict then?' Jenny asked leaning forward to place her coffee mug and plate on the desk as Ella replaced the receiver. 'Guilty or not guilty?'

Ella sat back in her chair and smiled. 'Oh guilty,' She said, 'very, very guilty.'

Thursday 7th September

'What are you thinking about?' Nina propped herself up on one elbow and gazed down at Andy, as they lay together drowsy from a long love making session.

'How good freedom feels.' He smiled up into her face, teasing his finger around a tendril of her long hair.

'Aren't you being a little premature? There's a divorce case ahead of you.'

'Piece of cake.' He said confidently, easing himself against his pillow, 'It's just a formality. Ella doesn't seem to be arguing about anything. In fact she's been quite generous. I get to keep the house without even having to buy her out.'

'I suppose you'll sell it.' Nina rolled onto her back again, gazing up at the ceiling. 'Not much point living somewhere that's a constant reminder of her is there?'

'On the contrary,' He said thoughtfully, 'despite what's happened, I actually like the place. It's a nice house; I've got privacy, and a gardener. And although I'm losing Helen, I'm sure I can get another housekeeper. It seems a shame to get rid of it somehow. Anyway, if I did, where else could I go?'

'You could always move in with me.' She said seductively, running a red tipped finger down his arm.

'What? Live in this shoe box?' He started to laugh. 'You must be joking Nina. We'd be falling over each other all the time.'

'Well, if it's that small,' She gave him an impudent smile, 'perhaps I should move in with you.'

He looked at her for a moment, unsure. Her words mirrored the exact thoughts that had been circulating in his mind for some days now. He hated the to-ing and fro-ing; their hasty partings each morning. The drive back to Chelwood Lodge to shower and change before driving to the site. Living together would the perfect answer - if it wasn't for his father. He thought again. But did his father really have to know? He never came near Chelwood Lodge and if he did visit he always rang first. The house was on the edge of Abbotsbridge, tucked well back off the main road. There was an element of risk, but it was far outweighed by the benefits. And maybe it was time he started doing the things he wanted, it was his life after all.

'Actually,' He said with a thoughtful nod, 'I think that would be a great idea.'

SIX

Friday 8th September

Ella sat behind her desk gazing out into the cobbled courtyard at the leaves on the cherry trees which were just beginning to turn colour. What a difference a few days had made. She'd just celebrated her twenty fourth birthday quietly at Nick and Jenny's where the kitchen had been turned over to Issy for the evening. The result, with Mick assisting, had been a wonderful, memorable meal with wine and, for the first time since that dreadful Monday, laughter. She'd woken up the next day determined to move on, to get on with her life and detach herself from Andy as quickly and painlessly as she could.

The first thing she did was rent a house. With Mick's help she found just the thing, a three bedroom Victorian bay windowed semi in Byron Avenue, a ten minute walk from work. She took it on short term rent promising herself that once she came into her inheritance next year she would buy a place of her own; somewhere new where Lucy, Helen and herself could make a completely fresh start. Chelwood Lodge had been a wedding present from Bob, she was entitled to half, but as far as she was concerned she wanted nothing from the Macaynes. Andy was welcome to it. Still thinking of houses she looked at the gold edged card on her desk, lifting it with the edges of her fingers and tilting it upwards.

'Change of Address' it proudly announced. Her mother and Liam were moving to Conniston Drive, the cul de sac adjacent to where Tad and Faye Benedict lived, at the end of October. Now how could they afford to buy a house there and why hadn't either one of them mentioned it before? Liam's father, Philip had been in hospital in the States for many years following a bad hit and run accident. His care bills had always been paid for by Liam and although he had now been transferred to a care home there, that financial support still continued. His financial support had always been a bone of contention with her mother, who said these enormous costs kept them 'downmarket' as she termed their old house in Cambridge Crescent. So what had caused this sudden change in fortune? It was all very mysterious. Setting the card to one side she picked up the business card Jenny had left tucked into the

other edge of her blotter, her mind returning to her present situation in general and the divorce in particular. Marcus Goddard would be the ninth solicitor she had met with. He was coming to see her this morning. Please, she prayed, let him be the last.

Over the past few days she had approached local solicitors with a view to handling her divorce. Many, she discovered, as friends of Bob Macayne, were reluctant to assist, whilst others obviously with scores to settle were rather too eager. One by one she crossed them off her list. What she needed was someone with no hidden agendas to act on her behalf; someone totally impartial. But finding that in Abbotsbridge was rapidly becoming like looking for a needle in a haystack. Everyone, it seemed, knew or had had some contact with Bob. Everyone except the man she was waiting for now.

The intercom buzzed and she swung her chair round to answer it, her finger connecting with the button.

'Ella, Mr Goddard is here to see you.' Trudi's voice sang loudly through the grill.

'Show him through will you please?'

He was not at all what she had imagined. He entered the room, not wearing the customary suit she associated with solicitors, but instead a denim jacket, light cords and desert boots. His hair, thick, straight and black, framed a face with blue eyes so unusually dark they were almost violet. As he spoke he had a presence about him which despite his slenderness, gave her the impression he might be quite formidable in a court of law. She relaxed immediately, feeling a little more confident about Jenny's recommendation as he smiled and shook her hand. A strong handshake she noted, with a warm, dry palm.

'May I call you Ella?' He asked as he sat down opposite her.

She smiled. 'Please do.'

'Well…Ella,' he said, opening his briefcase and pulling out a pad. 'Your sister-in-law tells me you're having difficulty finding someone to assist you in your divorce proceedings.'

She nodded. 'They're either friends of my father-in-law who are understandably reluctant or enemies looking to settle their own scores.'

'Well I'm thankfully neither of those.' Marcus smiled his teeth very white. 'In fact as far as Bob Macayne is concerned I'm probably just small fry, a back street boy, picking up scraps. I have no high flying reputation like many others in Abbotsbridge. But then,' he laughed, 'I guess that may work to our advantage. I may look a push over but as we all know, Goliath, to his cost, assumed much the same about David. Now then,' he opened the pad and pulled a pen from his breast pocket. 'If it's OK with you I'd like to start by taking down a few details.'

Thursday, 5th October

Parking her Mercedes in the driveway of Chelwood Lodge, Ella made her way to the front door. Looking at its redbrick walls and fancy portico she decided she wasn't going to miss it at all. Although she was well settled in Byron Avenue now, Laura, on learning of the divorce, had generously advanced her money from her inheritance which was enabling her to go ahead with the purchase a beautiful property in Kingsford with a glorious garden which backed onto the river. Trying to tie up all the loose ends in her private life she had been promising herself all week that she would come here to look for the few forgotten items left behind when she moved out. There was the diamond ring Andy had given her for her twenty second birthday, her pearl drop earrings (a present from Laura) - both in the top drawer of her dressing table and her blue silk dressing gown, no doubt still hanging behind the bedroom door. She also felt it would be an opportunity to leave her keys and say goodbye to the house for good.

The divorce was well under way and it appeared Andy was actually looking forward to his freedom, to making a fresh start; happy to stay on in their old house. It was so unlike him; no arguments, no recriminations, eager to end their marriage in as adult a manner as possible. She wondered whether he was missing Nina, who since the abortive wedding to Alex, seemed to have disappeared into thin air. Ah well, whatever he did or felt it didn't matter any more, she had her own life to think about. Lucy, Helen and herself would hopefully be in the new house just before Christmas and she promised herself that 1973 would be a fresh start for all three of them.

Letting herself into the hall, she closed the door quietly behind her. Above her, she could hear the sound of a radio. The Supremes were singing *Automatically Sunshine*, a woman's caterwauling voice keeping pace with them. A housekeeper in already? Ella smiled to herself. She wouldn't last long if she sang like that when Andy was in the house.

Slowly she climbed the stairs, treading softly along the landing carpet, cocking her head to one side, listening. She could hear the music clearly now and she knew exactly where it was coming from. The main bathroom at the end of the landing. Reaching it she pushed open the door, fully expecting to see someone round and homely in the middle of an energetic cleaning session. Instead she found herself looking down at Nina, her head protruding from a bath overflowing with suds. Her cheeks were swathed in a ghostly white face pack, cucumber slices covered her eyes and she was singing for all she was worth. Ella recognised the pearl drop earrings and the diamond ring amongst other jewellery lying on the glass shelf above the basin and her silk dressing gown was draped across the toilet seat. She stood there for a moment staring at Nina, a woman who had not only taken her husband, but who it also appeared had no problem in taking her things for her own use. The animosity bubbled up inside her, bringing with it the need to do something quite reckless. Bending slowly over the bath she placed one hand over the other and lowered them gently over Nina's head. Then with one swift downward motion she pushed her head under the water.

Friday 6th October

Trudi Thompson, One Plus One's receptionist, had just put a call through to Jenny when the main office door flew open with a bang, causing her to drop the receiver with a shriek of fright.

'Where is she?' Andy took two steps forward and leaned over the desk, ignoring her white face and horrified expression.

'In her office,' Bending to retrieve the handset she pointed shakily to the door in the corner. 'But you can't go in, she's busy.'

Andy leaned farther over the desk, his eyes very black as he pushed his face close to Trudi's. 'Little fat girl,' he said quietly, 'Don't tell me what I can or can't do!'

Trudi sat rooted to the spot holding her breath as he left her and crossed the reception area, colliding with a palm plant as he went. He reached Ella's door, grabbed the handle and shouldered it open.

Ella sat with Alex Nicholson drinking coffee. He had called in this morning, newly-returned from the States to make her acquaintance once more and to talk generally about his recruitment needs. Despite the recent trauma in his private life Ella thought he seemed very relaxed. The Estate Agency, he had told her, was only one of his many business interests in the area and she was amazed to discover that he employed over three hundred people locally in small specialist companies and retail outlets. He was just starting to tell her about a new venture which he and Miles were interested in getting off the ground - a cash and carry on the local trading estate, for which he would need to recruit a whole range of staff - when the door was thrust open noisily and Andy stood there looking as if he was about to explode. Seeing Alex, he hesitated, his eyes wide in shocked surprise; then without a word he made an immediate exit, closing the door quickly behind him.

'Problems?' Alex raised an inquisitive eyebrow.

'Nothing I can't handle. Excuse me a moment.' Ella got to her feet and left the room. She caught up with Andy at the reception desk.

'What do you want?'

'I came here to see you,' He said turning angrily, 'about yesterday.'

'What about yesterday?'

'Breaking into the house like that, frightening Nina!'

'I did not break in, I used my key.' Ella said calmly. 'I came to look for the few missing items I mentioned to you. What I did not expect was to find her there, having a bath and obviously using them.'

'She said you tried to drown her. You pushed her head under the water!'

'It was the only way of stopping that dreadful noise she was making. Does she know she's tone deaf?'

'Very funny Ella.'

I guess your father's mellowed then?'

'What do you mean?'

'Well the fact that she's living with you, I gather he approves.'

'What's it to you?'

'Just curious.' Ella shrugged.

'Curiosity can be a dangerous thing Ella.' He eyed her darkly.

'Are you threatening me Andy?'

'I'm just telling you to mind your own business.'

'That's exactly what I *am* doing. I collected everything and left my key on the hall table. You won't see or hear from me again. Satisfied?'

'You'd better mean that Ella,' He said waving a warning finger at her, 'because if I find you've been stirring up trouble for us...'

'Oh just go away will you?' She waved a tired hand at him and turned back towards her office.

'I mean it!' He called after her. 'Mess with me and I swear I'll destroy you *and* your bloody business, do you hear!'

SEVEN

Tuesday 7th November

'I wish you'd change your mind Matt!' Marcie Maguire said with a painful smile. 'I'm not sure I can do Hawaii without you.'

They were standing at the TWA check in desk at La Guardia, where Matt Benedict was just about to surrender his suitcase en route to Europe. Exotic, coffee coloured Marcie, Matt's discovery and Maverick Records latest star was, as usual, dressed in a collision of colour - green, pink and purple - her hair a wild, dark halo surrounding her face.

'You'll be fine.' Matt pulled his ticket from his jacket. 'Besides you won't be on your own.'

'But Charlene's not you.'

'No but she's her father's daughter and like Doug knows Maverick Records inside out. He wants to give her a chance to prove herself and managing the Hawaiian tour in my absence is ideal. It's only three weeks, all the venues are tried and tested, there'll be no hassle and the bonus is you get to entertain the Navy for Christmas. It's going to be televised so you'll be even more famous! What more could a girl want?'

'You, there with me.' She said sticking out her chin stubbornly.

Matt shook his head as he handed over his ticket. 'No can do Marcie. It would be far too distracting. I need to find somewhere to write, alone. And that, I'm afraid, is not Hawaii.'

'But Spain, Matt!' She protested. 'It's so far away - why not California or Mexico?'

Why indeed? Matt thought. It was a complete gamble. In the three months since Marcie's tour had finished he had been trying to settle down again to produce fresh material for her next album. But inspiration had eluded him; most of his efforts ending up in the trash can. He paced the floor, played everything from Lou Reed to Beethoven on his stereo, trying to find the inspiration to kick start his writing. But still nothing came. Now the green of Central Park blazed red and gold. Autumn was here and time was no longer on his side. He began to despair. And then a telephone call from Baz Young changed everything.

The Attitude had just returned from two months in Europe. Baz, who had been the only member of the group to keep in regular touch with Matt since his departure from the band, phoned to see how he was and to tell him that now the band were home he was planning to spend a long, relaxing vacation in Spain.

'Fancy joining me for a couple of weeks? I've just bought this brilliant house. You'd love it.'

'Sounds great.' Matt tried to appear enthusiastic, knowing there were too many bad memories on the Costa del Sol for him to want to return there. 'But Marbella's not really my scene...'

'It's not Marbella you berk.' The gruff voice replied. 'It's Cordoba, a hundred miles from the coast. A beautiful white city, oozing with history. It has everything - amazing food, inspirational music! You'll love it!'

The instant he heard the words 'inspirational music' Matt's curiosity was roused.

'I'm going for the music,' he said as the girl on the check in desk handed him his boarding pass, 'and to catch up with Baz. Haven't seen him for over a year. He's on his own. Between girlfriends at the moment. I also had an idea,' he added, 'that I might make it home for Christmas!'

'Home?' Marcie looked surprised as they walked to passport control. 'You're going back to the UK for Christmas? You never said.'

'Well nothing's definite. But if the writing goes to plan, I'll give them a call. We seem to have drifted apart. My fault I know. If I can make it, I know they'll be pleased to see me.'

'Matt I'm gonna miss you so much!' Her brown eyes misted over. She had at least hoped to entice him out to Hawaii for Christmas. She felt disappointed, even cheated slightly that this was not now going to happen. But she knew he hadn't been home for nearly three years. It was a trip he needed to make.

'Don't worry; Charlene has given me your hotel numbers. I'll keep in touch.' He assured her, tugging her away from her thoughts as he pulled her against his chest and smiled down at her. 'I'll let you know how I'm getting on,' he laughed, 'whether the vibe is with me!'

'Is that a promise?'

'It's a promise.' He confirmed, kissing her forehead. 'Have a great time in Hawaii. Go out and do the business and please, trust Charlene. She knows what she's doing. She'll give you all the support you need.' He released her with a smile, 'Now, I really must go.'

Marcie stood watching as he went through passport control. She adored everything about this six foot Englishman; she loved his unconventional good looks; his thick dark hair peppered with auburn highlights and eyes the colour of smoky cognac. His voice sent shivers down her spine and she was totally overawed by his ability to write the most amazing songs for her. She melted when he put his arms around her just before she went on stage and gave her a kiss for luck. But this one gesture although guaranteed to make her go out and give her all, was tinged with sadness. As he gave her a final wave and strode off down the corridor towards the boarding gate, she wished with all her heart that his kisses were more than just brotherly; that he could love her in the same way she loved him. But that part of him she knew was still tied to the memory of a dead woman he could not forget. She wanted so desperately to help him end his grieving, to set him free from his ghost and show him how to love again. But exactly how to do that she had no idea. No idea at all.

Thursday 9th November

Baz Young, a huge mountain of a man with a mass of brown curly hair, opened his front door to find Matt standing there. 'Matty!' He said, his face breaking into a huge grin. 'Good to see you mate!"

Matt dropped his case and guitar to the floor and gave the big man a friendly hug and a slap on the back.

'You look well!' Baz held him at arms length, the big grin still splitting his face. 'It's been a long time. Come on in.'

Pushing the door open wider he helped Matt in with his luggage.

At the end of the narrow hallway, beyond an intricate wrought iron cancela Matt glimpsed brightness. He followed Baz and found himself standing in a large open tiled courtyard, a fountain in its centre.

'Wow!' Matt gazed around in admiration at his surroundings. 'You'd never believe this was on the other side of that door! It's like Dr Who's Tardis!'

'Yeah, looks like a little two up two down from the street don't it? The Moors built their houses in a square around a patio and fountain. The constant circulation of water kept the place cool and the entrance and passageway deliberately concealed everything from the road. No one would know whether the owner was rich or poor; it was his private place. And...' Baz indicated the galleried rooms above with their terracotta window boxes of red and purple flowers, 'now it's my private place.'

Matt grinned and shook his head in amazement.

'Come on,' Baz indicated an ornate flight of stairs. 'I'll show you to your room. There's plenty of space here for house guests.' He said as they climbed the stairs. 'Not that I'm much of a party animal. I come here for peace and quiet. Now then,' reaching a heavy door he swung it open to reveal a light, airy bedroom, 'make yourself at home. Lunch will be ready in an hour. We'll have a wander later. I guarantee you'll be glad you came!'

Mel Carpenter eased her blue Spitfire into a vacant space on the first floor of the Anderson Gate shopping centre's multi storey. She had been looking forward to this morning's little shopping trip. The new house, coming out of the blue, had been a wonderful surprise. As an empty property with no chain; the purchase had gone through very quickly. And Liam had been most generous, his lucrative contracts for the Civic Hall and Shopping Precinct had enabled him to put quite a substantial sum of money aside for furnishings. So, today she was on her way to look at curtain material and carpet samples.

This time she decided things were going to be completely different; the decorators were in and she had opted for plain walls in neutral shades. Her furnishing choices therefore would be a complete departure from the traditional Sanderson patterns she usually favoured. With very specific ideas firmly in her mind she took the lift down to the main hall and crossed its marbled floor to the new and impressive Langleys department store.

Heading for the carpet section first she spent nearly an hour deliberating; feeling textures, thickness of pile, weighing up the advantages of Axminster over Wilton. A most obliging manager hovered by her side, seeing to her every need, making her feel important. Once her choices had been made, the manager was quite happy to arrange for carpet samples to be sent up to the Soft Furnishing Department to make sure the curtain matches were just right, suggesting that in the meantime 'Madam' might like to take refreshments in their newly-opened Coffee Shop.

It was there that she quite unexpectedly ran into Sheila, wife of Taylor Macayne's solicitor Charles Fitzallyn. This gave her an excellent opportunity not only to catch up on the latest Ladies' Circle gossip, but also to tell her all about the new house and invite her and Charles to dinner at the end of the month. Forty minutes later, feeling buoyed up by her morning's activities, she waved goodbye to Sheila and took the lift to the second floor.

The Soft Furnishing Department bore no resemblance to its predecessor in the old store. No more boring bales of material housed in ugly racks standing on beige linoleum. Instead, sample curtains had been produced and were suspended around the room in colour co-ordinated sections. Following the theme, chairs and settees draped with swatches of colour options were displayed on low plinths and, and set into little alcoves around the walls were an array of brightly coloured cushions. It was an Aladdin's cave of colour and styles. Mel was impressed, she had a good feeling about the day, convinced her shopping spree was going to go very well.

The manageress produced the carpet samples from under the counter and after making some recommendations, left her to wander at leisure. The department wasn't particularly busy, only half a dozen people browsing as the gentle sound of Mozart floated overhead. Mel was relaxing, tucked away amongst the hangs of greens and beiges, almost sure the material she was holding would go just right with the lounge carpet, when a loud voice interrupted her concentration.

'What do you call *this*?'

'Is there a problem Madam?'

'Yes, I asked for three inch headings.'

'These are three inch headings Madam.'

Mel frowned, curious to see who was making such a loud complaint. Slowly she pulled back the curtain she was standing behind.

In the far corner at the counter, she saw the manageress talking to a young woman wearing sun glasses and fashionably dressed in dark green gaucho pants, beige leather jacket and boots, a black suede Stetson set elegantly on her head.

'There we are.' The manageress had picked up one of the curtains and was holding a tape measure against it. 'Three inch headings, Madam.'

'OK,' the woman shrugged arrogantly, 'so I made a mistake. Just wrap them and charge to the Macayne Account.'

The woman nodded. 'The other three pairs should be ready by Thursday. They're three inch headings as well. I assume that's correct?'

'Yes, fine!' The young woman waved an impatient hand. 'Just ring me and I'll come in and collect them. Have you the number? No? It's Abbotsbridge 492561.'

Mel clutched at the curtain tightly. Macayne account - and wasn't that the number for Chelwood Lodge? Who was this stranger making purchases? Hadn't Bob been keen to tell her Andy now lived alone -a workaholic who was totally avoiding women?

She continued to hover behind her curtain while the transaction took place, then watched as the woman walked off with a confident stride, carrying her purchases. There was something familiar about the arrogant tilt of her head and the fine wisps of tawny hair that protruded from under the hat. She crossed to the desk, carpet samples in hand, determined to find out the identity of this stranger.

'Ah, Mrs Carpenter.' The manageress smiled. 'Have you come to a decision?'

'Yes I think so.' Mel smiled indulgently at the woman. 'A wonderful choice you have here! Unlike your last customer, you won't get any complaints from me.'

'I'm pleased to hear it.' The woman replied. 'But please believe me, that little scene was thankfully a rarity here.'

'Who was she?' Mel looked in the direction the woman had taken.

'No idea. Her name's Dominique Tyler. Andy Macayne has given authorisation for her to purchase on his father's account. Having his house done up apparently. She's been in a few times. We have two new leather Chesterfields on order and of course all the new curtains. As you've just seen, she can be a very difficult lady.' 'However, I shouldn't complain.' She laughed. 'She is doing an awful lot of business with us.'

'How interesting.' Mel replied, her polite smile suppressing the anger she felt. Interior designer indeed! She was convinced she knew just who Dominique Tyler was and that Bob should be informed about her at the earliest opportunity.

'How long have you had the house?' Matt asked as he and Baz wandered through the narrow streets later that afternoon, taking in the sights.

'Just over a year. Rupert Sheppard, one of our record company's A & R guys was looking to offload it to help fund a rather expensive divorce. Got a maid thrown in too.'

'A maid?'

He nodded. 'Rosa. Cooks, cleans, keeps the place ticking over when I'm not here.'

'Do you come here much?

'Not as much as I'd like to.' He looked at Matt with a broad smile. 'Unfortunately, we don't get the same generous holidays as you lot across the pond.'

'I'm not on vacation!' Matt laughed. 'This is work. I've got less than two months to come up with the raw material for Marcie's next album and at the moment I'm struggling.'

'Well you've come to the right place. There's a good vibe here. Especially in the Tablaos.'

'Tablaos?'

'Flamenco clubs. They're all over Andalucia. There's a really good one a few doors down from the restaurant we're eating in tonight. Fancy taking a look after dinner?'

'Sure,' Matt nodded, intrigued, 'Why not.'

'Could I speak to Bob Macayne please?'
'I'm sorry; he's out of the office today.'
'Do you know when he'll be back?'
'The end of the week, he's in Scotland.'
'Scotland! What's he doing there?'
'Who's calling please?'
'It's Mrs Carpenter.'
'Ah Mrs Carpenter,' Bob's secretary Marion Westwood smiled, tapping her pencil against her typewriter, 'I thought it was you, good afternoon. He's gone up to Pitlochry with a group from Rotary on an exchange visit; he'll be back on Sunday evening.'

'Then can I leave a message for him please, I need him to call me. Urgently!'

'Certainly,' she began to write on her pad. 'I'll see he gets it as soon as he's back.'

Saturday 11th November

Matt sat in his bedroom window, looking out across the city as the evening sun turned its pale walls a warm gold. He turned his attention to the pad on his knee and the music he had just spent all afternoon composing. Flamenco - whoever would have dreamt that would be the key?

He remembered that first evening after dinner, entering the unassuming whitewashed walled hall where the devotees of flamenco gathered. Paintings by local artists hung there, vivid splashes of colour against the pale walls. Tables and chairs circled a central wooden dais; people stood around drinking wine and chatting - the place was full of noise and cigarette smoke. He and Baz found seats and settled themselves down. The room quickly filled; people of all ages, watching, waiting and chatting. More jugs of local wine were brought round, glasses filled. Then suddenly a hush settled itself on the gathering as an old grizzled man dressed in black got to his feet and climbed onto the dais. He cleared his throat and began. A hoarse, guttural sound with its own unique rhythm. Gradually, other members of the audience joined in, adding their voices to his.

A young man, his long hair pulled neatly back in a pony tail, stepped forward with an acoustic guitar. He began to add musical accompaniment and then finally two girls entered. They were dressed in simple scoop necked white blouses and turquoise patterned skirts. Both had a black fringed shawl tied around their shoulders, their dark hair, woven with flowers, hanging loose down their backs, castanets in their hands. Mounting the dais they raised their arms and began to dance, circling each other slowly and deliberately. The rhythm grew, strong and solid aided by clapping, the accompaniment of castanets and the staccato drumming of the girls' heels. Flamenco, Juan Camenara, their host, told Matt, expressed many feelings; loneliness, hopelessness and the pain of unrequited love but also joy, love and great happiness. Opposites woven through with a common thread: passion.

The girls whirled energetically, twisting and turning their elegant wrists, their fingers manipulating the castanets, bringing them alive with a chattering language of their own. By the time it had ended Matt was sitting, breathless from singing, his palms stinging and his feet sore. He looked at Juan, then at Baz. Smiling he grabbed Baz's shoulder excitedly. 'Amazing; absolutely amazing!' He said, his thoughts already focusing on how he could develop this for his own use.

Now with a smile he lodged the pad on the window ledge, picked up his guitar and began to play. He nodded. This was good, very good. Tomorrow he would start on the lyrics.

Monday 13th November

'Is there anything pressing amongst this lot?' Bob asked as Marion laid the post folder in front of him.

'No, most of its just routine stuff.' She replied, taking a seat on the other side of the desk. 'I sent out holding letters for most of it. A couple of contracts arrived mid week, they need to be signed by this Wednesday; Charles Fitzallyn has them at the moment. I've booked him in to see you at 10.30 tomorrow so he can brief you before signing. Oh and I drafted a letter to Alex Nicholson concerning the next Marina Project Meeting and I've been through the trade journals and highlighted new building projects I thought you might be interested in.'

'Great, thank you.' Bob gave her an appreciative smile. Marion was worth every penny he paid her, an excellent secretary who not only used her initiative but was totally trustworthy. After a brief look he set the file to one side.

'What about messages?'

She began to read from the small pile of notes she held, placing them in front of him as she finished. 'Oh and I nearly forgot, Mrs Carpenter rang.'

'What did she want?'

'Didn't say; sounded rather agitated and wanted you to ring her back urgently.'

'Ah I think I know what that is about.' Bob made a face as he picked up the note and looked at it. 'I'll give her a call tomorrow.' he said, sliding it under the edge of his blotter.

Wednesday 22nd November

'Marion told me I'd find you here.'

It was Wednesday afternoon and Bob had just finished his usual round of golf at Kingsford Golf Club. After lunch in the club house and a brief chat to a couple of his fellow Rotarians on the success of the Scottish visit, he made his way to the car park and was stowing his clubs in the boot of his Jaguar when he heard her voice.

She was standing directly behind him, looking at him with those brilliant blue eyes of hers, coat collar shielding her face, the wind teasing her hair. Seeing her there made him realise how much he was in the mood for sex, but the determined set of her mouth told him he'd obviously have to deal with her urgent problem first. The one still ledged under the edge of his blotter; the one he had forgotten all about.

'Mel.' He approached and kissed her cheek. 'It's good to see you and I do apologise. I still have your note *and* I was meaning to ring but it's been a bit hectic at work.' He smiled affably. 'You can't imagine what my desk looks like after a week out of the office.'

'Never mind Bob,' she smiled up at him. 'You're here now that's the main thing.' She looked towards the club house. 'Could we discuss my urgent issue over a drink?'

'Of course.' He nodded, gesturing towards the front door.

They found a quiet spot by the window overlooking the 18th hole. The day had turned grey and cold and rain had begun to streak the window by the time he returned with the drinks and sat down opposite her.

'Now then, what's the problem?'

'It's Andy.' She looked hesitant.

'Well...go on.'

'I think he has someone living with him at Chelwood Lodge.'

'Whatever makes you say that?'

'I was in Langleys two weeks ago and there was a young woman in there collecting curtains which had been ordered against your account. Signed herself as Dominique Tyler.'

'Really?' Bob's dark brows came together in a puzzling frown.

'Don't you realise who that is?'

'Yes,' the frown faded suddenly and he nodded amicably, 'I think I do.'

'You do?' Mel's eyes widened.

'Yes. Andy's been talking about making changes to the house, getting in an interior designer. That was probably her.'

'What do you mean probably? Don't you know?'

'Does it matter?'

'Of course it does when she's putting her purchases on your account. Don't you see? It's Nina Taylor!'

'Don't be silly Mel, of course it isn't. After this business with Ella, she's the last person he'd want around him.'

'He could be lying to you Bob.'

'My son doesn't lie. Not to me anyway. He daren't! Come on Mel, you're beginning to sound paranoid.' Bob sighed. 'Did she look like Nina?'

'I don't know. She was wearing a hat and dark glasses. I only really saw the back of her. She did have red hair though!'

'Mel,' Bob reached over and stroked the back of her hand reassuringly, 'believe me this whole divorce thing's really turned Andy around. He's very anti-women at the moment. He has a new love in his life. It's called work. No, don't look at me like that, he's turning into a very committed individual, in fact it's the one thing that seems to be helping him cope with his current situation. Now, please,' he slipped his hand over hers and gave her one of his most sensual smiles, 'I insist we stop all this craziness and talk about something else.'

'Such as?'

'Your current project: furnishing the new house. How's that coming along?'

It was no use. Mel looked into his eyes and knew she had hit a brick wall. Bob simply would not believe what was going on under his nose. Andy had covered himself well. But it couldn't last. And when Bob eventually found out he was not only going to be very angry, he was also going to feel extremely foolish.

Tad Benedict looked around the deserted interior of the club. It was just after lunch and he had come here to meet Liam Carpenter to look over the final designs for the refurbishment. It wouldn't be long now, just over a month, till the old Club closed its doors for good. Seven years this place had been in existence, he thought, running his hand along the smooth edge of the bar; seven successful, profitable years. All with a wealth of good music and warm memories to look back on. At its peak this had been *the* place to come to, but now things were different, the club scene was changing and numbers had dwindled, lured away to more sophisticated offerings which had now opened in Taunton and Weston Super Mare. The generation which had flocked here on a regular basis were now in their twenties, with the income which had once funded nights out being spent on mortgages and babies. It was the end of an era, but Tad had never been one to dwell on the past. Besides, the Mill wasn't really ending, it was being reborn. And he hoped would become a crowd puller for the nineteen seventies.

The sound of footsteps interrupted his thoughts and he looked up to see Liam crossing the dance floor, briefcase in hand.

'Caught you.' Liam smiled as he reached Tad and shook him warmly by the hand, then seeing his puzzled expression, said. 'You were remembering all the great moments this place has had weren't you? The laughter and the music.'

'I have to admit I was.' Tad gazed around. 'We attracted chart topping acts here at one time you know. The Attitude was discovered while playing on that stage. But today's bands would laugh if you suggested they play in some backwater like Abbotsbridge. Oh I'm going to miss it, no doubt about it, but it's time for a change. Time to do something completely different. As we discussed, I want to attract a completely new type of punter.'

'Well,' Liam replied, lifting his briefcase onto a barstool and releasing the catches, 'here are the final plans.' He pulled out a bundle of drawings and placed them on the bar. 'I've done all the changes you asked for. Can you check through each one, initial them and then drop them back to my office as soon as possible? We need to get the application in by the 29th at the latest in order to catch the next committee meeting.'

'Fine,' Tad gave an enthusiastic grin as he patted the drawings. 'I can't believe it Liam; we're on our way at last.'

'We certainly are.' Liam said, closing his briefcase. 'And if everything goes smoothly the builders can make a start in early March. Have you decided on a name for the new place yet?'

'Yes, as a matter of fact I have.' Tad replied, gazing thoughtfully at the stage. 'I'm going to call it Zeffirelli's.'

Thursday 30th November

'Dad: what a surprise! What brings you here?'

Andy Macayne, seated behind his desk flicking through paint cards, was suddenly aware of someone in the doorway of his office and looking up saw his father standing there, hands pushed firmly into his overcoat pockets, his breath clouding the air around him.

'Oh just wanted to see how you were getting on out here. What's the latest?'

'Plot 6 went this morning.' Andy said with just a hint of smugness. 'It's been an absolute bastard to get rid of. No one wanted it, the garden was like a postage stamp and for some reason the lounge and dining room have ended up as one big room because someone didn't read the plans properly. Until today I'd despaired of ever selling it.'

'Well done!' Bob gave a satisfied smile. 'That's wrapped up this site nicely then, next stop is Kings Moreton.'

'Yes, Liam showed me the plans, they look really good and the location's just right, tucked away down by the church, we'll have no problem moving them.'

'Well, as you know, the new site is nowhere near ready for sales to move in yet.' Bob edged towards the portable gas heater in the middle of the room and stood for a moment warming his hands. 'So it might be an opportunity for you to take some time off.'

'I'd rather not.' Andy shook his head, tossing the paint cards into one of the trays on his desk. 'I'd only be bored, besides there's nothing to keep me at home at the moment.'

'Not even your new lady friend?'

'What?' Feeling his stomach churn Andy took a deep breath and gave his father what he hoped was a calm smile. His mind raced, had he been rumbled? No, of course not. If Bob knew Nina was living with him, the last thing he'd be doing would be standing there with a friendly smile on his face.

'Dominique Tyler.' Bob raised curious eyebrows. 'Seems she's been buying furnishings on my account.'

'Oh that. Yes. Sorry Dad. I completely forgot.' Andy gave a relieved sigh. If he just kept calm he could get out of this one. 'You know we had that chat about redecorating? Well Dominique was recommended to me by someone who came to look at one of the houses here. Thought I'd try her out, see if she could come up with some good ideas. Change the place completely.'

'And has she?' Bob rubbed his hands and moved away from the heater.

'Yes, I'm very pleased so far.'

'In that case, maybe I could drop by one day; have a look at what she's doing. Who knows, I might be able to use her myself if I like what I see.' I've a couple of rooms at Everdene which could do with the feminine touch.'

'Yes, of course.' Andy gave a thin smile as he felt his stomach lurch again. Just as he thought he was in the clear the whole thing had unexpectedly swung back and hit him again. It had seemed such an easy thing to do, creating the fictitious Dominique so that Nina could buy goods from Langleys without creating suspicion. She had quite enjoyed the role, the hat and dark glasses giving her an air of mystery. Things were going well; the house was beginning to take on a completely different look. But he now realised they had been so engrossed in planning and executing the facelift that it had caused them to become dangerously complacent.

'Better go.' Bob was saying as he turned towards the door. 'I've a meeting at three with Miles and Alex. You'll have to come down to Stonebridge Bay, see how the Marina project's coming along. I think you'll be impressed.'

'Thanks Dad, I'd like that.'

Watching his father cross to his car, unlock it and climb in, Andy picked up the phone and began to dial.

Friday 15th December

'Hi Matt, how are things?' At the sound of Marcie's voice, Matt lay back on his bed, cradling the receiver against his chin.

'Fine! How's the tour going?'

'It's been a breeze. You were right, I take everything back. Charlene has been terrific. What's the weather like there?'

He turned his gaze to the open window where the evening sun hovered on the horizon. 'Quite warm; very pleasant in fact.'

'You don't say. We had rain this morning. How's the writing going?'

'I'm stuck.' He gave a heavy sigh and looked across the balls of paper littering the floor of his bedroom. 'Number ten. It's not coming! You wouldn't believe what the floor of my room looks like.'

'Can't we run with nine?'

'No, Doug said ten, so ten it's got to be. So it looks as if...' he hesitated, biting his lip, 'I might not make it home for Christmas.'

Wednesday 20th December

'Still nothing?'

'Nope.' Matt looked up from his pad to see Baz hovering in the bedroom door. He shook his head. 'Inspiration has totally abandoned me.'

'I know just what you need.' Baz eyed thoughtfully.

'What?'

'Some fresh air; sitting in here is doing your head in. Come with me.'

The sky was a vivid blue above the white of the buildings as they stepped into the street, the sun high overhead. Even though it was December and they wore jackets, Matt could feel the sun's warmth reflecting off the walls as they walked through the maze of tiny streets. They stopped for coffee in a small café opposite the Roman Temple on Calle de Claudio Marcello. Later, lingering for a while on the Puente Romano, watching the river and feeling the breeze on their faces they reminisced about the old days on the road before they were discovered and how simple life had been then. Eventually they wandered back, the brightness of the buildings mellowing to warm yellow as the sun lowered itself in the afternoon sky.

'These songs that you've written,' Baz said as they strolled past the Mesquita, 'what are they about?'

'Oh the usual roller coaster of emotions.' Matt replied. 'Love, happiness, loss, regret.'

'No betrayal then.'

'No betrayal,' Matt shook his head, 'or unrequited love. I've done them both to death.'

'You're good at it though. I bought a copy of Marcie's first album. There was a lot of Ella in it.'

Matt nodded. 'Writing seemed to be the only way to get her out of my system for good.'

'Did it work?' Baz held his gaze.

'No.' Matt gave a hopeless shrug. 'Sadly the ghost is still hanging on in there.'

'All the more reason then...'

'For what?'

'For someone to give you a hand to exorcise this ghost of yours.' Baz said as they turned into Calle Maimónides and the Jewish quarter.

'Like who?'

Baz grinned. 'Like me, of course. Two heads are better than one ain't they? Come on!' he gave Matt a friendly pat on the back. 'Let's go back and frighten the living daylights out of it by writing a blaster of a song!'

1973

EIGHT

Monday 1st January

Ella tucked herself into the back seat of the taxi, Issy following her, while in the front, Mick eased in beside the driver, a thin faced swarthy man.

'What a great evening! Shame about Jen, she really wanted to be there.' Issy said inclining her head towards Ella in the darkness as the taxi pulled away.

'Yes; what a time to have gastric flu.' Ella said. 'Poor Jen.'

Issy nodded in silent agreement.

'Tad certainly knew how to bring the final curtain down tonight though didn't he?' Mick said, with a smile, turning to look at them both in the darkness. 'That firework display was amazing! It must have cost a fortune!'

'And free champagne to toast in the New Year!' Issy added. 'He really spoiled us didn't he?

'Yes, I should think everyone will remember the Mill's final evening.' Ella agreed, her eyelids heavy, recalling Tad and Faye on stage together, hand in hand, wiping moisture from their eyes as they said goodnight and goodbye amid loud applause and whistles from an appreciative crowd.

'And now that's it.' Issy said despondently, turning in her seat to take a last look at the Club. 'It's all over.'

'No it's not,' Ella argued, resting her head sleepily against the back seat, 'it's just going to be different that's all. Bigger and better Tad said in his closing speech.'

'Liam showed Dad the plans.' Mick interrupted. 'He's very impressed, says he thinks Tad's hit it spot on, just like he did with the Mill.'

Ella took one last look at the lights of the Club dancing across the water and through the trees. As the taxi swung into River Street it was finally lost from sight. The next time they visited the place it would be Zeffirelli's opening night - and if the rumours circulating were right Matt would be there. She closed her eyes realising that fact no longer held any fear or apprehension for her. The divorce had toughened her up, given her strength and made her even more focussed. She was standing on the threshold of a new year, about to make a fresh start on her own, leaving Andy and her marriage behind. Perhaps, she decided, it was about time she closed the door on Matt for good too.

'Well, what do you think?'

'It's great. I love Chinese food.' Marcie said looking around at the rich red and gold silk screens and brightly coloured lanterns. 'The sharks fin soup was the best. Where did you find this place anyway?'

'Arnie Ross. It's his favourite restaurant. He eats here all the time.'

'You're kidding me! I always thought he was a burger and fries guy. Well, I guess that's another myth blown.'

'Would you like another drink?'

'Sure.'

Matt raised his hand to attract the attention of the waiter. As he took their order so a second waiter appeared, setting down two food warmers and lighting candles under them. He was followed by a third who cleared away their soup bowls and replaced them with hot empty plates. The wine arrived ahead of a selection of dishes, sweet and sour, special chow mein, fried rice, spicy beef and assorted vegetables. Smiling, Marcie picked up a fork and spoon and began helping herself.

'Well, I have to say this is a wonderful surprise; being met at the airport and taken out to dinner.' She said. 'I thought I'd be curled up in front of the TV watching Perry Como, I didn't expect you to be back yet, thought you'd might still be in the UK.'

'Never got there.' He said taking a mouthful of wine. 'The last song; it took ages to come and even longer to get right. If it hadn't been for Baz giving me a hand I'd probably still be there now. I couldn't leave till it was completed, so I stayed on and spent Christmas in Cordoba.' He saw her disapproving look. 'Marcie it was never a definite arrangement. There'll be other opportunities.'

'When Matt? It's been three years. I know how close you were to them. Letters and phone calls are no substitute.' She saw the guilty expression on his face. 'You don't keep in touch?'

'Hardly,' He shook his head sheepishly. 'Mum and I had a bit of a falling out which we sort of half patched up. Dad calls, but it's been a while now since I spoke to him.' He shrugged. 'My feet haven't touched the ground since I've been working for Doug.'

'No excuses.' She lifted her glass. 'Let's make '73 the year you make that journey home so you can spend some quality time with them. Rebuild those bridges.'

He nodded thoughtfully. 'Maybe.'

'Matt!' She looked sternly at him from under her halo of hair.

He hesitated then smiled. 'Oh, all right, yes. But it will have to be after the next album's finished.'

'Just as long as you do.'

They touched glasses.

'Right!' She said, setting down her drink and continuing with her meal. 'Now, I want to know all about these songs you've been writing. When do I get to hear them?'

'Right after this meal, back at my place, that's why I invited you here tonight. Of course it'll only be with an acoustic guitar, but tomorrow we'll go into the studio.'

'You can't do that! The studio's closed. Doug's vacationing in Europe for two more weeks.'

'Yes I can. Charlene's setting it all up for us.'

'Is that why she was on the phone to you all last week? But Matt, no one goes into that studio unless Doug's here. It's the rules. It's how it is.'

'Marcie,' Matt gave her the benefit of his wonderful smile, 'I need to start this project; it's important. So on this occasion it won't hurt for the rules to be bent a little. Now please, forget about Doug and tell me all about Hawaii.'

'Oh Ella, it looks wonderful!'

Mick's voice woke Ella from her gradual drift into sleep on the back seat of the taxi. She opened her eyes, noticing they had just passed through the gates of her new home. The old red brick house with its white colonnades was a blaze of lights and the majestic blue spruce which lined the driveway sparkled with small white fairy lights.

'I'm glad you like it.' She said as she pushed herself up into a sitting position. 'Do you know, when I first saw this house all I could think about was how good those trees would look decorated with lights for Christmas. I just had to do it.'

'It's beautiful.' Issy said leaning forward to look out of the window as the Zodiac pulled up outside the front door. 'And the house looks so inviting.'

'In that case I insist you both come in for coffee.'

'Are you sure?'

'Yes.'

Paying the driver and asking him to return in an hour, Mick followed Ella and Issy up the steps towards a heavy white door, decorated with a huge holly wreath. Inside the beige carpeted hall, they took off their coats. A door opened and closed upstairs and Helen appeared.

'How's Lucy?' Ella asked as she took the coats and hung them in a small closet.

'Fine, went off without any trouble. Would you all like coffee?'

'Please.' Ella nodded, showing Mick and Issy through into the lounge, a room of creams and rich browns where comfortable toffee coloured couches were set and a warm fire burned in an Adams style stone fireplace.

As they settled themselves comfortably and Ella began telling them about her plans for the house, the shrill of the telephone in the room beyond interrupted their conversation.

'I expect that will be Nick and Jen wanting to wish us Happy New Year. Won't be a minute.' Ella said jumping to her feet. She slid back the connecting doors to the dining room and entered, closing them gently behind her. Issy and Mick sat quietly, watching the fire as they listened to the muffled sound of her voice, then heard the receiver being replaced. They both looked up as the doors parted once more. Ella entered the room, her face pale.

'What's wrong?' Issy got slowly to her feet looking anxious. 'What's happened? Is it Jen?'

'No it's Grandfather.' Ella stood looking at them both, trying to hold back tears. 'He collapsed at the village's New Year's Eve party this evening. He's had a heart attack!'

Marcie sat looking at Matt as he set the guitar down on the floor. The clock on the wall said two thirty but she didn't feel a bit tired. She felt full of energy. Alive! And she knew it was all down to the fact that she was beside him again. He was so special, so different from anyone else she had ever known. A remarkable talent she had heard him called; and he was just that. What a strange way to see in the New Year and yet how wonderful, for she had experienced the strangest sensations as she sang and he accompanied her on his Spanish guitar.

He had done it again, produced ten incredible songs, but there was one which stood out from the others. The one he'd had all the trouble with. *'Never Quite Over You.'* That, she told herself, would be the first single and the one she would also take transatlantic. For Doug had decided that 1973 would be the year to introduce her voice to the UK and European markets.

'Happy?' Matt watched her, a smile on his face.

'Absolutely!' She got up and crossed to where he sat, linking her arm in his, resting her cheek against the thickness of his sweater. 'I'm amazed Matt Benedict. They're all wonderful. I still don't know how you do it.'

'And,' he said ignoring her praise. 'I thought about calling the album *Spanish Steps*. What do you think?'

'I think it's a great title.' She said, reaching up to kiss his cheek. 'You're wonderful. You do so much for me, you know.'

'Ah but you do so much for me too.' He smiled at her. 'Because all this is nothing,' he held out the sheaf of music to her, 'without you to bring it to life. When I hear you sing what I've written, it's amazing. Just now, when you sang *Never Quite Over You* it...' he broke off, shaking his head and turning away from her.

Marcie stared at him. She'd had no idea her voice affected him this way. But then they had always been in the recording studio before, surrounded by other people. Not exactly the place to let his emotions show. Her voice interpreting his lyrics had just brought tears to his eyes; instantly her mind grasped the importance of this. It could be the key. She wanted him to love her, to wipe the ghost of his dead girlfriend away and now she knew there just might a way to make that happen.

Tuesday 2nd January

'To be sure,' Mary Evas said in her soft Irish accent, 'your grandfather must be one of the most cantankerous men on earth.'

Mary and Ella were making their way through Taunton's Musgrove Park Hospital's car park to the Cardiac Ward where Richard Evas had been since the first hours of the New Year.

'First he keeps his heart condition to himself for months.' she continued, 'then he frightens the life out of us all by collapsing on the floor of the Village Hall in the middle of *Auld Lang Syne*. And now he's giving the nurses a hard time, telling them he can't stay because he has a farm to run! If he wasn't wired up to that blessed monitor I'm sure he'd have escaped back to Willowbrook by now.'

'What did the consultant say when you saw him?' Ella asked, feeling considerably calmer now she was in full possession of the facts surrounding her grandfather's collapse.

'Rest, rest and more rest.' Mary answered as she pushed through the doors of the main entrance and made her way up the grey tiled corridor. She stopped for a moment, turning to look at Ella, her hands tightening over the bag of fruit she carried. 'We have to face it,' she said, her expression serious, 'he is not a well man and he just cannot go back to doing what he did. Those days are over for good.'

'How are you going to manage?' Ella looked concerned as they moved off again, taking a left turn through swing doors. 'Is Jake able to take over?'

'No. Good as he is at the foreman's job, I don't think poor old Jake's up to running the place long term. I think there's only one thing for it. We'll have to hire a Manager.'

They had reached the Cardiac Ward now; dark red doors punctuated with white lettering. Mary hesitated, her hand resting on the handle. 'Now then,' she said, 'whatever you do, don't mention *anything* about Willowbrook. And for goodness sake don't tell him what I'm planning or he'll have a relapse. As far as he's concerned, he's in for another week then back to Kingsford General for a fortnight. By the time he comes home I'll have it sorted, but at this stage, the least we say about anything the better.'

Wednesday 3rd January

Jenny emerged from Langleys with a huge sigh of relief, glad to be free at last from the rugby scrum of their January sale.

Walking to her red Ford Escort, the cold easterly wind chilling her cheeks, she stowed her shopping in the boot and turned back towards the town, one last purchase firmly in her thoughts. The bag had been on her mind for days. It was just the thing she had been looking for, in beautiful soft tan leather. As she reached Faye Benedict's shop *Handbags and Gladrags* she checked the window. Yes it was still there, and now with a ten percent reduction; even better.

Pushing through the front door into the cosy interior, she stood quietly waiting to be served. Faye's two girls were both busy; one with a customer purchasing shoes, the other behind the counter wrapping gloves. Faye appeared suddenly from the back of the shop, pushing through the beaded curtain with a box of silk scarves.

'Hello Jenny.' She said, sliding the box onto the glass top of the counter and brushing a strand of dark hair out of her eyes. 'Happy New Year. We missed you and Nick at the Club on Sunday. What happened?'

'A touch of gastric flu over Christmas.' She made a face as she patted her stomach. 'You know I really did want to be there too, what with it being the Mill's last big evening before it closed, but I just didn't feel well enough. Issy tells me you went out in real style.'

'Yes we did and now we're both very excited about the future. I think the new club will be even better.' Faye's eyes lit up with enthusiasm. 'Tad is so thrilled about the project; I can't wait to see the finished result. But what about you, are you OK now?' She asked as she took the scarves one by one from the box and arranged them on a nearby stand.

'Yes, much better, thanks.'

'So,' Faye stowed the empty box under the counter, 'what can I do for you?'

'I'd like the tan bag in the window please.'

'Ah yes, I know the one.' Faye lifted the flap and crossed to the metal and glass structure housing a host of multi-colour handbags in the main window, gently removing Jenny's prospective purchase and bringing it back to her.

Jenny took the handbag with a smile and opened it, exploring its interior. 'Great, I'll take it.' She looked pleased as she handed it back to Faye, slipping her bag from her shoulder and retrieving her purse.

'Are you in a hurry?' Faye asked as she cut the price tag off and began wrapping Jenny's purchase carefully.

'No. Why?'

'Well, I'm just about to make a coffee and there's a spare slice of sponge going begging. Thought you might like to join me.'

'I'd love to.' Jenny said, handing over the cash and taking possession of the green and gold plastic carrier.

Faye dropped the money into the till and closed it, then lifted the flap and ushered Jenny through the beaded curtain into the kitchen.

'Paula.' As she pushed back the curtain to let Jenny through she called out to one of her assistants who was busy serving a middle aged couple. 'Just going for a coffee, give me a shout if things get busy.'

Mick Taylor turned his blue Stag off the main road and into the quiet village of Kings Moreton where Taylor Macayne Residential had just begun building another new clutch of luxury homes. The site, formerly the orchard and paddock of a large Victorian vicarage was flat and even with good access and planning permission had been given for five four bedroom detached houses. Now the site infrastructure was in and the roof on the first house, Mick had driven out today as part of his weekly site visit programme to see how things were coming on.

As he turned into the cul-de-sac he saw the ambulance with its rear doors open standing outside Plot one. A site accident; that was all he needed. Pulling up beside it he ducked under scaffolding and ran quickly into the house. A group of men were standing in a huddle towards the back of the building watching two ambulance men transfer someone carefully onto a stretcher.

'What's happened?' He called out.

Dave Meredith, the Site Foreman turned and walked back to meet him. 'A fall, from up there.' He looked up at the joists.

'How bad?'

'Broken leg, compound fracture, nasty business. Could be off a while.'

'Who is it?'

'Your ex-father-in-law.'

Mick and Dave watched as the ambulance men manoeuvred the stretcher through the gaping hole that would eventually be the dining room doorway. As they passed by Mick looked down at the small man whose left leg was now encased in a splint, his face grey with pain.

'What have you been up to Ron?' He said. 'Out on the beer again?'

'No! It's that bitch of a daughter of mine!' The little man replied angrily as he tried unsuccessfully to push himself up onto one elbow. 'The little cow, if I ever get hold of her I'll kill her, I swear to God I will! Aahhh.'

'You need to lay still Sir.' The ambulance man holding the back of the stretcher called out to him. 'That's a bad fracture; you don't want to make any it worse.'

Ron Harrison lay back against the pillow and closed his eyes, clenching his teeth in agony. The stretcher passed by, leaving Mick and Dave alone.

'What was that all about?' Mick looked curiously at Dave.

'He was there, just by the stairwell about to get on the ladder to come down.' Dave pointed. 'He overheard Gus Chapman talking to Terry Wilson about your ex and Andy Macayne.'

'What about them?'

'Gus was in Langleys with his wife last Saturday.' Dave replied. 'Saw this woman, dressed up to the nines, wearing a big hat and dark glasses. Ordering this and that she was, treating the place like she owned it. He suddenly realised it was Nina. Seems she's redecorating Andy's house, new furniture, the lot. Rumour has it she's moved in with him too. Well, Ron went apeshit when he heard. Ranting and raving about the disgrace she'd brought on the family and what he was going to do to her when he got hold of her. He was so lathered up he missed a rung as he came down the ladder. Hit the concrete floor pretty hard. Talk about mad, I've never seen anyone in a worse temper.'

'You will.' Mick said with a grin, 'When Bob finds out!'

'Well that's my news, what about yours?' Faye asked, chasing cake crumbs around her plate with her fingers. 'Anything exciting going on in the Kendrick household?'

Jenny finished her coffee and slid the mug along the worktop towards the draining board. She had insisted on hearing all about Tad's plans for the new club first and now thinking about her own life, it seemed filled with ordinary day-to-day living and the expected arrival of the new baby, which they had already touched on briefly.

'Exciting?' She thought for a moment. 'I don't think so. Child rearing and housework don't really come under that heading do they?' She laughed. 'If there's anything exciting going on in the family I guess Ella's cornered the market there. Her decree nisi came through two weeks ago.' She said nibbling at her cake. 'Four weeks to the absolute and she's certainly not letting the grass grow under her feet.'

'Oh?' Faye eyed Jenny curiously. 'New man in her life is there?'

'No; nothing like that.' Jenny replied, finishing off her cake and wiping her hands on a tissue she'd found in her coat pocket. 'She comes into her trust fund this September but her grandmother has allowed her to use some of the money early to buy another house. It's on the edge of Kingsford. A lovely place; lawns right down to the water, huge sun terrace off the main bedroom. Helen's moving in with her too. As Ella's come back to work part time she'll be looking after Lucy as well as the house.'

'Well, well, so Andy's on his own is he?' Faye looked amused as she consigned her empty plate to the draining board. 'Can't see him coping with his own domestic chores without a housekeeper, can you? I bet it won't be long before he's knocking on Bob's door begging to come home.'

'I thought that too.' Jenny said brushing the crumbs from her lap. 'But Ella said he likes the Lodge, wants to keep it. I think he's making arrangements to employ someone.'

'Blonde and Swedish no doubt.' Faye smiled. They both laughed.

'What's Matt up to these days?' Jenny asked curiously, sliding off her stool and slotting her plate under Faye's. 'I heard he'd split with the band just over a year ago.'

'Yes he did.' Faye's expression tightened suddenly. 'It was all very sudden.

We never did get to the bottom of it.' She shrugged, being deliberately vague. 'He lives in New York now, you know.' She added quietly getting up to rinse her mug under the tap. 'Doing very well so we hear.'

'Good.' Jenny's eyes brightened with interest, 'I heard rumours Tad was going to ask him to open the new club.'

'Yes, he keeps talking about it - hasn't contacted him yet, of course.' Faye's voice began to waver and her hand went unsteadily to her lips as she turned off the tap. 'Anyway I'm not sure whether Matt will come. He's been away for three years now. He did promise he'd be home in December, but then at the last minute he said his writing had reached a critical stage and he wouldn't be able to make it.' She stemmed the trickle of a tear from the corner of her eye and looked despairingly at Jenny. 'I'd like to think that was true, but sometimes...' Her voice trailed off. 'I wonder if we'll ever see him again!'

'Of course you will! He's bound to say yes isn't he?'

'Do you think so?' Faye said pulling a handkerchief from her pocket. 'I'm not so sure.' She sniffed and blew her nose loudly. 'There's bound to be some reason why he can't come.'

'Oh come on, think positively.' Jenny said encouragingly. 'Pick up the phone! Ask him! If he's as busy as you say he is he is going to need as much notice as possible, isn't he? And just think how pleased and surprised Tad would be if you pulled it off!'

'Yes, of course, he would. But what if Matt says no?' Faye looked doubtful. 'I couldn't bear it if that happened.' She pulled her handkerchief to her face again.

'Oh Faye,' Jenny smiled softly and gave the older woman's shoulder a comforting squeeze. 'This is a very special occasion; he'll do it, I know he will.'

NINE

Tuesday 9th January

Marcie and Matt stood with the other members of the recording team in the studio listening to approaching footfalls in the corridor outside.

'I only hear one set of footsteps.' Marcie said in a hoarse whisper, her head tilted, listening. 'Do you think Charlene's managed to pull it off?'

'Sure.' Matt nodded confidently. 'He's putty in her hands.'

'What'll you do if she hasn't?'

'That isn't going to happen.'

'Don't worry Marcie, the worst Doug can do is fire him.' Recording engineer Arnie Ross winked at her as he relaxed back in his chair in front of the console.

'Oh shut up Arnie!' Marcie said shooting a worried glance towards the door, hearing the footsteps stop and watching the handle of the door move. She closed her eyes, crossed her fingers and offered up a small prayer for their deliverance. She should never have gone along with this and she knew it. She was as guilty as the rest, and now feared the consequences of Matt's rash decision to lay down tracks while Doug was away. The door swung open and Doug stood there like Al Capone. Wearing a dark pinstripe suite, a black cashmere coat draped over his shoulders, he stood gazing around the studio at the assembled team, his dark eyebrows drawn together severely.

'I understand from my daughter that this studio, which is normally off limits, has been in use while I've been away.' He said, his gaze falling on each of them in turn,

Nobody in the room moved. Marcie looked at everyone around her. All wore uncomfortable expressions apart from Matt. He stepped forward to face Doug.

'Yes, I know it was out of order boss, but I've put together a new album of songs for Marcie and it was important to get moving on them as soon as possible. If I'd waited for you to come back I know I would have lost the momentum.'

Doug didn't answer; instead he paced slowly around the room looking at them all.

'And I don't want you blaming Charlene or any of the guys here.' Matt continued. 'It was all my idea.'

Settling himself on a spare stool in the corner, Doug lit up one of his regular Havana cigars. As the smoke drifted slowly upwards to the ceiling his eyes came to rest on Matt once more.

'I also understand from my daughter,' he said, pulling the cigar from his mouth, 'that she thinks this album is going to be - how did she put it?' He waved his cigar in the air. 'Simply awesome. So,' he nodded thoughtfully, 'before I decide whether I should fire you or not, maybe I ought to hear what you've done so far.'

Wednesday 10th January

Faye sat in her drawing room amongst the pastel peaches and greens she loved so much, a warm fire burning in the hearth. Outside, beyond the protection of the curtains, a cold north wind beat at the window. Sitting at the small oak bureau, she was going through the shop's books, analysing how well the sale was going when she heard the clock in the hall chime ten and got to her feet. Tad was visiting one of his hotels this evening, The Blue Lion at Ilminster, saying he would be back by ten thirty. Her free evening, she decided, would be just the opportunity to make her call to Matt, the one she had been putting off for days.

Jenny's visit had left her confident; ready to pick up the phone and tackle her son there and then, positive that she could entice him home for Tad's opening night. But she had delayed the moment; the daily bustle of the shop had intervened and so she decided make the call later that evening instead. However, when she got home, she discovered Tad had made arrangements for them to eat out. Unable to argue without revealing her secret plans, she went. She had to admit she enjoyed the meal, a new French restaurant in Taunton which someone had recommended and after a couple of glasses of wine any concerns about delaying her phone call began to evaporate. However, the next day when she woke up she found everything was different. Her confidence seemed to have deserted her and doubts had crept in again. There were so many 'what ifs' it made her head spin. For the last eight days she had been agonising over the whole thing. And now she knew she had to do something. Standing in the hall, address book in hand, she realised she couldn't delay any longer. Her stomach churned, she knew she would fall to pieces if he said no. But that isn't going to happen she told herself. She knew he hated the limelight, but this was different, it was a family thing and it would be so quick. A moment on stage, a few words then he could slip back to the anonymity of their table for the rest of the evening. Finger in the dial she closed her eyes.

'Please.' She whispered. 'Please be there.'

'I didn't realise shopping could be so much fun!' Marcie said, pulling off her coat

The Ghost of You and Me

and dropping all her designer bags into a chair. 'Do you really think the hot orange dress will go with the pink suede shoes?'

'In your case definitely.' Matt confirmed, stacking the bags he was carrying into the other corner of the settee. 'Although I don't think the woman who served you in Bloomingdales was convinced.'

Marcie giggled and kicked off her shoes before sinking into a chair, remembering their afternoon of shopping and how she had spent over an hour mixing and matching colours - much to the horror of the blue rinsed matron who hovered attentively. Now they were back at Matt's apartment and all she wanted to do was curl up and relax.

'So, what's it to be tonight?' Matt asked, lodging himself on the arm of her chair as he unbuttoned his sheepskin. 'Italian, Greek or shall we just do a takeaway?'

'Don't mind. I'm easy.' Marcie said, grabbing the remote and scanning the channels for something to watch. 'Hey, look at that!' She laughed, settling back to watch *Hawaii Five-0*. 'I bought a shirt just like that one when I was in Hawaii, do you think it would work as one of my stage outfits for the UK tour? I've got some fabulous red boots and great green flares, I could do the bare midriff thing, big flower in my hair...'

'Marcie Macguire.' Matt interrupted, gazing at the TV screen, his face creased with amusement. 'Now I know you're completely mad!' They were still laughing when the shrill of the kitchen phone interrupted and took him from the room.

As Matt disappeared, Marcie settled down to watch the last half of the programme. Later, as the credits rolled, she realised Matt had not returned from the kitchen. Puzzled she turned off the TV and went to find him.

He was leaning on the draining board, looking out of the window across Central Park's wintry landscape. Quietly she crossed the kitchen and stood next to him, resting her hand on his shoulder.

'Matt? What is it?'

He took a step back and looked at her, his face pale, his eyes huge. 'It's nothing. Really, it's nothing.'

'Who was on the phone?'

'No one, please I'm fine, really I am.' He pushed her towards the door. 'Just go back and watch TV.' He flipped the switch on the kettle. 'I'll make us some coffee.'

'Matt, stop it. You look awful. Please, tell me who were you talking to?'

'My Mother.'

'Oh boy!' She put a hand to her face. 'Something's happened hasn't it? Has your dad been taken ill or something?'

'No, no, he's fine. They're both fine.' He waved a calming hand at her.

'Well what is it then, what's upset you so much?' She frowned, frustrated, wanting desperately to cut through the invisible barrier he had retreated behind. 'I don't understand. Matt, tell me please.'

'They want me to come home.' He said in a flat voice. 'My Dad's club.

The Ghost of You and Me

Remember I told you about it? Well it's having a face lift. Going up market. They're re-opening this summer. It's going to be called Zeffirelli's.'

'Matt that's great!' She clasped her hands joyfully. 'And just the excuse you needed.'

'Yes, but...'

'What?'

'They want me to open it.'

'That's wonderful.'

'That's just the thing; it isn't.' He screwed his face in to a frown. 'And I can't think what made me agree to do it.'

'Matt, I don't understand, what's the big deal?' Marcie's heart went out to him, still so shy, even after all his fame. 'You're the local boy made good; everyone will be so pleased to see you. What's this? Stage fright?' She laughed. 'You've been in front of thousands without any trouble. Your Dad's club will be a breeze.'

'That's where you're wrong.' Matt shook his head stubbornly. 'It won't.'

'Matt.' Marcie looked at him uneasily. 'Is there something you don't want to face back in England?'

'What?'

'What *really* made you walk out on the Attitude?'

'I've already told you. It was all over!' He shouted. 'We'd seen it all, done it all. There was nothing new left to experience! I was bored!'

'No way; I believed that once but not anymore. Something real bad happened didn't it? And that's why you've been here in New York ever since. Is she the reason you haven't been home?'

'Who?'

'Your old girlfriend. The one who died? Did it happen while you were away on the American tour? Weren't you able to get home? Does that make you still feel guilty in some way? Is that why you're scared to go back?'

'What is this Marcie?' He rounded on her angrily. 'Some sort of interrogation?'

'No! I just think it would help if you sat down and talked to me about whatever's bugging you; get it off your chest.'

'There's nothing to discuss.'

'Don't give me that, you've a major hang up about something.' She replied, tired of the way he kept evading the issue. 'Isn't it about time you got everything out into the open? Finished your grieving. Laid those ghosts to rest? Because if you did then maybe, just maybe you could get on with the rest of your life.'

'Butt out Marcie!' He stepped back from her, his expression explosive. 'I don't need a shrink and if I did it wouldn't be you!'

She stared at him, feeling the force of his anger almost like a physical blow, shocked and frightened by such a sudden and unexpected outburst. 'Matt,' she said quietly, 'I was only trying to help.'

'I don't need *help*.' He said through gritted teeth. 'I really am all right.'

'But that just it, you're not...'

'Marcie, just piss off and leave me alone!' His temper exploded once more.
'What?'
'Leave! I'd like you to leave now!' He pointed towards the door.
'Right!' She stared at him, her dark eyes blazing angrily. 'Right, if that's the way you really feel! If you want to wander around tied to all these bad vibes then OK, you do that. Me? I've better things to do than stand here having my concern for you pushed back into my face! You don't need me? Fine! It's your loss!'

Snatching up her coat and shopping from the lounge Marcie threw open the front door and left, hot tears blurring her vision as she ran down the corridor, towards the elevator.

Thursday 11th January

'You've got a nerve showing your face here after what you've done!' Elsie Harrison said irritably as she ran the iron over a folded candy striped cotton sheet.

'Mum! Don't be angry please!' Nina watched her mother's strangle hold on the iron suddenly intensify as she pushed it across the material, her face pale and tired. 'Look I haven't been to the hospital. I knew that would only make matters worse. I thought maybe if I could talk to you then you could tell him that I do care, and I want to help if I can.'

'We don't want your help.' Elsie said stubbornly. 'And as for caring, if you'd cared anything about this family my girl, you wouldn't have caused all the trouble you have.'

Her mouth set in a thin line of displeasure as she glared at her daughter standing there like some well dressed stranger, totally out of keeping with the shabbiness of her kitchen and her own faded clothes.

'That Mick was a nice lad.' She shook her head. 'Your father was horrified when he heard you were getting divorced. And then that other nonsense with that toff, Mr Nicholson. Nearly old enough to be your father he was! What did you think you were playing at you stupid girl? You made us all a laughing stock. And now here you are again, living in sin with Macayne's boy. And how do we get to hear about it? Through some brickie at work telling one of the labourers! Your father went spare, that's how he fell off the ladder!' She shook her head despairingly. 'And now he'll be laid up for months with his broken leg. A bad break the doctor said. Compound fracture.' She pointed the iron at Nina angrily before attacking the sheet again. 'And where's it all going to lead to I ask myself? In tears like it always does with you!'

'I'm happy now; I'm settled. You should be pleased for me.' Nina said, wanting to move the conversation away from her father's troubles and focus on more positive things like herself and her good fortune. How could his accident possibly be her fault? She hadn't pushed him; he had fallen off the ladder all by himself. Silly old fool.

'If I remember rightly, you were very keen for us to settle down together once.'

'Not like this.' Elsie replied, folding the sheet neatly and placing it on the kitchen worktop next to the other things she had ironed. 'Not without churching, it's not decent.'

'Oh Mum, this is the nineteen seventies, everything's more casual now.'

'Just like your relationship.' Her mother eyed her scornfully. 'You're just a convenience to him, till something better turns up.'

'It's not like that at all!'

'Oh no? Do you honestly think if that housekeeper of his was still there he would have been as keen to have you under his roof? Wake up girl!'

'I'm not a housekeeper!' Nina tossed her hair indignantly. 'I'm his live in girlfriend; I have a clothes allowance and my own car, see!' She pointed out of the kitchen window where her new yellow Triumph Spitfire was parked. 'I came to help too.' She pulled an envelope from her handbag. 'I know Dad's going to be off work for a while and as Bob's not exactly the most generous of employers, I brought this for you.' She held out a brown envelope.

'What is it?' Her mother looked at it suspiciously as she rested her iron and took it from her.

'Two hundred quid, it should tide you over for a while.' She smiled, watching her mother's mouth open in amazement as she pulled the notes from the envelope.

'More than you've seen in a long time eh?'

Elsie Harrison stared at the money in her hand then at her daughter.

'It's OK Mum, take it.' Nina nodded enthusiastically. 'There's plenty more where that came from. Andy gives me a very generous allowance.' She laughed. 'Besides this is Macayne money, no more than Dad should have really.'

'I don't want it!' Elsie said pushing it back at her daughter, her face flooding with anger.

'But Mum, Dad's not working, you need it!'

'No I don't, we'll manage.'

'I insist.'

'You can insist all you like.' Her mother said churlishly. 'If it was honestly earned I'd accept, but it ain't. You can call yourself what you like Nina, but this is whore's money.' She shoved the envelope at Nina.

'Mum!'

'Oh Nina!' She gave a sarcastic laugh as she pulled a blouse from the washing basket and picked up her iron again. 'Look at your face, so offended. But can't you see how it looks to everyone? You're just a kept woman. All your fancy gear and money is just the window dressing he provides to make you feel better about yourself. He's just paying for regular sex. If he really thought anything of you, he'd have asked you to marry him by now. After all, he's single ain't he? Nothing to stop him putting that ring on your finger, showing the world you're good enough to be his wife. But he won't do that, never in a million years. And there's nothing you can do to make him!'

'Who says I want him to? I'm quite happy as I am thank you!' Nina retaliated angrily. 'I don't need marriage! Look what it's done for you. Made you old before your time.' She gazed around the kitchen, with its worn curtains and peeling paintwork, unchanged since the day she had left to marry Mick. 'I'd rather be the whore you think I am than piss poor like you, living in this dump! You can keep respectable! Who needs it?' And without another word she pushed the envelope back into her bag and left the kitchen, slamming the door behind her.

Elsie Harrison stood there for a moment, watching as her daughter climbed into her car and drove off into the distance. 'As I said it'll all end in tears, my girl.' She said. Then with a weary shrug of her shoulders she returned to her task, concentrating on the run of the iron through the blouse, banishing the creases one by one.

Nina rammed her foot to the floor of the Spitfire, her anger burning. She had expected her mother to be pleased, to be even grateful for a share of her good fortune. She had gone home genuinely wanting to help, to show she wasn't the selfish, uncaring daughter she had been branded. But instead of being happy for her, her mother had launched a personal attack on her morals and with a few brief words, had turned the elation on its head, making her feel that she was cheap and worthless. Ah well, she was glad it was all out in the open now. It was about time they realised they couldn't get away with criticising her, not when they were more embarrassing than she was. Marriage! What did she need that for? She was happy with the way things were; public vows and a piece of paper didn't make a relationship any better, in fact in some ways it made it more complicated. Look at the endless visits to the solicitors she had been required to make when splitting with Mick.

She smiled to herself as she turned in through the gates of Chelwood Lodge; the feel good factor returned instantly as she took in the opulence of her new home. Things were different this time; she was with a new changed Andy, one who adored and spoiled her. A man whose only wish was to make her happy. And if her mother chose to be cynical about it, well that was her problem.

Marcie arrived at Maverick still smarting from the events of the previous evening. She was not only angry with Matt at being so stubborn and not wanting to confide in her but also with herself. The way he had been emotionally moved by her singing on New Year's Eve had given her a false sense of her own influence over him. She'd really blown it hadn't she? She wondered whether he was still mad at her. Perhaps, she decided, the best thing to do was act as if nothing had happened, contenting herself with the fact that once he heard her sing, hopefully he would soon come round.

Doug was chatting to Arnie as she entered the recording studio.

'Where's Matt?' She said, pulling off her coat.

'He phoned in; said he was taking the day off.' Doug said chewing on freshly lit Havana.

The Ghost of You and Me

'Did he say why?' She screwed her face up in a frown.

'Hey, the guy wants a day off.' Doug pulled the cigar from his mouth. 'Is there a problem somewhere?'

'Yes - no - oh forget it!'

'Well c'mon then.' He opened the door to the recording booth and ushered her in. 'Let's get going. Time's money.'

Isolated in the soundproof booth, she began to worry about Matt, wondering how he was, what he was doing. Thoughts ran around her head so wildly that she began to find concentration almost impossible. She made mistake after mistake, Arnie threw his hands up in exasperation, Doug raised frustrated eyes to the ceiling, chewed ferociously on his cigar and when she eventually came to record *Never Quite Over You,* which she considered the most important track of the album, the whole thing turned into a bad tempered confrontation between her and the recording team.

An irritable Doug eventually called it a day at lunch time and everyone pulled on their coats and went, leaving her alone to struggle into her green Astrakhan coat and yeti boots.

Outside the studio she hovered in the compacted snow on the edge of the sidewalk, watching the flow of traffic, her arm half raised in anticipation, waiting for an empty cab to come into view. Now she was out of the studio, the most important thing was to get to Matt's apartment, and make sure he was all right. She closed her eyes, fearing the worst, suddenly turning the blame on herself. She had been arrogant, pushing uninvited into his private life. This was all her fault.

A yellow cab left the main stream of traffic and pulled up to the pavement a few yards away, the back door swinging open as it came to a halt. She hurried forward, eager to claim it then stopped. It pulled away, leaving its passenger standing there, hands pushed deep in the pockets of his sheepskin.

'Matt!' She threw herself at him like an enthusiastic puppy. 'Oh Matt thank goodness, I've been so worried.'

'Hey, hey, calm down.' He said placing a firm grip on her shoulders.

'Matt, I'm sorry, I'm so sorry!' She continued, unaffected by his restraining hands. 'It's been such a pig of a day. I've been useless. Doug's mad at me. He's closed the studio and sent everyone home. I couldn't concentrate. Sang like a turkey!' She clasped him tighter than ever, so glad he was safe and well.

'Marcie!' He pushed her away, holding her at arms length. 'Will you listen please? There's something I need to say.'

She looked up at him eagerly, watching his face, waiting for his words.

'I'm sorry too.' He said gently. 'I behaved like a complete heel. I know you were worried, that you only wanted to help.'

'I still do Matt.' She looked at him her eyes bright. 'It was about the girl who died though wasn't it? That's why you didn't want to go home.'

'Yes.' He looked at her for a moment before continuing. 'But the thing is she isn't dead.'

'Not dead?' Marcie frowned.

'No.' He hung his head. 'I lied to you. It was unforgivable I know, but I had to. It was too painful to talk about at the time. But you were right; it's about time I got everything out into the open. I met her years ago when we were both at college; we were always together as friends but I couldn't tell her how I really felt, that I loved her. The band took me away and I lost her; she married someone else. Then a couple of years later we met up again. She said it was me she'd always loved. That she was going to leave him and spend the rest of her life with me. I was so happy. But she lied. She went back to him again. It happened just before the American tour. Everything fell apart after that. You're right; I didn't want to go home. That's why I left the Attitude and stayed on to work for Doug. Lately I was beginning to think I was OK - that I was over it. Then last night after my mother rang I suddenly realised what going home would really mean. I didn't know whether I could cope. You know, seeing her again.'

'But you were planning to go back for Christmas. You seemed quite happy then.'

'I know. But I was so involved with getting the new album written that I didn't really stop to take in the implications of what I'd decided to do. Just as well I never made it. The old club bowed out with a massive New Year's Eve party. She'd have been there with him. It would have been awful.'

'Oh Matt!' Marcie looked up at him, feeling his distress. 'Poor you.'

'You're not mad with me then?'

'No, I could never be mad with you. Not for long anyway.' Her smile surfaced, familiar and affectionate.

He hugged her then, glad things were back to normal, but at the same time filled with a strange regret that warm and generous hearted as she was, what he felt for her could never be more than friendship.

'So where have you been all day?' She asked, still locked in his embrace.

'In Central Park, wandering. Went to the Zoo. Talked to the animals!'

'And what did they say Dr. Dolittle?'

'That I'm big enough to face June 30th. It's not going to be the end of the world.'

'June 30th?' She broke away from him. 'That's five days away from the start of my UK tour.'

'I know. I thought I'd fly up to Edinburgh on the 1st, join you there.'

'No Matt, I'm coming with you.'

'What?'

'I want to be with you. Help you get through this. I'll sing! I can make it my first public performance in the UK - for free.'

'Marcie.' He was taken aback by her generosity. 'I don't know what to say.'

'Just say yes Matt.'

'Well...Yes! And thank you!'

With a satisfied smile she moved away from him to the kerbside and spotting an approaching empty cab, flagged it down.

'Come on then.' She called back to him as she opened its rear door.

'Where are we going?' He asked as he ran to join her.

'Lunch. And on the way you can tell me all about this heartless woman of yours.'

'Ella.' He said. 'Her name is Ella.'

TEN

Monday 12th February

'Is this it?' Ella held up the sheet of paper up in front of Marcus Goddard, a look of bewilderment on her face.

'I'm afraid so.'

'A photocopy with the court's stamp on it? I can't believe it.'

'What were you expecting?' Marcus smiled as he took off his glasses and laid them on his blotter, 'Parchment with an official seal?'

'No.' Ella placed the paper on her lap. 'But I did think it would look a bit more professional than this, you know, like an examination certificate.' She studied the sheet, running her finger over her name, then over Andy's, finally coming to rest over Nina's. 'This doesn't feel like freedom at all.'

'Well it is,' Marcus assured her, 'and I insist on taking you to lunch to celebrate. Where would you like to go?'

She thought for a moment. 'The Red Lion would be nice.'

'Oh come on.' He looked offended. 'A back street boy I may be, but I think I can run to something a bit more exotic than a pub lunch.'

'No, honestly, the pub will be fine Marcus,' Ella insisted. 'I'm not really dressed for restaurant eating anyway.' she indicated her jeans,' and I can't stay long, I promised to be in Meridan Cross by three; my grandfather's coming out of hospital today and I want to surprise him.'

Bob Macayne swung his Jaguar through the gates of Chelwood Lodge. He was on his way to see Andy, who for some strange reason, seemed to have taken himself out of circulation for the past few weeks. He had rung the site earlier that morning to talk to him, only to be told that he was at home but expected in after lunch. Andy's blasé attitude towards the divorce was worrying Bob. There did not appear to be any trace of remorse or regret; he was approaching his divorce from Ella in a cold, clinical business-like way. Bob wondered whether he was just putting a brave face on things. Knowing the decree absolute was imminent, he decided perhaps the time was right for a visit, to show some fatherly support and also to see what Andy's fancy interior designer had been up to.

Fresh from lunch with Mel, he was in an extremely good mood. For that lunch had thrown up a very interesting update on the situation in Meridan Cross. Mel's father was coming out of hospital today, with express instructions that he take things easy. Knowing she was probably the last person he'd want to see, Mel had decided to stay away from the village. Instead she had sent a get well card and kept in touch with her step mother, who had informed her that their foreman was now running Willowbrook. Bob didn't know much about farming, but he guessed that this foreman's experience and seniority would be on a par with one of his own site foremen. They were team players but certainly not up to running the business themselves. Therefore he guessed it would not be too long before Richard Evas would need to review his current situation and hire a manager. And when that happened he would be waiting, ready to give financial assistance in return for Fox Cottage and the land he needed.

With this in his possession it would be easy not only getting the right price out of Miles and Mirage Holdings when he sold it on to them, but to also become their contractor of choice for the build. And when that day came it would more than make up for the losses he had incurred on the Shopping Precinct due to Miles Anderson's trickery.

Parking next to Andy's Mercedes, he walked to the front door, confident that everything was at last going his way and the whole thing was practically in the bag. He smiled as he rang the door bell. When Mirage Holdings' Scandinavian holiday village project was they were all going to be very rich. On the second ring the door opened and Andy stood there, holding a sandwich. Despite the smile Bob decided Andy wasn't really that pleased to see him.

'Dad! Ah, actually you've caught me at a really bad moment.' He said, placing one foot across the threshold, barring his father's way. 'I'm about to leave for the site. What's the problem?'

'I was a little concerned; you haven't been in touch lately.' Bob peered beyond Andy, wondering what it was he was hiding. 'I wondered whether this divorce thing was getting you down. Thought I'd better come round and make sure you were all right.'

'I'm fine, just fine.' Andy nodded nervously, taking another bite of his sandwich and then looking at his watch. 'Actually Dad I'm running late, I'm due to meet Tom Ransome of Ransome and Ridley at two fifteen. They're keen to handle the marketing, thought I'd give them a go.' As he took a step backwards into the hall and pulled his coat from the rack, Bob noticed the new decor.

'Good grief!' He said, spotting the heavy flock wallpaper in the hall. 'Where has all that lovely old oak panelling gone? Are you sure this woman knows what she's doing?'

'Of course she does.' Andy said indignantly. 'I wanted something completely different if you must know,' he added defensively

'Well it's certainly that.' Bob raised puzzled eyebrows. 'I do hope you're not letting yourself be taken in by a load of arty-farty nonsense.'

'Of course not. Come on Dad, I'm going to be late.' Easing his father off the doorstep, he stuffed the remainder of the sandwich into his mouth, pulled on his coat and slammed the front door behind him.

'Fancy a trip to the site with me? See how we're getting on?' He said unlocking the door of his Mercedes. 'The show house is almost finished.'

'Thought you were in a hurry; you said you were meeting Tom Ransome at two fifteen.'

'I am, but I think I might be able to squeeze you in for a quick guided tour before Tom arrives.' The old smile returned.

'Yes, I'd like that.' Bob replied, noticing how Andy seemed more relaxed now they were out of the house. Inside he had been nervous and edgy. It meant he was hiding something - but what, and why? Had he been embarrassed by the obvious fiasco the hall had turned into? Or was there something else? Whatever it was, when they got to the site he was determined to find out.

Bob followed the Mercedes down the driveway and through the main gates, watching it speed away towards Kings Moreton. Waiting for a gap in the traffic, he eased the Jaguar to the edge of the road and eventually pulled out. As he accelerated away three vehicles passed him, the last of which was a yellow Triumph Spitfire with a familiar face at the wheel. Glancing in his rear view mirror he saw it was indicating to turn left into the Lodge. Suddenly he understood the reason for his son's nervous behaviour, bundling him out of the house, eager to get back to the site. He was expecting Nina Taylor.

At the first opportunity he turned the Jaguar back towards Chelwood Lodge where Nina was in the process of retrieving bags of shopping from the boot of the Spitfire. He watched as she made her way to the front door and let herself in. Bob sat motionless behind the wheel, cold anger seeping its way through him. So Mel had been right after all; it was her in Langleys spending money on his account. With a roar of anger he slammed the car into gear and headed towards the house.

'Well, what a wonderful surprise!' Mary's soft features broke into a broad smile as she opened the door to find Ella standing there. Reaching out she kissed her cheek. 'No prizes for guessing who you've come to see. Actually, I was just about to go out for a ride. Fancy joining me? Merlin could do with some exercise.'

'I'd love to, but is there enough time? I do want to be here when Granddad arrives.'

'Plenty, the ambulance car will be bringing him home around 4.30.' Mary said picking up her riding crop from the hall. 'Come on, I'll find you a hat.'

She closed the door and they both crossed the yard to the long, low wooden building which housed the Trekking Centre.

'Is Rachel around?'

'She's looking after the shop today, her mother has the flu.' Mary said producing a key and unlocking the door to the clothing store. 'It's a brave bug that dare attack the likes of Margaret Sylvester. I doubt it will stay very long.'

Ella smiled.

'And how's that beautiful daughter of yours.' Mary asked, rummaging through a rack of riding hats.

'She's fine. And growing up fast, I can't believe she's nearly a year old.'

'You must bring her out here to see us all. We haven't seen her since the christening you know. We miss her.'

Mary's words made Ella realise how absorbed she had become in both the divorce and her business. 'I'll bring her out soon, I promise.' she said.

'You make sure you do now. Here,' Mary said handing her a hat and picking one for herself, 'this one looks as though it might fit.'

Ella pulled it on. 'Good guess, it's just my size.'

'Great.' Mary gave a satisfied grin. 'Let's go then.'

They left the Centre, Mary relocking the door and slipping the keys into the pocket of her jacket

'Laura tells me your divorce has come through.' She said as they made their way towards the stable block.

'Yes, in fact the decree absolute came through today.'

Ella followed Mary into the warm depths of the stable where she caught the familiar scent of hay and horse. A shaft of sunlight from the roof light played around them momentarily as Mary's blue eyes caught hers.

'And how are you feeling now it's all over? Sad: happy, relieved?'

'A little of all of those I guess.'

Ella moved across to her grey hunter Merlin's stall and ran her hand affectionately over his velvet nose. 'No one likes to feel they've failed do they? But on the other hand I knew I couldn't stay with him any longer.'

'Never mind,' Mary replied, leading her black mare Cassie from her stall and throwing the saddle over her back, 'You'll get over this, I know you will, and who knows, perhaps next time...'

'There isn't going to be a next time.' Ella replied as she released Merlin from his stall and reached for his saddle. 'I'm in an enviable position. My own business, money, freedom. I'm perfectly capable of bringing Lucy up on my own. We've settled everything quite amicably. Andy gets to spend time with Lucy at the weekend so she'll still grow up with two parents; it's just that they won't be living together. I'm a single, independent woman and that's the way I want it. I'm better off on my own Mary, every man I've ever had anything to do with has only brought me pain.'

'Including Niall.' Mary said straightening up from tightening Cassie's girth.

Ella nodded, taking off Merlin's halter and slipping on the bridle, easing the bit between his teeth gently. 'Yes, including Niall.'

'Ella what would you say if I told you he'd changed. That he'd become the person he talked about in his letter all those years ago. You know, the son I deserved.'

'Then I'd say some Australian girl is going to be very lucky.'

'But Ella!' Mary said giving Cassie a slap on her rump with her gloved hand as she moved her forward and out of the stable. 'He's not in Australia. He's on his way home. He's going to help out here. The new manager let me down, he's not coming. I'm putting in another ad next week! Niall will stay till he arrives.'

'Mary, you do know you're talking to the wrong person, don't you?' Ella said as she made a final adjustment to Merlin's girth before letting down the stirrups and mounting up.

'Am I?'

'Yes. It was Rachel he said he loved, remember?'

'Rachel? No! He got involved with her on the rebound from you! You're the one.' Mary was insistent. 'You always were.'

'Mary I don't think so...'

'Ella!' Mary raised a silencing hand. 'Believe me, I know my son. Ever since he left he's always asked about you. And I can tell you, he's looking forward to seeing you again. Very much.'

Nina held the curtains up to the window. They had cost a small fortune, but cost wasn't really an issue, was it? After all, someone else was paying - Bob - and he could afford it. Yes, they were just right. Well anything had to be better than the awful Laura Ashley stuff currently hanging here; the sooner that went the better. She folded the curtains with a satisfied smile and placed them back in their bag. Now all they needed was Dave Lloyd the painter. He should have been here three days ago. She found the delay annoying but Andy had promised to chase him up when he got to the site today.

The sound of the doorbell drew her from the room. She could see the blur of a large dark figure behind the opaque of the glass as she reached the foot of the stairs.

'About time.' She snapped, swinging the door open. 'I've been waiting for....'

The words died in her throat and she froze, confronted not by the painter she expected, but by Bob Macayne.

'Me? Surely not.' He smiled genially as he walked past her into the hall.

'The decorators, they should have been here yesterday.' She said eyeing him curiously. What was he doing here? Had he come by chance? She didn't think so. He was smiling as if he knew and accepted the situation here. She relaxed. Andy must have plucked up the courage to tell him. Everything was going to be all right after all.

'Can I make you a coffee?' She smiled at him graciously.

'No thank you.' He returned the smile. 'You won't be stopping that long.'

'Don't you mean you won't be stopping that long?' She looked amused.

'No.' He said, taking her by the arm and pushing her towards the stairs. 'I mean *you* won't. I want you out of here before I do something I might regret.'

'You can't order me about!' She said, pulling away from his grasp. 'This is Andy's house and what goes on here is none of your business.'

'Don't argue with me, just get up there and pack!' He shouted, pushing her up the stairs. 'And I'm going to be really generous. You've got fifteen minutes…'

Ella rode behind Mary along the edge of Forty Acre thinking about the news she had just received. Fate was such a strange thing. If the man Mary had appointed as the farm's new manager hadn't let her down, opting to take a job elsewhere at the last minute, Niall would still be in Australia working on his brother's cattle ranch. But now he was coming home to plug the gap for a couple of months until another advertisement and more interviews could be arranged. And of course Mary being Mary, was dreaming about reunions and romance. Ella knew she meant well, but what she did not need right at this moment was someone with good intentions trying her best to push her into another relationship. True Niall had been her very first love and whilst she had never forgotten him, the thought of getting back together now with a man who was almost a stranger, held very little appeal. And what about Rachel? Did she know he was coming back? Ella remembered their conversation back in the summer of '71 when she was planning to leave Andy. For Rachel there had been no one else but Niall. She was totally committed to waiting for him, no matter how long it took. Of course, time could possibly have changed all that; but somehow, knowing Rachel, she didn't think it would have. It might be safer, therefore, to keep away from Meridan Cross all together during the few weeks Niall was planning to be here.

Andy stood at the lounge window of the show house watching Tom Ransome drive off and wondering where his father had got to. He was quite sure he had been right behind him when he pulled out from Chelwood Lodge. Unfortunately he hadn't really been paying much attention to his rear view mirror on the way, as the radio had distracted him. So when he reached the site and Bob wasn't immediately behind he just put it down to traffic. Now he had been here nearly an hour with still no sign of him, he was beginning to worry. Perhaps he'd better go and look for him. Retrieving his briefcase from the floor, he turned and walked into the hall, feeling in his pocket for his car keys. As he opened the front door he saw the blue Jaguar pull up sharply outside.

'Dad!' He gave a relieved sigh as he saw his father emerge from the driver's seat. 'Where've you been? I've been so worried.'

Andy watched him lock the car and walk up the drive towards him. 'I was just about to leave to look for you, thought you'd had an accident.'

'No I'm fine. Some urgent business came up which I had to attend to first.'

Andy hovered there waiting for his father to cross the threshold, ready to launch into his committed workaholic routine, wanting to distract him from more questions about Chelwood Lodge. 'Come on in.' He stood back with a broad smile as Bob walked into the hall. 'I think you'll be impressed. You must see the kitchen. I had one or two good ideas and Liam has come up with some really impressive designs.'

He hovered there, talking enthusiastically as his father closed the door and leaned hard against it, his eyes dark and angry.

'Shut up Andy.'

'What?'

'I don't want to hear about work. I think you owe me an explanation.'

'Sorry?'

'Nina Taylor or whatever she calls herself now. She's been living with you hasn't she? That's why you wanted me out of the house.' He gave a bitter laugh. 'I caught sight of her turning into the driveway as I pulled out. So I went back for a little chat. Very interesting it was too. She tells me she's been living with you for the last three months!'

'Dad, I can explain!' Andy's mind struggled, trying to work out some half sensible excuse to placate his father.

'I don't think I need you to, thank you. I think I can work it out quite easily for myself. What's the matter with you for God's sake! It's bad enough you getting involved with her again, but trying to pass her off as some fancy interior designer with free access to my bank account - how dare you! I fought your corner for you, you know.' He said quietly, his dark eyes fixed on his son. 'When I first heard a rumour that she might be living with you, I thought not my son, this divorce business has hurt him badly. He's not interested in women and her least of all after what she's done. His work is all he lives for.' He pushed himself away from the door and closed the gap between them, his eyes full of rage. 'And all the time you had her under your roof.' He gave an unpleasant smile. 'But not any longer.'

Andy looked at his father uneasily. 'What have you done?'

'Sent her packing, back to where she came from. And if she knows what's good for her she'll stay there. There's no way a little tramp like her is going to live off the back of my hard work. And as for you...' He waved a threatening finger. 'If I find you anywhere near her again, I'll pull the plug on you, do you hear? And I'll write you out of my will! I'll leave the whole bloody lot to charity!'

'Just a minute,' Andy frowned at his father. 'Did you say you heard a rumour she was living with me?'

'Yes.'

'Who from?'

'Someone.' Bob said warily.

'Tell me!'

'Why?'

'Because if it's who I think it is, she's going to wish she'd never been born.'

'Actually, it was Mel.' Bob snapped. 'And thanks to you I owe her an apology!'

'Is that so?' Andy looked at his father, his mind following the route this news must have travelled to reach Mel. Mel, who had blamed Nina for breaking up her daughter's marriage and who no doubt, had taken great pleasure in passing the news on to Bob. Now Nina was gone he realised the difficulty he was in; as long as his father bankrolled his lifestyle he would be expected to do as he was told, to tow the line. The happiness he believed so close had been snatched away. The frustration of his situation bubbled around inside his head. He wanted revenge; to destroy the person who had destroyed his world. Without another word he grabbed his briefcase, pushed past his father and tugged open the front door.

'Andy come back here, I haven't finished with you!'

But Bob's words were lost in the heavy slam of the door. He watched his son go, knowing that if Andy was about to have a showdown with Mel he might have bitten off just a little more than he could chew.

Friday 16th February

Charlotte Grace Kendrick came into the world at approximately 11.20 p.m. on Thursday 15th February 1973 weighing 7lbs 10oz. She was small and pink with a thin dusting of black hair, a small button nose and the striking blue eyes of Mel Carpenter.

Ella and Issy arrived the next morning with flowers for Jenny and gifts for the baby. After a thirty minute visit with a tired but extremely happy new mother, they left the hospital together. Having no diary appointments that morning, Ella decided to delay her arrival at the office and spend some time shopping with Issy.

As they chatted over a coffee, Ella realised how free time had become a luxury; her whole world seemed caught up in a cycle of work and child care. With the move to the house at Kington Heights she had now extended her working hours, happy to leave Lucy in the capable hands of Helen, but moments such as this morning's shopping trip had become a rare interlude and she promised herself that she would in future take herself out of the loop more often and treat herself to pockets of freedom like this, giving herself time to relax and enjoy herself. Looking at the business, maybe the time had come to promote internally.

Trudi had proved that she was capable of far more than reception duties. Ella had been toying with the idea of appointing an Assistant to support her and to give support to Jenny and Joan when she was out of the office. And who better than Trudi, who had been there from day one and knew the business inside out? She made a mental note to discuss it with her as soon as she got back.

A small balding man sitting in the corner got to his feet as they both entered One Plus One's reception. He was clutching a black leather brief case and his dark suit and sober expression spoke of something official.

Trudi nodded in his direction. 'Mr Samuels is here to see you Ella.'

Ella slipped her coat over the Bentwood hat stand and turned to face him. 'I'm sorry, have we an appointment?'

'Looks like Inland Revenue to me.' Issy whispered suspiciously.

'Actually no,' He gave a polite smile. 'I'm from Fitzallyn Martin and Stevens.'

'So what can I do for you Mr Samuels?'

'I have been asked to deliver this.' He dropped his briefcase onto the reception desk and opened it, pulling a long envelope out and handing it to Ella.

Ella looked at the envelope with curiosity, then at him.

'What exactly is this?'

'Notice to quit. Mr Macayne has decided to sell the premises.'

'What? Just a minute he just can't throw us out!' Ella protested. 'I know a bit about the law. He has to offer us alternative premises.'

'He has. Paragraph 4.2. A suite of offices in Silver Street.'

'But most of the buildings there are derelict.'

'That's all that's on offer I'm afraid, otherwise we're looking at the statutory rate of compensation.'

'Well you can go back to Macayne and tell him if he's selling this building I'll buy it.' Ella said waving the envelope at him.

'Buildings, Mrs Macayne. There are three.'

'Three?' Ella frowned.

'Yes, your other premises are included, either separately or as a package.'

'But he doesn't own them.'

'Actually he does.'

'But I had no notification of a change of landlord. When did this happen?'

'They were purchased in 1971, I believe.' He pointed at the envelope again. 'If you wish to purchase, Mr Macayne has, in fact, allowed for that option. The price is set out in the letter.'

Ella walked over to the window, ripping the envelope open as she went. Extracting the letter she opened it and searched through its sheets. Turning from the window she looked at Samuels in amazement. 'Fifty thousand pounds! Has Bob Macayne gone mad?'

'Oh this has nothing to do with Mr Macayne senior.' Samuels replied with a shake of his head. 'We are representing Mr Andrew Macayne.'

'I checked with Dad today.' Mick said seated in a quiet corner of the Red Lion that evening between Ella and Issy. 'Bob purchased the other two properties in the summer of 1971 and they were transferred to Andy back in August last year.'

'The devious bastard!' Ella looked at both of them. 'Last August we were rowing about my returning to work. He said there was no way I was going back. He must have got everything transferred over from Bob to make sure I didn't.'

'But why do this now?' Issy asked, chasing the lemon slice around in her drink with her finger. 'I don't understand. I thought you'd parted fairly amicably.'

'We had, except...'

'What?'

'In October, I went back to the house to collect the last of my things. I found Nina in the bath complete with face pack and cucumber slices, singing like a demented cat. Not only that, she appeared to have taken ownership of the items I had come back to collect, would you believe it?'

'And?' Issy leaned forward eagerly.

'Well I pushed her head under the water to shut her up for a start. Then I told her what I thought of her, retrieved my belongings and left. The next thing I know I get a visit from Andy complaining that I had tried to drown Nina. It was obvious from our conversation that Bob didn't know Nina was living there. Andy got quite nasty about it - Trudi was there, she witnessed it all. Basically he threatened that if so much as a whisper about Nina living with him reached his father's ears he would destroy me and the business.'

'That,' Mick said, 'ties in with my next bit of news. Bob does know. Dad told me this morning. He threw Nina out of Chelwood Lodge two weeks ago.'

'And Andy obviously thinks I'm the one who blew the whistle on him.' Ella shook her head. 'But I didn't.'

'It doesn't really matter whether you did or didn't.' Issy shook her head. 'Andy would never believe you anyway. The thing is, what can you do now?'

'Relocate and re-open I suppose. I should be able to find something in six months.'

'Don't be too sure Ella.' Mick shook his head. 'Just because this has come from Andy, don't expect Bob to sit back. Knowing his feelings about working women in general and you in particular he will use his influence to try and block any sale or lease you go for. And he has a hell of a lot of influence.'

'Surely he wouldn't do that.' Issy was horrified.

'I'm afraid he would Iz.'

'I won't give up Mick.' Ella shook her head obstinately. 'I won't let the Macaynes beat me. In six months time all my businesses are going to be thriving in new locations and that is a promise!'

ELEVEN

Wednesday 21st February

'So how's the new baby?'

'Small, pink and leaks at both ends.' Mel looked at Bob over the top of her menu. 'Why the sudden interest?'

'Just curious, that's all.'

'Well please don't be.' She frowned irritably. 'When I'm with you I like to forget about the more mundane aspects of my life like grandchildren.' Giving the menu a peremptory glance she smiled. 'I think the salmon would be nice don't you?'

'Yes, looks good.' Bob cast his eye over the options then placed the menu on the table. 'I think I'll go for that too.'

The dining room of the Ragbourne Grove Hotel with its discreet bamboo screening was half full and with Liam on his annual sabbatical to California to see his father, Mel and Bob were making the most of their time together.

'A little bird tells me you evicted a squatter recently,' Mel said with a malicious glint in her eye. 'seems I was right after all.'

'Yes.' Bob looked uncomfortable. 'I was going to talk to you about that, I owe you a big apology. I hope Andy wasn't too abusive.'

'I haven't see Andy.' Mel said watching her glass being refilled. 'Why should he be abusive to me Bob?'

'But I thought...' Bob frowned. 'I was sure he said....'

'I haven't seen him for weeks.' Mel interrupted.

'God, he was so angry when I said you had already tipped me off about her living with him. He slammed out saying something about making you wish you'd never been born.'

'I don't think he had me in mind when he said that. I think it was Ella.'

'Ella?'

'Mmm. He's just issued her with a notice to quit all of her premises. He's going to sell them.'

'What?'

'It's true, Liam told me.'

'Well, well.' A slow smile spread across Bob's face.

'I'm glad you find it all so amusing.' Mel said waspishly. 'Personally I think you should put a stop to all this at once. Tell him it was me who saw her in Langleys. That it's my fault not Ella's.'

'I can't do that Mel.' Bob shook his head calmly. 'The properties are legally his. It's not for me to interfere.'

Mel looked at him sourly. 'All right then, forget Ella. Do it for me.'

'For you?' He started to laugh. 'Since when have you been a champion of your daughter's business activities? I thought you disliked them as much as I did.'

'I do. I'm just a little concerned about the fallout from this. Ella will fight this and she will do it very publicly to embarrass us all and that's the last thing I want, having just moved. What will my neighbours think?'

'Mel.' Bob shook his head. 'Lighten up will you? Stuff the neighbours! Do they really matter that much? I think not. Now,' he looked up with a smile as the waiter arrived to take their order, 'I believe we'd decided on the salmon hadn't we?'

On the other side of the screen two men were having lunch. One of them, a heavy set business man with a florid face was talking about his proposed move to the area and the money he would have available to purchase property.

'Something in the country,' He said, dabbing his napkin against his chin as one waiter cleared the table and another began setting up for the sweet. 'It must have a paddock and stables. My daughters like to ride when they're home from boarding school. Oh and a few acres. My wife's determined to embrace the whole country life thing; wants to keep chicken and goats. And a small lake would be nice, stocked with trout of course. I do so enjoy fishing.'

His grey suited companion smiled and nodded politely as beside their table the waiter added a generous measure of Cointreau to the crêpes he was cooking over a small copper burner. With a practised ear he listened to the requirements of his client, but his attention was also drawn to the other side of the screen and the conversation going on there.

The waiter lit the alcohol with professional precision, it flared blue and he watched it carefully until the flame had died down before turning the crêpes onto sweet plates and placing them in front of the two men. A jug of smooth thick cream followed, placed in the centre of the table.

'Will there be anything else Sir?' He asked, taking a respectful step back.

'No thank you Manny.' The man in the grey suit smiled as he lifted his spoon. 'Mr Jackson and I will take coffee in the lounge when we've finished.'

'Very good Mr Nicholson.' The waiter gave a courteous bow to both men. 'Bon Appetit Gentleman.'

Niall O'Farrell paused at the top of the track leading up to Willowbrook. It was late afternoon and he had just returned from taking the herd back to the south pasture after milking, Willowbrook's sheepdogs Laddie and Gaffer trailing at his heels. He gazed for a moment across the valley towards Hundred Acre. Two days now he'd been back. Two days after an absence of almost five years. And yet the familiarity of the place and its people made him feel he'd never been away at all. He shivered slightly and turned up the collar of his wax jacket to protect his face from the damp, raw wind that had started to blow down the valley from the east.

On the summit of Sedgewick Hill, a low pale finger of wispy cloud had detached itself from the damp sky to lace itself through the blackness of the trees. Watching its subtle movement, Niall realised, despite the coldness which numbed his face, he was glad to be back.

He remembered the call from his mother which had brought him here. Of course there was no question of him not being there for her when she needed him. But coming back, he knew, wasn't just about his mother. It was about Rachel too. Over the years there had been regular mentions of her in his mother's letters. He knew she worked full time at the stables. Ran the trekking centre during the months it was open. She had a natural way with horses his mother said and was a great asset to the business. In fact, she didn't know what she would do without her. All this, of course, he read with interest, but found amongst all the accolades there was not one single fragment of information which gave him any clue as to what kind of woman she had become. And so for him, she still remained locked in his memory as the fragile, pale haired child-woman whose warmth and gentleness had captured his heart. An image he had carried with him since leaving Meridan Cross, and which no other woman he had known in his years away had been able to erase. Now he was back, he knew he needed to see her. There were things he had to say. Things, even after all this time, he felt she should know.

The sound of an engine broke suddenly into his thoughts. He looked up, saw a car approaching from way off, labouring steadily up the track towards the farm. The dogs began to bark loudly, rushing back and forth. He frowned, wondering not only who the owner of the red Triumph Herald was, but what could possibly have brought them to the farm at this time of day.

The vehicle eventually stopped a few yards from him. The dogs rushed over, still barking and he called them back. Almost reluctantly they returned. A young woman wearing a wax jacket and riding breeches emerged from the vehicle and began walking towards him. The dogs bounded towards her, tails wagging. She bent to fuss them, her fair hair falling over her face. Then she looked up and smiled at him.

'Hello Niall, Mary said you were coming home.'

'Rachel?' For a moment he didn't recognise her.

'Yes, it's me.' She stopped in front of him, burrowing her hands deeply into her jacket pockets. Shivering slightly, her gaze drifted across to Sedgewick Hill.

'Bitterly cold day isn't it? Bit of a shock to the system for you I expect after Australia.'

'Oh I don't mind.' He shrugged. 'It's a welcome change really. After all the heat and dust of Maurundi.'

She turned back to him, watching him carefully for a moment and then smiled. 'It's good to see you again.'

'Is it?' He hung his head as the memory of that day came back to him. Her face; pain mingled with anger. The sting of the whip as she lashed out. It had had never left him. 'I'm surprised you can say that Rachel after...'

'Niall,' she interrupted. 'Look at me, please.'

He raised his eyes to hers; they were still the beautiful blue he remembered.

'It's me who should be saying sorry, lashing out at you like that. I had no idea, you see, until I read the letter.'

'Letter?' He looked confused.

'The one you left for Ella.' She said softly. 'The one which contained the truth. You'll never know how much I hated my mother after that, knowing what she'd done.'

'And you still remained here?' He shook his head. 'You should have gone Rachel, started a new life on your own somewhere else. It's the least you deserved.'

'I couldn't do that Niall. I had to stay.'

'For her?' He was amazed at such sacrifice.

'No, to wait for you to come back to me.' She reached out and touched his face gently. 'And now you have.'

Friday 20th April

'Come for Easter Ella.' Laura had insisted on the telephone earlier in the week. 'There's nothing to keep you in Abbotsbridge. And bring Lucy. The whole village is dying to see her.' So here she was at last, putting all her troubles on hold for a few days, Hundred Acre on her left and Meridan Cross nestling in the spring sunshine below her. Of course she was looking forward to seeing everyone; her last visit to the village had been back in early February when her grandfather had come out of hospital. He had looked pale and tired, but his eyes had still held their determined spark. Since then she had been in regular touch by phone, keeping the conversation centred on his progress, ready when Mary turned to talk of Niall or coming back to the village, to listen then make her excuses to end the call. But now, well into April, he would almost certainly be back in Australia. It was safe to return.

Reaching the valley floor she passed the entrance to Willowbrook and glimpsed the pale stone farmhouse, tucked comfortably into the lee of the hill. For a moment she hesitated, wondering whether she should drop in there first and surprise them all, but noticing Lucy was still sleeping peacefully in her car seat decided to continue on towards the village and Little Court.

It was as she rounded the last bend, the one before Ross's garage and the village proper that it happened. The brilliance of the afternoon sun breaking from behind the wood temporarily blinded her and as she raised a hand to shield her eyes, a tractor pulling a slurry spreader suddenly appeared from nowhere out of a gateway on the right. There was no time to think, she went with her instincts, pulling the car to the left and accelerating through the small gap between bank and tractor. Once clear, she braked and stopped, immobilised for a moment by what had just happened and winded by the restraining pull of the seat belt. Then all her responses came back and she turned to the back seat, her only concern for Lucy. To her amazement she still slept peacefully in her child seat, unaware anything had happened.

With a gasp of relief she released her belt and got out of the car. Emerging from the gateway the tractor had been crawling and had come to rest half way across the road, the slurry spreader still coupled to the back of it. She ran towards it, recognising the red Massey Ferguson belonging to Willowbrook. Jake Carr would have been at the wheel. She hoped he wasn't too shaken. She saw the door open on the far side of the cab and a figure jump down into the road.

'Jake? Are you OK?' She called out as she reached the vehicle. 'I'm so sorry, the sun blinded me, I couldn't see a thing...'

But the figure, who appeared around the front of the tractor, wearing jeans and a heavy sweater, wasn't Jake at all. He was younger and taller, his tanned face accentuating the blueness of his eyes. For a moment he just stood there gazing at her with shocked surprise, then pushing a hand through his thick blond hair he walked right up to her and gave her a hug.

'Ella!' His face was warm against her own, his voice holding a slight trace of Australian accent. 'It's so good to see you. Mum said you were coming down for the weekend.' He pulled back with a laugh. 'Little did I know that I'd be the first person to run into you - literally.'

'Niall! What a surprise.' She answered hesitantly, aware of his close scrutiny.

'What is it?' He frowned. 'You don't seem very pleased to see me.'

'Forgive me.' She shook her head. 'I'm just a little shocked; I thought you'd gone back. Shouldn't the new manager be here by now?'

'He is,' His handsome face broke into a grin. 'It's me.'

'You?'

'Yep.' He nodded enthusiastically. 'She didn't click with any of the guys she interviewed. So I thought well this must be an omen. I'm destined to be here. I asked Mum how she felt about me staying on and she was all for it.'

'Really?' Ella was taken aback; it was not at all what she expected. Then unexpectedly the awkward moment was rescued by a familiar sound.

'I think Lucy's woken up.' She said. 'Excuse me a minute.'

'Can I see her?'

'Of course.'

Following Ella to the car he looked in and smiled at the wide eyed child.

'She's lovely.' He said. 'And I have to say not in the least like that ex-husband of yours.'

'Everyone says that.' Ella laughed, relaxing a little as she distracted her daughter with her soft toy rabbit. 'I think it's their way of humouring me.'

'So, any chance of seeing you down the Arms tonight for a welcome home drink?'

'It's a nice thought, but I've only just arrived.' Ella gave a gentle shrug, wanting to avoid an embarrassing evening with Mary and her matchmaking plans. 'I really need to get Lucy settled in. Maybe tomorrow?'

'Oh come on, surely you can make time for a quick one.' He looked disappointed. 'Rach is dying to see you, you know.'

'Yes,' she smiled awkwardly, 'I'm sure she is.'

'It's all right Ella.' He looked at her seriously. 'I know what Mum's been up to. She means well but time's moved on for both of us hasn't it?'

'Yes.' Ella nodded. 'I'm sorry but it's not what I want Niall. Not at all.'

'Neither do I.' He hesitated, then said shyly. 'So I made a point of telling her about Rachel.'

'You're back with Rachel?'

'Yes. All the time I was away I never stopped loving her.' He hung his head for a moment then looked at her again. 'You know, I thought she'd hate me. But she didn't. Said she'd been waiting too. That she knew I'd come home one day. Of course the fact that you'd shown her the letter I wrote you made all the difference. Under the circumstances I think that was a very generous thing of you to do.'

Ella shook her head. 'I couldn't let her go on believing her mother's lies about you. Besides, by the time I read it I was already in love with someone else.'

'Anyone I know?'

'No. But needless to say that went wrong too and I caught Andy on the rebound. And now he's gone. Bit of a mess all in all isn't it?'

'It's not been all bad.' He said, gazing down into the car. 'You have Lucy.'

She followed the direction of his gaze, saw her daughter cuddling her rabbit tightly, her thumb in her mouth, eyes gradually closing. 'Yes,' she said with a smile, 'I do don't I?'

Saturday 21st April

Nina sat in front of the dressing table mirror and pulled the brush through her hair. In thirty minutes time Andy would be arriving to pick her up. For the first time since she had moved here they were eating out.

With a sigh she rested the brush in her lap and looked at her reflection. Trapped, that's how she felt; stuck in a claustrophobic ground floor flat with no job, no car and no real social life other than Andy. And even his commitment to her was now beginning to feel hollow. True he picked up the weekly rent and she still had money in the bank from the sale of her flat so she wouldn't starve. But now she was no longer in Chelwood Lodge she felt somehow she had become a nobody, living among all the other nobodys in this quiet backwater of Abbotsbridge.

Of course Andy was happy enough; in his father's good books again; the obedient son, behaving himself, towing the line. Still living in the luxury of Chelwood Lodge with his new live in housekeeper Freya, found for him by his father. Nina had deep suspicions about someone with a fancy name like that. She saw a pale model's face, high cheekbones and cool aristocratic eyes. Another Ella with long straight hair tied carelessly back, elegant hands rolling pastry, ironing shirts, caressing Andy in bed.

The fact that he had been unable to see her for the last three weeks because he said business was taking him out of the area clearly indicated to Nina that he was beginning to slip away from her. Despite all he had said, he had, in the end, returned to his old ways. Of course she knew Bob was directly responsible for this. Not satisfied with parting them, he was making sure, with distractions like Freya, that his son would eventually make a clean break from her.

Setting her brush down she began to apply her makeup. But maybe all was not lost. She had one valuable trump card left up her sleeve. And tonight she was going to play it.

Andy sat opposite Nina in the dining room of the Harvest Moon Hotel, Kingsford, thinking how wonderful it was to be with her again. Frustrating though, that their relationship still had to be conducted in secrecy. If only there was some way round this. The thought trailed away. It was hopeless. Currently he might be in his father's good books for his efforts at work, but Nina was still number one on his father's hit list. Why else had he gone to the trouble of employing that old dragon of a housekeeper Freya Nash, if not to spy on his every move and make sure he didn't sneak her back to Chelwood for the night?

It had been just over three months since his father had evicted her. Just over three months since he had walked out of the show house in Kings Moreton and driven straight to the Parkway Estate to find her. Pushing through the front door, past a gaping Joan Harrison, he had taken the stairs two at a time, calling for her. She had emerged from one of the bedrooms at the sound of his voice, her face pale and tearstained. He had thrown his arms around her and held her very tightly, telling her he was sorry and despite all his father had said there was no way he was going to give her up.

Insisting she came with him, he waited while she re-packed her things then stowed the suitcase in the boot of his Mercedes and drove her straight to Ashley Grove, a lime tree lined avenue of Victorian bay windowed houses deep in Abbotsbridge's bedsit land. Leaving her in the car he disappeared. The landlord was a friend. He always had the odd property empty. He returned moments later and handed her the key to a small basement flat with a pretty plant filled patio located at the end of the next road. Leaving her to settle in, he'd driven straight to Fitzallyn, Martin and Stevens and demanded to see Charles immediately.

He emerged from their meeting leaving Charles to prepare the paperwork which would terminate all of One Plus One's leases. The sites, he decided, would be sold off to the highest bidder. 'And if she wants to buy,' he'd told Charles, 'they'll cost her fifty thousand.'

His father phoned a few days later offering advice. 'She'll try and relocate.' He warned. 'You'll need to cut off the commercial property supply. Grease palms, lean on people if necessary. If anyone gives you trouble, call me. I'll deal with them.'

And so in the weeks that followed he worked long and hard, travelling across west Somerset, meeting people, making sure that every open door was closed in Ella's face. He was rarely home and slept little; only his determination kept his energy levels from flagging. He knew Ella. She would fight until the six month deadline was up. But now he was back, his work completed. There was nothing she could do. No one would touch her. One Plus One was well and truly finished.

And now another challenge - he sat facing a quiet, resentful Nina across the table. He knew he should have told her the reason for his absence but he couldn't. It had been Macayne business, its details for his father's eyes and ears only. So there was no alternative but to leave her for three whole weeks with what she must have taken as the vaguest of excuses. She probably thinks I found someone else, he thought. But I'll show her how much I care, I'll make it up to her, I really will.

'Darling you look so sad and I know it's entirely my fault.' He gave a guilty sigh. 'I've neglected you, running off like that. I'm so sorry.'

'Are you?' She looked at him sceptically as she raised her wine glass to her lips.

'Yes I am! Something very important came up you see. Dad and I had to deal with it straight away. It took me out of the area for a while. But I was thinking of you all the time. I saw these.' He reached into his pocket and pulled out a small black velvet box, sliding it across the table towards her. 'Bought them for you as a surprise.'

She took the box and opened it, a pair of dark pearl drop earrings lay nestling against the blueness of the silky lining. Something to keep me sweet, she thought. As always he's keeping his options open. Wants the best of both worlds; Freya and me. Good old Andy. But I'm afraid that's not possible. The time has come for him to make a choice.

'Thank you, they're lovely!' Her eyes glinted as she closed the box. 'Actually it's quite a coincidence because you see I've a surprise for you too. A very big one in fact.'

'Big eh?' He looked at the small black leather clutch bag lying on the table. He laughed. 'Where are you hiding it then?'

With a smile she got to her feet and moved around the table to stand beside him. Taking his hand she placed it gently onto her stomach. 'In here,' she said, 'I'm pregnant Andy.'

Tuesday 24th April

'Pregnant!'

Bob Macayne's bellow broke through the connecting door into Marion Westwood's office. Fingers whipping across the keyboard of her red electric Adler, she tried to concentrate on transcribing the shorthand from her pad, but the volume of the conversation going on next door was beginning to intrude so much that this was becoming impossible. She stopped for a moment, hands hovering above the keys, to listen.

On the other side of the door Bob Macayne was pouring a whisky and trying to convince himself that this was some terrible dream that he would wake up from in a moment. Sitting on the leather couch, white faced but determined, Andy waited for his father to resume.

'So, how far gone is she?' Bob turned back to him, glass in hand.

'Two months.'

Bob's face set in tight concentration for a moment then he smiled. 'I kicked her out on the first of February, that's almost three months ago. You can't be the father.'

'I'm afraid I am.' Andy's dark eyes looked huge in his pale face as he bit his lip and slowly looked up at his father.

Bob stood there gazing at his son in stunned silence then setting the glass down heavily on the desk he moved closer. 'You've still been seeing her?'

Andy nodded.

'Why?' He asked, his voice a harsh whisper. 'After all I've said, all I've tried to do to keep you out of trouble. Why dammit do you always disobey me where she's concerned?'

'Because I love her.'

'Love!' Bob found his voice again, loud and angry, 'How can you love *that*? She's a parasite; her only interest is herself and her own needs. She will *ruin* you. Have you thought about an abortion?'

Andy looked horrified. 'You can't ask me to kill my own child!'

'So what do you propose to do then? Raise a bastard?'

'No.' Andy said calmly. 'I'm going to marry her.'

'Andy, are you completely mad? You've just untangled yourself from one mistake. Don't jump straight into another.'

'This is not a mistake.' Andy got to his feet. 'It's the most sensible thing I've ever done. I realise now that all the time I was chasing around, looking for the perfect girl, she was already there. The trouble was I treated her badly; drove her into Mick's arms. But I've got her back now and I'm going to keep her. And you more than anyone should understand about love. You and Mum. Nina and me. Isn't it the same thing?'

'How dare you!' Bob caught Andy by the throat and pushed him back into the couch. 'I won't have you cheapen your mother's name by comparing her with that slut!'

Stunned, Andy pushed himself upright, rubbing his neck, watching his father cautiously as he retreated to the other side of the room.

'What am I going to do with you Andy?' Bob said, turning as he reached the window, his expression bleak. 'No matter how I talk to you or threaten you, you still manage to disobey me. To have your own way. You may think I'm hard and unsympathetic, but believe me, I only have your welfare at heart.'

'No you don't Dad,' Andy said, getting to his feet. 'You have your own. That's how it's always been. My life has been steered in the direction you wanted. The one you thought best for me and look what's happened. Your vision of Ella and me may have been your dream but it became my nightmare. Nina isn't interested in a career. She'll be a good wife, running the home, looking after the children, something Ella would never have been capable of.'

'Please Andy, don't do this.' Bob's voice was a desperate whisper as he saw his son turn for a moment to look at him before reaching the door.

'I'm not scared any more Dad.' Andy said with a shake of his head. 'Disinherit me if you must. Throw me out onto the street. Take my job away. I don't care. I've got Nina and the baby now. Nothing else matters.'

TWELVE

Saturday 12th May

Mick Taylor, carrying a large bunch of flowers and a bottle of wine, stood outside the door of Issy's flat waiting for a response to his ring on the doorbell. All at once it flew open and he was greeted by her smiling face and the delicious smell of cooking.

'Right on time, come in.' She ushered him in, accepting his gifts with a gentle peck on the cheek.

'Smells good,' He said, following her into the kitchen, 'but then everything you cook always does.'

'It's Hungarian Goulash.'

'Great, I'm starving.' He rubbed his hands together enthusiastically. 'Would you like me to uncork the wine?'

'Good idea.' She handed him the corkscrew and pulled a bottle of white from the fridge before returning to the cooker to check on the pans gently simmering there. The cork left the bottle with a healthy pop and retrieving two glasses from the cupboard he filled them, handing one to her.

'So, what's new?' He asked. 'Has Ella managed to find premises yet?'

'No.' Issy said solemnly. 'He's a complete bastard that Andy isn't he? He and Nina deserve each other, I expect their baby will be born with horns and a forked tail.'

'Baby?' Mick frowned. 'What baby?'

'She's pregnant, didn't you know?' Issy said taking a mouthful of wine and turning to give the goulash a quick stir. 'It's due at the end of the year.'

'Pregnant. Are you sure?'

'Yes.' Issy nodded, noticing the puzzled expression on his face. 'Mel told Ella last week. Apparently Bob is furious. The wedding's next Saturday. Of course, he's refused to go.'

'But Nina told me she couldn't have children because of some accident when she was fourteen.' Mick's face twisted painfully. 'How could she have lied to me like that? She knew how much I wanted us to have a family. That was one of the reasons she wanted me to give up the farmhouse. No point having a great rambling place like that she said, when there was only ever going to be the two of us living there.'

Issy reached for Mick's hand and took it in hers. 'Mick,' she said calmly. 'She's best forgotten.'

'It's easy for you to say that.' He said miserably. 'You're not the one she made the complete fool of.'

'You're not a fool.' Issy touched his face gently. 'You're a decent man with a lot to offer a woman.'

'Am I? I don't think so; be sensible who'd really want a no-hoper like me?'

'I would.' She said looking up into his face. 'And you're not a no-hoper.'

'You're just trying to make me feel better, aren't you?'

'No, I'm deadly serious. Remember the night of the Civic Hall opening when she appeared in the car park? You were about to kiss me, weren't you?'

He nodded.

'You've never tried since.' There was a note of disappointment in her voice.

'That's because all the wine we drank that evening gave me Dutch courage.' He confessed. 'Afterwards I was glad I hadn't, you'd only have shouted at me or hit me.'

'No I wouldn't.'

'Of course you would. Issy,' He laughed. 'You've been brilliant but I know where the boundaries lie. Oh I know my Dad has all these romantic notions about you and me, and so did I at one time. But I'm a realist, I know now all we will ever be is good friends.'

'Actually Mick,' she looked at him very seriously. 'You're wrong. I've not said anything before, but I really do believe I'm falling in love with you.'

'Issy.' He looked hurt. 'That isn't funny.'

'But I'm telling the truth.' Gently sliding her arms around his neck, she smiled at him, her eyes very blue. 'You've got under my skin Mick Taylor, don't ask me how, but you have.' She looked up into his face. 'Amazing isn't it, that you used to drive me crazy. And now you still do, but in a different way. So, do you think maybe it would be a good idea if we had that kiss now?'

Mick bent his head, felt her lips touch his and he was lost, his senses totally overwhelmed by the smell of her skin, and the texture of her hair. Her mouth tasted unbelievably sweet and when eventually he pulled away, he heard her sigh, saw the brilliance of her smile and the unmistakeable look of passion in the blue of her eyes.

'Oh Issy.' He pulled her hands from his neck, realising where this was all heading. 'We can't do this, not now.'

'Why not?' She looked up at him innocently.

'Dinner will be ruined.'

'Dinner will be just fine, Mick.' Issy laughed, reaching over and turning off the burners one by one. 'Come on.' And taking him gently by the hand she led him out of the kitchen towards the bedroom.

Monday 14th May

Elaine Lester opened her front door to find her sister standing there.

'Well, well, what's blown you round our way?' She said looking Nina up and down, her eyes on the expensive leather jacket she was wearing. 'Thought you'd be busy with your big event. This Saturday isn't it?'

'It's not a big anything Elaine, it's just me, Andy and a couple of witnesses, so please don't think you'll be missing out on something.' Nina replied irritably. 'Are you going to let me in or not?'

'I suppose so.' Elaine reluctantly held back the door as Nina walked into the hall.

'This is nice. Has Barry been decorating then?' She said, eyeing the gold striped wallpaper.

'Yeah, job lot of paper; said he got it real cheap off some bloke in the Red Lion.'

'Do you know this looks just like the stuff they've been using at Kings Moreton.' Nina said lightly, turning to look at her sister. 'Barry been up to his usual has he?'

'I don't know what you mean.' Elaine held her sister's stare brazenly.

'Light Fingered Lester, isn't that what they used to call him?' Nina said running her fingers slowly over the wall before turning with a smile to her sister. 'Been inside before for receiving hasn't he?'

'What do you want Nina?' Elaine sensed danger. Her sister was a self-centred taker. If she was here, she was after something and the discovery of the wallpaper was just the lever she needed to make sure she got it.

'I want you to do something for me.'

'And what could I possibly do for the likes of you?'

'John Tanner.'

'What about him?'

'Does Barry still see him?'

'Of course, they're old drinking mates.'

'I need to speak to him.'

'What do you want with a butcher, for God's sake?'

'None of your business. Now are you going to help me or...' Her fingers caressed the wallpaper again.

'Oh all right!' Forced into a corner by her husband's unlawful activities, Elaine knew she had no alternative but to agree to this bizarre request. 'Barry should be home in half an hour, you can speak to him about it then.'

Friday 18th May

'Any luck?' Trudi looked up from her typewriter as Ella walked back into the office.

'Not a thing Trude,' Ella said, setting her briefcase on the reception desk. 'Every door in west Somerset appears to be firmly closed in my face, unless I'm prepared to open shop on one of the out of town trading estates, and you know as well as I do we won't do much business there. I had no idea Macayne's influence was so great. Here, yes, but Taunton and Wellington are miles away. It's really scary.'

'Isn't there anyone who can help us?'

'It doesn't look like it,' Ella replied, picking up her briefcase and making a move towards her office. 'We've got just over two months left, but nothing's going to change. It seems as if the Macaynes have got everywhere well and truly stitched up.' she gave a tired sigh. 'Be an angel would you and hold my calls for the next hour? I'd really like to have some time to myself.'

Behind the closed door of her office Ella slid into her chair and for the first time since Samuels' visit she realised she might be looking at the end of all she had worked for. But it wasn't just her, there were others involved too. She remembered the hours Mollie Flanagan had generously donated to give advice to the two young and inexperienced girls who were taking over her business. And hadn't everything fallen into place so well? OK so Mollie had not been able to keep her promise to stay on for a while, but when one door closed another had opened with Joan Trimble retiring from the Tech College and coming in to help with the shorthand testing. Then there was Trudi and the temping team plus George Martock who ran the company's small printing outlet. And what about all the people in the other branches she now owned whose hard work and commitment had helped to make One Plus One such a success?

She put her hands to her face feeling desolate. All these people were going to lose their jobs; families would suffer; lives would be changed for ever. And all because of Andy Macayne's spiteful actions. His fight was with her, not them; it was so unfair.

The intercom buzzed and she pressed the button irritably.

'Trudi, I'm sorry, I really don't want to be disturbed.'

'But Ella...'

'Please, just take a message! I'll call them back in half an hour.'

Releasing the button she swung her chair around to look out of the window, feeling the warmth of the afternoon's sun on her face.

'There has to be a solution to this!' She called out in frustration. 'There just has to be!'

'You'll get locked up talking to yourself like that.'

She swung her chair around sharply.

'Alex!'

He stood there, solid and handsome, a smile on his face as he closed the door behind him.

'Sorry Ella, Trudi said you didn't want to be disturbed, but I do need to see you now. It simply won't wait.'

'Have a seat.' She indicated the nearby chair, curious to know what the emergency was; glad in some ways that he had interrupted, forcing her out of her grey mood.

'Can I get you some coffee?'

'Actually, I took the opportunity to organise something a little more glamorous with your receptionist before I came in. Ah, here she is.' He looked up as the door opened and Trudi walked in carrying a bottle of Moet and three glasses.

'Champagne? What is this Alex?' Ella frowned as she placed the glasses on the desk and handed him the bottle.

'We're celebrating.' He said matter-of-factly as he grasped it by the neck, despatched the gold foil and undid the wire. The bottle opened with a heavy pop and an explosive spray of foaming liquid. Quickly he grabbed each of the flutes and filled them.

'Here.' He handed one of them to her.

'Thank you.' Ella took her glass, shooting a bemused look at Trudi, who gazing into her own glass could only look equally mystified. 'So what's the special occasion?'

'A rather successful business deal.' He touched his glass with hers. 'My agent has just completed the purchase of three fine commercial properties in the area. Got them for a song. The owner wanted to off-load them pretty quickly.' He gave her a roguish wink. 'Something about a dispute with his ex-wife......'

The champagne finished, Trudi returned to her desk, leaving Ella to discuss the new leasing arrangements with Alex. It was after three before he finally left One Plus One. After he had gone, she phoned Jenny and Joan then each of her branch managers to relay the good news to them. Afterwards, in the privacy of her office, she broke down and shed the tears of relief she had been holding back. Her prayers had been answered; with Alex's help she had beaten the Macaynes, it was all over.

Letting Trudi go early she stayed on to collect the timesheets from the girls as they came in, eager to let them know their futures were safe. She closed the office at five thirty and as she locked the front door and stepped into the street she took a deep breath, turning to look at One Plus One's smart gold and black façade with a smile of satisfaction.

Home; reaching her car and unlocking it, she knew that was where she wanted to be now, bathing her daughter and putting her to bed in her primrose yellow nursery with its soft toys and Noah's Ark patterned curtains. The perfect ending to a perfect day.

Tuesday 22nd May

'Ah there you are. Good day at work?'

Mel's head appeared around the lounge door to greet Liam as he stepped into the hall, discarding his jacket and briefcase.

'Actually it's been hell.'

'Oh, how's that?'

'I had a meeting with Bob this afternoon. He is not in the best of moods. I think the wedding is still very much in the forefront of his thoughts. He was extremely irritable, argued over things he would usually endorse and was generally disagreeable. It soured the whole afternoon.' He followed her from the hall into the lounge and sank into a soft chair, watching as she unstopped one of the decanters and poured two large whiskies.

'Did he go to the wedding? I can't imagine he did.' She said as she handed him one and sat herself down beside him.

'No, he didn't.' Liam shook his head and tipped his glass to his lips. 'I spoke to him after the meeting; he seemed a lot calmer then. Apparently Andy and Nina had a quiet registry office wedding. They've gone to Paris for a week.'

Mel's face creased with distaste. 'I expect he's devastated. His only son married to that awful common girl and all because a baby's on the way. How could Andy do that to him?'

'Andy,' said Liam quietly, 'is a fool. A spoilt boy whose only interest is in what he hasn't got. Now he has Nina, although my feelings are that it's more likely that Nina has him. She may have lost Alex and the big prize, but marrying Andy means she can still be one of Abbotsbridge's minor princesses. He must be blind if he can't see he's just a means to an end.'

'Poor Bob.' Mel looked sadly down into her glass. 'That's the trouble with children today, they are so wilful, so hell bent on having their own way. Look at my two! We hardly ever see them now!' She gave him a mournful look. 'Sometimes I feel so abandoned Liam!'

'Mel, stop it!' He shook his head. 'You drove Nick away with your prejudices and Ella with a pair of scissors. You only have yourself to blame.'

'I do not!' Mel pouted defensively. 'Nick is too gullible for words and Ella, well controversy seems to follow her wherever she goes.'

'What do you mean by that?'

'Andy's not the only reason Bob's in a bad mood. Ella's back in business.'

'How?' Liam concealed his relief with a curious frown. 'I thought they'd successfully blocked all her attempts to relocate.'

'They had. And found a buyer for all three properties. Bob was pleased that everything had gone so well.'

'So what went wrong?'

'The buyer was Hurst Developments. Have you heard of them?'

Liam shook his head.

'They're one of Alex Nicholson's many subsidiaries apparently.' She said resting her glass in her lap. 'Of course once the properties were in his possession he offered Ella back her leases straight away. Getting his own back one might say. Poor Bob,' she said with a sympathetic shrug. 'He is extremely upset about the whole thing and will no doubt be looking for an explanation from Andy when he returns from Paris'

'Yes, no doubt.' Liam said in a calm, uncaring voice as he savoured his whisky.

Friday 1st June

Tad Benedict was standing in the Mill surveying with satisfaction the state of the renovations. The painters were in with long ladders giving a final coat to the walls while by his side, Denny Murray, his electrical contractor was unrolling the lighting plan on the top of a table covered with a paint splashed dust sheet.

'Look.' He pointed to the ceiling, 'I thought spotlights all over. With the dark blue ceiling, they'll give you a great atmosphere when the stage is in use. Then there will be wall lights around here, to light each of the tables on the outer perimeter of the dining area. Liam suggested Tiffany lamps on the other tables to keep the intimate theme going. Gave me this.' he pulled a catalogue from his bag and thumbing through it placed it on top of the plans. 'He suggested this,' he gestured, retrieving the pencil lodged behind his ear and marking the item. 'Or alternatively' he flicked over a couple of pages and marked another. 'This one. I can get some samples for you if you like.'

'Yes, that would be useful.' Tad nodded, pleased. Everything was falling into place very nicely, well on schedule

'We're doing the final testing of this new state of the art lighting system for the stage and dance area on Monday.' Denny continued, 'I've been guided by your new DJ, he seems to know what he wants.'

Tad nodded. 'Another good find. He's going to do the business; I have great faith in him Denny.'

Denny laughed. 'No offence Tad, but all this poncy stuff just so people can dance. Didn't have this sort of thing in my day,' he laughed again, 'in fact we seemed to manage quite well without it.'

'That was my era too, but times have changed. It appears this is what the punters want now.' Tad shrugged. 'And if that's what it takes to bring them in and spend their money that's what I'll do.'

'So what's this going to be? Mill Club Mark Two?'

'No,' Tad shook his head, 'the Mill belongs to the sixties. This place will cater for a more sophisticated audience. It's a dinner and dance club and I've decided to give it a movie theme. Fill it with film posters and photos of stars. And I'm calling it Zeffirelli's.'

'After Franco Zeffirelli?' Denny smiled as he began to roll up his plans.

'You've heard of him.'

'Yeah, film director isn't he?'

'That's the one.' Tad smiled.

The heavy creak of the club's swing doors opening caused both men to turn.

'Morning Mrs B.' Denny said as Faye walked over to join them. 'How are you this morning?'

'Morning Denny.' She beamed at him. 'I'm fine thank you.'

'Hello love, finished your shopping?' Tad smiled down at her as she reached him.

'Mmm.' Faye nodded, pleased with herself. 'I've got a lovely dress from Christiana's for the opening. Pale apricot and black chiffon. Marianne chose it. It's really gorgeous. You'll love it!'

'Good!' Tad turned to Denny with a grin. 'If the wife's happy, I'm happy.'

'Tad mentioned that Matt's coming back for the opening,' Denny said, securing the drawings with an elastic band he had found in the back pocket of his jeans.

'Yes.' Faye positively glowed at the mention of his name. 'He's not been home for three years. I can't believe it. He's due here at the end of the month. Bringing a new American singer with him. It's her first British tour and she's agreed to sing for us on the night.'

'You don't say?' Denny looked impressed. 'I'll look forward to that then.'

'Yes, 'Tad looked around the room before letting his gaze fall on the little electrician. 'All in all I think it's going to be a pretty spectacular evening.'

'It's all looking good.' Faye said gazing around with a satisfied smile. 'Have you much more to do?'

'No, Mrs B,' Denny said tucking the drawing under his arm. 'We're almost finished.'

'I know something we haven't discussed.' Faye said suddenly. 'Table lamps.'

'We're ahead of you there.' Tad winked at Denny. 'Denny's going to drop some samples round so we can make a decision.'

'When?'

'Tomorrow evening, if that's OK.'

'That would be great.'

Tad nodded in agreement. 'I really do want to wind everything up by the 22nd Denny. What I don't want are any last minute panics. We open to the public on the 30th and the last thing I want to do is hold up the invitations. They're just about to go out.'

'Actually, they went last week Tad.' Faye interrupted. 'All two hundred of them.'

Thursday 28th June

Abbotsbridge seemed a strange, alien place to Matt as he viewed it from the back of his father's car. New York, with its vast buildings, yellow cabs and big city energy had been his home for the past two years and the memories he had carried in his mind of his home town had in no way prepared him for what he was seeing today.

At the end of the park where the pedestrian footbridge crossed the river to the old part of the town, a red bricked multi storey car park now loomed coupled to a similar sized building which his mother told him was the new shopping precinct. But where were the Victorian bay windows of Brown Street and Waterloo Avenue? Gone under the bulldozer his father had said. For this was progress. Abbotsbridge had to move with the times, attract new business and shoppers from all over Somerset if it was to survive. New occupants of the precinct alongside a very impressive new Langleys included British Home Stores and Littlewoods. Abbotsbridge Tad had said, was now the best place to shop outside Taunton or Weston Super Mare.

They drove past the new elegant glass fronted Civic Centre, occupying the site of the old furniture factory which had now relocated on the Blackdown Trading Estate on the edge of town. Matt noticed even the road system had changed. A new one way system was in place and the town centre itself had been partly pedestrianised. The Town Hall hadn't escaped either, its Victorian façade swathed in scaffolding and plastic sheeting while a specialist contractor cleaned the grime from its ornate stonework.

'Like a different place isn't it?' Faye turned to look at him.

Sitting beside him, Marcie grinned, 'I love it!' she said enthusiastically. 'Back home when someone mentions England everyone automatically thinks London. But this, well it's kinda small, but it's really groovy!'

'Have we got time to see Gane Street?' Faye asked Tad as they left the town hall behind and turned into Church Street. 'I must show them the shop. You do want to see the shop don't you?' she called out anxiously to them both.

'Of course we do.' Matt shot his father a conspiratorial grin, seeing his expression in the rear view mirror as the BMW took a left into Market Street. 'And I'm sure Marcie would love to look around. Scarves and shoes are her thing, so this will be a real treat.'

Proudly Faye showed them over the shop, telling them how it had been set up, including the link with Christiana's which brought it quite a lot of extra business, and the new young fashion accessory area they had just opened. It was as she introduced them to Jane and Paula, her two assistants, that Marcie spotted the red shoes and asked to try them on.

'I think we may be some time.' Faye raised an amused eyebrow as fifteen minutes later Marcie sat surrounded by shoes of every shade totally overwhelmed by choice and style.

'Don't worry Faye,' Tad squeezed her shoulder, 'Matt and I will wait in the car.'

'Is she always like that?' Tad asked as they reached the BMW and he pulled his keys from his pocket.

'Yes, everything with Marcie is completely over the top.' Matt laughed. 'She's crazy, but a great tonic. You never feel down when she's around, she just won't let you.'

'And can she sing?'

'Oh yes.' Matt said confidently as he slid into the passenger seat beside his father. 'You'd better believe it.'

Once the key was in the ignition, Tad turned on the radio and fiddled with the station buttons, searching for Radio Four. 'Ah!' He said with a smile of satisfaction as Vivaldi floated through the car speakers. 'Now all I need to do is tune it in properly. By the way,' he continued, head bent, frowning in concentration as his finger and thumb performed the delicate operation. 'Did I mention that Sonny's bringing the Attitude to the opening?'

As Matt was about to answer, a silver Mercedes glided by and slowly slotted itself into a space just up ahead on the opposite side of the road. He watched as the driver, a young woman in black jeans and a white T-shirt, got out and leaned back into the car to retrieve something.

'No,' He said, only half listening, his eyes fixed on her as she crossed the road to the dry cleaners carrying a grey holdall. 'No, you didn't.'

'Did you know Todd Graham's gone too? He's decided on a solo singing career of all things.' Tad chuckled. 'A voice would help of course. Still, BVM have taken him on, so they must think they can do something with him...Matt?' He looked up. 'Are you OK? You look a bit pale.'

'I'm fine.' Matt looked at his father and stretched. 'A bit jet lagged, that's all. Nothing a good night's sleep in a comfortable bed won't fix.'

'Ah, at last, here come the ladies.' Tad smiled as Faye appeared helping Marcie with a collection of bags. 'Looks as though Marcie's bought half the shop, I'll just get it all loaded into the boot, won't be a minute.'

As Tad got out of the car, Matt saw the driver of the Mercedes appear again, crossing the road with graceful ease, the empty holdall tucked under her arm, dark hair tumbling around her shoulders. Unlocking the Mercedes she lowered herself in and slammed the door. Matt heard the engine fire and saw the vehicle nose its way out slowly into the road before making a wide sweeping turn back towards them and accelerating effortlessly past. As he watched the car gradually recede in the BMW's wing mirror, for a split second he wondered if he'd been wrong. But no, there was no mistaking someone like Ella Macayne; in fact she was even more beautiful than he remembered.

THIRTEEN

Friday 29th June

Helen Baker looked at the pretty blue Murano glass vases in the window then at her watch, knowing there was just under half an hour left before she would need to be making her way home. There was Lucy's tea to prepare and the finishing touches to be made to the evening meal.

Tonight was special. Ella had decided to invite Nick, Jenny, Issy and Mick round. So throughout the morning she had been busy preparing food, getting everything ready so that it wouldn't be such a rush when she got back. She spent ages laying the table, wanting to make it look decorative and pretty. Picking marguerites from the garden, she had placed them in two small crystal vases, but looking at these deep blue ones in Langley's window she knew they would set off the whiteness of the daisies to perfection.

Ella had an account here which she was authorised to use to make purchases for the house. Normally it was things like bed linen or kitchen utensils, but she didn't see why it shouldn't stretch to these two more frivolous items, especially when they would make such a difference to the dinner table.

'What do you think then Lucy?' She said to the dark haired toddler in the pushchair. 'Shall we buy them?'

The child looked up at her and gave a big smile, showing small white teeth.

'I think so too.' Helen smiled. 'Come on then, let's do it.'

Friday afternoon in Langleys meant business was brisk. The new location in the precinct with a bigger store and close parking had pulled people in from all over the area. Helen manoeuvred the pushchair around displays of ladies' summer clothes and headed for the lift which would take her to the first floor where the china and glass department was situated.

When she reached it, however, a large hand written notice stuck to the lift doors advised it was out of order. Helen tutted irritably, annoyed at the thought of this mechanical failure standing between her and the purchase of the coveted blue glass.

'Helen! How nice to see you again.'

She turned at the sound of the familiar voice and saw Joyce Kent, who worked in the dress materials section standing there beaming at her.

'Hello Joyce.' She said eyeing the green suit. 'Does the change of colour mean what I think it does?'

Joyce nodded. 'I'm Manageress now.'

'Congratulations.'

'So,' Joyce bent over to make a fuss of Lucy, 'what are you and the little one doing here today?'

'Trying to get to glassware, which is proving impossible as you can see.' Helen pointed to the lift. 'I'm beginning to think I'll just have to call it a day. It's so annoying; there are a couple of vases up there that would set Ella's dinner table off a treat, but...' she indicated the pushchair.

'If the buggy's a problem, I can keep an eye on Lucy for you.'

'Would you?'

'Of course, it's no bother; you won't be that long will you?'

'Just a few minutes, that's all. Thank you so much.'

Marcie slid the white MG Midget into a parking space on the top deck of the multi storey. How quaint this place was, she thought as she got out and locked the car. None of the rush and push of New York. Everything was calm, well-mannered and so microscopic. Even the car was a Dinky Toy in comparison to what she was used to driving back home.

She was glad to have some time to herself to explore the place. The Benedicts had been very good, showing her around all the old stuff here; the woollen mills, the old lock up on the town bridge, the hotel where some famous English guy called Oliver Cromwell had stayed the night. Everything was so old. There was nothing like it back home. It was good of Mrs Benedict to loan her the car too; brilliant in fact to put such trust in her, seeing she hadn't driven in the UK before. But Abbotsbridge she said was quiet; traffic minimal and she knew she would be just fine.

Matt and his father had left earlier for the new club to run through the final arrangements for Saturday. Tomorrow she would start rehearsals for her contribution to the opening night, but right now she was about to hit the shops. Of course shopping here was going to be completely different to back home, but that was the fun of it; it was an experience she could tell everyone about when she returned.

The lift from the car park took her directly into the precinct with its sandy marbled floor and high glass roof. She saw Langleys up ahead, its windows bright with colourful clothes and soft furnishings. Mrs Benedict had called it a department store and although it would never match Bloomingdales or Macys, she was interested to see what sort of things it had to offer.

Once through the doors she headed for the ladies fashion department, an Aladdin's cave of colours and styles, all of which she found were more suited to ageing matrons. Then tucked away down a small flight of stairs she noticed the in-house boutique Faye had mentioned. *'Annabels'* looked as if it might well have something far more interesting to offer she thought as she caught sight of a pale mannequin with stiff black hair guarding the top of the stairs. Standing on a high circular base, it was clothed in a bright green and purple patchwork jump suit. The colour combination was irresistible; Marcie was hooked. At the foot of the mannequin was a small card indicating the price. As she looked at it, trying to calculate the equivalent in dollars, she heard raised voices, someone shouting hysterically and the sound of a child crying.

She peered curiously around the dummy. A group of people were clustered in the far corner at the bottom of a broad flight of stairs which led to the next floor. There was a policeman talking to two women in green suits as he held onto a sobbing woman with short blonde hair. Beside them a brown haired woman in a blue dress clutched a small child in dungarees as she chatted to a police woman. After an animated discussion with one of the green suited women, the policeman led the blonde woman away. Marcie watched fascinated; she never imagined anything like this happening in a place like Abbotsbridge. She guessed the woman must have been caught shoplifting.

Turning her attention back to the jump suit she considered it again and decided if they had it in her size she would buy it. Feeling for her purse, she wondered whether they took American Express here, then deciding they probably didn't, checked on the amount of English money she had. Finding a five pound note stuffed untidily in amongst coins she tugged at it, only to find they came with it, cascading all over the floor. Annoyed with herself for being so careless she squatted down and set about retrieving them.

'Here's one you missed.' She looked up to see the woman in the blue dress standing over her, the child with her now firmly secured in a buggy. Standing beside her with a calm smile was the police woman.

'Gee thanks.' Marcie smiled up at the woman as she took the coin from her outstretched hand. As she returned it to her purse, she felt a light touch on her shoulder and looked up to find the child watching her with bright eyed curiosity.

'Hi there.' She eyed the small serious face then reached out and touched the child's hand. 'Cute kid!' She said to the woman with a smile. 'What's his name?'

'Sorry, I can't stop.' The woman shook her head, turning the buggy towards the door. She indicated the policewoman by her side, then seeing Marcie's concerned face said. 'It's all right; I'm not under arrest, they just want me to make a statement.'

Marcie nodded and stepped back, watching as they disappeared out into the main mall, then eyeing the jump suit again went in search of a Sales Assistant.

Ella, in the middle of a short-listing session with Trudi, was interrupted by the buzz of the intercom and the voice of Fiona, the new receptionist.

'Helen's on the phone Ella, it sounds urgent. Shall I put her through?'

'Please.' Ella frowned, wondering what was wrong. Her first thoughts were of Lucy. Had she had a fall? Did she have a temperature? Stop panicking she told herself, it's probably just something to do with tonight's meal.

'Hello Helen, what's the problem?' She asked calmly as the phone clicked to indicate the call had been connected.

'Ella, I'm really sorry to disturb you,' the voice sounded frantic. 'But I think you'd better come straight away.'

'What is it?' Ella looked across the desk at Trudi. 'Has something happened to Lucy?'

'No she's fine; she's with me, but......'

'What, Helen?'

'Well, we're at the police station. Please, can you come now; I'll explain everything when you get here.'

'Is that you Marcie?' Faye called out from her preparation of sandwiches as she heard the front door slam.

'Sure is Mrs Benedict.'

'Well,' Faye looked up as Marcie walked into the kitchen, 'How did you find our little town?'

'Interesting - and I actually found something in *Annabels*.' She held up the blue plastic carrier before pulling the garment from it. 'You like it?'

'I think it will grow on me.' Faye replied diplomatically as she took in the explosion of colour. 'I'm a pastels girl myself.'

'Thought so.' Marcie grinned, as she folded the jump suit and returned it to the bag, aware that her taste in clothes had the same affect on almost everyone.

'Is there anything I can help with?' She asked looking at the worktop and the sandwiches Faye was working on.

'No, I'm almost finished. You go on out and join the men on the patio. Get Tad to sort you out a drink, there's wine out there. Or a cold beer if you prefer.'

'Thanks.' Marcie nodded and left the kitchen.

'Oh Mrs Benedict,' She was back suddenly, hovering in the doorway.

'Yes?' Faye turned to look at her, knife in hand.

'Do you have folks in town?'

'No.' Faye said as she turned back to the worktop and quartered the stack of sandwiches she'd just prepared. 'Why do you ask?'

'Oh just someone I saw today. Thought it might have been a relation. A woman, thirty, thirty five. Hair the same colour as yours. She had this cute little boy in a buggy.'

'Not one of my relations I'm afraid.' Faye laughed. 'They're scattered pretty far and wide, but definitely not anywhere near here.'

Marcie looked at the sandwiches Faye was arranging on the plate. 'Shall I get Mr Benedict to organise you a drink? You look almost done.'

'Thank you Marcie. I could murder a glass of white wine.'
'One white wine coming up.' Marcie said and left the room.

Ella arrived at Abbotsbridge Police station and after speaking to the desk sergeant was shown into the small waiting room. There she found Helen sitting quietly, Lucy fast asleep in the buggy beside her.

'What's going on Helen?' She eased herself into the seat next to her. 'The police said something about an attempted abduction.'

Helen nodded, biting her bottom lip. 'I wanted to go to the china department in Langleys but the lift was out of order. Joyce Kent said she'd mind Lucy. It was only going to be for a moment that was all.' She looked up tearfully.

'And...'

'Someone distracted Joyce. And when she turned back to Lucy there was this woman. She'd taken her out of the buggy. She had her in her arms about to make off with her.'

'Here? In Abbotsbridge?' Ella was horrified. 'Surely not. Who would do that sort of thing?'

'Excuse me, Mrs Macayne?'

Ella looked up; the desk sergeant was standing in the open doorway.

'Would you come with me please?' He asked politely. 'Inspector Newton will see you now.'

Sergeant Dix was dealing with a lost property matter when a young man in a light suit pushed angrily through the front doors of the station. Dix watched him hover impatiently as he finished off the paperwork and handed the watch back to its owner.

'Yes sir.' He said politely as the woman left. 'What can I do for you?'

'I'm Andrew Macayne. I had a call this afternoon to say there had been an incident. That someone had tried to abduct my daughter.'

Sergeant Dix looked at him warily. The Macaynes were known by all and disliked by many in Abbotsbridge and he knew behind this young man's thin veneer of politeness lurked the potential for arrogance and rudeness and a word in the Super's ear if he felt he wasn't being dealt with properly.

'Actually I think the matter's been settled sir.' He replied pleasantly.

'Settled? And what exactly does that mean?'

Sergeant Dix caught the agitation in his voice. 'I believe your wife's already discussed the matter with Inspector Newton.' He said soothingly.

'So am I to gather that everything's sorted and the culprit's been charged?'

'I really don't know sir.' Dix said hesitantly.

'In that case Sergeant, I suggest you find me someone who does!'

Ella stood in the kitchen, watching Helen at work putting finishing touches to the prawn cocktails. The guests were imminent and despite the upheaval of the afternoon, everything was on schedule. Within the confines of the oven the leg of lamb looked wonderfully crisp, saucepans of vegetables simmered on the hob and the Charlotte Russe nestling in the fridge was an absolute triumph.

'Here.' She handed a large glass of red wine to Helen. 'I think we could both do with this.'

'I think you were wonderful.' Helen said her voice full of admiration. 'I don't know whether I could have been so generous given the circumstances.'

'She was ill Helen. I spoke to Dr Savage. I think if I'd been through what she had, losing a child like that, I would have gone crazy too. Poor woman.'

'How do you think Andy will take all this?'

'I don't know. I tried to contact him but no one knew where he was this afternoon. All I could do was leave a message on his answer phone at home. I've asked him to call me tomorrow, we'll discuss it then.'

The sound of the doorbell interrupted their conversation.

'I'll go.' Ella got to her feet. 'Can you put the starters on the table? We'll have a drink first and sit down about 9.15 if that's OK.'

Helen nodded and returned to the prawn cocktails.

The doorbell was being rung repeatedly as Ella walked down the hall.

'All right, all right I'm coming, I'm coming.' She called out, visualising a hungry Mick on the other side of the door with his finger on the bell push. She swung the door open with a smile, ready to greet her guests.

'Andy.' Her smile faded. 'This is not a good time. I did say tomorrow.'

'Yes I know you did. So sorry to interrupt, I can see you have far more important things than our daughter welfare on your mind this evening.' He nodded at the glass of wine she was holding.

'How dare you!' She reacted angrily. 'I phoned you as soon as I got to the police station. As Lucy's father I felt you should be there too, but as usual no one could find you. What else was there for me to do but leave a message? Look.' She ran a tired hand through her hair, eager to calm the situation and avoid the fight he was obviously spoiling for. 'It's OK, Lucy's fine, she wasn't harmed. Please, let's do this tomorrow. I'll explain everything then.'

'Sorry Ella.' He stood there obstinately. 'I want some answers now. I've been down to the station and spoken to Inspector Newton. I want to know what possessed you to let that bloody woman walk free.'

'Because she was ill; she'd suffered a nervous breakdown.' Ella replied, willing him to understand. 'Taking her to court wouldn't have helped.'

'And how did you reach that conclusion?' He gave a contemptuous snort. 'Some slick solicitor turn up with a convincing load of bullshit did he?'

'No, Dr Savage did actually. And it wasn't bullshit. Monica Jefferies' eighteen month old daughter fell into their garden pond and drowned last summer. I decided pressing charges was inappropriate. The poor woman obviously needs help not punishment.'

'Inappropriate! You're just like your bloody grandmother; full of misguided upper class benevolence. You're not fit to be a mother Ella, not when you compromise our daughter's safety like this.'

'I didn't compromise her safety Andy.' Ella said calmly. 'If the circumstances had been different I would have pressed charges, but on this occasion, taking everything into consideration, I was reluctant to do so.'

'Well that's not quite good enough Ella.'

'What?' She frowned at him standing there waving a finger at her like some overbearing parent.

'Your judgement's flawed and dangerous. You leave me with no alternative.'

'Andy.' Ella stepped over the threshold towards him. 'Before you do anything you regret, please, talk to Dr Savage first.'

'I think we're talking at cross purposes Ella.' Andy's tone was patronising as he looked down at her. 'You see I'm not interested in the issues surrounding your poor demented housewife. I intend to secure my daughter's safety for the future.'

'In what way?'

'I think I should be granted custody of Lucy.'

'Then I think you're on a loser straight away there.' Ella replied with a shrug, knowing the only way to win this war of words was to respond in a relaxed manner. 'I can't imagine Nina will want to be saddled with the responsibility of a baby and a toddler. Have you spoken to her about this yet?'

'No, but if she doesn't then we'll...'

'What? Employ a nanny?' Ella was ahead of him. 'I can do that just as well as you, in fact it's not such a bad idea, it will leave Helen more time to look after the running of the house. Sorry Andy, the courts just won't support you. Lucy is best left with me. Of course, if you'd like to spend more time with her then I'm quite willing to arrange it.'

'You don't think I'll do it, do you?' Andy looked at her, feeling the frustration seep through him. She had taken refuge behind that calm mask of hers again, the same one that drove him crazy when they were married. It meant she neither heard nor cared what he said, she would do what she felt was right and with the conviction and single mindedness only she possessed.

'I think,' Ella said quietly with her hand on the door, 'you are over-reacting. We'll discuss it in the morning.'

'Don't bother! I'll see you in court!' He said angrily as the door closed firmly on him.

Ella watched him climb into his car and drive away. Helen came to stand beside her, a worried look on her face.

'I'm so sorry Ella.' She said. 'I seem to have caused such a lot of trouble.'

'Nonsense Helen, it's just a storm in a tea cup.'

'But you heard what he said.'

'I did but it's all bluster.'

'Oh Ella, please, do be careful. Remember what he tried to do to your business.'

'That was different. I believe Bob was behind all that not Andy.'

'I hope you're right.' Helen was still sceptical.

'Of course I am Helen. Believe me, by tomorrow he'll have got all of this out of his system and be thinking about something completely different.'

Pulling up outside Chelwood Lodge Andy checked his watch. Seven thirty. He hoped Nina wouldn't be too put out at his late arrival. He'd better not tell her where he had been, or what he had been discussing. He was angry that Ella in her usual irritating know-all way had been partly right, for at this present moment in time the last thing Nina wanted was a small child to add to her problems. The pregnancy was making her tired, she complained of headache and backache and cried a lot. Pregnancy turned women into strange creatures he decided; even the perfect Ella had suffered similarly during her nine months. Still this time he felt no revulsion at this new life he had been responsible for helping to create. He even planned to be with Nina at the birth, convinced every man should be present at the birth of his son, for that was what he was sure she was going to have. A son who would inherit the family business and finally bring his father round.

As far as Lucy was concerned he would need to talk to Nina, of course. Slowly and carefully outlining his case; persuading her that it was only right and proper that his children be raised together. He would consult his father, get the best nanny that money could buy and also get some advice about putting a custody case together, with the help of his solicitor Bill Matthews. And this time Ella was not going to win, because he would move heaven and earth to make sure she didn't.

Finding his front door key he let himself in, calling out Nina's name as he always did.

'Up here.' The response sounded tearful, she was obviously having a bad day again. He scaled the stairs quickly reaching the landing.

'Where are you?'

'In the bedroom.'

She was on her hands and knees with a bowl of soapy water and a cloth, rubbing at a huge dark stain on the carpet.

'Good God!' He looked horrified. 'What's happened? Are you hurt?'

She stopped what she was doing and sat back on her haunches, brushing her hair from her eyes. He noticed she had been crying.

'What is it? What happened?' He stared at the carpet again and realised he was looking at blood.

'It's the baby Andy!' She said, tears choking in her throat as she looked up at him. 'I've lost the baby!'

Calling David Savage was his first thought as he knelt down on the bedroom floor and took her in his arms.

'Dr Savage was here.' She said, as if she'd heard his unspoken thoughts, her voice muffled in his shoulder. 'I called him as soon as I felt the dreadful pains. I knew there was something wrong.' She sniffed then rested her head against his shoulder again. 'It was all over by the time he got here. He was so kind you know; told me it was nature's way of sorting out things that weren't quite right.'

Andy stared at the blood again. "Shouldn't you be in hospital after losing all that?'

'No. Dr Savage said I just needed to rest. He wants to examine me again in a month, make sure I'm all right. Says we have to leave things for six months then we can try again.' She looked up into his face, her eyes bright through her tears. 'We can try again, can't we? I really want us to have a family.'

'Of course we can.' He hugged her tightly. 'But right now the most important thing is for you to rest.' He took the cloth from her hand and dropped it into the bowl. 'Come on now, into bed with you.'

'But the mess, I can't leave it.'

'It's OK, I'll sort it.'

She undressed and he helped her into bed, bitterly disappointed. The dream of having a son was over for now. And yet there was a spark of hope in all this. There was still Lucy and with Nina no longer pregnant, maybe if he went about things the right way, there was a chance he might be bringing her back to Chelwood Lodge sooner than he first thought.

FOURTEEN

Saturday 30th June

After answering the intercom and buzzing Mick in, Issy stopped to take one last look at herself in the mirror and adjust a stray tendril of hair. Then she scooped up her bag and rushed out of the bedroom and down the hall to answer the front door. Dropping the bag onto the hall table as she passed, she moved on towards the door, grasping the catch and swinging it open.

'God, Iz!' Mick's eyes were wide with surprise as he stepped into the hall and stood there looking at her. 'You look simply amazing.'

As Issy saw a glint of moisture appear in his eyes she wondered how a big man like him could get so emotional over something as simple as a strapless powder blue dress and high heeled sandals.

'Mick Taylor don't you dare cry!' She scolded, retrieving her bag and propelling him out of the flat. 'Come on now, out to the car with you!'

'Sorry Iz, you just look so lovely! It really got to me for a moment.' He said as she gently closed the front door behind them. As they stepped into the street, he turned to her, his face serious. 'Before we go to Tad's,' he said, 'I'd like to take a small detour. There's something I want to show you.'

The drive took fifteen minutes. As soon as they were out of Abbotsbridge she realised where he was heading but said nothing, not wanting to spoil the surprise. They finally reached their destination and Mick killed the engine and turned towards her with a smile.

'What do you think then?'

'It's wonderful.' Issy replied looking up at the farmhouse with its freshly thatched roof and the riot of colour in the front garden.

His blue-grey eyes scanned her face for a moment and then he said. 'Why did you do it Iz?'

'Do what?'

'Get Dad to hang on to the farm house for me?'

'Because,' she looked at the house then back at him and smiled, 'I knew how much you loved this place. How much time and effort you put into it. When you gave it up for her, it seemed almost criminal to sell it off to strangers.' She turned back to look at the house once more. 'You see I knew she'd do it again - you know, go off with someone else. And when she did your pride would be too strong for you to want to stay with her any longer. I knew when that happened, despite the bad memories here, the one thing that you'd need would be the farmhouse.'

'Has anyone told you,' he said running a finger down her cheek, 'that you're a wonderful woman.'

She gave a self-conscious laugh. 'Can I see inside?'

'Of course,' He said, opening the car door. 'Come on.'

The place smelt of fresh paint and preservative, their footfalls echoing as they walked from room to room. It was perfect. Everything had been done with such detail and loving care; from the restored inglenook fireplace to the oak kitchen with its green Aga. The only major change he'd made was to the bathroom, where he had discovered Andy and Nina together in the shower. Now it stood, just a square and empty room with magnolia walls.

'It seems a shame just to leave this empty.'

'Don't worry, I have plans for it. It's going to be a nursery.'

'A nursery?' She smiled.

'For my babies.'

'Haven't you forgotten one rather important item?'

'What's that?'

'A woman; you need a woman to have a baby. Preferably a wife.'

'Oh, I'm in the process of getting one of those.' He pointed a finger at her.

'Me?'

'Yes, you!'

She laughed. 'Are you proposing?'

'I guess I am.' His face broke into a wide smile.

'But what if I say no?'

He reached for her, pulling her into his arms and kissing her. 'I don't think there's any chance of that do you?'

'No,' she smiled up at him. 'Not in a million years.'

Half an hour later, slipping his hand in hers, Mick guided Issy through the maze of parked cars towards main entrance of Zeffirelli's. As they reached it the door swung open automatically to reveal Tad's suede headed bouncer Max kitted out in dinner jacket and bow tie.

'Well, aren't you just the smart dude tonight Max!' Issy said with a mischievous grin.

'It was the boss's idea.' The huge bouncer grinned back. 'Said he wanted to create the right image for his new club.'

'Well he's done that all right; I think you look great.' Issy replied as they moved forward into the foyer.

'Thanks.' Max gave her a broad grin,

Inside the guests were gathered in small groups; the women bright and colourful, the men sombre in their suits, all chatting and sipping their complimentary glass of champagne as they waited to be called through to the restaurant. Grabbing two glasses from a passing waiter Mick handed one to Issy.

'To us,' He said, as his glass touched hers. 'I wonder what the others will have to say when we tell them.'

'What's taken you so long, I expect!'

They both laughed.

Tad, Faye, Matt and Marcie, were standing in Tad's office above the club having a drink. They had arrived an hour before the doors officially opened. Tad had disappeared straight away to make sure everything backstage was OK. Marcie followed, wanting to check everything was in place in her dressing room and Faye headed for the kitchen to see how the preparation of food was going. Left alone Matt walked slowly around, taking time to absorb every new feature of the building. He had been here with his father on several occasions this week, but there had been distractions; people to talk to and last minute changes to make. Only now, on his own, was he able to appreciate the extent of the modifications. The new external wooden gallery suspended over the river, the extended ground floor dance area with its smart chrome railings and carpeted seating area and then, of course, the real pièce de résistance; the restaurant. The carpet was a light grey; the tables were glass and chrome and the seating and walls French blue.

Above the black ash dado rail hung photographs of nearly every movie star in existence, from Chaplin to Olivier, Bacall to Hepburn. They were all here, captured in crisp monochrome. Matt looked around. The contractors had done an excellent job; nothing of the old club was left. No ghosts, no memories, it was a completely neutral place and he knew even with Ella here tonight he would have no problem in fulfilling his promise to his father.

Now it was nearly time and they all stood together the clock ticking towards that moment, watching the guests arrive below, Faye pointing to individuals, telling Marcie who they were.

'Who's the pretty blonde in blue?'

'That's Isobel Llewellyn. Her parents have a hotel in a neighbouring town about five miles away. She's the Function Manager there. They do wedding receptions, conferences, that sort of thing.'

Matt stood behind Marcie, looking down at the clusters of people who had just arrived and were taking advantage of a complementary drink.

'What's Mick Taylor doing with his arm around her?' He frowned at his mother. 'Where's Nina?'

'They...um...divorced last year.' Faye said uncomfortably.

'Why? What happened?'

'Well you know her,' Faye gave a casual shrug, 'Flighty as they come. It was never destined to be long term, was it?'

'So who's she with now?'

'So many questions.' She smiled at Marcie. 'He was like that as a small boy you know, wanting to know the ins and outs of everything. Matt.' There was gentle reproach in her voice as she glanced up at him before turning her attention to the window once more. 'Is it really that important?'

'I suppose not.' He replied with a shrug, aware that his father was looking at his mother with some discomfort. 'I was just curious that was all.'

'Well let's see if we can put that curiosity to some good use.' She turned back to look at him with a smile. 'Rustle up some more champagne will you?' She pointed to the main doorway below. 'Sonny and the band have just arrived.'

'If you don't feel up to going this evening, I don't mind giving it a miss, honestly.' Watching Nina sitting in front of the mirror brushing her hair, Andy decided that after the events of the last twenty four hours, being involved in celebrations was the last thing he needed.

'I'm fine, I really am.' She gave a pale smile as she set the brush aside and stood up, reaching for the lilac dress that hung on the outside of the wardrobe door. 'Besides, I wouldn't miss Tad's opening night for the world, everybody will be there and it will be my first outing as Mrs Andy Macayne.' She pulled on the sheath of sparkling material, and zipped it up. 'You do want to show me off I hope.' she said teasing her hair back off her shoulders.

'Of course, you look lovely.' He gave a weak smile. 'But what if someone asks about the baby?'

'Are they likely to?' Nina turned to look at him, sitting on the bed inserting gold cufflinks into his shirt cuffs. 'I think they'd be too embarrassed to don't you? Especially after our rather hurried wedding. But if anyone does, well, I'll cross that bridge when I come to it.'

'I think you're being very brave my darling.' He said quietly, preoccupying himself with the final adjustments to each cuff, his mind carefully working out the route he intended the conversation to take. 'If only I had your strength.'

'The baby was really important to you, wasn't it?' She said, noticing the sudden sadness in his face.

'Yes, I miss Lucy.' He looked up at her, his eyes dark and melancholy. 'Having the new baby would have helped enormously.'

'It's not the end Andy.' She answered quietly, 'Dr Savage said it was just a setback. We've a six month wait, then we can try again.'

'But there is no guarantee though is there? What if it takes months, even years for you to get pregnant again? At the moment all I have is Saturdays to look forward to. You can't imagine how wonderful it is to hear Lucy's laughter, to be able to hold her. Without her the house seems so empty; at least if we'd had a baby.........' He lowered his head and gave a ragged sigh.

'Andy what is it?' With a frown of concern Nina sat down beside him.

'I'm probably over-reacting,' He leaned his head into her shoulder, looking into her face, his dark eyes troubled, 'but since yesterday and the business with that dreadful woman trying to steal Lucy, well I just don't trust Ella with her any more. I can't believe she didn't press charges. She's far too blasé about Lucy's safety. She just dumps her on Helen and goes off to that bloody business of hers and although I think Helen's a good housekeeper, she has absolutely no idea about child rearing. I lie awake at night and imagine all sorts of awful things happening to her. Being taken again, wandering off and drowning in that river at the bottom of Ella's garden.' He put his hands to his face. 'It's a totally inappropriate place for a small child to live.'

'Are you saying you want her here with us?'

He looked at her and nodded. 'I did. I thought about challenging for custody, but of course, with you pregnant it wasn't really an option. I mean, taking on a small child as well as a new baby would have been a lot to ask.'

'But there is no baby anymore.'

'I know, but that makes it worse in some ways doesn't it? I couldn't possibly ask you to take on the responsibility of a child now, not after yesterday. It's out of the question.'

'No it isn't.' She said, sliding her hand over his and giving it a reassuring squeeze. Her mind worked quickly. Having Lucy to live with them might be just the distraction Andy needed. He was besotted with the child and once she was living with them, another pregnancy might not seem such an important issue to him. Although she had made it clear they could try again after six months, now she was Mrs Andy Macayne she wanted to enjoy her new life properly and put stretch marks, nappies and sleepless nights on hold for a while.

'Andy,' she continued, patting his hand, 'I'm really upset about the baby, but I'm used to disappointment and the one thing I've learned each time is that you can't afford to dwell on things, you have to move on and keep positive. So if you want Lucy to be with us go ahead and see a solicitor, start the ball rolling...'

'Well if you're really sure.'

'I am, definitely.'

'Thank you my darling.' Andy kissed her. 'You don't know how happy you've made me. Of course, we'll employ a nanny.' He reassured her, eager to make Lucy's arrival less of a burden now he had agreement. 'I wouldn't expect you to look after her yourself.'

'I think a nanny is a brilliant idea Andy.' Nina smiled, envisaging the new carefree life she would have. 'Now come on, we'd better go. Tad will never forgive us if we're late.'

Tad stood with a huge grin on his face, his arms flung open as Max ushered the diminutive Sonny and his entourage into the office.

'Sonny.' He hugged the little man enthusiastically.

'I've brought my good lady too.' Sonny reached for the hand of the small plump blonde in pink who stood quietly by his side. 'We got married last month;

this is Linnie. She was the one who looked after Matt when he first lived in London, remember?'

'I certainly do.' Tad shook hands warmly and called Faye over for introductions before turning his attention to the members of the band.

'Great to see you all again,' He said as he gave each man an enthusiastic hug and pat on the back. 'And you must be Guy.' He extended a friendly hand to Todd's replacement, a lean young man with long curly black hair and dark eyes.

'The one and only,' He grinned as they shook hands. 'Pleased to meet you.'

'Have a seat everyone.' Tad indicated the collection of leather couches in the middle of the room. 'Make yourselves comfortable. Matt won't be long, he's gone to organise some champagne, but in the meantime,' he crossed the room to where Marcie sat gazing out of the window. 'I'd like to introduce you all to Marcie Macguire. I expect you've read all about her in the newspapers. She's flown in for her first British Tour and I have to tell you, everything that's been written about her is true. Her voice is just amazing!'

Ella sat in the back seat of Nick's Volvo listening to Jenny's enthusiastic account of their recent boating holiday on the Norfolk Broads, wishing she'd accepted the glass of red wine which had been so temptingly offered before they had begun their journey here tonight. If she had it might have gone a long way to steadying the nerves fluttering in her stomach.

Of course, there was a reason for Jenny's exuberance, a blissfully free evening stretched ahead of her. Precious time to be enjoyed and savoured without the worry of getting back for the babysitter. For Helen, treasure that she was, had suggested that it would be a good idea for Lucy to join her cousins at Tennyson Avenue for the night and she would sleep over with them. I should be looking forward to having a good time, she thought. But I'm not, not at all.

The week had started badly and got worse. First a lucrative contract for temps had been cancelled because the firm, based in Taunton, was relocating along the M4 corridor. Then there was all the bother with Monica Jefferies necessitating the cancellation of appointments and a dash to the police station, followed by Andy on her doorstep with his threats to take Lucy away. And finally, the news that Matt was back in Abbotsbridge.

Returning from lunch on Thursday, two girls were sitting in the main foyer waiting for interviews and as Ella collected her messages from the reception desk she heard one of them mention his name. A morbid curiosity caused her to linger at the desk, thumbing absently through each note while her real attention attached itself to their conversation. He had been spotted shopping in town with his black haired protégé Marcie Macguire. Wasn't he a dish? Rumour had it they were living together in New York. Well, lucky her, wouldn't any woman kill to wake up beside a man like that each morning? Both girls heaved shoulders and gave huge *if only* sighs and Ella found herself transported back to Meridan Cross on that June morning when he had appeared like a wraith from the depths of the wood, riding

Cassie. The memory of that moment was so overpowering she found herself on the verge of tears.

Returning to her office, she closed the door and seated herself behind her desk, her head in her hands. This was stupid and irrational; she was over him. He was out of her life - gone; he meant nothing. But if that was true, why had the mention of his name triggered such a strange reaction?

The Volvo was turning into the car park now, coming to rest under a tree, facing the river. Nick got out and opened the rear door for her. She stood there for a moment looking at the water, feeling the warm evening breeze on her face. They began to walk together towards the club entrance; Jenny's conversation had now turned to the subject of Mick and Issy, but Ella took little of it in. She found herself wishing she had a partner for the evening, someone to act as a distraction; a shield to protect her. But what exactly from? Him? Why? Exactly what was she so frightened of?

Grey doors, which she remembered once being blue, opened and the familiar figure of Max hovered; he looked her over appreciatively as he nodded a greeting to them all. The main foyer had been enlarged, the ladies cloakroom now on the right. She stood looking at French blue walls covered with chrome framed film posters. The beautiful soft skinned Catherine Deneuve, star of Luis Buñuel's Belle De Jour staring down over her bare right shoulder; Audrey Hepburn in Breakfast at Tiffany's, cigarette holder in one black gloved hand, while the other stroked the ginger and white cat on her shoulder. It was clever and distracting she thought as she gazed at them, almost like an art gallery. She wondered whether any of the décor had been influence by Liam. An act of deliberate selfish sabotage by her mother, meant he would not be here for the opening. Mel had booked and paid for two weeks in Minorca without telling him, denying she knew it clashed with the opening of Zeffirelli's.

A passing waiter came to a halt in front of them with a tray of drinks. Mechanically she took a glass and looked around her, identifying individuals among the small groupings of guests. There were nods and smiles, all friendly faces. No Bob here tonight either she thought with relief; he was in Scotland playing golf. Then she saw the stairs. They were wider now, set in a semi circular sweep and covered in blue carpet. So they had kept Tad's eyrie. He could still watch everything going on in the club. She looked to where the window had once been and saw it was now a giant circular mirror. But it wasn't was it? Liam had told her, it was one of those two way things which meant they were still up there watching. The thought made her feel uncomfortable.

'Ella, Jenny!' A familiar voice was calling. Then Issy was standing in front of them, her face flushed, Mick by her side, his arm around her waist.

'Guess what? We're engaged!'

'Issy that's wonderful!' The news brought a smile to Ella's face, making her forget her anxieties.

'Congratulations!' Jenny hugged Issy and then Mick.

'What took you so long?' Nick shouted kissing Issy and pumping Mick's hand enthusiastically.

'I told him someone was bound to say that!' Issy laughed.

'So when's the wedding?' Ella asked.

Issy looked at Mick and smiled. 'April, I want a spring wedding.'

People around them turned with curious smiles at their noisy encounter, some adding their good wishes when they realised what was going on.

'I'm having a topaz engagement ring.' Issy told them all once all the fuss had died down. 'Mick said the stones will match my eyes.' She looked at them all with a brilliant smile. 'He's so romantic!'

'Right then, let's organise a bottle of champagne to celebrate.' Nick turned, scanning the crowd for a waiter and seeing a dark suited figure making its way through the crowd clutching two bottles of Moet to his chest, set off to intercept him.

'Excuse me!' Working his way through the crowd he managed to catch up with the man. 'Could I possibly order some champagne please? Table ten. The name's Kendrick.'

The figure halted immediately and turned.

'Oh, sorry,' Nick suddenly realised his mistake; although the man was carrying glasses and clutching two bottles, he was clearly not a waiter.

'Don't worry.' The smile was friendly. 'I'll make sure it's organised for you. Table ten you said, didn't you? Sorry, can you give me your name again.' He leaned closer to Nick. 'I didn't quite catch it.'

'It's Kendrick, Nick Kendrick.'

'Kendrick?' The man frowned.

'Yes, that's right, is there a problem?'

'No, of course not.'

Nick noticed the man was now gazing past him somewhere over his left shoulder. He swung around to see Ella, glass in hand, had left their group and was now deep in conversation with Alex Nicholson and Miles Anderson.

'Ah, the lady in red; my sister Ella.' He glanced at the stranger's pre-occupied look. 'Do you know her?'

The man nodded. 'It was a long time ago though.'

Thoughtful dark eyes met Nick's then gazed around the room. 'No Andy?'

Nick looked at her affectionately, then turning back with a smile he said. 'Long gone. They divorced last year. Look, why don't you come and say hello, I'm sure she'd be delighted to see you.'

'I'm sorry, I can't.' The stranger indicated the champagne. 'I'm overdue with these already.'

'Give me your name then, I'll tell her I've seen you.'

'I doubt she'd even remember me. As I said, it was a long time ago. Sorry, I have to go.' He backed away with a polite smile. 'I'll get someone to organise the champagne for you. Table ten wasn't it?'

Nick nodded. 'Thank you.'

Matt made his way towards the stairs, carefully negotiating a clear path through the press of bodies at its foot. He tightened his grip on the bottles as he climbed, aware of how precarious his hold had become on them since seeing Ella. As he got to the top of the stairs, he heard the voice of Orlando the Restaurant Manager from somewhere below, calling the guests through to be seated. He knocked the door. It opened and he stepped into the small kitchen where Faye and Marcie were waiting to rescue the bottles from him.

'Are you OK Matt? You look as if you've seen a ghost.' Marcie looked concerned as she prised the two bottles from his fingers and handed them to Tad, who immediately began to uncork one.

'It's a bit of a rugby scrum down there.' He said breathlessly as the first cork popped. 'And I was very aware I was carrying a lot of glass.'

'Never mind, you made it, that's the main thing.' Faye said abruptly. She paused for a moment, watching Tad as he uncorked the second bottle then carried them both from the room, followed by Marcie and a tray of glasses. With a last look at the door she leaned forward and lowered her voice. 'What did Nick Kendrick stop you for?'

'He mistook me for a waiter,' Matt replied, 'wanted to order champagne for his table. I'd never met him before; I had no idea who he was until he told me his name.'

'You were chatting for some time.' Faye said suspiciously.

'So?'

'Did he mention...'

'Ella's divorce? Yes he did as a matter of fact. Which is more than you did.'

'It's because I thought...'

'What? He interrupted. 'That I'd let her bewitch me all over again? You don't give me credit for much do you? Yes, she's beautiful and yes, she still takes my breath away; but I also know how dangerous she is.'

'Oh Matt.' Faye stepped forward and put her arms around him, hugging him tightly. 'I'm so sorry! It's just where she's concerned I still worry!'

He suddenly found anger melting, he couldn't be mad at her for long; she had, after all, been right about Ella and it was wrong to punish someone whose only crime was caring.

'Well don't.' He said giving her a gentle squeeze. 'Come on, let's join the others, they'll be wondering where we've got to.'

FIFTEEN

Saturday 30th June

'Well, I think we've had a great evening so far, don't you?' Mick gave a satisfied smile as the waitress arrived with the coffee. 'Great food, Frank Sinatra floating through the speakers and a brilliant spot right here on the balcony.'

'All that's missing is that celebratory champagne my husband said was coming.' Jenny turned a critical eye on Nick.

'That's a point,' Nick laughed, 'to tell you the truth, I think the guy I spoke to was so mesmerised by the sight of Ella it must have gone straight out of his head. Mick,' he nodded towards the next table where a waitress was clearing plates. 'Could you ask for a bottle and six glasses?'

'Who's this guy then?' Issy asked curiously as Mick left the table.

'Wouldn't give me his name,' Nick said, reaching for the sugar bowl. 'But he definitely knew Ella. It was the he way he said *a long time ago* and the way he looked at her. Still,' he gave her an affectionate smile, 'I have to say, she has that affect on most men....'

'Nick, you're embarrassing.' Ella laughed.

'Well, it's the truth,' He laughed. 'Everyone fancies you.'

'I bet it was someone from the old Club days.' Issy said stirring her coffee.

'Or college.' Jenny suggested.

'Craig Winter.' Issy made a face.

'Oh shut up Issy,' Ella protested, 'he was awful.'

'All blond hair and flash mohair suits.' Jenny added. 'Thought he was God's gift, didn't he?'

'Can't be him then.' Nick interrupted. 'This guy had dark hair.'

'What did he look like Nick?' Issy frowned, elbows on the table, resting her chin on her hands.

'Well...' Nick frowned, concentrating as he tried to find the right description.

'Oh come on!' Issy rolled her eyes in despair. 'Can't you remember anything about him?'

'Tall, broad shouldered.' He paused. 'I reckon he'd look great in a suit of armour.'

'What?' Issy frowned.

'You'll have to excuse him.' Jenny interrupted. 'He spent most of the day marking second form home work - a project on mediaeval Britain.' She gave him an indulging smile. 'It's obviously left a lasting impression on him.'

'Suit of armour apart, does that description ring any bells with you?' Issy looked at Ella curiously.

Ella shook her head, determined not to get involved in a quizzing session with the relentless Issy. To her relief, Mick appeared followed by the waitress carrying the Moet and six glasses.

'First class service here.' He smiled as he poured the bubbling liquid into each glass. 'They even uncorked the bottle for me.'

'To Issy and Mick!' They raised their glasses solemnly.

Looks as if we've timed things just right.' Mick glanced above him as the lights began to dim. Voices softened with the fading of the light, the room eventually falling into a silence broken only by an intermittent cough or chink of glass. All eyes turned to the stage, where a spotlight was now directed onto a thin stem of microphone which had just periscoped up through the floor. There was movement behind the black velvet curtains, a drum roll and then a figure appeared, standing for a moment to adjust the microphone to friendly applause, waiting until it had died down before he began to speak.

'Good evening ladies and gentlemen...' The voice was friendly and confident.

'Ella!' Hissed Nick. 'Ella!'

'Shh!' Several people on adjoining tables turned disapproving faces towards him.

'Ella...' Nick mouthed, his face caught in the light of the Tiffany lamp as he pointed in the direction of the stage. 'The guy I spoke to, that's him.'

Marcie sat in her dressing room carefully applying eye liner, leaning into the brightness of the mirror, keeping her hand as steady as she could. She felt strangely nervous. A silly emotion given the size of the venue, but maybe it was because it was more important than any performance she'd given before. Because it was for Matt. To show everyone he'd returned home as successful as he'd left.

'Five minutes Marcie.'

The call and knock on the door interrupted her thoughts. Five minutes to her first public performance in the UK, she could hardly believe it! She stood up, reaching for her outfit, a sleeveless, low backed dress in a glorious burst of shocking rainbow patterned shimmer. Her favourite tight bright leather jump suits, Matt had told her with a laugh, when she was debating what to wear, would probably send Abbotsbridge matrons reaching for their smelling salts! Remembering his words she smiled as she took the dress from the hanger and slipped it on. Once the high silver wedge shoes were on her feet she took a look at herself in the mirror. Marcie the girl seemed to recede into the background as Marcie the performer stood there in a glorious explosion of metallic colour. Standing back from the door, she fixed her gaze on the blue wall clock, watching the second hand skim its face, anticipating the final knock. It came as the sweeping hand touched the twelve.

'Come in.'

Tad appeared in the open doorway, his smile reminding her of Matt.

'You look absolutely stunning!'

'Thank you, how's he doing?'

'He's doing just fine. Are you ready?'

'You bet!' She slipped her arm in his. 'Let's go!'

Ella was glad of the darkness. Her face burned with anger and embarrassment.

'So, it was Matt you ran into.' Jenny said to Nick, then looking down at the stage smiled. 'That explains it. I have to say though, I wouldn't recognise him. He's changed so much.'

'Yes! He's certainly filled out in all the right places.' Issy's tone was distinctly lustful.

'Behave yourself Issy Llewellyn!' Mick hissed.

'I'm just admiring!' Issy responded her eyes still firmly fixed on the stage. 'He used to look like a pipe cleaner. Boy what a transformation.' She looked at Ella thoughtfully. 'He's a real dish now. Don't you think so Ella?'

Ella ignored Issy's torturing comments, unable to take her eyes off the figure on stage. She watched the confidence with which he moved and the casual ease with which he interacted with audience. His hair was longer now, thick and dark, curling down over the collar of his shirt. He looked tanned, healthy and incredibly handsome. She imagined the lean hardness of his body beneath the suit he was wearing, saw him clasp the microphone and gave a small shudder as she recalled how it felt to be touched by those hands. He smiled; the mirror image of his father and Ella felt her heartbeat go into overdrive. She sat up straight, glaring down at the stage, trying desperately to summon up anger, rage, hostility - anything to blot out this other overwhelming and totally unwanted emotion which now seemed to have taken hold of her.

Matt had finished and stood clapping as his parents joined him on stage. Faye held his hand tightly, Tad hugged him and after a few words there was more applause after which he and Faye left the stage. Matt then stepped forward waiting for the noise to die down then, completely at ease, he began to talk about his time in the States, Maverick Records and last of all Marcie.

'And so Ladies and Gentlemen,' He finished, taking a step to one side. 'The time has now come for you to judge for yourselves. Please welcome Miss Marcie Maguire!'

Matt threw out his arm and the audience applauded once more as the curtain parted and the spotlight caught and held a sparkling figure swathed in a rainbow of colour. Ella watched transfixed as Matt blew her a kiss and left the stage.

Marcie stepped up to the microphone, pulled it from its stand and moved across the stage. Behind her, the band Tad had hired for the evening kicked in with the introduction to *'Never Quite Over You.'* Swaying to the gentle rhythm, she moved forward. As the first chords of the Spanish guitar came in, she lifted the microphone and began to sing.

Backstage Matt stood watching Marcie; it was an electric performance, the power and clarity of her voice breath-taking. Doug had made a good choice suggesting this should be her first British release; his most difficult composition had hit written all over it. He was glad she'd agreed to do this for his father too; it had made all the difference to the evening. As the song came to an end to enthusiastic applause he suddenly felt at peace. All the frustrations and uncertainties of his visit here melted away. The audience was still clapping, some were whistling and then she began to speak, announcing the next song she was going to sing. He frowned; only one song had been planned. What was she doing? A special song, she said, for Matt because she owed him so much and to accompany her, Tad, the man who had once made it famous. Everything went quiet, the lights dimmed, she stood immobile in the spotlight with Tad by her side. They turned to each other, sharing the microphone and with a smile, began.

Ella sat mesmerised by the figure on stage, thoughts of Matt suddenly forgotten. Marcie's voice was incredible; the song brilliant. It appeared that Matt hadn't lost his talent for writing. Matt. She gritted her teeth summoning up her most antagonistic feelings. I hate him, I really do, she thought. He's a liar, a user and a womaniser. Just like Andy.

The song ended and she applauded enthusiastically with the others. The musical interlude had been calming, distracting the others around the table. Matt as a topic of conversation seemed to have run its course. She was glad, she didn't want to dig up the past, she wanted to bury it in a huge dark hole and forget it ever happened. Marcie was talking now, a girlish transatlantic voice, full of enthusiasm as Tad joined her on stage. Ella closed her eyes for a moment as a sudden hush descended and then she heard their duet begin… *'Oh Danny Boy,'*
She opened her eyes immediately and sat there listening, transfixed, as unaccompanied, Tad and Marcie's voices, filled with emotion, sang. This song was all part of a past that no longer meant anything, she assured herself. Everything was fine, she could cope. And then she heard the words. His promise to her as they lay together on that warm June night in the woods near Otter Falls.
'For I'll be there, in sunshine or in shadow….'
Empty, hollow words he didn't really mean.
She stood up quickly and immediately felt Nick's steadying hand on her arm.
'Are you OK?'
'Fine,' She whispered. 'Going to the loo…'
She made her escape as quietly as she could, down the stairs, skirting the dance floor and out towards the foyer. Alex and Miles were seated on a large table just inside the door. Alex caught her hand as she passed. 'Everything all right?'

'Too much champagne I think. Some fresh air should do the trick.' She hid her lie behind her smile.

'There's a balcony just through there.' He pointed to the archway. 'Overlooking the river. Are you sure you're OK?'

'I'll be fine thank you...'

'Catch you for a dance later?'

'Of course,' she smiled at him and the other occupants of the table and walked on.

Out on the balcony she stood for a moment leaning on the railings, watching a sky shot with reds and purples, trying to convince herself she was merely having a mad moment which would pass. *You're just over reacting. Calm down* was her silent mantra. Then with a sigh she relaxed, losing herself for a moment in the dark depths of the river and the lengthening shadows. I need a break, she told herself, trying to remember the last holiday she'd had, realising it was all of two years ago when she was still married to Andy. Somewhere hot. Endless sand. The gentle wash of a warm sea. Barbados maybe. Or perhaps Bermuda. I'll drop into the agents on Monday, book something for July, after Charlotte's christening.

'Ella.'

She froze at the sound of his voice and moved away from the railings to face him as he walked out of the shadows.

'Andy?'

'I saw you come out, thought it might be an opportune moment to get you on your own.' He smiled. A malicious cold smile reminiscent of his father.

'Whatever for?' She eyed him calmly.

'Just to tell you to expect a solicitor's letter in the week.'

'What?'

'I'm going ahead with it.' He looked pleased with himself. 'The challenge for custody. I've spoken to Nina and she's more than willing for us to have Lucy.'

'As well as a baby?' She eyed him coolly. 'Is that really sensible, Andy?'

'Actually,' he looked out across the river, 'there is no baby any more. Nina miscarried last night. I found her when I got home.'

Ella looked at him, unable to speak. She should be saying she was sorry, offer a few words of comfort, but how could she when people as hateful as them were involved?

'Cat got your tongue?' There was a bitter edge to his laugh. 'Don't know what to say do you? Well, please, don't feel sorry for either of us, you see when one door closes another opens. We may have lost a baby but the way is now clear for us to take Lucy off your hands.'

'You will not have Lucy!' Ella rounded on him angrily. 'She stays with me! I'm her mother! As I told you before, I'm happy to increase the time you have with her, but I won't have her brought up under the influence of that..!'

The movement was so swift she had no time to avoid it. His hand caught her by the throat, pushing her against the railings and pinning her with his body so she was unable to move.

'Now you listen to me!' He brought his face very close to hers, his eyes dark and angry. 'I *will* have my daughter. I *will* take her from you and she *will* be brought up as a Macayne at Chelwood Lodge along with the other children we plan to have. And if you attempt to fight me on this, I'll make you sorry. Very sorry!'

Matt was standing in the wings listening to Marcie and Tad's duet as it came to an end when he felt a hand on his shoulder and turned around to see Max.

'There's a bit of bother, outside on the balcony.'

'Someone drunk too much have they?'

'No, it's a row and it's getting a bit heated.'

'Well, you're the bouncer Max, just chuck them out.'

'The problem is...' Max said hesitantly, 'one of them is Macayne. If I go out there on my own and try to break it up he's bound to get nasty. You know as well as I do he likes nothing better than to cause trouble and the last thing the Boss needs on his opening night is bad publicity.'

'I guess you're right.' Matt said thoughtfully, then alerted by the applause, he turned to add his own appreciative hands before turning back to Max. 'What do you want me to do?'

'If you could just come down with me, hang about in the shadows. Just in case he starts anything funny.'

'OK,' Matt nodded, watching his father disappear off stage and return almost immediately to give Marcie a big hug and present her with a huge bunch of flowers. 'But I need to see Miss Maguire first. You go on; I'll be down as soon as I can.'

'This has got nothing to do with Lucy, has it?' Ella held Andy's gaze defiantly. 'You don't really want her at all. This is all about revenge isn't it?'

'That's right. You made a fool of me Ella.' Andy's eyes were hard and black in the paleness of his face. 'Going behind my back, getting Alex Nicholson to bail you out like that.'

'I didn't approach Alex.' Ella replied, struggling against the weight of his body. 'When he came to me, he'd already bought the properties.'

'And how many shags did he charge for saving your precious business?' He gave a coarse laugh. 'Five, six? Or is it on-going?'

'You're disgusting!' She spat at him, wriggling furiously to free her right arm. 'Not all middle aged men behave like your father!'

'What?'

'Nothing!' Realising her mistake, she bit back the words quickly.

'What did you say?' He leaned on her harder and she felt the wood of the parapet press painfully into her back.

'Let me go!' She threw her weight against him angrily.

'Not until you explain yourself you bitch!' He forced her back into the railings, making her cry out in pain.

'Your father and my mother.' She said, giving in. 'It's been going on for ages.'

'Liar!'

'It's true! I saw them together last August. In the maze at Miles' house.'

'No!' There was madness in his eyes, 'He wouldn't do that! He doesn't want anyone else that way! He still loves my mother!'

'I used to believe that too.'

'What do you mean?'

She shook her head.

'Tell me!' His hands reached for her shoulders and he shook her violently. She felt the wood embedding itself painfully in her back once more.

'When we were in Italy,' she said, her anger returning as she pushed against him, 'your Aunt told me that at the time your mother died your father had a mistress. His secretary; they were together on the afternoon your mother went to meet him at the house on the park. He forgot the time. He was late. Your Aunt's family still blame him for her death; that's why he's never been back to Italy.'

'Rubbish!'

'Is it?' Her eyes held his and for a moment she thought she caught uncertainty in their dark depths.

'Of course it is! They never approved of my mother marrying an Englishman; they weren't happy that she hadn't married into a good Italian Catholic family. Worse still, he took her away from them.'

'Well I suppose there's an element of truth in that, but...'

'It's *the* truth.' He cut across her words, his voice hard and arrogant. 'As far as I'm concerned he is an honourable man. And if he wasn't, the last person on earth he would want is someone like your mother!'

'I know what I saw.'

His hands slid along her shoulders until his fingers met either side of her throat.

'You didn't see anything,' He said as she felt his thumbs begin to press down painfully and he began to shake her again. 'You're just a liar and a troublemaker Ella and it's time someone put you in your place.'

Pinned by her arms to the balcony Ella found herself unable to fight back. She lashed out with her feet, catching him in the shins. He swore at her but held on, his eyes black and violent. He was mad with rage and she knew she was about to pay the price for her outspokenness.

Max arrived on the balcony to find Andy Macayne pinning someone to the railings at the far end, his voice angry and loud. He hesitated for a moment, looked back into the club to see if he could see Matt, but the foyer was empty. He sighed. He would just have to hang around until he came. Then the sound of choking came to his ears and he knew he could leave things no longer.

'What's going on?' He stepped forward, his deep voice booming out in the darkness.

Andy immediately released his grip on Ella and spun round, concealing her behind him. 'Bugger off Max, mind your own business.'

'This is my business.' Max said politely. 'I'm employed to see that everything goes smoothly this evening, without any incident. This is an incident.'

Taking advantage of her freedom and having Andy with his back to her, Ella hovered behind his right shoulder. If she could get past him and to Max she knew she would be safe.

'Well just look at you.' Andy taunted. 'A gorilla in an evening suit sounding like Robbie the bloody Robot! Whatever gimmick will Tad think of next?'

Max's face remained impassive. 'Please go back inside, I don't want any trouble.'

'You won't get any if you just bugger off and mind your own business.'

'Can't do that, I'm afraid,' Max frowned, realising that it was Ella standing behind Andy.

'So what are you going to do then Max? Eh? Throw me out?' Andy began to laugh.

'If I have to...'

'If I have to,' Andy mimicked. 'Come on then you big ape!'

As Max stepped forward Ella saw an opportunity to escape.

'Oh no you don't!' Catching the movement out of the corner of his eye, Andy lunged at her. She dodged around him, but in doing so, the heel of her shoe caught in the boards and she fell forward with a cry.

With amazing speed Max reached out with one large arm, catching her around the waist, breaking her fall and setting her gently back onto the decking. In a continuation of the same movement he turned and grabbed Andy by the collar of his jacket.

'Let go of me!' Andy protested, swinging a punch at empty air as Max held him at arms length.

'Only when you've calmed down and promise you'll leave quietly.'

'Get stuffed! I'm not taking orders from the likes of you.'

'Suit yourself.' Max continued to hold him. 'We can stay like this all night, I'm in no hurry.'

Eventually Andy quietened, grimacing resentfully.

'Good, that's better.' Satisfied, Max released him.

Andy stood there glowering at Max as he straightened his jacket and pushed his hair back off his face.

'You can leave now, go on scoot.' Max said quietly and stood back, making sure that Ella was safely behind him.

Ella watched Andy pass. As he drew level with Max, he smiled and then twisted quickly, aiming his knee towards Max's groin. The bouncer had not anticipated this, but Ella had. As soon as his foot left the ground she darted out from behind

Max and pushed Andy in the chest, sending him sprawling backwards towards the railings. With a surprised cry he disappeared into the black void. Moments later there was a loud splash.

Hand to her mouth, Ella realised she had pushed him towards a spot where the balcony was roped off to give river users access to the club. He had fallen over the rope and straight into the water. She rushed forward, joining Max at the railings, looking down into the blackness for signs of movement.

Andy surfaced almost immediately, spluttering and cursing as he grabbed at a nearby metal ladder and began to haul himself out of the water.

'You bitch!' He said, hanging there, spitting weed from his mouth. 'You tried to drown me.'

'If I'd had any intention of drowning you,' Ella said peering over the railings into the water. 'I'd be down there with my foot on your head, making a proper job of it.'

Max grabbed Andy by the arm and hauled him back onto the balcony where he stood covered in weed, his suit clinging wetly to his body.

'Look at my clothes, they're ruined!' He glared at Ella, his black hair plastered to his head. 'What the hell did you think you were playing at?

'I was doing you a favour actually.'

'Favour!' Andy was almost hysterical with rage.

'Everything all right Max?'

Max looked towards the creeper covered archway with a relieved smile as a shadowy figure emerged.

'Tad,' Ella turned with a thankful smile.

'Hello Ella.'

Ella's eyes widened with surprise as Matt walked straight past her and over to where Andy stood.

'Moonlight swim?' He asked, looking at Andy's wet suit and dripping hair.

'Vicious ex-wife,' Andy said, eyeing Ella with hostility, 'pushed me in the river.'

'Oh dear - Max,' Matt turned to the bouncer. 'Help Mr Macayne inside will you? Get him dried off. We don't want him catching a cold. Oh and you'd better let his wife know what's happened. I'm sure they won't want to prolong their stay after this unfortunate incident.'

Emptying water from his shoes, Andy scowled at Matt then padded after Max. As he reached Ella he paused for a moment.

'This is not over.' He waved a vicious finger at her. 'I will have her and you are not going to stop me!'

'Are you all right?' As they left, Matt turned to Ella, his face filled with concern.

'Yes. Thank you.' She said abruptly, stepping away from him, her hand at her throat as she watched Andy depart. 'I must get back to my table; the others will wonder where I am.'

'You're shaking.' He said, placing a gentle hand on her shoulder. 'What did he do?'

'Nothing.' She shook his grip off impatiently. The last thing she wanted was any fuss, especially with him. He was too close; the warmth of his hand on her skin had sent her pulse racing. Quickly she fought to gain control of herself.

'How can you say that Ella? Why make excuses for a thug and a bully?'

She laughed, moving back, away from his touch.

'What's so funny?'

'I'm flattered that my welfare should concern you at all.' She said, maintaining her distance and folding her arms protectively against herself. 'Given the circumstances.'

'Well, if you want to take that attitude.' He said with equal sarcasm, 'Given the circumstances, maybe I should really be saying that you deserved it.'

'Me?' Ella reacted angrily. 'Why?'

'Well, you went running back to him, didn't you?'

'I did not!'

'Second honeymoon in Italy I was told. What was that all about then?'

'I was forced to go!' She said fiercely. 'Besides, after you'd gone what alternative was there?'

'I didn't go anywhere!' He rounded on her angrily. 'You were the one who went, after you'd got what you wanted! How could you lie to me like that?'

'Me? Lie? I didn't lie!'

'Yes you did!'

'No Matt, you lied. And you were the one who ran away; to Spain.'

'Sonny sent me to Spain. Todd was in jail, I had to sort things out before the tour.' He put his palm to his forehead. 'Why am I telling you this? You already know, it was all in the note!'

'Note? There was no note!'

'Yes there was...'

'Matt, I can assure you there was no note.'

'I left it with the keys.'

'Ah the keys,' Ella nodded, making a supreme effort to hold onto her temper, 'yes I do know about them, they were pushed through the letter box at Willowbrook. Mary was not amused.'

'I didn't push the keys through any letter box, I...'

'I really don't care what you did or didn't do!' Ella interrupted him, her patience at breaking point. 'If you feel better blaming me, you just go ahead, because I know the truth and that's all that matters to me.' She gave a wry smile. 'Your ex fiancée Belinda and me? I'd say we've both had lucky escapes.'

'Will you stop and listen for a moment!' His hands were on her shoulders again, 'I think there are a few things we should get straight, starting with Belinda......'

'Get lost Matt.'

Pushing him away angrily she turned and ran as fast as she could towards the ivy covered archway. Emerging into the main foyer she heard the throb of the disco, saw the brilliant pulsating lights over the heads of those gathered on the steps to the dance floor. Slipping easily between the clusters of people, she looked for a quiet corner to give herself time to think; time to calm herself before returning to her table.

She was aware that her hands were shaking and her mind was see-sawing between confusion and anger. She had hated his duplicity, now she hated the way he had tried to blame her for all that had happened with some cock-and-bull story that didn't make sense. How could she have possibly still been attracted to the kind of man had he turned into?

'Well, well, look who I've found.'

His Cockney accent was instantly recognisable. Small, balding and still wearing suits that were too big for him, five years had changed very little about Sonny Scott. Tonight he had a companion with him; a short round middle aged woman in pink chiffon, who apart from the difference in hair colouring, blonde to his dark, could easily have been his twin.

'It's great to see you!' Sonny stepped up to her and hugged her tightly. 'Well chick,' He looked her up and down appreciatively, 'you look a million bucks. That's some outfit...red's definitely your colour. Don't you agree Linnie?'

The woman nodded and gave Ella an enthusiastic smile.

'Have you seen Matt? Looks great too doesn't he?' He enthused. 'And the music! Hasn't lost his touch. It's better than ever. That Marcie, she's got a tremendous voice, you know. A second Streisand, that's what she is.'

'Sonny,' The woman tugged his arm. 'Will you shut up a minute and mind your manners. You haven't introduced me.'

'Sorry my angel,' He looked at her with an indulgent smile. 'This is Ella. Remember I told you about her? She used to get around with Matt in the old days.' He gave Ella a wink before turning back to his companion. 'Didn't I say at the time that he was mad not hanging on to her? Well, here she is, and was I right or was I right?' He shook his head. 'He was always bleedin' useless where women were concerned!'

'Language, Sonny!' The woman dug him in the ribs with mirthful reproach. 'Can't take him anywhere,' she said to Ella. 'A couple of drinks and he's off, effing and blinding.'

'Sorry!' Sonny looked embarrassed. 'Ella, this is my good lady wife Linnie.' He said proudly, giving her an affectionate hug. 'She's a little treasure, you know. Friend of my first wife. We met up by chance when Matt first moved up to London. I was looking for a place for him to stay. Linnie ran a small hotel just round the corner from the recording studios. Like a second mum to him she was. He stayed with her for nearly six months before he got that posh Chelsea pad of his. But blimely chick,' He waved a small fat hand at her, 'I'm probably telling you something you already know. Matt's bound to have mentioned her. Belinda Walsh she was in those days...'

SIXTEEN

Saturday 30th June

Watching Ella leave, Matt felt angry and confused. Walking onto the balcony and seeing her standing there beside Max, all he wanted to do was hold her in his arms. The moment he touched her, however, he could feel her hostility. At first he thought it was the aftermath of the confrontation with Andy, but the contempt in her face as they spoke made him realise it was also directed at him. The anger in her eyes had been frightening, her attack on him savage. How dare she, he thought; how dare she take the moral high ground after what she's been responsible for herself.

He leaned on the railing, watching the river and trying to get his head around the things she'd said. Weird things that didn't add up. Why had she deliberately lied about the note? And what did she mean about the keys? The moon rose above the trees, trailing its pale reflection across the river. Matt checked his watch, ten fifteen; the night was still young. It was time to go back and join the others, time to enjoy himself and put this unfortunate confrontation and Ella behind him for good. Hearing soft footfalls he found Max by his side once more.

'Everything all right?'

Matt nodded.

'I've left Macayne with Trixie, she's sorting him out a shower and a change of clothes.' He said in his familiar deep voice. 'Of course her Gingership was not amused at having her evening ruined, started to kick up a fuss but your Dad intervened, offered them both dinner on the house whenever they want to come back. That seemed to bring the smile back to her face.'

Matt nodded, realising the fact that his father had got involved meant he'd probably have to face his mother about this incident later on. 'I should have known anywhere Ella would be there would be trouble.' He shook his head.

'Weren't her fault,' Max replied. 'He was going to kick me in the balls, that's why she pushed him. Is she OK?'

'Oh yes.' Matt gave a painful smile. 'In fact she sharpened her claws on me afterwards. She was in a hell of a mood.'

'That's down to Macayne.' Max said seriously. 'He's led her a dog's life by all accounts.'

'She chose him.' Matt shrugged uncaringly.

'That's not what I heard. They say the marriage was mostly old man Macayne and her mother's doing.'

'Listening to gossip Max? Big mistake,' Matt said with gentle reproach. 'It rarely has much to do with the truth. Believe me, I was with Ella long enough to know she's not the kind of girl who does anything she doesn't want to. Now, come on,' he turned and gave the bouncer a friendly pat on the shoulder, 'let's go back in. If my mother's got wind of this, I'll have some explaining to do.'

'I was just about to send out a search party!' Nick said as Ella sat down next to him.

'Sorry, I ran into a few people, stopped to talk...'

'Are you OK? You look a bit pale.'

'It's this lighting, does strange things to your complexion.' Ella said with a convincing smile, still reeling from her unexpected meeting with Sonny and Linnie. 'Where are the others?'

'On the dance floor; Jenny was abducted by her father.' He nodded to where Jenny and Jack were dancing to the New Seekers *Beg, Steal or Borrow*. 'They've left me all alone.' He said mournfully.

'Better put you out of your misery then.' She said standing up and offering him her hand, 'Come on.'

They reached the edge of the dance floor and taking her in his arms, Nick eased his way between the other dancers. The tempo had slowed. Gladys Knight's *The Look of Love* now had couples in close contact, slowly circling the dance floor. Expertly guided by her brother, Ella was aware of moving among familiar faces. She nodded and smiled at people they passed, her thoughts returning to Sonny and Linnie again. How strange fate was pushing her into their company straight after her confrontation with Matt. Of course once she realised the truth about Belinda Walsh she had to know about Spain. Yes, Sonny confirmed, Todd had been in jail, and yes, he had sent for Matt. The American tour was imminent, there was such a lot at stake and Matt was the only one he could trust to sort it out. Of course he didn't want to go, and when pressurised had asked for a twenty four hour delay. But Sonny had insisted he had to go at once and so he had left Meridan Cross that morning to catch the late afternoon flight to Malaga.

It seemed part of the puzzle was solved, but there were other unanswered things, like the keys and the note and, of course, Shandy. I have to see him, she thought, I need to clear this up.

'Penny for your thoughts,' Nick whispered in Ella's ear as the music stopped and they came to a halt.

'Sorry.'

'Thinking about your knight in shining armour were you?'

'Matt you mean?' She gave him an amused smile. 'What makes you say that?'
'Big brother's intuition; you've seen him haven't you?'
She nodded. 'And I need to talk to him again before he leaves for Scotland.'
As the DJ keyed in the Sweet's *Blockbuster* Nick made a face. 'Do you want to give this a go?'
She shook her head. 'Let's sit this one out.'
As they reached the top of the staircase, he stopped, pausing to scan the dance floor below.
'If you're planning to go looking for him now, he's down there.' He pointed to where Matt was standing with his arm round Marcie's shoulder, talking to a couple of members of the Attitude.
'No.' she shook her head, 'What I have to say is best done somewhere less public. It'll keep until tomorrow.'

'I can't believe this of you!' Faye said, looking at Matt in dismay. 'After all you said to me!'
She had been aware of a ripple in the club earlier on that evening. Tad had disappeared for fifteen minutes, returning to sit quietly by her side. Matt, she also realised had been absent for a good half hour but returned soon afterwards and took Marcie out to dance. When they returned, they joined Baz and the other members of the Attitude on their table and spent the rest of the evening drinking and chatting with them. Through the evening she watched them both suspiciously; she recognised all the signs, Tad was exceptionally jovial whilst Matt was making sure he kept a discreet distance from her. Once they were home, behind closed doors she was determined she would have it out with both of them.
They left the club a little after 2.30 a.m. Sonny, Linnie and the Attitude were staying overnight in the George Hotel in town and they had all arranged to meet up for ealy lunch the next day before Matt and Marcie left for Edinburgh.
The journey home took little more than ten minutes, the car sweeping quickly through the deserted streets of Abbotsbridge, before it headed out of town towards East Portway. Tad and Matt talked in muted tones in the front, while beside her Marcie rested her head against the seat, her eyes closed.
By the time Tad turned the BMW into their driveway she was more than ready for them. As she walked towards the front door she knew that the moment it closed behind them all she would make sure she had her answers. As she faced them, demanding to know what was going on, she saw Tad and Matt give each other embarrassed glances, while Marcie the innocent bystander, hovered in the kitchen doorway, trying to diffuse the situation by suggesting she make coffee.
'It's something to do with her isn't it?' She said accusingly, feeling almost hysterical with rage. 'What's happened?'
And then it all came tumbling out, first Matt with his story of Andy Macayne falling in the river. His clothes saturated. Having to get him dried off. Max and Ella's involvement.

'It sounds like a right bloody pantomime! And how did you get involved?' She said, turning her attention to Tad.

'They got him upstairs. Dried him off and gave him a change of clothes.' He said calmly. 'Of course we had to let Nina know what had happened and predictably she hit the roof. So, to calm things down I offered them both dinner on the house.'

'You did what!'

'It's not a problem Faye, really it isn't.' Tad protested.

'But why should we be out of pocket because Ella Macayne takes it into her head to push her ex-husband into the river? What's the matter with you two?' She looked from one to the other, 'What is it about *her* that turns you both into mindless morons! I can't believe this of you Matt, after all you said to me this evening.' She held her hands up in exasperation. 'Why didn't you just walk away, leave him to strangle her? He'd be doing us all a favour!'

'Faye.' Tad crossed to where she stood and put his hands gently on her shoulder. 'Please. You don't really mean that.'

'Oh yes I do!' She looked determinedly into his face and then beyond him, at Matt. 'Every single word!'

Marcie had retreated to the kitchen where she busied herself with the percolator, searching the cupboards for coffee, sugar, cups and saucers. As the percolator began to bubble she retrieved the milk from the fridge. Boy was Mrs Benedict one angry woman!

By the time she had loaded the tray and carried it through they were all in the lounge. Matt stood facing the window, hands in his pockets, gazing silently out into the floodlit garden, while across the room Tad was sitting beside Faye on one of the two large couches, holding her hand and listening patiently to her.

'Please understand, I only feel like this because I care about Matt.' she was saying, gazing sadly into her husband's face. 'I wasn't sure about her when I first met her, but I was prepared to be open minded. Then when I saw what she was doing, playing Matt and Andy off against each other, well that convinced me she was like her awful mother. And what she did to him two years ago was unforgivable, it was so destructive, so cruel!'

'Faye, you mustn't upset yourself, you have to put this into perspective.' Tad replied quietly, as Marcie set the tray down on the nearby coffee table and took a seat on the other couch. 'Matt is here on a flying visit. Tomorrow afternoon he'll be on his way to Edinburgh. His meeting with her tonight was purely by accident. Max asked him to help because he knew Andy was out on the balcony arguing with someone and it was getting out of hand. With Macayne being a known trouble maker Max wanted someone in authority to nip it all in the bud.'

'So why didn't you go?'

'Because I was on stage with Marcie.'

Marcie served him with coffee and he accepted his cup with a smile and a nod of thanks before continuing. 'They both went out there under the impression

Macayne was with a man.' He went on. 'They had no idea she was there. And the only reason Ella pushed Andy in the river was to stop him kneeing Max in a rather vulnerable place, so as far as I'm concerned his swim was well justified. And as for the meal,' he shook his head wisely, 'well that was just a small compromise I had to make to get them off the premises without a fuss.'

As they drank their coffee, the room fell silent; the only sound the measured tick of the grandfather clock. Returning her empty cup to the tray Faye shot a sideways glance at her husband.

'I'm sorry.' She whispered, leaning to rest her head softly against Tad's shoulder. 'It's just whenever I think of her, something inside me seems to react quite violently.'

'You've had a long day.' Tad bent his face to kiss her cheek. 'We all have. Time for bed I think.' He looked at Marcie then across to Matt who was still staring out of the window. 'If you'll both excuse us.' He got to his feet and took Faye by the hand, helping her to her feet.

As the door closed, leaving Marcie alone with Matt, she waited for him to say something, to break the silence he seemed to have enforced upon himself since his mother's outburst. Eventually he turned away from the window, his face solemn and leaving his coffee cup on the tray, he sat himself down next to her.

'Are you OK?' She asked quietly.

He nodded, leaning forward, clasping his hands together.

'Your Mom really hates her doesn't she?'

'She certainly does.' He gave an embarrassed smile. 'I apologise. She's not normally given to such outbursts.'

'I guess she was only trying to protect you.'

'From what? Ella can't stand me; she made it quite clear I'm the last person she has any interest in.'

'You *spoke* to her?' Marcie said in astonishment. 'Matt was that wise?'

'Marcie,' His tone was icy, 'it really isn't any of your business.'

'I'm sorry.' Marcie apologised quickly, remembering how similar outspokenness on her part had triggered their row in New York. 'It's just that...'

'What?' He frowned.

She looked at him uncomfortably. 'Well, you told your mother you could handle it, that you were over her, but it looks to me like you're anything but.'

'She said some awful things to me tonight. Things that made no sense and she was so angry.' He turned to Marcie with an exasperated shake of his head. 'Getting divorced from Andy Macayne seems to have turned her into one bitter woman. Do you know something Marcie?' He managed a tired smile and raised his hand to her cheek. 'I can't wait to get out of here.'

Sunday 1st July

Marcie woke to find sun streaming through her bedroom window. She stretched comfortably and looked across at the clock. Nine thirty.

The first sound that came to her ears was the slam of the front door. Quickly she got out of bed and went to the window. Below her Tad and Faye were getting into the BMW while just in front of the car, Matt, in T-shirt and shorts gave them both a final wave before jogging off down the driveway. She returned to bed and fell into the softness of the duvet, her thoughts on the next eight weeks and the tour. Her lids began to feel heavy and she closed her eyes only to find when she opened them again it was ten past ten.

Pulling on her dressing gown and running a brush through her hair she made her way down to the kitchen. A note in Matt's handwriting was propped against the percolator. *'Dad and Mum have gone to the club'* it read *'I'm out for a run - help yourself to breakfast - see you later.'*

She set up the percolator and when the coffee was ready poured herself a large cup and sat herself down at the kitchen table to browse through the Sunday papers which had been left there. Halfway through the News of the World's celebrity gossip page she felt her stomach rumble. She got up and cut two thick slices of bread for the toaster, then pouring herself a second cup of coffee, she went back to her paper.

The noise of bread being ejected from the toaster coincided with the sound of door chimes in the hall. Quickly juggling the two slices of hot toast onto a nearby plate, she made her way to the front door. Opening it she found herself face to face with a young woman, dressed casually in a green shirt and black jeans; a stunning woman with wide grey eyes, high cheekbones and long black hair which tumbled in wild corkscrews over her shoulders. Instantly she knew. It was Ella.

'Hello Marcie.' The voice was gentle, educated, the smile benign. 'Is Matt in?' Marcie smiled pleasantly. 'Who's askin'?' she said as she leaned casually against the door jamb.

'I'm...I'm an old friend,' There was a self-conscious half smile. 'I just wanted a very quick word if he's around.'

'Hang on...' Marcie moved away from the front door, deliberately leaving it open. She sauntered over to the stairs, climbed up to the half landing and shouted. 'Matt, honey, there's someone here to see you. You decent?' She held her position on the stairs for a few seconds then walked back down into the hall.

'Sorry, late night.' The friendly smile materialised again. 'We've only just got up. He's in the shower right now, might be some time.'

'OK.' Ella nodded her face an expressionless mask. Marcie knew her words had spoken quite plainly of an involvement with Matt beyond a professional one, but if Ella had been shocked or upset, it certainly didn't show.

'If you'd like to leave your name and number, I'll ask him to call you back.'

'No,' Ella shook her head then smiled. 'Although on second thoughts, yes perhaps I will.'

'I'm Ella.' She said pulling a pad and pen from her bag. 'And I need to talk to him quite urgently. It will only take a few minutes. I'll give you my home number. I'll be there most of the day.'

'We're leaving for Scotland later today, but I'll see if he can squeeze a call in to you before we go.' Marcie said as she watched Ella write down the phone number. 'A friend from the old Mill days are you?'

'Yes.' Ella finished writing and handed Marcie the piece of paper, slipping her pen and pad back into her bag. 'If you could just give him this,' she smiled, 'he can make up his own mind whether he has time to call me or not.'

'Sure, be glad to.' Marcie's smile was wide and friendly. She waited at the door, watching as Ella got back into her Mercedes and the car moved off down the driveway. As it disappeared from view, she turned and walked back into the hall, closing the front door gently behind her. Returning to the kitchen she gazed at the note thoughtfully for a moment before tearing it into small pieces and throwing them casually into the pedal bin.

Matt was on the home stretch. Since arriving back in Abbotsbridge he had worked out a route which would cover most of the eastern side of the town in an hour. Today he had really enjoyed it; a typical English Sunday morning - dog walkers, paper boys and other joggers sharing the quiet leafy suburban streets with him. He loved New York with its mix of city and park, enjoyed the bright lights, rush of traffic and the cosmopolitan feel of the place but there was something about provincial England on a warm summer morning that was quite unique, a nostalgic reminder of his previous life which still managed to tug at his emotions.

As he turned into Mountbatten Drive he knew he was only five minutes from home. He could feel the dampness of his body as it clung to his cotton T-shirt. Warm water and the fresh feel of soap on his skin beckoned as he ran along the tree shaded pavement, searching for a gap in the line of parked cars. Finding one, he crossed over to the other side of the street and picked up his pace again for the hundred yards which took him to the junction.

As he reached the corner, the Mercedes passed him, a gleaming silver bullet in the morning sunlight. He stopped to look but it passed him so quickly he had no time to see who was driving. He ran on again, his mind racing. Could it have been her? If so, what was she doing here, so close to where he was? Did it matter, another part of him said. She was history - unpleasant, rude history. She didn't figure in any part of his life any longer. Turning into his parent's driveway he slowed to a walk.

Reaching the back of the house he stopped outside the utility door, bending his back, resting his hands on his thighs, letting his breathing gradually return to normal. When he stood up again he caught sight of Marcie, staring out of the kitchen window, eating toast.

'You look pooped.' She grinned, as he joined her in the kitchen.

'I am.' He answered, wiping his face with a towel he had retrieved from a pile stacked in the utility room. When he had finished he slung it around his shoulders, went to the fridge and pulled out the milk. As he was finding a glass, he heard the front door slam and voices in the hall. Tad and Faye walked into the kitchen.

'Everything OK?' He looked at both of them.

'Fine,' Tad smiled. 'As always, Trixie's done a brilliant job. The place looks wonderful. You wouldn't think we'd had a full house last night.'

'Heavens Matt!' Faye stared at him. 'Look at the state of you!' She touched his T-shirt, 'You're soaked. Yuk! Get out of here at once!' She waved a hand at him. 'Go and have a shower!'

Finishing off his milk Matt left the room.

'Well,' Tad smiled at Marcie, 'And how's your morning been? Bombarded by fans and autograph hunters at the door no doubt.'

'Nope.' Marcie looked up from her coffee with a grin. 'No one's been here all morning Mr Benedict.' she said resting her cup gently in its saucer. 'In fact it's been real quiet.'

Wednesday 4th July

'So nice to have met you Mr Johnson. If there are any questions about the contract do give me a call.'

Ella stood by the front door of One Plus One, shaking hands with Kevin Johnson, the Personnel Manager of Stewarts Engineering, who had spent most of the morning with her discussing the contract for temporary labour which he and Ella had just finished negotiating. Stewarts were a company who always placed their own ads and handled their own shop floor recruitment, but owner Oliver Knight was keen to farm out their constantly fluctuating casual labour needs to an external source so that his company's only involvement would be to turn up and interview.

To Ella this was something of a coup. Stewarts was a large company, employing in excess of a thousand people. Their demand for additional labour ebbed and flowed according to the contracts they had on their books. To take this process out of their hands set a precedent; it was a service she could now market to other local manufacturing companies and being able to advertise her connection with an old and established firm like Stewarts was just what she needed.

Returning to her office she slipped behind her desk once more and checked her diary. Tad was coming to see her at two thirty to talk about recruiting more staff for his new club. Thoughts of Zeffirelli's made her think of Matt. She wondered if he had ever got her message; she very much doubted it, not while he was being guarded by the American Doberman whose smile and eagerness to help she had most certainly not been taken in by.

She felt frustrated that she hadn't been able to speak to him in person. After talking to Sonny she had felt a real need to clear the air before he finally left Abbotsbridge. There would never be a possibility of them getting back together now, there was too much bad history between them, but she hated the thought that he would be returning to America carrying awful memories of her. At the very least he deserved an apology.

She closed her diary with a sigh, realising quite sensibly that it was pointless dwelling on things outside her control and she should be giving her concentration to other more pressing issues, like what Andy's next move would be. Quickly she scribbled a note on her pad as a reminder to speak to Marcus Goddard after Tad had gone.

'Hi,' Jenny's head appeared around her office door, interrupting her thoughts. 'I thought I'd come up and see whether you had time for a spot of lunch with me.'

Ella looked at the clock. One forty five.

'It'll have to be a quick snack; I'm expecting Tad at two thirty.'

'It's a good job I'm clairvoyant then isn't it?' Jenny replied, emerging into the room carrying two mugs of coffee. 'Fiona's gone round the corner for sandwiches,' she said easing the door shut with her foot, 'chicken salad OK for you?'

Ella nodded, watching as Jenny placed the coffee on her desk and pulled up a chair.

'So, who's minding the children?'

'Nick, he's taken the day off.' Jenny picked up her coffee. 'He's a very proficient nappy changer - loves it really. Actually this lunch was his suggestion.'

'Was it? Why?'

'He's a bit concerned about you after Saturday night.'

'There's no need for him to be. I appreciate your concern about what's going on with Andy, but look...' She pointed to the pad, 'there, see, I've made a note to speak to Marcus as soon as Tad's gone.'

'It's not Andy that's causing the concern Ella, it's Matt.'

'Matt?' Ella frowned, as she picked up her mug 'What's he got to do with anything?'

'More than you're letting on I think.'

The mug hovered at Ella's lips for a moment. 'Meaning?' She answered sharply, placing it firmly back on the blotter.

'There, you're getting all stroppy, just like you were on Saturday night when Nick was talking about him.'

'I am not!'

'Nick tells me you had to sort something out with him.' Jenny rested her mug on her knee, her dark eyes bright with curiosity. 'Ella, what's going on?'

'Nothing,' Ella shook her head. 'Nothing at all.'

'So did you go to see him?'

'Yes, but he was in the shower. The lovely Miss Maguire took my phone number to give to him but from the look of her I think that's the last thing she intended doing. She made it very clear when we spoke that their relationship is, well...'

'They're sleeping together?'

Ella nodded.

'And that's obviously upset you.'

'No it hasn't!'

'Yes it has! It's written all over your face. It was just the same when you came to Cornwall with us. Worse in fact!'

'I was upset!' Her grey eyes flared. 'At the time I thought he'd...'

'Let you down.' Jenny finished the sentence. 'I realise that, but knowing the kind of person you are, I would have thought four years would have been plenty of time to have got over that sort of flaw in a *friendship*.'

'What are you driving at Jen?'

'I think something deep went on between the two of you. Something that none of us knew about.' Jenny went on, ignoring Ella's obvious irritation. 'I know you always had a soft spot for him, but something now tells me it was more than that.'

A knock at the door halted the conversation, and Fiona, the new receptionist, arrived with the sandwiches, tottering in on high yellow platforms, her pale blonde hair falling like a curtain round her face.

'Well?' Jenny resumed her interrogation as soon as Fiona left and the door was closed behind her.

Ella gazed into her coffee mug, and shaking her head slowly said. 'I really don't want to talk about this, it's so pointless.'

'Ella.' Jenny reached across the desk and touched her arm. 'What is it? Why are you so angry?'

'I don't know.' Ella bowed her head, putting her hands to her face. 'Everything was fine till I saw him again. Now it's become complicated.' She looked at Jenny. 'And there's no one I can talk to about it.'

'You can talk to me,' Jenny said calmly, 'you know you can.'

'I wouldn't know where to start.'

'How about January '68.'

'What?'

'College Car park? Flat tyre?'

Ella laughed. 'Jenny what are you talking about?'

'The beginning Ella, where all stories start.'

Monday 9th July

Bob looked out of his office window at a brilliant summer morning; the sky clear blue, the sun warming through the glass. His expression arranged itself into a self-satisfied smile. Miles had just phoned to say now that the North Somerset Marina project was back on target, Martin and Gavin had raised the issue of the holiday village again. They had come to the conclusion it was too important to leave, sure that if someone else got a whiff of such a ground breaking development, they'd steal the idea from under their noses. The next Mirage board meeting was due to be held in early August and reactivating the project was top of the agenda. So, Bob mused contentedly, things were coming round to his way at last. Thoughts of the scheme naturally moved his thoughts on to Richard Evas. Swinging his chair around to face his desk again, he reached for the phone and began to dial. Mel answered on the second ring.

'Mel it's me.'

'Bob. Is anything wrong?'

'No, just thought I'd give you a call. I've just heard that Mirage are planning to restart the holiday village project.'

'Really?'

He could feel her smile.

'It's early days yet of course, but we really do need to talk to your father about selling Fox Cottage.'

'The christening's imminent. I could try to get him on his own - he'll be in a good mood. Nick's his favourite grandchild.'

'Excellent, let's hope something positive comes out of it. If not then maybe I ought to approach him direct.'

'That won't be necessary Bob.' her tone was confident. As you are aware, he told me the farm was mine at Lucy's christening last year. And now he's a semi invalid, paying someone to manage the place, I think he'll be quite amenable to a deal. If the truth be known, I expect he could do with the money.'

'That thought had crossed my mind, but be careful Mel, he's a wily old devil.'

'Was a wily old devil Bob. The illness has changed him; he's not the man he used to be. You need have no worries; this is going to be like taking candy from a baby.'

SEVENTEEN

Friday 20th July

Faye set the burglar alarm and closed the front door of *Handbags and Gladrags* with a relieved sigh, glad to be finally escaping after a totally exhausting day.

It had all started with a phone call from Paula's mother to say her grandmother had just died. Paula fled into the kitchen and sat there tearfully with a large handkerchief, unable to cope with anything but catching the first bus home. This meant that Faye, usually only there for a couple of hours each Friday morning, had been left with no alternative but to stay for the rest of the day to help Jane.

The second disaster was a phone call mid-morning notifying her that an expected delivery of evening bags would be delayed for several weeks because of a strike at the manufacturers. Knowing there had been several orders placed by customers who were due to attend a Rotary dinner dance in Kingsford in a weeks' time, Faye spent nearly an hour phoning around to apologise and offer alternatives or refunds.

The day had brought frustrations within the shop too. It was the summer holiday, a time when groups of schoolgirls wandered in and out of Abbotsbridge shops trying on clothes and shoes in an effort to amuse themselves and pass the time. Four came in around eleven; they chose shoes, tried them on, admired themselves in mirrors, changed their minds and selected alternatives, all while Jane hovered, unable to assist Faye in the busy main shop. Twenty minutes later they all casually drifted out of the shop, leaving a chaotic pile of footwear scattered around the fitting area to be picked up and repacked into their boxes.

By twelve Faye's feet ached and she was dying for her usual Friday lunch time gin and tonic with Tad. However, she knew today that was going to be out of the question. So she rang him at Zeffirelli's to explain, making do instead with a half hour break in the kitchen and a ham sandwich from the bakery around the corner. As she finished her coffee she made a mental note of the time, knowing she must get to the bank earlier rather than later that afternoon to avoid the long queues that always built when small businesses were paying in their weekly takings. To avoid the rush she decided to go just before two but as she was about to leave a salesman arrived. It was a cold call and usually she would have turned him away, but he was carrying some very high quality costume jewellery which she thought would sell very well. So she delayed her journey to look at the samples and eventually placed an order. Hurrying down to Lloyds immediately afterwards she discovered only two cashiers on duty and a queue stretching to the front door. Determined to salvage one calm moment from the day, she let Jane go at four thirty and closed early, using the hour left to create a new window display of co-ordinating bags and scarves.

And now it was five thirty. The door locked, the alarm set; time to get home for that much missed gin and tonic. Slinging her bag over her shoulder she made her way to the end of Gane Street and turning left, headed for Catherine Street car park where her car was located. Passing through the black wrought iron gates which marked the entrance to the park, she walked on, deep in thought. She had switched off completely as far as the shop was concerned, concentrating now on the coming evening at Zeffirelli's and things to be done there. People were amazed that at her age she had so much energy - running her own business as well as helping out in Tad's. The truth was she enjoyed what she was doing. It kept her busy and together with Tad and Matt, it provided the main focus of her life. Matt, she thought warmly, he's due to phone tonight. I wonder how the tour's going.

As she reached the war memorial she was vaguely aware of someone there and turned to see a young man in well worn jeans and a denim jacket leaning against the monument, the sole of one foot resting against the pale stone. He was thin faced with a shock of brown, untidy hair and an irregular crescent of stubble around his chin. As she passed he finished the cigarette he had been smoking and pushing himself away from the stonework, headed away from her towards the band stand. He looked as though a good square meal would do him the power of good she thought as she watched him go.

She walked on, past the Bowling Green and the pavilion, following the narrow path which skirted them both before it disappeared behind a high hedge. Two women approached, clad in tennis whites, racquets over their shoulders, on their way to an evening game on the far side of the park. Moments afterwards heavy footfalls made her turn sharply and a man in a grey suit carrying a briefcase overtook her at a brisk pace, heading in the direction of the multi-storey.

Seeing him reminded Faye of home and that relaxing drink waiting out on the patio before they left for their evening at the club. With this in mind she upped her pace as she came to the high hedge at the end of the Bowling Green. The bridge was only a hundred yards ahead now and beyond that the car park. The drive home would take her less than fifteen minutes.

As she came around the corner she found the young man she had seen at the memorial standing directly in front of her, blocking her path. She realised he must have cut behind the bandstand and the pavilion to intercept her.

'Gimme the bag!' He pointed at her handbag.

'Certainly not.' She said defiantly, clutching it even tighter. 'Get out of the way!'

'Not till you give me the bag.' He said squaring his shoulders and standing there stubbornly.

'There's nothing in it you could possibly want,' she argued. 'Nothing at all!'

'Don't give me that, you got money. Give it here!'

As he made a grab for the bag, all the events of a bad day collided in Faye's head. Feeling his fingers close around the leather she gave an outraged cry and pushed him hard. As he stumbled backwards and fell onto the grass she began to run. The bridge was yards away from her now and beyond that the car park where she could see the movement of vehicles, meaning people were still about. If she could get close enough to shout, to draw attention to herself, she was sure she could frighten him away. But suddenly he was there again, coming from behind, his arm around her throat like a vice, pulling her up sharply.

'Lady!' she heard him whisper in her ear. 'You really shouldn't have done that!'

Ella slammed and locked the boot of the Mercedes and swung her holdall over her shoulder. She crossed the first floor of the multi storey where she had parked and pushed open the door to the flight of concrete stairs. At the bottom of these the car park opened out into a small walled balcony with more steps down to the park itself. She paused for a moment, shading her eyes as she looked out at the early evening shadows cast by the poplars across the lush green expanse of grass.

Well, Bob's generosity certainly had made its impact; flower beds full of co-ordinated colour, the ornate Victorian bandstand glorious in its new coat of shiny black paint, the newly turfed Bowling Green and refurbished club house. And of course there was the new gym, opened on the site of the old library. A gym which she had recently joined and which she was currently heading for. The brass plaque set into one of the pillars of the park gates marking the improvements in the park and acknowledging him as one of the town's leading benefactors was just another physical indicator of how great Bob's authority was here in Abbotsbridge.

She thought of the custody battle to come. The courts were supposed to be impartial, to uphold the law. She felt her case was waterproof, Marcus had said as much. But could a judge be bought? Bob's influence had almost destroyed her business. Could he use that again to sway a verdict? It was a worrying thought.

A woman's cry interrupted her thoughts. She frowned, trying to place where it had come from. And then she saw them; a young man struggling with an older woman over by the bowling green. Without hesitation she ran down the steps and headed out across the grass towards them.

Gary Nix looked at the woman struggling with him and wanted to hurt her. Silly bitch, why wouldn't she just let go of the handbag? All the others had. After she'd pushed him over he had got back onto his feet and chased after her. He thought that grabbing her from behind would finish it all, frighten her enough to give in, but no, she'd stamped on his foot and elbowed him in the ribs, another painful and humiliating experience which had caused him to release her instantly. And now they looked like a comedy turn, both holding onto the handbag and refusing to let go as they pulled against each other. She had money; he was even more convinced of that now. Why else would she fight so hard? Reaching into his pocket he felt the knife. He had no home, no job and no money. He was hungry and out of cigarettes. His dry throat ached for a beer. With the money in her purse he could sort himself out, perhaps even have a few quid left over to get him the train fare to another town and the next handbag or wallet. She could afford to lose it. With all that gold round her neck, she probably had loads of money stashed away in the bank. He felt the knife again; he hadn't planned on using it but now he'd have to, it was the only way. Difficult cow, she deserved it really.

He pulled it from his pocket, the blade bright and the bone handle warm against his palm. 'Let go damn you!' he said through gritted teeth, 'or you'll get this!'

The woman looked at the knife fearlessly and tightened her grip. 'You wouldn't dare!' she shouted at him.

'Wouldn't I?' He smiled as he watched the knife move in a blur before him. He heard her scream, felt the bag fall into his hands and then he was running, across the park, towards the shopping precinct.

Ella saw the struggle come to its conclusion; saw the woman fall over, releasing the bag. She watched the young man as he turned and ran. Two men appeared and gave chase across the grass. The young man climbed a wire fence on the perimeter of the precinct with the agility of a monkey and was gone. Ella ran over to the woman who lay sprawled face down on the grass moaning. Kneeling by her side she gently reached to turn her over.

'Are you all right?'

The woman turned her head towards Ella and frowned up at her as if she had difficulty focusing.

'Faye!' Ella wasn't sure what shocked her the most, the identity of the woman she was holding or the blood which she could see seeping through the front of her blouse.

One of the men came panting up to her. 'The little bastard got away!' he said, drawing in deep lungfuls of breath.

'We need an ambulance!' Ella said. When the man didn't move she turned and seeing the frozen fear on his face as he stood there looking down at Faye, shouted at him. 'Please! Get to a phone!'

As he ran off Faye looked up at Ella, her face creased into a frown.

'Ella? Is that you?'

'Yes.' Ella pulled her sweatshirt from her shoulders and folded it under the older woman's head. 'I'll just make you a little more comfortable while we wait for the ambulance.'

She looked at the blood on the front of Faye's blouse, the stain was spreading rapidly. 'Just try and relax, I'm going to take a look.' She said in as calm a voice as she could manage.

Faye nodded feebly. 'It's gone all numb.'

Ella leaned forward and gently eased the edges of the torn blouse apart. Blood oozed from a six inch slash under Faye's rib cage. Leaning across the older woman she reached into her holdall.

'Is that my blood? Faye said weakly, looking at the stain which had seeped into the front of Ella's shirt. 'There seems to be such a lot of it. I'm going to die aren't I?'

'No, you're not Faye.' Ella said pulling out a white vest and folding it into one long strip before compressing it against the wound. 'Believe me; you're going to be just fine.'

Tad arrived at A & E fifteen minutes after he had received the call. He ran into reception, his face white, his heart thudding. The receptionist calmly asked him to take a seat saying the doctor would be with him shortly. He sat down obediently, wanting to argue but knowing it was pointless. Hospitals had their own way of doing things. His mind strayed back to the time Matt was born. He had been helpless then too, forced to leave it to the experts. He remembered countless cups of coffee and the hours of waiting. He put his head in his hands. He couldn't lose her, please God not now, not like this, just when everything was going so well.

'Mr Benedict?'

He pulled his hands from his face. A slim, middle aged man with a stethoscope protruding from the pocket of his white coat stood in front of him.

'I'm Dr Sanders.' The eyes were kind, the smile relaxed.

'My wife?' He got to his feet anxiously.

'Weak but comfortable. She's going to be fine. It was a flesh wound but we'd like to keep her in overnight, just to make sure everything is OK. That there is no infection.'

Tad nodded. 'Can I see her?'

'Of course; come with me.'

He was led away from reception and down a brightly lit corridor which seemed to run on forever.

'She was very lucky indeed,' Dr Sanders said. 'There was a lot of blood but the wound was not that deep. Luckily the young lady who came in with her knew first aid. She compressed the wound, which reduced the bleeding.'

'Young lady?' Tad frowned.

'Yes, your wife seemed to know her. She didn't want her to leave.' He smiled. 'She held onto her hand so tightly. She called her Ella. Do you know her?'

'Yes, I do. Where is she now?'

'In our relatives' room giving a statement to the police.'

'Could you ask her to wait please? Tell her I'll drive her home after I've seen my wife.'

The Ghost of You and Me

Marcus Goddard sat in his VW Beetle outside Abbotsbridge station waiting for the 7.05 from Penzance. He had been looking forward to his father's visit for some time now. His father Henry, a senior partner in a GP practice in rural Cornwall, had since his mother's death from cancer five years ago, thrown himself into his work, his only recreational pleasures being fishing and his regular visits to Abbotsbridge to spend time with Marcus and his growing family.

Tonight, for a change, the train was on time. The reverberation of the diesel engine followed by the noisy protest of slowing carriages and brakes announcing its arrival. Minutes later Henry, in a pale cotton suit, light brown brogues and Panama, appeared outside the station with the other passengers, clutching his familiar battered suitcase. Father and son embraced warmly, delighted to see each other.

'Hungry?' Marcus asked as he deposited the case onto the back seat of the car.

'Absolutely starving,' Henry, now firmly installed in the passenger seat, grimaced. 'After looking at what was on offer in the buffet car, I thought it was best to avoid the culinary delights of British Rail! What's Natalie got waiting for us tonight?'

'Cold beef salad with new potatoes and apple pie and cream for pudding.'

'Sounds wonderful.' The older man said, closing his eyes in delight as Marcus pulled on his seat belt, started the engine and eased the car forward to wait for a gap in the traffic.

'So, are the legal problems of Abbotsbridge still keeping you fully occupied?'

'Oh yes.' Marcus smiled as they joined the main flow of traffic. 'People will always need a solicitor.'

'A crusader you mean.' The older man smiled. 'I know you; you've never been able to resist a challenge.'

'Well, I've certainly got one at the moment.' Marcus slowed down for a pedestrian crossing, 'A divorce which seemed fairly uncomplicated and over with has flared up again. The father's decided he wants custody of the child.'

'Anyone I know?'

'Dad, you know I can't discuss my cases with you.' Marcus tutted. 'As a GP you should know all about confidentiality.'

'It's obviously someone well known then.' Henry continued to prod. 'Well if it's confidentiality you're worried about, then don't be. My lips are sealed.' He ran an imaginary zip fastener across his mouth. 'Now then, come on, who is this client of yours?'

'Ella Macayne.'

'Bob's remarried?' Henry looked surprised. 'Well, well, I thought the memory of Lucia was too strong for him to ever commit himself permanently to anyone else.'

'Ella is Andy's wife, or should I say ex-wife.'

'And they have a child?'

Marcus gave an amused laugh. 'Is that so strange?'

'Actually it is. Andy's infertile.'
'Infertile?' Marcus laughed again. 'I don't quite understand.'
'Ah, perhaps I'd better explain then…'

Tad found Ella sitting in the relatives' room. She got to her feet with a tired smile as he reached her and gave her a tight hug, whispering his gratitude in her ear.

'Are you OK?' He pulled away smiling down at her. 'You look exhausted.'

'I am.' She nodded. 'It's been quite a day.' She looked at her blood spattered shirt, 'I'm desperate for a bath.'

'Better get you home then.' He took her holdall from her and guided her towards the automatic doors.

'I can't thank you enough, I really can't.' He said in a voice full of emotion as they crossed the car park. 'When that call came, when they said she'd been knifed, I honestly thought I'd lost her. If it hadn't been for you...'

'I did very little.' Ella replied as they reached the car. 'The hospital staff were the heroes.'

'That's not what Dr Saunders says.' Tad insisted as he unlocked the BMW. 'He tells me you made all the difference.'

'Basic first aid, that was all.' Ella said as she tucked herself into the passenger seat. 'I'm glad I had the presence of mind to do it.'

'You're too modest.' Tad said as he slotted the key into the ignition. 'Anyway as far as Faye's concerned it was you who saved her life. She said something told her as long as she held onto your hand she'd be all right. She also spoke of the conversation she had with you about Matt.'

'Yes.' Ella said quietly as they pulled out of the car park. 'We had quite a heart to heart in the ambulance.'

'She was pretty amazed at what you told her, you know. Until today she had you down as the bad guy.'

'And I thought Matt was the villain. If it hadn't been for Sonny the other night I'd still believe that. Crazy isn't it?'

Tad nodded.

'He phoned Faye from Marbella once the Todd thing was sorted. Said when he got back he wanted to talk to us, before he went to the States.' Tad took his eyes from the road for a moment to look at her. 'He said he loved you. That you were leaving Andy to be with him.'

'I was.' She nodded. 'So how did it all go wrong?'

'I don't know.' Tad said as they pulled up at traffic lights. 'But now we know the truth, don't you see? It makes things easier.'

'Easier?' Ella frowned.

'Yes.' He said eagerly 'Matt's in the UK. We can sort this whole thing out. You can be together again.'

'No Tad.' She cut him off gently. 'It's too late. Besides, he's with Marcie now.'

'Only in a professional way.'

The lights changed and he pulled away.

'I think you're mistaken there.' The briefest of smiles crossed Ella's face.

'Believe me Ella, I know my son.' Tad insisted.

'Maybe not as well as you think.'

'What do you mean?'

'I called round the day after Zeffirelli's opening night. I wanted to talk to Matt about what Sonny had told me. Marcie answered the door in her dressing gown. She said Matt was in the shower. It was very obvious from the way she spoke that they had a thing going on. I left my phone number, asked him to call me. But I wasn't at all surprised when he didn't.'

'What time was this?'

'I don't know, around ten thirty I think.'

'But Matt wasn't in the house then. We followed him out of the gate at 9.30. He was going for his usual morning run, which takes just over an hour. We got back around ten fifty.'

'Was he there then?'

'Only just, he had a towel round his shoulders and was drinking a glass of milk.' He laughed. 'He'd had quite a hard run. He was sweating and his T-shirt was stuck to him. I remember Faye pushing him out of the door and telling him to go and have a shower.' He shot a sideways glance at Ella's still sceptical face. 'None of this adds up you know.'

'Tad, the last thing I want to do is make trouble for Matt.'

'Matt's not the one who's going to be in trouble,' Tad replied. 'But I think the lovely Miss Maguire may have some explaining to do.'

EIGHTEEN

Sunday 12th August

Jenny and Nick emerged from the church into the afternoon sunshine carrying Charlotte, the small Christening party trailing in their wake. The group halted for a moment, stopping to chat among themselves as they waited for the photographer to set up his equipment for outside shots.

Liam wandered away to the edge of the graveyard, down the well mown grass paths, killing time by reading epitaphs on the lichen covered tombs, amazed at the longevity of some of those buried there. His contemplation was suddenly disturbed by an agonised cry. He looked up to see a plump grey haired woman in a blue dress and navy cardigan standing just a little way back from the group outside the church door. She had dropped the flowers she was carrying, her hands going to her face momentarily before she turned and fled across the churchyard towards the yew trees in the far corner.

Liam saw Richard detach himself from the group, pick up the flowers and go after her, catching up with her by one of the large Victorian memorials. She appeared quite agitated, waving her hand in the direction of the Christening party. Liam could hear the murmur of their voices, but was too far away to hear what was being said. He frowned, wondering what was going on. Richard's hand had now drifted to the woman's shoulder in a calming gesture. She pulled a handkerchief from the pocket of her cardigan as the conversation continued and began to dab her eyes.

'That's Missus Masterson the schoolmaster's wife. Lost 'er 'usband a couple o' months back.'

Liam swung around immediately to see Meridan Cross's odd job man Doggie Barker leaning on the stile which breached the hedge between the field the churchyard. He smiled at the old countryman as he walked over to him. Reaching through the stile he ruffled the head of his black and white collie cross Toby, who sat patiently at Doggie's feet, his long pink tongue scissoring back and forth as he panted in the heat.

'She seems very upset about something.' Liam said turning back to look at the woman for a moment.

'Don't worry, Mr Evas'll sort her out.' Doggie said comfortingly. 'He's good like that.' He nodded towards Mel, who was busy organising parents, baby and godparents for the first photo. 'Very glamorous your wife; bossy too.' he began to chuckle.

'Yes, grandmother of the baby.' Liam smiled. 'Must have everything just right.'

'Her's been here a lot lately you know.' Doggie fixed Liam with a steady, watchful eye, leaning forward and resting his arms on the top of the stile. 'Driving around with that bloke in the big car.'

'Which *bloke*?'

'Dunno his name. Car's a big blue thing. I think he must be some sorta solicitor fella with a car like that.'

'What does he look like?'

'Black 'air, what's left of it. Black eyes too. Got the look of the devil about 'im. First time they came Mr Evas was real upset. Shouted at 'er to go away and leave 'im alone. Jake Carr overheard all the shenanigans, said her were trying to get him to sell part 'o the farm. Still,' he gave a knowing smile. 'Mary's boy's back here now so there's no chance 'o that happening.'

Liam watched his wife as she turned her attentions to Christopher, who had helped himself to flowers which had been left on one of the nearby graves. She snatched them from him, causing droplets of water from the ends of the small bouquet to spray the front of her. Dabbing her red silk dress with a tissue she waved a dictatorial finger at him as she disposed of the flowers and returned him, wriggling like an eel, to his father. What exactly had she had been doing out here with Bob Macayne, Liam wondered? Once the celebrations were over and they had returned home, he promised himself he would find out.

'Granddad?' Jenny held a plate of vol-au-vents out to Richard Evas as he sat on the edge of the terrace at Little Court, turning his face up to the warmth of the late afternoon sun.

He opened his gentle blue eyes and smiled at her. 'No thanks Jenny, I'm full to bursting. Got a touch of indigestion too.' He patted his chest. 'Serves me right really, never could resist a good spread!'

Jenny continued through the small gathering with the plate, eventually returning it to the table where Ellie, Laura Kendrick's housekeeper was beginning to clear away. Across the lawn she noticed her mother, busy at work with her camera, Christopher trailing behind.

'Betty seems to be in her element.' Elegant grey haired Laura Kendrick, every inch the lady of the manor in her pearls and royal blue suit smiled up at Jenny, Charlotte nestling quietly in her arms.

'New camera,' Jenny smiled. 'No one's safe today!'

'And she's got an assistant I see.' Laura's face lit with amusement.

'Christopher! Oh no!' Jenny stifled a laugh as she watched the antics of her small son, standing behind his grandmother, striking the same pose as her each time with his own invisible camera.

'He's a dear little chap.' Jack Taylor, sitting opposite Laura and Mary, watched his grandson with amusement. 'We love having him over. Keeps us amused for hours with his antics.'

'Yes, they are all beautiful children.' Laura looked down at the peaceful Charlotte. 'We are extremely lucky.'

'We certainly are.' Mary agreed, Lucy sitting on her knee, her head resting against her shoulder, thumb in her mouth. 'Hey,' she nudged Lucy. 'Look Aunt Betty's going to take a picture of us. Come on now. Smile!'

After the photograph had been taken, Richard pushed himself out of his chair. 'If you'll excuse me, I think I'll just collect the dogs and Land Rover and go up to the south pasture. Check on the herd.'

'Are you all right Richard?' Mary eyed him with concern as Lucy snuggled back into her shoulder, still sucking her thumb.

'Me? Yes, fine.' He stood there rubbing his chest. 'Just a touch of indigestion that's all.'

'There's a box of Rennie in the kitchen medicine chest if you'd like Ettie to find it for you.' Laura offered. 'I suffer myself. It's one of the banes of old age I'm afraid!'

'Thanks Laura, I'll make sure I take a couple before I go.'

'Are you sure you're OK?' Mary looked up at him, shading her eyes with her hand.

'Of course. You know I take my tablets regular as clockwork. I've just over indulged a bit that's all.' He patted her shoulder affectionately.

'I don't mean the indigestion Richard. You look troubled. Is it something to do with Mrs Masterson? I saw you talking to her when we came out of the church. She seemed very upset.'

'Mrs Masterson? Yes she was.' He nodded then simply turned and walked away.

'I saw Richard talking to Mrs Masterson in the churchyard too.' Laura said much later as they strolled slowly across the lawn, Lucy toddling between them, all of them heading for the river to feed the ducks who now congregated there in noisy anticipation of food.

'He's keeping something from me, I know it.' Mary shook her head.

'I should ask him when you get home if I were you. I saw him talking to Liam earlier as well. Do you think that's why he's gone off on his own now?'

'Oh definitely,' Mary agreed. 'When he's got things on his mind he always heads for the south pasture and a wander around his girls.'

'Very strange,' Laura shook her head. 'I thought he was a bit off with Mel too, didn't you?'

'Maybe that's why she decided to go home.' Ella answered, joining them from the shadow of the beech trees with Mick and Issy.

'Gone?' Laura looked puzzled. 'Without even saying goodbye to anyone. What about Liam? How's he expected to get back to Abbotsbridge for heaven's sake?'

'Don't worry, I'm dropping him home.' Ella replied. 'Nick's with him at the moment, picking his brains about sun lounges.'

'Ella's just been taking us round the gardens.' Issy smiled. 'They're very beautiful Mrs Kendrick. I love the fountains.'

'Thank you.' Laura acknowledged the compliment. 'They're eighteenth century Italian. A wedding gift, I am told, from the parents of Alessia Beauman when she married my husband's…' she counted on her fingers, 'great great grandfather.' Turning to the little group she waved a bag of bread crumbs at them. 'Actually we're just off to feed the ducks, please, do join us.'

Godparents Issy, Mick and Ella fell in behind Mary and Laura, Mick hoisting Lucy onto his shoulders.

Shading her eyes against the late afternoon sun, Laura saw Jenny sitting on the old swing which hung from the elderly beech tree just a few yards away from the river. Charlotte, still in her christening robe, was tucked into her arm, sucking noisily on her bottle while Christopher was chasing around, stick in hand, pretending he was riding a horse. He stopped when he saw Lucy and the others and with a whoop dropped the stick immediately and ran over to join them.

'Nearly finished,' Jenny called out as Mary took Christopher by the hand. 'We'll be with you in a minute.'

Richard walked slowly between the golden flanks of his Channel Island herd. The day was still warm, but clouds were gathering towards the west. He wondered whether it would rain before sunset. He rubbed his chest. The Rennies had not shifted his indigestion. Ah well, he thought, as Laura said, such inconveniences came with old age. He moved away from the herd and back towards the Land Rover. He smiled as he saw Gaffer sitting sedately in the back of the vehicle watching the younger dog, Laddie tearing around barking playfully.

If only I could have a moment of your carefree existence, he thought, pondering on the events of the day. *To be able to forget all the hurt, all the deceit, for just one second.* Seeing a small piece of broken branch lying near his feet he picked it up and threw it, pursing his lips thoughtfully as Laddie gave chase.

'Dad?'

He turned sharply to see Mel standing there, her blue eyes fixed on him.

'Mel.' He said abruptly. 'I thought you'd gone.'

'No, I followed you. I wanted to get you on your own. I thought it was time we had a talk.' She said as she closed the gap between them, picking her way carefully across the uneven surface of the pasture in her high heels.

'What about?' He turned and scowled at her, bending to retrieve the stick Laddie had just dropped at his feet.

'The farm; I've a proposition for you.'

'A proposition eh?' He gave a harsh laugh as he heaved the stick into the air once more.

'I'd like to buy Fox Cottage and a swathe of the wood that surrounds it. '

'He turned to look at her, frowning.

'The cottage? Part of Hundred Acre? I thought we'd settled all this. I told you, nothing's happening to Willowbrook until I'm gone.' He stopped, frowning. 'Your friend Mr Macayne's put you up to this hasn't he? Why does he want it?'

'Don't be silly Dad, it's for me. I want it.'

'Why?'

'Nostalgia I suppose.' Mel shrugged. 'It's so peaceful here, it could be my weekend cottage where I could come and relax when I wanted to. The woodland around it would give me complete privacy. I'd pay a good price, and think about it, the extra money would come in handy now you're having to pay Mary's son to manage the farm.'

Richard stared at her then he rubbed a tired hand across his cheek. 'They just roll off your tongue don't they?'

'What?'

'The lies.'

'What do you mean? I haven't lied about anything.'

'Oh yes you have. Remember Mrs Masterson in the church yard this afternoon? She recognised you. Strange thing Fate isn't it? She just happened to be passing by on her way to visit her husband's grave when we all came out of the church. It was the red outfit that did it.'

'Are you talking about that hysterical old woman?' Mel's face creased into an irritable frown. 'I've never seen her before. *How* did she know me?'

'She says you were the woman on the platform at Abbotsbridge station the day your mother was killed.'

'Well you know that's impossible, we were still abroad then!'

'I thought that too. So I checked with Liam. He says you returned from the States in April that year, not November.'

'I...'

'Don't even attempt an excuse! It *was* you there wasn't it?'

'Yes.' Mel gave a deep sigh and wandered across to the Land Rover leaning against it. 'I came to pick Liam up that day, off the London train. I'd been on the platform about ten minutes when I noticed this woman staring out at me from one of the carriages of Taunton train. I suddenly realised it was Mother. I could see by her expression she wasn't sure about me - because my hair was blonde and not brown like it used to be I suppose. I knew the train was almost ready leave, so I deliberately walked along the platform, out of her view, waiting for it to go. Then I heard the express in the distance and turned round. I could see Mother. She'd got out of the train and was on the platform opposite, smiling and waving out. The express was getting closer. I knew I couldn't stay there any longer. It wasn't safe. So I ran.'

'You ran away from your own mother?'

'Liam knew nothing of my old life Dad. We'd had ten wonderful years together. I couldn't see that all destroyed. I had so much to lose.'

'Your mother lost her life!' He shouted at her angrily.

'That was not my fault!' She rounded on him, pushing herself away from the Land Rover. 'I didn't ask her to run after me!'

'What else did you expect her to do? Don't you understand? You were everything to her. When you walked out of our lives, it affected her badly. It did something to her mind. She was never the same. You became even more of an obsession with her than when you lived here. Every knock at the door, every letter landing on the mat. She never gave up hope that you'd return. Can you imagine how she must have felt, seeing you there? Her dream had come true. She was within moments of being with you again,' he shook his head, 'and what did you do? You ran away!' His tone was scathing. 'When she crossed that line all she was thinking of was catching up with you. She probably didn't even know the train was there until...' His hand went to his face and he swallowed hard, as the memory of that day came flooding back.

'It was not my fault! Don't you dare say that!' Mel protested. 'I would have come back eventually, I just needed time.'

'How long Mel.' He looked at her tiredly, 'A week? A month? A year?'

'Oh I don't know!' Her expression was bitter, 'Look Dad, no matter what you think. I did love her.'

'Love? You know nothing of the word!'

Mel opened her mouth to reply but Richard silenced her with a raised hand.

'Strange isn't it that you didn't worry too much about your precious anonymity when you came back here to check your inheritance was still intact.'

'That was different.'

'Of course it was, there was money involved. You thought you might lose the farm because I was marrying Mary.' He shook his head. 'So cold blooded, so avaricious and so you! And now you want to buy the cottage and woodland. To come and stay weekends. Tell the truth! You're going to sell it on aren't you?'

'No!' She stared at him, wondering how the conversation had suddenly taken this turn. 'I would never do that.'

'Another lie! You see Nelson Miller got talking to someone from a visiting team playing skittles in the Blue Boar at Higher Padbury last week. He told Nelson about how his boss was hoping to buy a cottage out this way. When Nelson asked where, it turned out to be Fox Cottage of all places. Nelson's curiosity was naturally roused so he bought him a few drinks, tried to find out more. Turns out it was your friend Macayne. And he intends to sell on to Mirage Holdings for access so they can build a holiday village on land up in Sedgwick Wood. With him getting the building contract!'

'I don't know anything about that.' Mel shook her head vigorously.

'I don't believe you! I think you'd sell your grandmother if the price was right!

How could you even *think* of becoming involved with that detestable consortium! You traitorous bitch! I always suspected your motives and at last I see you for what you are!' He shouted. 'Well I disown you! You're no daughter of mine! Just get out of my sight! I never want to see you again!'

He turned then, whistled for Laddie and began to walk back to the Land Rover.

'Dad, come back!' Mel shouted and began to run after him, pulling off her high heels as she went.

Richard wrenched open the door, pausing for a moment to let Laddie in before he climbed in.

'Dad, don't go,' She tugged at his arm 'We can work all this out, I know we can.'

Sensing trouble, the dogs began to bark angrily.

'Get off me!' Richard threw off her grip and slammed the door with a heavy thud.

Mel stood there helplessly, watching her father prepare to leave. She heard the engine fire and closed her eyes, feeling a black nausea envelop her. Events in Mirage Holding's board room had forced Bob's hand. The scheme was about to be resurrected, there was no more time, they'd had to act. She felt sure that with his heart condition her father would be amenable to a sale. But she had totally misjudged him. Bob was right; she should have left it to him. Now the will would almost certainly be changed. Everything was in ruins. There would be no money, no new life with Bob. Miserably she slumped onto the grass, discarded her shoes and began to sob.

After a few moments she sat up, blinking back the tears. The Land Rover was still there, the engine running. Her father was sitting in the driver's seat, motionless, staring straight ahead.

Frowning, she got to her feet, walked over to the vehicle and pulled open the passenger door. The younger of the two dogs jumped out and ran over to where the stick lay. Picking it up he ran back and dropped it at Mel's feet, sitting there, his head cocked to one side. Ignoring him, she leaned inside the Land Rover. The older dog Gaffer had started to whine and was nudging his nose against Richard's hand which was still outstretched and covering the gear lever.

'Dad?' She looked at him and frowned.

He didn't speak. A strange gurgling was coming from his throat, a sound which gradually trailed away to nothing. She reached over, her fingers searching for the pulse in his neck, finding only stillness through the warmth of his skin.

She shook him and he fell against the driver's door, sightless eyes staring into space. The movement frightened Gaffer who began to bark.

'My God!' Her hands flew to her face. 'He's dead!'

Carefully leaning across him she turned the ignition off. Then easing herself from the passenger seat she carefully closed the door on her father and Gaffer. She attempted to catch the younger dog, but he was too boisterous. Leaving him she retrieved her shoes and walked quickly back to her car. She thought of driving back to Little Court to break the news but then realised how impossible that was. Whatever she did she mustn't be implicated in any of this. They must never know she had been here. Home, she thought. I'll go straight home. That's where I need to be when they call to break the news to me.

She drove away from the south pasture, turning east towards Abbotsbridge. As the car ate up the miles the trauma of her confrontation with her father and his death began to ease. It was going to be all right. The project was saved. Nelson Miller was the only other person who knew about her and Bob's plan and no one was going to believe a scruffy gypsy who sold scrap for a living. They were fine. They were safe. Bob. I must phone Bob she thought. I must tell him.

She found a phone box just outside Moredon. Mrs Catt answered the phone and she sent her off to find him immediately. Eventually he picked up the phone.

'Bob!' She blurted out. 'I just had to call you.'

'How are things?' Bob sounded wary. 'Did he go for it?'

'He's dead!'

'Have you been drinking Mel?'

'No! Listen. He's had a massive heart attack.'

'I don't believe it!' Bob sounded irritable. 'There'll be even more delays now. The funeral. The will. Dealing with the new owner. This could set us back months!'

'I'm the new owner!' She said excitedly.

'What?'

'You don't listen do you? I've already told you; at Lucy's christening, when I went over to talk to him. He told me then. It's mine Bob!' She laughed out loud. 'The farm's mine! Break open the champagne!'

Bird feeding over, the small group had returned from the river. After putting the little ones up for a nap, Ella and Jenny joined Nick, Issy and Mick, who were in the process of setting up a game of croquet on the lower lawn. Reverend Farr had taken his leave to prepare for the evening service and those who remained sat on the veranda waiting for the arrival of Ettie with the tea. Betty and Jack were deep in conversation with Mary about their recent holiday in Rome while Laura sat with Liam, wanting to sound him out on new plans she had for the house.

'It's the smallest wing.' She said. 'There's a large bedroom, dressing room, bathroom and a small study. It was my son Christopher's part of the house before his marriage to Mel. I've kept everything of his. Toys, books, even his RAF uniform is there, with his medals. I thought it was time you see, after thirty years, to breathe some life back into the place.' She laughed. 'Because I shall need somewhere for my great grandchildren, when they come to stay. Christopher was quite a gifted painter too; I have a fine collection of his water-colours, and some charcoal sketches. I thought I might have them framed, perhaps turn the dressing room into a little gallery. What do you think?'

'I think it sounds an excellent idea.' Liam smiled. 'I'll give you a call from the office tomorrow. We'll fix a date for you to show me around.'

'Wonderful.' Laura clapped her hands together. 'Make it early - we can discuss things over lunch. Do you like fish?'

Liam nodded.

'Excellent. Ettie's very good with trout.' As she spoke her gaze drifted towards the house where a figure had just appeared carrying a huge tray. 'And talking of Ettie here she is with the tea.'

The sun began to fall slowly towards the distant trees as tea was poured and they settled themselves once more to enjoy what was left of the afternoon. The croquet began again in earnest, Jack and Betty joining in. Amused laugher floated across the lawns interspersed with the sound of wooden mallet against ball and then unexpectedly Ettie was back on the terrace again, Jake following closely behind her.

He looked at each of them in turn as if he did not know who to address first.

'What is it Jake?' Laura broke the silence.

'It's Laddie, Missus Kendrick.' He said, taking off his cap and clasping it tightly. 'He came back to the farm about twenty minutes ago. Running round and making a terrible racket he was, so I brought him along here, tied him up at the front door. I thought Mr Evas would be here, but he's not.'

'No, he went up to the south pasture, to look at the herd. I thought he'd gone straight back to the farm.' Mary frowned.

Jake shook his head. 'No, ain't seen him since he come back to collect the Land Rover. I best go to the south pasture, maybe it broke down or got stuck somewhere. It's still a bit boggy in places after all that rain we had last week.'

'I'll come with you,' Nick got to his feet, 'you might need a hand.'

'I'll come too.' Liam offered.

'Come on Dad.' Mick said, nudging his father.

The small group of men made their way around the house and disappeared from sight. Excited barking was followed by the banging of car doors and the sound of engines starting.

'I hope everything's all right.' Mary said looking at Laura uneasily.

'Don't worry,' Laura gave her arm a reassuring pat. 'I'm sure there's a perfectly sensible explanation.'

It was their third night in Liverpool and Matt was having dinner with Marcie at the Adelphi when the Restaurant Manager came over to tell him that his father was on the phone. He was directed to a small private cubicle just outside the dining room.

'Dad, you beat me to it! I was going to call you later.'

'No matter, how are things going?'

'Fine, it's been great; a full house every night so far. This is our last night in Liverpool, we're due in Manchester tomorrow. The *Echo* did a really good a feature on her.' He said enthusiastically. 'And big TV news; Granada want to interview her on Thursday and after that we're dashing across to the BBC studios to record *Top of the Pops*.' He gave a relaxed laugh, 'It's all happening! By the way Doug has decided to release *'Never Quite Over You'* as a UK single. Everyone seems to love it. But you didn't phone me urgently just to get an update on the tour, surely?'

'No, I thought I ought to let you know that your mother's been in hospital.'

'Why? What's happened?'

'Some tearaway grabbed her handbag while she was walking through the park. When she wouldn't let go he slashed her with a knife.'

'Oh no, poor Mum, how is she?'

'She's fine; thankfully it was a only flesh wound. The hospital kept her in overnight, just as a precaution but I'm pleased to say she's back home now and making good progress.'

Matt gave a sigh of relief. 'Do you want me to come home?'

'No, but I'm sure she'd love to see you again before you go back to the States if you can manage it.'

'Of course, Marcie and I would be glad to.'

'Matt.' Tad sounded serious now. 'About you and Marcie.'

'Yes?'

'I didn't realise you were, how shall I put it, a little more than just professional colleagues.'

Matt gave a strange laugh. 'We're not.'

'Straight up?'

'Straight up Dad; what's brought this up?'

'Ella.'

'Ella?' He drew his breath in sharply.

'She was there when your mother was attacked. She carried out first aid until the ambulance came. I spoke to her afterwards. Matt I think there's something you ought to know...'

'No Dad.' Matt said abruptly, eager to end a conversation that had suddenly made him feel an unwanted past was being raked up again. 'That part of my life really is over!'

'Matt, she came to the house looking for you the morning after Zeffirelli's opening.'

'What?' He thought for a moment. Remembered coming back from his run, seeing the silver Mercedes pass in Mountbatten Drive.

'Marcie answered the door in her dressing gown. Said you were in the shower. She gave Ella the impression that you two were...well...involved.'

'What did she do that for?' Matt frowned.

'I have no idea.'

'Did Ella say why she came to see me?'

'After she had the row with you at the club she ran into Sonny. Said she'd met

Linnie and Sonny had also told her about Spain. She came to apologise. She also wanted to try and clear up some things that still didn't make sense. She left her number with Marcie. Asked if you'd call; did you get it?'

'No.' Matt shot a glance back at the table where Marcie was busy signing an autograph for one of the diners.

'I think Marcie owes you an explanation then.'

'Yes,' Matt nodded, gazing at Marcie's innocent smile as she handed the pen and book back, 'I think you're right.'

'Problems at home?' Marcie looked up anxiously at Matt's serious face as he returned to his seat.

'Mum's been in hospital.'

'What happened?'

'She was attacked in the park. A guy took her handbag, tried to knife her. It's OK,' he said seeing her concerned face, 'she's going to be all right.'

'You going home?'

'No.' He said pouring himself another glass of wine. 'Dad said there was no need. He did ask if we'd drop in and see her just before we fly back though.'

'Sure.' She nodded, then seeing the thoughtful look on his face said. 'Hey c'mon; don't worry. She's in good hands. She'll be fine.'

'It's not Mum that's worrying me Marcie, it's something else Dad mentioned; about you.'

'Me?' She looked taken aback.

'Why didn't you tell me Ella had called?'

His face was expressionless, only the hardness in his eyes showed the depth of his hurt at being deceived by her.

'I...' Marcie took a deep breath, struggling to find an explanation for her actions that would melt away the anger. 'Oh boy.'

'I understand she gave you her phone number.' He continued. 'Have you still got it?'

'No,' she shook her head. 'I tore it up and threw it in the garbage can.'

'And why did you make out there was something going on between us?'

'To get rid of her.' As his expression became harder with every question, Marcie's mind groped for a plausible explanation. Then it came, so simple, so perfect. He was bound to believe her. 'Honest to God Matt I was so scared!' She blurted out. 'Your Mom and Dad were due back any moment. After what had happened the night before I thought if your Mom found her on the doorstep she'd go crazy. I didn't know what else to do! I asked her if she wanted to leave a message because it seemed kinda polite. The last thing I wanted to do was slam the door in her face!'

'But I didn't get the message Marcie. You've just said you destroyed it. Why did you do that when you could have quite easily given it to me out of sight of my mother?'

'Because...' She shrugged. 'After she'd gone, I realised how stupid I'd been. I thought if she saw you again it would only mean more trouble for you and that's the last thing we wanted with the tour about to start.'

'Marcie.' He responded, his face still stony. 'I'm not happy with this. I'm an adult, I don't need someone taking control of my life and making decisions for me behind my back OK?'

'I'm sorry.' She said in a small voice. 'I was out of order, but I did it because I care about you and your folks. Is that so bad?'

'I guess not.' He answered, aware that it was difficult to be angry with someone as good intentioned as Marcie for long. 'But don't ever do anything like that again, please.'

'OK.' She nodded and gave him a hesitant smile. 'Are we friends again then?'

He nodded. 'I guess so.'

'Gimme a smile then, to show you mean it.'

He grinned at her.

'That's better.'

She picked up her wine glass and sat sipping slowly, watching Matt finish off his meal. As he set the knife and fork neatly together on his plate, the waiter appeared and cleared away, leaving them with the dessert menu.

Marcie scanned the list of sweets, her final decision caught between fruit salad and Black Forest gateau. But something else far more important than food niggled in her brain. Although she was sure Ella held no interest for Matt any longer, Ella's feelings for him were an unknown quantity and that, coupled with the fact she was now single, made her dangerous. So any chance of them meeting up had to be avoided at all costs. To ensure that didn't happen, Marcie decided their return visit to Abbotsbridge was going to be brief; very brief.

NINETEEN

Monday 13ᵗʰ August

Ella was having breakfast when Helen appeared to say Marcus was on the phone.

'Hi there,' He sounded upbeat. 'I need to see you. Any chance of sparing me half an hour this morning?'

'Actually you're lucky to have caught me. I wasn't planning to be around much this week.'

'You sound a bit down Ella.'

'I am. My grandfather died yesterday while we were at Charlotte's christening. I was planning to go out to Meridan Cross tomorrow and stay over with the family until the funeral next Tuesday.'

'Ella I am sorry. I know how much he meant to you. It was his heart I take it?'

'Yes, he was weaker than we all thought.' She paused for a moment. 'So, what's happened? Don't tell me Andy has changed his mind.'

'I'm afraid not,' Marcus cleared his throat. 'However, something rather interesting has come up that may mean we might be able to change it for him. Can we say ten thirty, my office?'

'Sure.'

Later that evening Ella looked down at her small daughter, dark eyelashes fanning the smooth skin of her baby face. Asleep without a care in the world she thought, as her fingers gently touched the dark curl of her hair; and totally unaware of this new controversy going on around her.

She had gone to see Marcus this morning, her curiosity burning, wondering what this new development could possibly be. He had welcomed her with his usual smile and ushered her into his office, where she found herself face to face with a man he introduced as his father.

Henry Goddard was an older version of his son, his dark hair shot with grey, his blue eyes gentle, his smile friendly. His grip was firm as he shook her hand. She took a seat, looking from one to the other expectantly. When Marcus asked her if she'd ever heard of orchitis she simply shook her head.

Henry smiled and with a nod from Marcus took over the conversation. Orchitis, he said, was a complication of mumps and only a danger to boys who contracted the disease in puberty. Andy Macayne had contracted mumps two months before his sixteenth birthday. Henry, then the family's GP, had advised Bob that because of the severity of the case and his age, it would probably leave him infertile. However,ature, Bob had dismissed his prognosis as rubbish and refused to discuss the issue further.

'I'm afraid,' Henry said gently, 'that facts are facts. The test results I filed on Andy's health record mean that there is no way your daughter can possibly be his. Unless, of course, some minor miracle has occurred.'

Ella sat there for a moment, digesting the information, her mind going back to the summer of 1971, to Tarvaggio. 'But I know exactly how and when it happened. We went to stay with Andy's relatives in Italy. My contraceptives were left behind. We used condoms. One split.' She said to Henry. 'That's when Lucy was conceived.'

'No,' Henry shook his head. 'You were already pregnant by then. A week or two at the most I would think, given the date of Lucy's birth.'

Ella looked them both and shook her head. 'But what about Nina?'

'Who?' Henry frowned.

'Andy has a new wife.' Marcus explained. 'She was pregnant when they married, lost the baby a month ago.'

'Then that child was also fathered by somebody else.' Henry insisted.

'I'm sorry,' Ella said, getting to her feet, 'I'm having real problems with this.'

'Ella.' Henry fixed her with wise eyes. 'Trust me. There's absolutely no way Andy could father a child. I'm sorry if you find this embarrassing, but the only explanation is that you *must* have been with someone else prior to the time you thought you conceived Lucy with your husband.'

'Ella?' Marcus looked at her curiously.

'I....' Ella gazed at him, then across at Henry and with a resigned sigh settled herself back into her seat. 'Yes, yes I was. But I don't understand how this could have happened.' she frowned. 'I was on the pill at the time.'

'The pill isn't foolproof you know.' Henry said. 'What was your usual regime for taking it?'

'Mornings, I took it each morning, when I brushed my teeth.'

'Did you have any sickness or tummy upsets on or around the date you had sex with this man?'

'Yes, just before.' She nodded, remembering the meal at the Charlton Cat.

'And did you continue your tablets after that?'

'Yes, the day after, but I still had a bit of a queasy tummy. Could that have affected it?'

'It's possible. And afterwards, what then?'

'No. No more tablets after that.' That had been the Monday morning. She had left the house without breakfast, late for her ride with Rachel. Afterwards she had rushed home to change to meet Matt for lunch. They had come for her after that and with her mother in charge of packing her things, the pills had been deliberately left behind.

'Are you still in touch with this man Ella?' Marcus asked gently.

'No, he's long gone.'

'Ella I know this is extremely hard for you,' Marcus replied, 'but with this evidence the Macayne's application for custody will collapse. We have no case to answer. Of course there may be repercussions, but personally I feel the last thing Bob Macayne will want the world to know is that his son's child has been fathered by someone else. He'll just drop the case. You may find, however, that Andy won't be as easy to get rid of; he's bound to come looking for answers.'

'And I'll be ready and waiting when that time comes.' Ella said calmly. 'But I honestly I think he'll be more interested in Nina and the explanation she gives about her miscarriage, don't you?'

Marcus smiled. 'It sounds as if you're happy for us to approach the Macaynes with this evidence then.'

'Yes, I am.' Ella nodded. 'I'll do absolutely anything to keep my daughter Marcus. And if achieving that means I end up with a reputation that's a little tarnished, well it's a small price to pay.'

Tuesday 14th August

'What is this Bill?' Bob Macayne stood with his back to the window of his office, his eyes scanning the piece of paper he had just been handed. He looked at his solicitor and laughed, 'What was Nina's pregnancy then? Scotch mist?'

On the other side of his desk Bill Matthews, heavy set and florid, sat with an opened brief case on his lap. 'They say they have medical proof Bob.' He looked uncomfortable.

'Rubbish!' Bob threw the paper onto his desk. 'I don't know where this has come from, but my son is not firing blanks. Who are they saying the father is then?'

'They aren't, but,' Bill said in a warning tone. 'No doubt that will become clear in due course. Unfortunately it means we're going to have to bring along evidence to disprove their claim.'

'What are you saying?'

'Andy will have to have to take a fertility test.'

Bob didn't answer. He turned back towards the window, staring out across the rooftops of Abbotsbridge.

'Bob?' Bill looked at him uneasily. 'Is there something you're not telling me?'

'Of course not, it's just a bloody nuisance, that's all!' Bob snapped as he swung round to look at his solicitor. 'OK, leave it with me, I'll speak to Andy and get everything arranged with his GP. Take it from me it will be a mere formality Bill. A mere formality.'

'Dad is this really necessary?'

Andy Macayne sat in his father's office staring at him across the desk, unable to believe what he was being asked to do.

'I'm afraid so. Your ex-wife and her solicitor are playing silly buggers with us. We have to put a stop to it. I've made an appointment with Dr Savage this afternoon so that he can arrange for the necessary tests. I want this settled once and for all.

'But Dad, why do I have to go through all this? Nina was having my baby, surely that shows I haven't any problems?'

'It does, but Bill says we'll be expected to take clinical proof to court.'

Bob Macayne's expression softened as he looked at his son.

'Just think about winning, about the look on that bitch's face when we take Lucy away from her for good.'

'Yes.' Andy said with a malicious smile as he visualised the eventual conclusion of this legal battle, 'OK, I'll make an appointment to see Dr Savage.'

Thursday 16th August

Bob looked out of his office window. It was a hot, oppressive day. The fan in the corner of his office was struggling. But the heat didn't worry him today. In fact nothing was worrying him at all. As he stared out at the heat haze shimmering over the roofs of the cars in the car park his expression arranged itself into a self-satisfied smile. Miles had phoned to say he'd just heard the sad news about Richard Evas. He was very sorry he said and asked for condolences to be passed on to Mel. And then after a moment's silence, came the words Bob had been waiting for.

So at last, retribution was at hand; Miles Anderson was about to get his comeuppance for his part in a deception which had cost Bob money on the precinct development. Swinging his chair around to face his desk again, Bob reached for the phone and began to dial. Mel answered on the second ring.

'Bob. Is anything wrong?'

'No far from it. Miles has just phoned. Sends his condolences and he wants to negotiate with you on behalf of Mirage for Fox Cottage and an area of wood around it.'

'Does he now?' There was amusement in her voice. 'How interesting, I'll have to consult my business adviser.'

'What business adviser?'

'You, of course.'

Bob began to laugh.

'What's so funny Bob?'

'Nothing, nothing at all. Oh Mel, do you realise, we're going to be seriously rich! Doesn't that make you feel excited?'

'Yes, it does Bob, but there's something else just as wonderful! You and I, we can start to plan our future together!'

Tuesday 21st August

'Well, whoever would have thought my dear father would have breathed his last surrounded by a herd of cows.'

Mel's face arranged itself into an amused smirk as she sat beside Liam in the Range Rover en route for her father's funeral.

'Must you be so spiteful Mel?' Liam slowed down for a sharp bend. 'I would have thought you would have had a little more respect for the dead. He was your father after all, an elderly man with a heart condition.'

'I didn't realise he had a heart.' She shrugged uncaringly. 'He's half the reason I left Meridan Cross in the first place you know. Driven out I was, by a bullying father and gossiping villagers.'

'I always found Richard a decent enough man and as for the villagers, well, they've always been more than friendly.' Liam reacted angrily, aware that events of the past week had prevented him finding an opportune moment to question his wife about her visits to Meridan Cross with Bob Macayne.

'And what would you know about anything here?' She turned to him angrily. 'It's surprising how friendly these people can be when they want to know something. Any friendliness I can assure you had more to do with finding out about me than anything else.'

'You flatter yourself my darling,' He smiled in a way he knew would annoy her. 'Do you really think these people are that interested in anything you do?'

'Maybe not at the moment Liam,' she said with an icy smile. 'But I can assure you they will be very soon.'

'Forasmuch as it hath pleased Almighty God of his great mercy to take unto himself the soul of our dear brother here departed, we therefore commit his body to the ground.'

The Reverend Farr stood, prayer book in hand, at the head of the open grave as members of the Evas family watched the casket being lowered into the black earth.

Mary, supported by Niall on one side and Ella on the other looked pale and drawn, Nick, Jenny and Laura beside them, white faced and serious completed the family group. The villagers congregated opposite, while Mel and Liam stood conspicuously alone at the foot of the grave.

Laura hated funerals. By the time you were beginning to come to terms with the initial shock and accompanying grief, you were put through it all again with the burial. She looked across the grave at Liam and Mel. Liam, bearded and distinguished in his dark suit, looked subdued. His eyes met hers for a moment, sad and gentle. He doesn't deserve to be tied to a woman like that, she thought. He's a good man, just like my son. What is it that attracts decent men to women like her?

Mel Carpenter dressed from head to foot in navy blue and wearing a hat with an impossibly wide brim raised her eyes to Laura at that instant almost as if she had heard her thoughts, and Laura saw that although her expression was solemn, there was a gleam in her eye that certainly was not tears. Willowbrook, she thought depressingly, remembering her conversation with Doggie Barker in the week about the strangers he had seen in Hundred Acre. She's thinking about Willowbrook and what she's going to do with it. But exactly what *is* she planning?

Dr David Savage sat in his office looking at the young man seated opposite him, feeling utterly confused. Andy Macayne, a personable young man with a pleasant smile and not a hint of nervousness had come to the surgery a little less than a week ago, quite happy to undertake the tests his father had asked for. This morning he had returned and it was now his job to break the news that the results showed that he could not possibly have fathered the child who was currently the subject of a custody dispute with his ex-wife.

When told, Andy had just smiled and said there must be some mistake, that there was a second child; a child miscarried earlier that year. And he, Dr Savage, had been called to the house by his wife when it had happened.

'I'm sorry Mr Macayne.' He shook his head, looking at Andy over the top of his glasses. 'I don't believe I've ever been to your house. Is your wife one of my patients?'

'Of course she is!' The impatience in Andy Macayne's voice was clear. 'It was the end of June. It happened in the bedroom. I came home just after you'd left. There was blood everywhere. I thought she should have gone to hospital, but apparently you didn't think that was necessary.'

Dr Savage looked at his patient and saw the insistence in his face.

'That's very irregular. Can I have your wife's first name?'

'Nina.'

'One moment please.'

He left the room and went out to reception where he found one of the secretaries. After a short conversation with her, she retrieved a set of notes from one of the nearby carousels and handed them to him.

'Yes, she is one of my patients.' He confirmed with a smile as he returned to his office and sat down in his chair again. 'Although I can't for the life of me work out why I don't remember her. After all, a visit to someone's house for something as traumatic as a miscarriage usually sticks in the mind. For a start I would have contacted you immediately to advise you of the situation. And if there was the amount of blood loss you say, she'd almost certainly have been admitted to hospital overnight.'

'But she came to you for a check up afterwards!'

David Savage pulled the contents of Nina's records out onto his desk. Finding the summary card, he checked through the dates carefully.

'No, there's nothing about a miscarriage here, or any visit afterwards.'

'But there must be!' Andy was insistent. 'The next thing you'll be telling me is she wasn't even pregnant!'

'Actually Mr Macayne, it doesn't appear she was.' Dr Savage shook his head. 'In fact, according to this, only two months ago she had a check up before being issued with a fresh supply of contraceptives. '

'That's impossible! She was pregnant then, why would she need contraceptives? There must be a mistake.' There was uneasiness in Andy's face, 'Are you sure you haven't got someone else's records?'

'I'm quite satisfied these relate to your wife.' Dr Savage said gently. 'Here, take a look for yourself.'

Andy took the record card eagerly, looking for something which would tell him the man sitting opposite him had made a mistake. His eyes were immediately drawn to one date. 25th January. He could see the doctor's notes beside the date, ending with the prescription details for a course of antibiotics. He remembered - she'd had a very bad throat infection and could hardly speak.

'I don't understand any of this.' He said with a dazed frown as he handed the card back.

'Mr Macayne, I really don't know what to say,' Doctor Savage gave Andy an embarrassed shake of his head, 'other than I'm sorry these results have raised rather delicate issues for you which obviously need to be discussed in private at home with your wife.'

Andy stood up. He was aware of the doctor opening the door, extending his hand, saying goodbye. Then he was back in the waiting room, heading for the front door. It began to rain as he crossed the car park, feeling in his jacket pocket for his car keys. He sat in the Mercedes for a moment collecting his thoughts. The doctor's concerned eyes still hovered in his mind. He thought about Nina, remembered the bedroom floor and the blood. She had a lot of explaining to do. But not as much as the person he was about to see. He turned the keys in the ignition, heard the engine come to life and felt the explosive force of his temper building. The car wheels spun on the loose gravel of the surgery car park and he was gone, speeding down the road towards the centre of Abbotsbridge and One Plus One Recruitment.

TWENTY

Tuesday 21st August

The small group of mourners left All Hallows churchyard, making their way slowly along the gravelled pathway under the stately cedars and out through the lych-gate. Both Nick and Niall stopped to shake hands with Reverend Farr before joining the rest of the family for the drive back to the farmhouse.

Liam and Mel followed behind in their Range Rover, Liam constantly slowing the car down to avoid small pockets of villagers making their way home.

'Don't they all just love a spectacle?' Mel cast a critical eye over them as they passed by. 'I bet some of them broke their necks to get here today. Thankfully, we don't have to put up with them at the farmhouse, it's family only because of the will reading.' She gave a small self-satisfied smile as she pulled her powder compact from her handbag.

Liam caught her smug expression. 'What's going on Mel? What are you up to?'

'I don't know what you mean Liam.' She interrupted her survey of her face to look at him.

'It hasn't got anything to do with Bob by any chance, has it?'

'Bob?' She swung around to look at him again, her face tight. 'Why do you say that?'

'I understand you've been out here with him on several occasions.'

'And where did you get that from?'

'Doggie Barker. He saw you both.'

'Social visits,' Mel said dismissively, still preoccupied with her face in the compact's mirror. 'I was making sure Dad was OK and Bob wanted to join me.'

'Didn't that strike you as a strange request?'

'No.' Mel said irritably, 'He was interested in the village and surrounding area that was all. He hadn't had the chance to see it properly when he came to Ella's wedding.'

'Bob Macayne interested in the countryside.' Liam nodded thoughtfully. 'Come on Mel. This is me you're talking to. What really brought him out here?'

'You'll see Liam.' Mel said, closing the compact with a loud click. 'You'll see.'

Arriving back at the farm, Mary led the small family group to the front door and let them in. While Niall disappeared to get the milking underway, coats and jackets were removed. Nick, feeling the heat, relieved himself of his tie and unbuttoned the neck of his shirt.

'Phew that's better.' He said, walking into the living room and unlocking and opening the French doors which led to a small south facing patio, warm from the afternoon sun.

He stood for a moment, taking in the garden, wondering why it seemed today that when he reviewed his life most of it seemed to have been spent as a passenger on an express train. The speed with which time passed was something which, in his day-to-day life as a teacher, preoccupied with his work, did not occur to him. It took things like death and the subsequent loss of someone close to make you realise how as you got older the process of life accelerated considerably and as a consequence, how precious every moment was. He felt someone squeeze his arm and found Laura beside him.

'Would you like to walk me down the garden?' She asked. 'There's a lovely view of the river and Willowbrook Copse from the field gate and I should very much like to see it again.'

Nick patted her arm gently, knowing this was a polite way of saying that she wanted to talk with him out of earshot of the others. Taking her arm he went with her, wondering what it could be about.

'Anything I can do?' Ella followed Mary into the kitchen where cups and saucers had already been set out.

'There are sandwiches and cake to take through if you will,' Mary said as Jenny joined them. 'Oh and plates and serviettes on the dresser.'

Mel, followed by Liam was the last to enter the house. She gave the occupants of the kitchen a cursory glance before unpinning her hat with a theatrical flourish and dropping it onto the hall table. She had put on heavy black sunglasses and took these off for a moment to gaze around her before she replaced them and walked into the living room.

Liam hovered in the kitchen doorway. 'Need any help?'

'No, I think we have everything under control.' Mary smiled. 'Kind of you to offer though Liam, make yourself comfortable, we won't be long.'

While Ella and Jenny laid everything out on the table, Mary brought in a tray of crockery.

'The kettle has almost boiled.' She said before returning to the kitchen.

Liam noticed Mel had left the room, selecting a chair on the patio and she was now sitting, legs crossed, staring into space. To the untrained eye it might have appeared that beneath her dark glasses she was lost in her own private grief, mourning for her father. Liam, however, knew better. She knew something the rest of them didn't. It made him feel uneasy.

Tea arrived; Laura and Nick returned from the bottom of the garden and Ella and Jenny made Mary take a seat while they took charge of serving refreshments.

The little group moved out to the patio to sit together, oddments of conversation passing between them as they ate. When they had all finished, Jenny and Ella cleared away and disappeared to the kitchen to begin the washing up, insisting that Mary sit and talk with the others.

'How's the harvest going?' Laura asked.

'We're about half done. Niall's overseeing it all.' Mary sounded business like. 'Perhaps I'll take a ride out tomorrow, see how they're doing.'

'Well, well,' Mel stretched out her legs and took off her dark glasses. 'Here are you two sitting discussing Willowbrook as if everything was normal.'

'Mel, I'm sorry if you find the conversation upsetting.' Mary was apologetic. 'There was no offence meant. I loved your father dearly and I'm devastated that he's been taken from us like this. But we still have the farm to run.'

'Correction,' Mel's cool but deadly gaze locked onto both women. 'You *had* the farm to run. Peter Merrick the family solicitor will be here soon and I will be the new owner.' She directed her gaze at Mary. 'And as soon as that is made official I will want you and your son off my land immediately.'

'What?' Mary frowned at Mel.

'You have your own farm. That's where you should be.'

'But *you* haven't a clue about running a farm.' Nick interrupted, putting his cup and plate on the table. 'Besides Mary has tenants at Paddocks; she can't just turn them out. Be sensible.'

'I don't need to have *a clue* as you put it Nick,' Mel replied coldly, 'Not for what I have planned.'

'And what exactly is that Mel?' Mary looked at her curiously.

'We're twenty miles from the sea, an ideal setting for a holiday village.' She looked at all of their faces. 'Oh don't look so shocked, we're not talking anything as common as Butlins or Pontins. This will be *far* more up market. And Sedgewick Wood will make an ideal setting. Once Fox Cottage has been bulldozed the developers will have the access they need to build. And as for the rest of the farm, well I shall simply dispose of it to the highest bidder.'

'But the herd!' Mary was horrified. 'Richard spent years building it.'

'Then it will make an excellent price at auction won't it?' Mel replied tartly.

'You can't be serious about this!' Nick now added his voice to the argument again. 'This is a green belt area. The planners wouldn't allow that sort of development to go ahead.'

'Ah but that's where you're wrong.' Liam got to his feet. 'I think my wife has got everything sorted.' He looked down at her. 'That's what you and Bob have been doing on your regular visits here isn't it Mel?'

'You mean Richard knew?' Mary's hands flew to her face. 'How could he be planning to do this to his farm?'

'Oh Dad knew nothing of the plans.' Mel flapped a hand at Mary 'As far as he was aware, I was just trying to persuade him to part with the cottage and some land.'

'And knowing Richard, he wasn't playing ball.'

'That's right,' Mel nodded. 'But in the end at least he had the grace to reassure me that everything was mine. ' She gave an amused smile. 'Although soon of course, some of it will belong to Mirage.'

'You're selling it to the Consortia?' Laura was appalled.

'That's right.' Mel said, enjoying the horrified looks on their faces. 'They're the developers of the holiday village.'

'So that's what the surveyors were doing in Sedgewick this week.' Nick joined the conversation. 'A Taylor Macayne van wasn't it Grandma?'

Laura nodded and seeing the surprise in Mel's face said. 'Oh dear, hasn't Mr Macayne been keeping you informed? That's a bit naughty.'

'Mel,' Liam said gently, 'have you any idea what you're dealing with here?'

'Of course I have!' She rounded on him. 'Bob and I have been close for a long time.' she gave her husband an unpleasant smile, 'Very close.'

Ella, standing in the doorway, stared at both of them. She caught the slight tremor of unease which momentarily crossed Liam's face. He knows now, she thought, watching his expression return to normal. But exactly what is he going to do about it?

Somewhere deep within the house the doorbell rang, temporarily halting the conversation. Mel got to her feet and brushed the creases from her skirt.

'This is madness!' Laura began again, shaking her head in disbelief. 'You can't do this.'

'Oh but I can Laura dear.' Mel smiled graciously as she walked to the French doors. 'You sleepy village folk are about to get a rude awakening. Now where's Peter?'

There were voices in the hall followed by the slamming of the front door. Peter Merrick, the family solicitor, wearing a dark suit and black tie, despite the heat, emerged onto the patio, briefcase in hand.

'Good afternoon, everyone.' He greeted them all with a polite smile.

Moments later, they had all gathered in the dining room where Peter had seated himself at one end of the large rectangular table. Pulling out a large buff dossier of papers, he snapped his briefcase shut before setting it on the floor.

'Right, ladies and gentlemen,' He smiled at them as he pulled on his glasses. 'Shall we begin?'

Margaret Sylvester, returning from the funeral quickly removed the black coat she had worn.

'Thank goodness for that, I thought I should stifle in this thing.' She said, draping it over the counter and casting her eyes around the shop with satisfaction. 'Very good Rachel, I can see you've done well while I've been out. I'll put the kettle on in a minute and we'll have a cup of tea, or would you prefer something colder? There's orange in the fridge.'

'As it comes, I don't mind.' Rachel, her long sweep of fair hair tied back in a pony tail, stood unpacking tins of processed peas and setting them out on the shelves behind.

Margaret leant on the counter watching her daughter work. 'There'll be fireworks up at the farm now.' She said smugly. 'I wonder who Richard's left it to. Can't be Mary I shouldn't think. I hope that bitch Mel doesn't get hold of it! We don't want her back in Meridan Cross again!'

'Are you referring to Ella's mother?' Rachel asked as she flat packed the cardboard boxes ready for the dustman.

'Yes, you should have seen her at the funeral. All dressed up like some American movie star. Big hat, sunglasses.' Margaret snorted indignantly. 'With her fancy husband dancing attendance on her. And the way she was looking at everyone in the church, as if they were dirt under her feet!'

'I wish you'd forget her Mum. Can't you see how pointless all your hate is? The only person you're harming is yourself!'

'Don't you speak to me like that my girl! Some things run so deep they'll never heal over. And you ought to be careful!' She wagged a threatening finger at Rachel. 'Don't think I don't know about you, taking up with that son of Mary Evas's again behind my back!'

'I love him!' Rachel declared, wishing she felt as brave as she sounded.

'Love!' Her mother scoffed, snatching up her coat. 'You're amazing you are! You really can't see you're being used again can you?'

'I am not! We...' Rachel hesitated; a tin of peas in her hand. It was on the tip of her tongue to challenge her mother there and then about the contents of Niall's letter to Ella, but sensibly right now, like all the times in the past she had thought about doing the same thing, she knew it would be a bad move. Her mother not only had an answer for everything but the ability to manipulate the truth and twist it to her own advantage. No it was not the time to raise the issue, she decided. But the way things were going between her and Niall, it would have to be raised and sooner rather than later.

'Well, go on! Say what you have to say! What's he been filling your head with this time?' Margaret hovered in the doorway waiting for a response, stiff with indignation, 'Don't tell me.' she gave a spiteful smile. 'More empty promises no doubt! Well you can tell him from me, he can sling his hook! You belong here with me and that's where you're going to stay!'

Rachel looked down at the tin of peas she was holding, feeling her fingers tighten around it as the anger welled up inside her. For a moment she was tempted to hurl the tin straight at her mother, to shout and scream out all the pain and frustration that had been trapped inside her over the years. But looking across the room at Margaret standing there, face pink and blotchy, traces of spittle at the corner of her mouth, she realised perhaps it wasn't the best thing to do. One mad woman in the family was quite enough.

Back at Willowbrook, Peter cleared his throat and opened the will.

'I Richard Evas, being of sound mind and body, hereby revoke all former Wills and testamentary dispositions made.........'

He then began to list a series of money and property gifts to employees, two hundred pounds for one, one hundred and fifty for another, taking his time, alternating his gaze between the papers in front of him and the gathered group. Mel was visibly agitated, wanting him to move on to the main bulk of his estate, to her moment of triumph. She stood up quickly.

'Peter must we go through all these trifling little bits of money? Can't you get to the part that matters? The part we're all here for?'

Peter Merrick looked over the top of his half glasses at her, his eyebrows met as his face creased into a frown.

'Mel I am merely reading out this will in the way your Father instructed me to. It was what he wanted.'

'How can what he wanted possibly matter now? He's dead!'

She sat down angrily, ignoring the angry gazes of the others gathered with her.

'I've nearly finished.' He said sternly. 'Please! Exercise a little patience!'

He continued with the list of bequests then turned the page and smiled at them all.

'Now then, the main bulk of the will.' He cleared his throat again. 'It's fairly simple in its instruction. Willowbrook Farm together with its outbuildings, Channel Island herd and other livestock plus all lands and assets, including Fox Cottage, will continue intact and as a working farm and is to be left in its entirety in the joint ownership of Nicholas Stuart Kendrick and Marcella Louise Macayne.' He looked at them both. 'And as neither is experienced in farm management, monies have been set aside for them to employ the services of a professional person to carry out this function. It will also remain my wife Mary's home for as long as she wants it to be.'

'No!' Mel was on her feet again. 'There must be some mistake. Willowbrook is mine!'

'I'm sorry Mel.' Peter took off his glasses and pinched the bridge of his nose. 'When he came to me, your father was very specific in his instructions.'

'This is wrong, it's not what he told me!' She was almost hysterical. 'It's mine; he said it would be mine! When was this will made?'

Peter turned the papers over. 'Monday 18th September, 1972, but it wasn't a new will, it was just updated. The farm had been left in trust to Nick and Ella since July 1956, but now they had both turned 21 he wanted to give them full ownership.'

Mel stood there unable to believe what she was hearing. She considered the date - July 1956; that was when she had left everything in Meridan Cross behind, including her children, to make a new life abroad as Mrs Liam Carpenter. He had written her out of his will years ago, the evil old bastard! Now as she felt Liam's hand reach up and try to ease her back down into her seat, she threw off his grip irritably. 'Don't touch me! I will have my say!' She redirected her anger at Peter Merrick. 'I'll contest this in court! I will!'

'On what grounds?' Exasperated, Peter pulled off his glasses and looked at her.

'That he was a senile old man who didn't know what he was doing. Sound mind and body indeed!'

'Then you will be wasting a lot of time and money and to no avail Mel.' Peter put his glasses back on and picked up the will. 'Your father's GP, Dr Beckwith was present; he was one of the witnesses on this last change. I'm afraid you'll have to accept what it says.'

'I will not!' Mel would not be put off. 'Willowbrook belongs to me, I have to have it! Keys Liam!' She snapped her fingers at him.

'Where are you going?' He asked as he dropped the car keys into the palm of her hand.

'Away, I'm not staying to listen to any more! I shall see you in court Peter, and as for the rest of you, well you can all go to hell!' She said venomously and picking up her handbag she swept out of the room. Pausing at the door she glared at Nick and Ella. 'You have both plotted behind my back; I don't know how you can live with yourselves!' Then she was gone, slamming the front door behind her.

It was one thirty when Helen Baxter eventually seated herself at the kitchen table to begin her lunch. Today she had volunteered to look after Christopher and Charlotte as well as Lucy while Ella, Nick and Jenny attended the funeral at Meridan Cross. It had at the outset looked like a simple enough task to look after a baby and two toddlers, working a few of her household chores in between. Unfortunately her experiences that morning had been completely different.

Whilst Charlotte slept and Lucy seemed quite happy amusing herself in her playpen in the nursery, Christopher was another matter. He made it quite clear right from the start that he didn't want to stay with his cousin, flexing his fingers towards Helen and making little grunting noises in his throat which indicated he wanted to be picked up. As soon as she felt his arms close tightly around her neck she knew she had made a mistake. Once lifted out of the playpen he wriggled until she set him down on the carpet and then promptly made his escape towards the open nursery door squealing with laughter.

She caught up with him on the landing, catching him mid-stride and swinging him around. He laughed gleefully as she set him on his feet again then looking at her with a face which mirrored his father's, stretched his arms out and demanded more.

She thought he would tire after ten minutes of being amused; but once the game was over he was off again, climbing into the landing window seat, pushing small starfish fingers against the glass. 'Pitty.' He pointed to the flowers in the window box outside, then stood up on the cushion and began jumping up and down as if he was on a trampoline. Helen realised at that moment that any thoughts of incorporating housework into the day were wasted ones and to ensure a peaceful afternoon, she would have no option but to put them all in the car and take them to the park where hopefully Christopher could run around and tire himself out. An hour and a half later she had returned to the house and after sorting out their lunch, settled all three down for a sleep upstairs. At last she could concentrate on the normal tasks for the day. It was as she emptied the washing machine that she noticed the rain against the window and realised the day was conspiring against her. Now, seated at the table with coffee, a sandwich and the sound of the tumble dryer in the background she ran through her 'To Do' list.

Later when she was asked, she honestly couldn't remember which she heard first, the doorbell or the telephone. They both seemed to start together and as she walked into the hall she decided that from the impatient pounding of the knocker, it was the door which needed be answered first. She swung it slowly open, expecting to see someone with a clip board canvassing or brandishing envelopes for Oxfam. Instead she found herself face to face with Andy Macayne.

'Where is she?' He shouted above the ring of the telephone his face white with anger, 'Where is the bitch?'

He pushed roughly past her into the hall and securing the door quickly she rushed after him, grabbing the phone, eager to make contact with whoever was on the other end, feeling the voice as remote as it was, offered her a kind of protection.

'Kingsbridge 659431.'

'Helen, Hi, it's Trudi.'

'Hello.' She tried to control the tremor in her voice.

'He's there with you isn't he?' Trudi said slowly.

'Yes,' Helen looked at the glowering Andy and gave a light hearted laugh. 'Is there a problem?'

'Yes, he's been here, almost wrecked the place. He's after Ella; been saying some crazy things about Lucy not being his. I don't know what to make of it all. The police are still here. They suggested I phone and warn you he'd probably be on his way to the house. Try to keep him talking, calm him if you can.' Trudi said as the muted sound of a siren broke into their conversation for a moment. 'They're on their way to you now.'

'OK will do. Thank you for calling. 'Bye.'

Helen placed the receiver slowly with both hands and looked down the hall to where Andy stood. During the time she had been their housekeeper she had seen his various moods. He was capable of immense charm, but also vicious temper when things didn't go his way. A quiet, understanding approach was needed. He had always trusted her in the past and despite the fact that she was now employed by Ella, she hoped he still would.

'Now then,' she said in a calm, matter-of-fact manner, 'Ella's in Meridan Cross at her grandfather's funeral today. She won't be back till later this evening.' She moved closer to him and placed a comforting hand on his arm. 'I can see you're upset Andy. Why don't you come into the kitchen? I'll make you a coffee.'

He looked at her for a moment, his eyes running from her face to her feet. Then he screwed up his face in a sneer of contempt.

'Have a coffee with you?' He shouted, pushing her heavily into the wall. 'The hired help! You must be joking!'

'In that case I think you had better come back.' She said pulling herself upright, her voice firm. 'She'll be home around seven; you can talk to her then.'

'Talk? I'll break her bloody neck for what she's done to me!' He said viciously and then stopped suddenly, gazing up the stairs. Listening.

Helen heard it too. The muted sound of Charlotte's cries from the nursery.

His face twisted. 'Lucy's here, isn't she?'

'I have all three children.' She said, hoping that would act as a deterrent. 'They're having an after dinner nap. I'd rather you didn't disturb them.'

'Piss off Helen!'

He was at the foot of the stairs before she could stop him, running up them two at a time.

She chased after him, shouting the most abusive things she could think of, trying to make him turn his attention to her, concerned at what he would do when he found Lucy. Andy ignored her and reaching the top of the stairs, he paused for a moment. The crying had stopped. He stood there frowning at the closed doors which punctuated the large square landing.

Watching him open the nearest door and disappear into the one of the spare rooms, Helen made a dash for the nursery. There was a key on the inside of the door. If she could lock herself in with the children, she could buy them time until the police arrived.

She burst into the room, much to the amazement of Christopher and Lucy who were out of bed and sitting on the floor playing with a stack of coloured bricks. They watched her silently as she slammed the door shut, her fingers grabbing for the key, twisting it in the lock. She heard him outside the door, shouting at her to let him in, punching at it with his fists, threatening her with untold physical abuse if she didn't let him in. Then suddenly there was silence. She closed her eyes, leaning with her palms against the wood of the door, listening. After a few moments she straightened up. He'd gone. It was all over. They were safe. She turned her head and gave Christopher and Lucy a reassuring smile.

A sudden explosive impact against the door knocked her backward onto the floor. She rolled over and sat up to find herself staring at a large gaping hole in one of the door's upper panels just above the lock. The children started to scream as a hand appeared, feeling for the key. As his fingers closed around it, she crawled back to the door and kneeling in front of the gap grabbed his hand, trying to lever his fingers back to make him let go. Suddenly and quite unexpectedly he withdrew his arm from the hole. Immediately Helen grabbed at the key, frantically trying to pull it from the lock, but as she leaned towards the door, Andy's arm came back through the hole, his punch hitting her full in the face. She screamed and fell to the floor, blood pouring from her nose. By the time she recovered, Andy was standing in the room, his gaze fixed firmly on Lucy who was sobbing as she clung tightly to Christopher.

He walked slowly towards the two children, stopping to look at them both for a moment before prising Lucy out of Christopher's arms.

'Daddy.' She looked up at him through her tears.

'Lucy,' He said, looking down at her with an unpleasant smile. 'Oh Lucy, Lucy, Lucy.' then bending down he reached out to grab her.

Helen reacted at once; despite the agonising pain in her face, she got to her feet and launched herself at his bending figure with a terrible scream of rage. He swung around too late and the full force of her hit him squarely in the stomach propelling him backwards. She heard the crack as they hit the floor together and felt his body go slack under her. Untangling herself from him, she sat up and pulled a handkerchief from the pocket of her jeans to staunch the blood still pouring from her nose. Then she gathered up Lucy and Christopher and placed them on the bed. When she turned to look down at Andy again he was still lying motionless on the carpet, his head resting beside the corner of the heavy oak toy chest.

'Andy!' She shook him. 'Andy come on, wake up!' She patted his face then felt for a pulse in his neck. 'Andy!'

She got to her feet shakily. 'Come on my darlings.' She said to the children, picking up Charlotte's carry cot and coaxing them from the bed and along the landing.

Getting them all into Ella's bedroom she locked the door then picked up the phone and with unsteady fingers dialled for an ambulance. She heard the faint wail of a siren just as she was giving the address to the operator. When she eventually opened the front door to the police everything seemed to collapse around her.

'He's upstairs, in the nursery.' She said, leaning weakly against the wall, as they came into the hall. 'I think he's dead.'

TWENTY ONE

Tuesday 21st August

Bob Macayne watched the navy Range Rover as it made its way up the twisting thread of road towards him. He sat; a lone figure on the wooden bench beneath a cluster of Scots pines on top of Lancombe Hill. The view here was breathtaking and now, as the vehicle approached, he smiled, realising the plans for the valley would soon be a reality. As the Range Rover pulled up next to his XJ6 he got to his feet and walked over to it, opening the driver's door, helping Mel out.

'I was beginning to think you weren't coming.' He said with a laugh, swinging her into his arms and kissing her. He looked down into her face, his black eyes alight. 'I called Miles this morning. He assured me he will have the champagne well chilled by the time we arrive for the meeting'

Her blue eyes met his and she shook her head. As she turned away from him to look out across the valley he caught the glint of tears.

'Mel?'

'I didn't get the farm.' Her voice was almost a whisper.

'What?'

'It's only a temporary setback, Bob,' She tried to sound positive but was aware of the waver in her voice, 'Of course, I'm contesting the will. It's totally unsound. The old fool can't have been in his right mind to have done what he did.'

'I don't believe this! You said the place was yours!' Bob Macayne hissed under his breath, pulling a packet of cigarettes and a lighter from his pocket. Mel watched him light a cigarette and inhale deeply. Expelling smoke into the air he turned back to her with an uncomfortable expression.

'It's not my fault,' she said, relieving him of the cigarettes and lighting one herself. 'I had no idea, I really didn't. He lied to me! The old bastard lied to me!' She slapped the cigarettes and lighter back into his open palm.

'Well,' He said harshly, 'Seems like my local tip off was right after all.'

'What are you talking about?'

'Four days ago I was standing at this very spot, watching the surveyors.'

'Ah yes the surveyors.' She looked at him, aggrieved. 'The whole village knew about them I hope you realise. Which is more than I did!'

'Well at the time you led me to believe the will was just a formality.' He said brushing away her objections. 'I was merely getting things underway. Anyway, as I was saying, there was this old man...'

'What old man?'

'Early sixties, swarthy, with a black and white dog.'

'Joe Barker.' She blew smoke in the air. 'Local riff raff.'

'Very knowledgeable riff raff I'd say.' There was a cynical smile. 'He asked me what the men were doing and I told him they were surveying for the new owner of Willowbrook. He laughed and asked who that might be. When I told him it was you he laughed again. He looked at me for a minute and then he said *Mr Evas leave her the farm? Hell would have to freeze over first.*'

'I'm not finished yet Bob.' Regaining some of her composure, Mel tossed her head back defiantly and tried to look confident as she blew smoke into the air. 'As I told you I intend to contest the will.'

'So, who *has* he left it to?'

'Nick and Ella!'

'Surprise, surprise!' He drew on his cigarette and looked at her thoughtfully before he spoke again. 'Of course, you do realise if you challenge this, Laura Kendrick is bound to give them her financial backing. And that will mean dragging it all through the courts, which will cost you a pretty penny.'

'But I'm not using my money Bob; I'll be using the Consortia's.'

Bob gave an odd laugh. 'You're expecting Mirage to pay for this fight?'

'Of course,' she looked at his blank expression. 'Well I haven't the money to fight this by myself, but then I didn't expect to. As we were going to be business partners I thought I could count on Mirage.'

'I don't think you can Mel, in fact I think it would be quite foolish of you to think that.'

'But Bob, they want the land and the cottage, it's in their interest to support me.'

'Is it?' He stared at her coldly. 'Do you honestly think Mirage will shell out vast sums of money on a court case they probably haven't got a snowball in hell's chance of winning?'

'But we can't just give up!' She was almost shouting at him now. 'We can't!'

'Mel, I have to go,' Bob looked at his watch. 'The meeting's in less than an hour.'

'Take me with you then.' She caught his arm as he turned to leave. 'I'll talk to them! Explain! They'll listen to me!'

'No!' He shook her off, turning his dark gaze on her. 'Right now all you'll end up being is salt in a very open wound. Just leave, please!' He waved an irritable hand at her. 'Go home; back to Liam that's where you belong now.'

'What are you saying Bob?'

'It's over Mel! Finished!' He said, throwing his cigarette butt into the grass and walking off towards his car.

'Over!' She shouted after him. 'But you said we'd be together!'

'Did I?' He wrenched open the door of his car and stood for a moment looking at her. 'I say a lot of things Mel. Most of which I don't usually mean. They're right for the moment, that's all.' He said coolly. 'As far as I'm concerned we had a business arrangement which, because of your incompetence I'm now terminating. Goodbye.'

Bob slipped into the driver's seat and closed the door; she heard the engine fire, saw it begin to move off down the track.

'No! Please!' She shouted after him as she watched him drive away. She felt desolate and alone, abandoned at a time when she needed words of support and strong arms around her.

'You can't leave me like this Bob.' She whispered, her eyes filling with tears she watched the car reach the end of the track and turn onto the main road. 'You just can't.'

Nick and Ella stood side by side watching Peter Merrick's black Gilbern disappear down the lane.

'Good old Granddad.' Nick rested an affectionate arm on his sister's shoulder. 'Sensible to the end.'

'Do you think he knew what mother was up to?' Ella looked up at him thoughtfully.

'Almost certainly,' He nodded, 'Do you think Niall will stay on now?'

'Definitely!'

'Oh?' He looked at her suspiciously. 'Something you know that I don't?'

'He's going to propose to Rachel this evening over dinner.' She looked up at Nick with a smile. 'Wants to get married after the harvest. Rowan's agreed to be best man and I think you're going to be asked to give the bride away.'

Nick looked both surprised and pleased. 'I'd be delighted to.'

'Not a word if you see her, mind. Niall told me in the strictest confidence.'

'My lips are sealed.' Nick said with a grin then paused to stare thoughtfully at his sister for a moment. 'And what about you?'

'Me?'

'Yes, everyone's settled. Rachel has Niall, Issy has Mick. You're the only one left now; we have to do something, can't just leave you running around on your own.'

'And why not?' She laughed. 'I'm quite happy.'

'Are you really Ella?' His gaze never left her face. 'Honestly?'

'Yes.' Her grey eyes challenged him then she laughed. 'Who had you in mind anyway?'

'Actually I was thinking of Matt.'

'Well please don't.' She raised a warning finger at him. 'I'm not interested.

OK, maybe he's not guilty of all the things I thought he was, but he's with Marcie now, so the whole exercise is pointless.'

Nick was about to argue his case when Mary appeared in the doorway of the farmhouse.

'Ella!' She waved out. 'Phone! It's urgent!'

Ella turned to look at her. 'Who is it?'

'It's Helen.' Mary said. 'She's at the hospital. There's been some sort of accident.'

'It's just a storm in a teacup Bill!' Bob Macayne said as he walked out of Abbotsbridge General Hospital, Bill Matthews at his side.

'Bob, I don't think you quite understand. Andy's looking at charges of criminal damage not to mention common assault.'

'Oh come on, he only gave Helen Baxter a tap!'

'A tap?' Bill came to an abrupt halt. 'Bob he broke her nose for Christ sake!'

'That's as maybe,' Bob waved him on, 'but I'm sure the judge will still look on him leniently. You know, extenuating circumstances. I think if I'd found out my child had been fathered by some other man I would lost it too.' He turned to Bill, waving an authoritative finger. 'And don't forget we could be pressing our own charges. You heard what the doctor said about keeping him in overnight. I thought we were calling in to take him home.'

'An overnight stay is normal procedure for anyone who's had concussion Bob.'

'Well I hope you're right Bill. Because if anything happens to him, I promise you, I'll make Ella and that housekeeper of hers sorry they were ever born!'

They had reached their cars now. With an exasperated sigh Bill stowed his briefcase on the back seat of his green VW Variant then leant on the roof watching with an uneasy expression as Bob unlocked the Jaguar. He was really wound up and that wasn't good, bearing in mind where he was planning to go next.

'Bob, do you really think it's wise you seeing Nina?' He said quietly, 'After all Andy was very specific about wanting me to do it. After yesterday's events he feels it's perhaps wiser to approach the issue with her in a calm manner.'

'And you know what that means don't you?' Bob looked at his lawyer for a moment. 'The bitch is going to get away with it again. No way Bill. As far as I'm concerned, she's done as much damage as Ella. Besides,' he said, opening the door and sliding in behind the wheel. 'This is just the opportunity I've been waiting for. I want her out of my son's life for good!'

Bill heard the car door slam, heard the engine come to life and watched the Jaguar glide gracefully out of the hospital car park.

'I hope you know what you're doing Bob.' He said to the departing car, 'for all our sakes.'

Ella stood with Jenny, both stunned at the damage which had been done to One Plus One. By the time they arrived, Trudi and Fiona had brought some normality back to the reception area. Furniture and plants had been righted, broken glass swept up, coffee stains cleaned from the carpet and a glazing company brought in to board-up the broken windows.

'Got a bit of a temper, your ex.' Trudi said casting solemn eyes around the room.

'So I see.' Ella surveyed the damage once more then went into her office, closing the door behind her.

'Frightened Fiona so much she locked herself in the stationery cupboard.' Trudi continued. 'The police have only just gone. There were at least three witnesses besides the two of us. I've never seen Andy like that before.' She lowered her voice. 'He's never been one of my favourite people Jenny, but this time he really scared me. Kept shouting he was going to kill her. Once he started smashing things I got everyone out and ran round to Parker's Bakery to call the police. How's Helen by the way? Someone said she'd been taken to hospital.'

Jenny nodded. 'Andy broke her nose.'

'Trudi's hand went to her face. 'Oh poor Helen!'

'Don't worry; he got the worst of it. Concussion, six stitches and hopefully a thick head.'

'How did that happen?'

'He tried to take Lucy. Helen rugby tackled him before he could touch her. He hit his head in the fall and knocked himself out.'

'He kept shouting about Lucy not being his? Is that true?'

Jenny looked up. Ella emerged from her office and was indicating they should join her. 'I think.' She said. 'We're about to find out.'

Chelwood Lodge looked peaceful in the late afternoon sunlight as Bob drove through its gates. Ahead he could see the yellow Spitfire parked outside the garage. Pulling up beside it he got out, taking his briefcase with him. As he walked to the front door he turned over the events of the day in his mind.

First a quite tense meeting with Miles and the Mirage Board which thankfully he had managed to turn to his advantage. He had to admit to having become increasingly unhappy with what was going on at Willowbrook. Despite Mel's assurances, his instincts told him things weren't going quite as well as she insisted they were. And so as always when these situations arose, he'd arranged a fall back. Four hundred acres of land just south of Dunster, one hundred and fifty of them wooded; not quite as good as Meridan Cross, of course, but nearer the sea and with a retiring farmer keen to sell. He'd done his research well too. The lie of the land was similar and so new plans would not be needed, the existing ones would just require reworking. Hopefully there wouldn't be too many hitches with the planning permission either. Miles knew several members on the local council. Tourism and new jobs were just about the biggest issues in the area. They would jump at it. And, if all went well after tomorrow's meeting with owner Elliott Marquis, everyone would have smiles on their faces. It was a win-win situation.

With this to concentrate on, he hoped the unhappy episode with Willowbrook would soon be forgotten.

He had returned home feeling pleased that he'd managed to salvage both his reputation and his dignity, but then found himself plunged into yet another drama. Andy was in hospital with concussion and six stitches in his face while Ella's housekeeper Helen Baxter had a broken nose and was going to press charges for assault. Much as he wanted to blame Ella and Nina for all of this, he knew to his shame that a large portion of the blame lay fairly and squarely with himself. He should have listened all those years ago to the experts, accepted what they'd told him about Andy's situation. But at the time he had been busy making a success of his business, with thoughts of the generations to come. To be told that his great dream was over had been unacceptable; he had worked so hard and become so successful he felt this couldn't be happening in his life. So he had chosen to rubbish the test results, holding onto the belief that there was always the possibility that someone somewhere might have made a mistake.

When Lucy had been born, his disappointment that she was a girl had been more than balanced out by the fact that medical opinion had been proven wrong. He looked to the future, hoping the next baby would be a boy. However, when Andy and Ella parted he knew that would have to be put on hold. And then out of the blue Nina's pregnancy had raised fresh hopes. Of course it wasn't what he had wished. He detested the girl, with her common pushiness and her dreadful family, but a baby was a baby and like Andy he felt certain this time it would be the grandson needed to carry on the family business after Andy. Then the unthinkable; the miscarriage. He remembered Andy telling him how upset Nina had been at the time. The tears; the disappointment. As he rang the door bell Bill's words of warning rang loudly in his ears, stilling his rising anger.

The door opened and she stood there, her smile fading as she saw him. She was wearing a low cut T-shirt and jeans, her hair loose around her shoulders. Bob looked her up and down. A self-important, arrogant little tart, he thought, but with a body like that almost certainly a first class lay. And sex, he knew, was the main reason Andy kept going back to her.

'Oh,' she said, her smile resurfacing, 'Bob! What a surprise. Andy's not here but he's due back any moment. Would you like to wait?'

'Actually, it's you I've come to see.'

'Really? ' She tilted her head uncertainly. 'What about?'

'Why don't you let me in and I'll tell you.'

He followed her through to the lounge, now transformed from the pastels of Ella's day to the heaviness of gold velour, matching Regency stripe and the smell of leather furniture. Bob sat down on one of the stiff leather Chesterfields and opened his brief case.

'What are you doing?' She frowned, easing herself onto the couch opposite.

'I'm leaving some papers with you.' He dropped the envelope casually onto the coffee table

'What are they for?' She picked up the envelope and looked at it.

'I want you out of my son's life for good. So I'm making you a very generous offer. You sign these papers and in return I hand over a very healthy five figure bank account in your name.' He gave her a penetrating look. 'And given the circumstances I think you'd be foolish not to take it.'

'I was wondering how long it would take before you tried this.' She dropped the envelope back onto the table with a smirk. 'You're wasting your time. I'm his wife unless you've forgotten. Your daughter-in-law.' she held his stare then smiled. 'I can see that sticks in your throat, but I'm afraid it's something you'll have to get used to.'

'Is that what you think?' He was dying to tell her, but he held back. Let her have her moment, he thought, let her dig herself a huge hole because I am going to take the greatest of pleasure kicking her into it.

'You can't stand it can you? She said lighting up a cigarette and curling herself into the settee like a cat. 'To think you've lost. To have to admit that your son actually loves me.'

'Is that what you believe?' He said in the sort of dismissive tone he knew she hated. 'Well that might have been true once but not any more I'm afraid.' He shook his head. 'In fact I'd say that when Andy does come home it will be safer for you if you're not here, after what you've done.'

'What are you talking about?' She tossed her hair back carelessly, blowing smoke into the room.

'The baby, the miscarriage.' Bob said, his dark eyes fixed on her. 'A very clever plan, but I'm afraid you've been found out.'

She leaned forward, flicking ash into the ashtray, her eyes immediately welling up with tears. 'How can you be so cruel? We desperately wanted that baby!'

'You can turn off the waterworks,' Bob said watching her, 'I think it's time you came clean. You see Dr Savage says he's never been here and his records show you've never been pregnant. So, how did you do it eh? You're an expert at tears, I can see that. But all that blood, where did that come from?'

'I *was* pregnant!' She stood up, bristling with indignation. Grabbing the ashtray she stubbed the cigarette out angrily. 'Andy made a mistake. I didn't say Dr Savage. I was still with Dr Saunders at the Riverside Practice at the time.'

'Nina, please, don't make things worse than they already are.' Bob raised his voice. 'You could not have been pregnant. Andy can't have children!'

'You're a monster, do you know that?' Nina looked at him with contempt. 'What about Lucy? I suppose you'll be telling me next she someone else's.'

'As a matter of fact she is.'

'That's rubbish! Everyone knows she's Andy's. That's it! I've had enough. I want you and your poisonous lies out of here at once!'

'Sit down and shut up!'

The power and menace in his voice took her legs from under her. She collapsed onto the Chesterfield, her eyes wide with fright.

'I wasn't going to bore you with all the details.' He said irritably, 'But as you're being such a difficult bitch, it looks as though I'll have to.' He settled himself again and began. 'We had correspondence from Ella's solicitors claiming they had evidence that Andy wasn't Lucy's father. We thought it was some sort of stalling tactic, so we called her bluff, but it meant that Andy had to undertake tests so we could disprove their claim in court.' He clasped his hands tightly and looked at the floor. 'Unfortunately, the test results showed he's sterile.' He raised his eyes to look at her. 'So if you're still saying all this is rubbish and still insisting you were pregnant I shall be withdrawing my offer and just kicking you out of here. And in a few days time Andy's solicitor will serve you with divorce papers citing your adultery. The choice is yours!'

She gave a great moan, her hands going to her face. 'It was pig's blood,' she said, her words muffled by her fingers. 'I got it from a butcher my brother-in-law knows.'

'So you did trick my son into marrying you after all!' Bob's eyes were dark and cold as she sat there, wiping her eyes with the back of her hand.

'It wasn't like that!' She protested. 'After you threw me out of here he found me a flat. I lived there for two months. I had no life, no job. He used to come round during the week but we rarely went anywhere, just in case someone spotted us and told you. It was like being in prison! Of course, Andy seemed happy enough; he was having what he wanted, when he wanted it. I had to do something. I felt used.'

'So you decided to use him instead.'

'No I didn't! I did it because I loved him and I wanted to be with him!'

'Oh come on Nina, cut the crap! Be honest, you made a mess of things with Alex, so you thought you'd grab the next available meal ticket. Well I'm afraid it's all over.' He pushed the envelope back towards her. 'Just be thankful I've been so generous.'

'No!' Nina picked up the envelope and threw it angrily across the room. 'I want to see Andy! I'll talk to him, not you! I know he'll listen.'

'He won't be coming back while you're here.'

'What have you done?' She was almost hysterical now, looking up at him with tears pouring down her face. 'Where is he?'

'In hospital, recovering from a little incident at Ella's.'

'What was he doing there?' Nina stood up in alarm. 'Is he badly hurt?'

'Concussion and six stitches in his head.'

'Oh my God!' She began to move towards the door. 'I must go to him.'

'You're not going anywhere.' Bob got up and stepped into her path, blocking her way, 'I've left strict instructions on who visits - you don't. Now, shall we get back to business?'

He retrieved the envelope, opening it up and placing its contents in front of her. 'It's this or nothing.' he said harshly, pulling a pen from his jacket pocket and handing it to her. 'I'll take the house and car keys once you've finished packing.'

She looked up at him, a glimmer of hope suddenly appearing through the tears. 'Of course, you must think I'm stupid. This house is half mine. As Andy's wife, I'm entitled...'

'To half of nothing;' Bob interrupted with just the hint of a smile on his lips. 'Everything is mine. You bought all the house contents on my account; I paid for them. And after the divorce I persuaded Andy to sell the house back to me.' He looked around the room. 'It's a lovely property. A good investment in fact,' his eyes fixed themselves on her again. 'I'm afraid it's just not your day is it?'

She turned from him then, her face tear-streaked and muddied with mascara and with a despairing shake of her head sat herself quietly down on the sofa.

'You've only got yourself to blame for this you know.' He said calmly. 'The irony is, if you'd had just a little more patience he'd have married you with or without my blessing. He told me it had taken him all these years to realise what a fool he'd been and how much you meant to him. But you were greedy, you couldn't wait, you had to lie and cheat your way to that ring on your finger. What Ella's done to him is bad enough, but what you've done is ten times worse. You've totally destroyed him.' He held out the pen and pointed to the bottom of the paper. 'Now, no more arguing please, just sign here, then you can start packing.'

It had been a wonderful meal Rachel thought snuggled into the crook of Niall's arm as they made their way across the car park of the Charlton Cat. Reaching the car, they paused for a moment to stare out at the dark countryside, listening to all its familiar night time sounds. Above them a dark velvet sky was scattered with stars, a round orange moon, courted by a passing thread of cloud, was about to break out from behind the edge of the trees.

'Happy?' He looked down at her with a smile.

'Very.'

'I think I can make you happier.'

'Do you?' Her face creased into a curious smile. 'How?'

'By giving you this.' He reached into his pocket and pulled out a small square green leather box. 'I was looking for an appropriate moment while we were eating, but with all those people around us I just couldn't do it. I wanted it to be romantic,' he looked out across the shadowed fields. 'And now we're here like this, it seems the perfect time and place.'

'Another ring,' she took the box from him with a laugh. 'To go with my pearl.'

'This one's different.' He said, watching as she slowly opened the box. 'It's my Grandmother's engagement ring. And I'm giving it to you here, tonight because I love you and I want to marry you.'

She stared down at the ring, a beautiful square cut solitaire diamond lying in the black velvet interior of the small box. Her hands began to shake. 'I can't touch it,' she said, panic in her voice, 'because if I do I'm sure I'll drop it and we'll never be able to find it here in the dark!'

'Here, let me.' He laughed, gently taking the box from her, removing the ring and slipping it onto the third finger of her left hand. 'Rachel Sylvester,' he said solemnly, 'will you make me the happiest man in the world and become my wife?'

'Oh Niall, I don't know what to say.' She looked confused.

'Yes, maybe?' He looked hopeful

'Oh yes. Yes! Yes! Yes!'

She threw herself to his arms and kissed him. The implications of his proposal exploded in her brain like a firework display. I'm going to be his wife! His wife! And I know I'll have to pick the moment, but when she realises he does really love me Mum will give us her blessing, I know she will.

TWENTY TWO

Wednesday 22nd August

'Are you sure there's nothing I can do to get you to change your mind Ella?'

'No Marcus, there isn't.'

'OK, so you don't care if he knocks twelve bells out of your property, but what about Helen?'

'That's an entirely different matter.'

'Ah so you are bringing charges?' Elbows on his desk, he brought his palms together, a spark of interest in his dark blue eyes.

'Helen is. I said I'd cover her legal costs. He had no right to do that to her.'

'I don't understand. The whole event was inexcusable and grossly anti-social. Why let him off the hook at all?'

'Because I realise I was wrong.' She hung her head. 'I know I said the identity of Lucy's father was none of Andy's business, but I realise how awful it must be, finding out that another man has been responsible for fathering your child. He doted on her.'

'Oh Ella!' He gave a sigh, resting his chin on his fingers. 'Feeling sorry for Andy shouldn't even enter into the equation. You lived with him long enough to know that he and his father have no thought or care for anyone or anything except themselves. They are totally unscrupulous, bend the rules and tread over anyone to get what they want.' He relaxed back into the comfort of his chair, staring at her thoughtfully. 'If you want to give yourself a few good reasons for not feeling bad about what's happened, just cast your mind back to the time you came to see me about the divorce.'

'What are you saying?'

'Well, think about it. For most of the two years you were married to Andy he was hopping in and out of bed with Nina behind your back. He was with her when you were giving birth to Lucy. His failure to show at her christening, with hindsight, convinces me that he was also with her then. He humiliated you. And this custody case was all about depriving you of your child to punish you for standing up to him. In my opinion, Lucy's real father, whoever he is, has got to be a one hundred percent improvement. You should be rejoicing! So,' he banged the desk with the flat of his hand and jumped to his feet, 'time to ditch the guilt trip. Be thankful you've finally got the Macaynes out of your life. You're free! And to kick start this new life of yours, we're going to do things properly this time. Don't even mention the word pub; I'm taking you to the Rotunda for a celebratory lunch.'

They ate at a window table with a view of the river. Ella watched the activity below her; boats passing by, people sunbathing on the far bank, mothers and children wandering leisurely along the bank. It was a warm and relaxing day and suddenly she realised Marcus was right, she should be happy. She really was free of the Macaynes. And as for Matt, well no one except Jenny and Trudi, who had been sworn to secrecy, knew anything about his connection to Lucy and that's the way it was going to stay. As she had told Mary, she was an independent woman both financially and emotionally and that's the way she intended to stay.

'So, what's happened to Nina?' she asked, as the waiter poured out two glasses of chilled Frascati.

'She's gone.' Marcus said as he picked up his glass. 'Bob kicked her out of The Lodge yesterday. Alex tells me Gavin Miller's been asked to sell it. When he gets out of hospital, Andy will be going back to Everdene to live with Bob.' he said, smiling at the surprise on her face as he raised his glass to hers.

'I can't imagine Andy agreeing to something like that.'

'I don't think he has a choice Ella. Bob's the one calling the shots now.'

Mel sat curled up on a couch in the sun lounge smoking a cigarette. It was a lovely warm afternoon and usually on a day like this, alone and left to her own devices, she would have been stretched out on one of the garden loungers, her mind devoid of anything but relaxation and reading the latest copy of *Vogue*. Today, however, as she stared out at the rich green lawn and pretty flower borders, she knew it was impossible to put her thoughts on hold. There were things that needed sorting. Things which would not wait.

For the last few days her emotions had been in turmoil. She felt betrayed by her family, outraged by the loss of her inheritance and filled with despair because the one man who had been central to her life for so long appeared to have turned his back on her. Now, with time on her hands to think, she began to realise that his reaction to the news that the farm had gone to Nick and Ella was no more than she should have expected. After all, since the beginning, hadn't he always been in the background, offering support, giving up his time? The loss of the farm had almost certainly put him in a very difficult position with Miles and Mirage. Something he had faced alone.

'Poor Bob.' She whispered to the garden. *'I should have insisted I went with you. I should have been by your side, facing them, giving you the support you*

deserve. But you wouldn't let me. You were so angry and yet so brave, going it alone like that.'

Now, whatever had taken place in Mirage's board room was over. Bob was a veteran of many such confrontations - tough, strong, able to weather the storm and move on. She was sure by now he would be regretting his outburst at Lancombe Firs; an outburst which she realised was only to be expected, given the catastrophic news she had presented him with.

But if there was one thing she knew it was that Bob wasn't a man to dwell on failure. He'd be moving on, planning the next deal. But what of Bob the man? She thought of him alone in that cold, austere house. Behind that hard, masculine exterior she knew he needed her. He was probably too proud to pick up the phone, she reasoned, which meant she'd just have to go to him.

In the days which had just passed, she had also thought long and hard about her situation with Liam and knew it was time to leave him. Ella had started it all, of course. She had been the cuckoo in the nest, driving a wedge between them, souring what had until her arrival had been a perfectly good marital arrangement.

Although he had always denied it, she suspected that Liam's sympathies lay with Ella. And only a few days ago, these suspicions had become a reality when she was chatting to Sheila Fitzallyn outside Langleys. She discovered that Issy Llewellyn's flat, which was going to be taken over by Sheila's youngest son once the Llewellyn-Taylor wedding had taken place, had in fact been the very one Ella had occupied prior to her marriage to Andy - and that Liam had been paying the rent. To take on such a burden, Sheila said, bearing in mind the fact that Ella wasn't even his daughter and he already had heavy financial responsibility for his father's home care bills, made Liam a husband in a million didn't it?

Behind her polite smile and nodding agreement Mel had seethed with rage. It was the final act of betrayal, one which now made her feel he deserved to be left behind once and for all. Not that he'd care very much about anything she did at the moment, she decided. He had been almost like a passing stranger ever since Ella dropped him back home after the funeral. This tendency to withdraw from her, to lock himself away in his studio was something he usually did when he was angry with her. This time she knew it had been triggered by the events in Meridan Cross. Well too bad. She no longer cared whether he snapped out of it or not. It was time to go, to leave a man she no longer respected, a man whose goodness she found she actually despised.

Stubbing out the cigarette she looked at her watch. Four o'clock. Bob always took Wednesday afternoons off to play golf, which meant he would be home just after five. She smiled and got to her feet. Time to go and pack.

'Well ladies, yet another profitable year. Well done both of you!' Accountant Tony Rutherford closed his brief case with a smile and prepared to leave. The mid afternoon meeting with Ella and Jenny had gone well. This year in particular, despite all Ella's problems, the company was again looking at a very healthy surplus.

He got to his feet and shook hands with both of them.

'I'm guessing,' he paused as Ella opened the door for him, 'that most of your profit will be ploughed back into the business.'

'Better ask the financial genius here.' Ella nodded towards Jenny.

'Yes.' Jenny confirmed. 'That's the general plan. Why? Have you got something in mind?'

Stepping through the doorway, Tony swung around to look at them both. 'Yes,' he said, 'how about using some of it for that farm of yours?'

'How do you know about the farm?' Ella laughed.

'I ran into Nick yesterday. He told me all about your unexpected inheritance.'

'Well, to be honest with you, grandfather was quite comfortably off.' Ella pursed her lips. 'And the farm was one of the best run in the district. He was a very prudent man, a first class manager as well as having an eye for a good animal.'

'In that case,' Tony said thoughtfully, 'what about creating a farming scholarship in his memory? Training ties in quite nicely with recruitment, don't you think?'

'To send someone to Cirencester?' Ella asked, remembering that was where Niall had studied.

'Actually I was thinking of closer to home. Maybe Cannington?'

She paused to consider his words for a moment then looked up at him with a smile. 'Tony, I think it's a wonderful idea! Grandfather would have loved it. And I'm sure Mary and Niall will feel the same when we tell them.'

'Excellent!' Tony's face creased into a broad grin.

'How do we get things moving?' Jenny asked.

Tony considered the question for a moment. 'Well, perhaps you should start by having a word with Marcus; he'll be able to investigate the legal side of things for you. And I know someone who teaches at Cannington. I can make enquiries; find out who you need to talk to there.'

'Thanks Tony,' Ella looked pleased, 'it's an excellent idea. Grandfather was very generous leaving us the farm and this way we'll be giving something back!'

As Mel turned into the winding driveway which led up to Everdene, she thought how austere the great house looked. Creeper clung to every inch of its front; gothic windows peering from the rich green foliage like mournful eyes. Even the front door was heavy and black. This was a man's house, a man in mourning for the long dead Lucia; a woman so special no one he had been involved with since her death had ever been thought of as important; until now. For today, Mel decided, things were about to change

As she reached the front door and rang the bell, her resolve was firm. She would get Bob back by hook or by crook, even if it meant ditching her pride and begging. But it wouldn't come to that, she told herself confidently. They had been together five years, she must mean something to him otherwise it wouldn't have lasted that long. Deep down he loves me, she told herself, but he's just too scared to admit it.

The Ghost of You and Me

Mrs Catt the housekeeper, grey and severe, opened the door, eyeing Mel with obvious dislike as she stated her business and was allowed into the hall. Mr Macayne had not returned from the golf club, she was told politely. He was expected soon and perhaps she would like to wait.

As she was shown into the drawing room, Mel made a mental note that removing Tabby as Bob always called her would be the first of many changes once she came to live here permanently. The house would need to be opened up, filled with colour, warmth and laughter. They would be the perfect couple; the envy of all, hosting dinner parties which would be the talk of the area. She smiled to herself as she gazed around the solemn green of the drawing room, seeing herself as a sort of urban Laura Kendrick, but with far more style and panache. Oh yes, she thought as she sat down and picked up a copy of Country Life, once I'm here I'm going to make everyone in Abbotsbridge sit up and take note.

Across town, Nina Taylor stood at the end of the street where she had grown up and took one last look back. After reluctantly putting her signature to the agreement which forfeited any rights as Andy's wife, she had dried her eyes, packed her clothes and called for a taxi. Handing her house and car keys over had been her last act as she crossed the threshold of Chelwood Lodge, her head held high. As the taxi drove her away she did not look back. Booking herself into the George Hotel, she spent a sleepless night deciding her future. As dawn broke; her decision was made. She was leaving Abbotsbridge for good. Because of this decision she had felt obligated to return home one last time to say goodbye to her mother.

It had been a fractious moment full of moral lectures and smug self-righteousness from a colourless little woman standing in a room which smelt of overcooked greens and cheap washing powder. Their meeting appeared to hold no hint of regret that she might never see her daughter again.

And so at last here she was, about to leave Abbotsbridge behind; for there was no future here any more. Life with Andy was no longer an option, Bob had seen to that. Picking up her case she turned and began making her way to the phone box at the end of the High Street to call for a taxi to take her to the station.

On her way she glimpsed familiar landmarks from her childhood; the Spar Foodliner where her mother did the weekly grocery shopping, trudging home up the hill afterwards laden with heavy carrier bags. Next door there was a small Woolworth. She had worked there as a Saturday girl while still at school. It had been a good laugh, filling shelves or serving on one of the tills. She remembered joining the other girls after work for a drink sometimes, easily able to fool any publican that she was 18.

Farther on she passed the Bunch of Grapes, the smell of alcohol and cigarettes wafting from its open doorway; its peeling façade a dramatic contrast to the bright green affluence of Targett's Turf Accountants next door. These were the two places where the majority of her father's time and money had been spent over the years, in a ritualistic cycle of drinking and betting.

It had been a dream come true leaving all this behind. Bettering herself as her mother had called it. She reflected on the men in her life as she walked. Mick the workaholic. Alex the father figure, making her feel safe and secure, offering her a lifestyle many could only dream of. And on either side and in between them Andy. Like a thread running through a garment. Selfish, disloyal, always playing the game to suit himself. Ironically as time went on she found he was the one she'd truly loved and had really wanted to spend the rest of her life with.

However, in the end she hadn't married him for love. He'd been in the right place at the right time, breaking her fall from Alex. A convenient safety net. A way in which she could keep the lifestyle she'd grown accustomed to. Self preservation had in the end turned her into a user, just like him. And she had not believed a word Bob had said about him really loving her. That had all been said to make her feel worse. In truth, Andy loved no one but himself. And now he was gone. She was on her own again - but not for long, she guessed. The world was full of opportunities and with a very healthy bank account courtesy of Bob and a plane ticket waiting for her at Heathrow, the possibilities, she decided as she reached the phone box, were endless.

Bob climbed out of his XJ6 locked it and walked across the car park towards the hospital entrance. Rain had meant an early finish to his round of golf and on returning to the club house he had found a message waiting for him from the hospital. It had been from Andy, phoning to say he was being discharged that afternoon and would wait for his father to pick him up after his round of golf was over.

Making his way to Wessex Ward, he pushed through the double doors and walked into the Sister's office, a small box like room to the left of the main ward. Sister Brannigan looked up from her desk with a smile.

'Mr Macayne!' Her dark eyes washed over him appreciatively. 'Oh dear, I'm afraid you're too late. He's gone.'

'Gone?' Bob frowned. 'But when I phoned him earlier he said he'd be ready for me to pick him up at four thirty.'

'Yes I know. But he made a telephone call about an hour ago. He seemed rather agitated afterwards. Said he couldn't wait for you. Phoned for a taxi and left.'

'Do you know who he rang?'

'No, Staff Nurse Brooks will though.' She looked through the glass partition down into the ward. 'Ah there she is. I'll just go and get her for you.'

Andy Macayne jumped a set of red lights, accelerating down Bridge Street towards the railway station. He felt tired and irritable; his stitches were beginning to hurt now, making his head throb.

As he lay in his hospital bed that morning his thoughts were tied into Nina and the things she had done. Like lying about her pregnancy and stage managing a convincing miscarriage. He had been so pleased the night she'd announced she was pregnant. Although a baby wasn't what he really wanted, it now meant he could be with her permanently and legitimately. It also made it difficult for his father to disown him without all of Abbotsbridge casting disapproving eyes in his direction. It had brought things to a head, ended the impasse and solved all their problems. A slow smile spread across his face as the penny suddenly dropped and he realised what she had been responsible for masterminding. 'You clever girl.' he said out loud. 'You clever, clever girl!'

'Are you all right Mr Macayne?'

He was aware of Staff Nurse Brooks standing at the foot of his bed, looking at him with a puzzled expression.

'Yes. Yes I am nurse! Thank you.' He smiled at her in his most enchanting way. 'I don't suppose you could get me the phone trolley could you?'

Bill Matthews' secretary put him through straight away.

'Andy.' He caught a hint of edginess in Bill's voice. 'Everything all right?'

'Yes. Bit of a thick head and some stitches but they tell me I'll live. Dad's picking me up later this afternoon. Look Bill, sorry to bother you but I just wanted to know how things went last night. You know, with Nina.'

'Nina. Yes; fine. Just fine!'

There was a pause. A thick silence broken only by Bill's heavy wheeze. Andy knew immediately.

'You didn't see her did you?'

'Andy I'm sorry. I was going to, but you know what he's like...'

'If he's laid a finger on her, so help me, I'll kill him!'

He slammed the phone down and redialled for a taxi, then hastily pulled himself into his clothes, knowing every second counted.

When the taxi eventually reached Chelwood Lodge he was surprised to find two men in overalls nailing a *For Sale* sign to the perimeter wall.

'What's going on?' He asked, leaning out of the taxi window.

'What's it look like? Place is up for sale.' One of the men said, banging in the last of the nails.

'There must be some mistake.' He waved at the man. 'Take it down at once!'

'But we were told...'

'Take it down you idiot!'

He urged the taxi driver on. The car moved through the gates and up the driveway. He noticed that her yellow Spitfire no longer sat beside his Mercedes. Paying the driver he found his keys and let himself in. The place was empty. Wardrobe doors open, her clothes gone. He stood for a moment trying to decide the most logical place to find her then ran downstairs to find his car keys.

Fifteen minutes later Elsie Harrison opened the door to him, her face hard and uncompromising.

'Oh it's you.' She said abruptly. 'What do you want?'

'I'm looking for Nina. Do you know where she is?'

'Putting as much distance between you and her as she can.' Elsie's acid features formed themselves into the semblance of a smile. 'First sensible thing she's done in her life. If you ask me your old man did her a favour throwing her out!'

'Where is she?' He heard himself shout. 'Tell me!'

'Station.' Joan said abruptly, as she shuffled back into the darkness of the house. 'Mentioned something about Bristol.' was all he heard before the door closed in his face.

Now the station was ahead of him. He pulled up outside and leaving the engine running, dashed past the booking office onto the platform, finding it dotted with half a dozen people and a porter half way up a step ladder watering hanging baskets.

Andy ran to where he was and looked up at him hopefully. 'When's the Bristol train due in?'

The man paused, battered watering can in hand. 'You've just missed it mate. Went five minutes ago.'

'Damn!' Andy turned and walked back down the platform. 'Damn! Damn! Damn!' He shouted, aiming an angry kick at a nearby empty fire bucket, ignoring puzzled stares and the yell of protest from the porter as he left it rolling around the platform.

He went back to the car and slouched irritably behind the wheel. Gone; she really was gone. He had no hope of finding her now. Misery seeped through him. How could this have happened? Then Elsie Harrison's words, the ones he hadn't taken in at the time, floated back into his mind. *If you ask me your old man did her a favour throwing her out.* So his father hadn't just scared her as he'd first thought, he'd got rid of her for good. Then something else hit him. The agent's men. The *For Sale* sign. In the twenty four hours he'd been in hospital his father had rampaged through his life, taking it over and wilfully dismantling it piece by piece. With a howl of rage he the rammed car into first gear and left the station car park, almost colliding with a dark blue taxi as he went.

'You bloody idiot!' The middle aged taxi driver swore as he swung the vehicle out of the Mercedes' path. Looking at his passenger in the rear view mirror as they pulled up outside the station, he grinned apologetically. 'Sorry love didn't mean to swear in front of a lady. That'll be one thirty five please.' He turned in his seat to watch her as she pulled out her purse and counted out the money.

'Here.' She handed him a note. 'Keep the change.'

'Thanks.' He smiled. Her wide green eyes and the cascade of pale ginger hair falling around her face reminded him of a girl he'd known in his younger days. 'Right then.' He said, shouldering his door open. 'Let's get that luggage of yours out the boot. Don't want you missing your train do we?'

Driving through the gates of Everdene, Bob saw Andy getting out of his Mercedes. On the drive here he had tried to work out the route Andy might have taken after his conversation with Bill. Chelwood Lodge first he decided, then Elsie Harrison.

The Ghost of You and Me

Hostile and unobliging, she wouldn't have helped him much. He hoped Andy hadn't found her yet. It would make what he had to do so much easier. The anger in his son's bruised face as he pulled up beside him told him nothing. He hadn't a clue what he was walking into, but he was prepared. Andy could be difficult, but he could also be controlled, it wasn't a big issue.

'Andy.' He said stiffly as he got out of the Jaguar, slammed the door and locked it. 'I've been looking for you everywhere. Where the hell have you been?'

'You couldn't leave it could you?' Andy's bruised and stitched face twisted itself painfully as he closed in on his father. 'I told you I wanted Bill to see her. But oh no, you had to interfere!'

The punch came, unexpected and frighteningly fast, connecting with Bob's left cheek, sending him sprawling back against the car. His feet slipped on the gravelled driveway and he felt himself sliding down the smooth body of the Jaguar. As he grabbed the car's door handle to save himself Andy was on him again, punching and kicking, his voice full of abuse and hatred.

'Andy!' He shouted, raising one arm in a desperate attempt to protect himself from the blows as he used all his remaining strength to pull himself to his feet. 'For God's sake! Stop this madness!'

'Mrs Carpenter! Mrs Carpenter!'

Mel opened her eyes to find Mrs Catt standing over her. She hadn't realised she'd fallen asleep and now, horror of horrors there she was faced with this sharp faced old harridan in front of her hopping about like a mad toad.

'What is it?' She said sharply. 'Is Bob home?'

'Yes, yes he is.' The old woman replied breathlessly. 'But they're fighting. Out on the driveway; you must stop them!'

'Bob fighting?' She got to her feet, still bleary from her sleep. 'Who with for heaven's sake?'

'Mr Andrew.' The old woman replied. 'Please, come quickly!'

Andy backed away at last, watching his father, his breathing deep, his eyes dark and full of hatred.

'That's better.' Bob breathed a sigh of relief, pulled himself to his feet and brushed the dust from his check golfing trousers. 'Whatever's got into you? I know why you're upset, but you are really out of order. You should be thanking me for what I've done. She was no better for you than Ella. Worse in fact.'

'No she wasn't.' Andy argued, close to tears. 'All she ever wanted was to be with me. But you drove her away.'

'Andy, listen. She loved your money and what it could buy her. Believe me, I know her type.'

'Of course you do!' Andy said stepping forward pushing his face right up to his father's. 'You're the expert on gold digging tarts aren't you!'

'What are you talking about?'

The Ghost of You and Me

'Mel Carpenter. Been going on for ages hasn't it?'

Bob looked at him warily. 'I don't know what you mean.'

'Don't you? Ella says different.'

'Ella?'

'Yes. She said she saw you all over each other in the maze at Miles' place last year!'

'Rubbish! Mel is Liam's wife. The only contact I have with her is when I see them together socially.' Bob said dismissively. 'Ella's a vindictive bitch; she's just trying to cause trouble.'

'Is everything OK Bob? Mrs Catt seemed to think there was a problem.'

The voice came from nowhere. Bob and Andy both turned to see the subject of their conversation approaching from the house.

Andy gave his father a malicious smile.

'Ah Mel, no everything's fine. What brings you here?' Bob gave a surprised if uncomfortable smile as she reached them both and pulled off her sunglasses.

'I had to come. The other day was so awful. I haven't been able to sleep properly. Bob I'm so sorry...' She said and then stared at Andy's dressing. 'What's he done to his face?'

'Mel what do you want?' Bob looked at her frostily.

'To see you Bob.' She sidled up to him, Andy's wound forgotten and looped her arm in his. 'Perhaps somewhere a little more private?' She gave him a pleasing smile.

Bob gave an uncomfortable laugh as he disentangled himself from her grip. 'Mel, if you want to talk to me privately about anything then really, my *office* is the place.'

'Are you suggesting I make an *appointment*?'

'That's what everyone else does.' Bob shrugged.

'Funny.' Her blue eyes iced over. 'Up until this moment I had the strangest feeling I wasn't everyone else. I had the distinct feeling that we...'

'Mel I'm sorry.' Bob interrupted. 'You've caught us both at a bad time.' He looked at Andy. 'We're in the middle of something really important...'

'I believe you were asking how I got this.' Andy said, touching the gauze pad and smiling charmingly at Mel.

'Andy not now!' Bob snapped. 'Mel, I suggest you leave please!'

'On the contrary Dad, I think Mrs Carpenter has a right to know. After all it was Ella's fault.'

'Ella did that?' Mel stared at them both. 'Surely not!'

'It's nothing Mel! Andy's just making a fuss about nothing! Please go. I'll catch up with you in the week.' Bob waved a dismissive hand at her, angry eyes fixed on his son.

'Nothing!' Andy spat at him. 'Concussion! Six stitches! The humiliation of finding out I'm not the father of my own daughter. And now to add to it all you've waded in like Mr Fixit and driven my wife out of town! How dare you call it nothing!'

The Ghost of You and Me

'Lucy isn't his? What's he talking about Bob?' Mel's hysterical voice now joined Andy's as she too turned to face Bob.

'Well go on!' Andy shouted. 'Tell her! Because if you won't I will!'

Mel let herself into the hall, still reeling from events back at Everdene. It had all gone horribly wrong. There was to be no new life with Bob. No redecorating, hosting parties or indeed ousting Mrs Catt. All her plans and schemes were over; totally destroyed. She closed the front door and leaned against it, her mind reliving the madness she had just escaped from.

While Bob stood there in a daze, Andy seemed to have taken malicious pleasure in detailing the events leading up to the discovery that Lucy was the result of Ella's one night stand with a nameless someone in Meridan Cross. She remembered her hands going to her face in alarm as he told her. This concern, however, had nothing to do with Andy, it centred on the identity of this unknown man. The dark gypsy faces of the Miller boys flashed before her and she'd groaned loudly. This had triggered mad hysterical laughter from Andy that seemed to get louder and louder as it bounced off the walls of the house and its outbuildings. It was then that Bob seemed to come to life, stepping forward to slap him hard across the face. In that instant the laughter turned to loud choking sobs as his arms went around his father's shoulders. His knees buckled and he clung to him, weeping like a small child.

Mel looked at Bob, saw his dark eyes well up with tears as he held his son tightly; heard his first choking sob. In that second, everything changed. The strong man, always in control suddenly looked pathetic and Mel knew; painful though it was, it was time to leave. Tears and emotion had diminished the very thing that had first attracted her - his strength and his power. Showing this weak side of himself had reduced him to the level of all other ordinary men. She no longer felt any respect for him and knew that if she stayed she would end up despising him in the same way she did Liam. With a final glance at them both she turned and walked over to her car, keen to put as much distance between herself and them as quickly as she could.

Now leaning against the door she contemplated her future. Much as she disliked the idea, there was no other option but to throw in her lot with Liam again. To do that, she decided, after the traumatic events at Meridan Cross, she would have to eat humble pie for a while. She pushed herself away from the door and walked towards the stairs. Apologise, that would be the first step. Then cut back on her spending, that too would help. Only one trip a week to the hairdressers instead of three. Limit herself to one item a month in Christiana's. Spend more time at home. Do things together. She stopped half way up the stairs, deciding doing things with Liam held very little appeal, and then consoled herself with the thought that it would only be a short term sacrifice. She'd probably only need to carry on the new regime for a couple of months at the most. Wrapped up in his work the way he was, he'd soon forget and she would be able to return to her old ways as if nothing had happened. And at the end of the day it was a small price to pay for the being able to continue her comfortable life in Conniston Drive.

Her thoughts turned to Ella as she resumed her climb. Although she felt she needed to vent her displeasure on her daughter for such humiliating behaviour, sensibly she knew she should concentrate on her own problems first. As she got to the top of the stairs she was so deep in thought she almost fell over a suitcase and holdall sitting there.

'Liam?' She had no idea he was home. Where was the Range Rover?

He appeared in the bedroom doorway dressed casually in slacks and a polo shirt.

'Mel,' he said calmly, 'I didn't expect you back. I was about to leave a note.'

'Liam what's all this about?' She pointed at the luggage. 'Where are you going?'

'To the States.'

'On business?'

He shook his head. 'I'm going to California to see Dad. I've hired a Winnebago; I'm taking him on holiday.'

'But he's an invalid.' She looked at him as if he was mad.

'They do have holidays too you know.' He said picking the suitcase and holdall and pushing past her impatiently. 'Besides, his doctor says he's strong enough to travel and that a change of scenery will do him good.'

'And how much is all this going to cost?' She called after him as he walked down the stairs. 'Another great drain on our income I suppose!'

'Mel.' He said reaching the hall and turning to look back up at her, hostility in his normally placid face. 'How I spend my money is none of your business!'

'Well how long are you going to be away?'

'I really don't know,' He shrugged. 'Mac Wilson's got the car and he's looking after the business for me in my absence. Could be anything up to three months, depends on Dad really.'

'Three months!' She descended the stairs rapidly. 'You can't leave me for three months!'

'I don't understand. Why the hysterics? You've got Bob now.' He faced her amicably. 'I've seen Marcus Goddard, by the way - about a divorce.' he smiled at her panic stricken face, 'well, no use in hanging around is there?'

'What?'

'It's my own fault really.' He said, pulling on his jacket. 'For years I indulged you, let you tread all over me. I didn't mind because I thought although you were spoiled and selfish, you loved me. Then I began to notice you and Bob together.' He shook his head. 'Of course, I pushed it out of my mind, told myself I was mad even thinking you'd get involved with someone like him. The day of your father's funeral, that was when I realised how naive I'd been. I knew then you weren't only planning things for the farm, you were planning to leave me too, but I still couldn't believe Bob would want that kind of commitment. Still,' he shook his head, 'seems I've been proved wrong. I notice your wardrobes are empty, seems I've timed my departure just right haven't I?'

As Mel opened her mouth to reply a car horn sounded outside.

'Ah that'll be my taxi.' He said, slinging the holdall over his shoulder and picking up his case.

'Liam, don't go. I need to talk to you. It's *important*.'

'What's left to say Mel? You've won, you've got Bob.'

'Liam...' Her voice was a desperate hiss. '*Please......*'

He opened the front door and waved out at the taxi driver before turning back to look at her. 'Mel, it's a bit late to have a conscience and it's very unlike you.' He gave her an indulging smile. 'Don't you worry about me, I'm fine, I really am. The break will do me good and it will give things here a chance to settle down by the time I come back. As I said, I've already seen Marcus Goddard, and of course, I've cancelled the lease on this place. They're collecting the furniture this coming Monday, putting it in storage for me. If there's anything you want, I suggest you take it before then.'

'Liam,' she looked at him uneasily, 'I thought you *owned* this house.'

'Heavens no, I could never have afforded a place like this, not with the outgoings we had.'

'So who *does*?'

'Bob of course.' He looked at her wide eyed with amazement, 'Didn't he ever mention it? Cambridge Crescent was his too.' He paused for a moment, staring at her shocked expression, 'It was an ideal arrangement. Dad's bills took such a big chunk out of my earnings and of course you had very extravagant tastes too.' He gave a cynical smile. 'Still, you'll be OK now. With his money, I'm sure Bob can afford anything your heart desires.'

The taxi's horn sounded again, two loud blasts of impatience.

'Must go.' He said, easing himself through the partially open door.

Mel stood watching the driver take his case, stow it into the boot and then join him in the front of the car. She knew she should be running out to stop the taxi, banging on the passenger window, begging Liam to come back, telling him what a mess her life was in. That she had no money and nowhere to live. But what was the point? The man looking at her from the taxi wasn't Liam any more. He was a man looking ahead. A strong man thinking only of himself. Turning back inside, she closed the door behind her and sinking onto the hall carpet, she began to weep.

TWENTY THREE

Friday 24th August

Standing at his bedroom window, Andy watched his father's gardener, Bert Jessop manoeuvring the ride on lawnmower with familiar precision, cutting regular swathes up and down the length of the long stretch of lawn at the rear of the house.

It seemed impossible that he had been in this room for two whole days. The last forty eight hours had pushed him through the full spectrum of emotions; from violent anger to exhausted indifference; the latter brought about largely by the medication Dr Savage had prescribed. He still felt resentful about all that had happened, but in a weak, powerless sort of way that rumbled around in his brain like the constant threat of a thunder storm. He tried to shake it off, to find some vigorous burst of energy to enable him to break out of this apathy and return him to normality. But the means eluded him and so once again he lingered by the window, watching others go about their daily business, unable to be anything but a spectator.

He reached up and felt the rough growth of stubble on his chin, thinking how well it complimented his crumpled pyjamas. He had always been so particular about his appearance, but suddenly it was the last thing that seemed to matter any more. Who was going to see him? He wasn't going anywhere. He was going to spend the rest of his life in this room, taking medication and sleeping.

There had been one moment, waking up with a violent start in the middle of the night when he had thought of ending it all. But pills frightened him and thoughts of dragging a razor blade across his wrists made him shudder. He had to admit he was a coward. Or was he brave? He didn't really know and he cared even less.

Bert had stopped the mower now and was wiping the sweat from his forehead with a large handkerchief pulled from his trouser pocket. As he pushed it back into his baggy brown corduroys he checked his watch and looked towards the house.

Andy knew exactly what that meant. He gazed at the radio alarm; it was quarter to eleven and Bert was keeping a watchful eye for Tabby at the kitchen window, calling him in for his morning coffee and biscuits. Andy's stomach rumbled.

He was normally left undisturbed to sleep through the morning, wandering into the kitchen around twelve thirty for a late breakfast. But today his stomach was telling him he needed something now and that meant he'd have to go down and submit himself to Bert's beady-eyed gaze. He moved away from the window. He'd need a wash and a quick shave first though, or details of his dishevelled state would be all over Abbotsbridge.

At exactly eleven o'clock Bert Jessop wiped his boots and walked into the kitchen. Seeing him, Dora Catt took the saucepan from the Aga and while he pulled up a chair to the large white Formica topped table, slowly poured milk into the two cups set out on the worktop.

'Here we are,' she said with a smile which looked out of place on her severe features, 'your usual, just as you like it.'

'Thanks Dora,' Bert screwed up his old brown face into a crinkled grin as the milky coffee was placed in front of him and the sugar bowl eased towards him. He spooned three sugars into his cup and stirred energetically, watching silently as she returned to the table with her own cup and a plate of chocolate biscuits, settling herself opposite him.

'That lawn's looking a treat,' Bert said, looking up after a mouthful of coffee, a thin crescent of froth covering his top lip, 'that special liquid feed I got Mister Macayne to buy was just the thing.'

Dora nodded. Gardening was lost on her. Although aware of the smell of newly mown grass through her kitchen window, the bright colour of the flower beds and the plentiful supply of vegetables left in her kitchen, her world was an indoor one. It revolved around cooking wholesome meals and applying beeswax to furniture and polishing it until she could see her face in it.

'So how's the young 'un?' Bert asked, reaching for a biscuit.

'No change.' Dora shook her head despondently. 'It's like all the stuffing's been knocked out of him. It's a bad business this and no two ways about it. Of course, I'll never understand why he left that first wife of his for that Nina. Ella was a lovely girl, a real lady. Nina wasn't a patch on her! Too flashy and common for my liking!' She heaved her shoulders in disapproval. 'Mr Macayne didn't like her either,' she dropped her voice to a whisper, 'thought she was a bit of a gold digger.'

Picking a biscuit up from the plate she took a bite from it and chewed thoughtfully.

'Of course,' She continued quietly, collecting up escaping crumbs from the table with the tip of her finger, 'I suppose I shouldn't be that surprised at the sort of things Master Andy was up to behind his wife's back.' She looked at Bert, 'After all, it's only history repeating itself.'

'Oh?' Bert closed one eye and tilted his head curiously, sensing something interesting was about to be divulged. He already knew about all the trouble behind Andy's arrival here. Now he was about to hear something about Bob.

Bob intrigued Bert; a man who it was said was totally heartless and ruthless when it came to business, but who kept a shrine in his house to his dead wife and refused to remarry. In the ten years he had been working here, Dora had always been discreet when talking about the Macaynes. But Bert knew events of the past few days had changed all that. Taking responsibility for Andy after his mother's death, she had become a surrogate mother to the boy. To see him returning to his home in such a state was more than she could bear. He knew she blamed Bob Macayne for all of this and that her anger was slowly eroding her loyalty to her employer and loosening her tongue.

'All that upstairs,' she sat back with an expression of distaste. 'That shrine! It's nothing but a shallow sham!'

'But I thought...devoted didn't they say?' Bert began, aware of the rumours he had heard about Bob's dedication to his wife both in life and death.

'Well you heard wrong Bert Jessop!' She picked up her coffee cup. 'Do you want to know the truth? Well I'll tell you!'

Andy looked in the mirror and ran his hand down his face. He felt much better now the stubble had gone. The wash had been a quick one, the continual rumbling in his stomach turning it into what he remembered Tabby calling a 'lick and a promise'. Quickly he pulled on jeans and a blue shirt, leaving the room, doing up the buttons as he went.

He ran down the stairs and into the hall. The kitchen, at the back of the house, was approached through a narrow corridor off the dining room. As he reached it, he heard the voices of Tabby and Bert. Hers was raised, insistent. Discussing the state of the kitchen garden, no doubt, telling him what vegetables she expected to be ready for the coming weekend. His father was lucky having someone like her. Dragon she might be, but she ran the house with frightening efficiency.

He was in the passage now and could hear the voices much clearer. He realised they weren't discussing the garden at all and stopped to listen.

'Wasn't long before he took a mistress,' He heard Tabby say. 'His secretary. Chloe Marshall her name was. Set her up in a flat on the Westbrook side of town. On the day he should have been with Lucia showing her over the house he planned to renovate, he was with her instead. He forgot the time apparently. When he got to the house...' Her voice trailed off. 'Well, the damage was done! Poor Lucia was lying at the bottom of the stairs with a broken neck!'

There was a pause. Andy moved forward slightly and was now able to see the two figures sitting at the table. Bert was handing a red faced Tabby his handkerchief.

'I'm sorry,' she sniffed, blowing her nose loudly, 'I loved Mrs Macayne. She was delightful; full of life. Italian you know,' she smiled through her tears, 'with so much to learn here in a strange country. So in love, so trusting!' She took the handkerchief away from her nose, her face red and angry. 'All he really wanted was her money. To get the bloody family business going again after the war! My

God there were times afterwards if I'd had a knife in my hand I'd have surely stuck it in him for what he did to that poor innocent girl!'

'But if you hated him so much Dora,' Bert frowned, 'why did you stay?'

'I had to, for Master Andrew. He needed someone - poor little mite. And now look what's become of him!' The handkerchief flew to her face again and she began to sob.

In the passageway Andy leaned against the wall, his hand pressed against the stitches in his forehead. After Dora's revelations he thought for a moment, remembering the conversation he'd had with Ella on Zeffirelli's opening night. So she hadn't lied after all. But his father had. Time and time again. Declaring himself celibate; a one woman man. Quick to rubbish the accusations of being involved with Mel Carpenter; holding up the purity of his own marriage as an example time and time again during his endless moral lectures.

Anger and hate curdled up inside him. He closed his eyes then opened them again, realising that with this new knowledge, the bonds that had tied him here, the heavy shackles of his father's influence were now well and truly broken. He was free at last. He pushed himself away from the wall and turned back towards the hall. As he reached the stairs he looked around at the subdued decor, the dark wallpaper, the solid furniture and decided that if he didn't have a reason to leave before, he certainly did now. But before he went, there was one final thing he had to do.

Bob Macayne was returning from lunch with Miles Anderson and the members of the Mirage Board to celebrate the signing of the contracts for the new holiday village on the outskirts of Dunster. The deal was now done. The contract for the project build signed and in his briefcase. Eager to be away, he left just as the coffee arrived. He had more important things on his mind. Like Andy and his future.

He thought of him as the Jaguar sped up the A396 towards Tiverton. The best thing was a completely new start, away from Abbotsbridge. And right now, sending him back to Tarvaggio seemed to be the most sensible option. He got on well with his uncle and his cousins, and spoke fluent Italian. It was warm and sunny there with no reminders of the past and he was sure Lorenzo could make good use of him in one of his companies. All the right ingredients to get him back on his feet again. And who knows, while he was out there he might even meet someone who would make him forget the past. A nice Italian girl from a respectable family.

Dreaming of wedding bells and happy ever after, Bob turned the Jaguar through the gates of Everdene and pulled up outside the house. As he opened the front door and walked into the hall, he found himself confronted by a frantic Mrs Catt.

'Mr Macayne I'm so glad you're back!' She rushed up to him. 'Something dreadful's happened!'

'What now Dora?' Bob looked at her wondering what domestic trauma had occurred.

'It's Mr Andrew!' She blurted out. 'He's gone!'

'Gone!' Bob grabbed her bony shoulder. 'Gone where for heaven's sake?'

'I don't know!' Her bottom lip wobbled fearfully. 'I was having morning coffee with Bert and suddenly we heard this banging and crashing. I thought it was the dustman.' She flapped an agitated hand at him. 'Anyway, I didn't think any more about it but then after a bit the front door slammed and a car started up. I came rushing out as quickly as I could in time to see Master Andrew's car disappearing down the driveway.'

'You were supposed to be looking after him, woman!'

Mrs Catt trembled as he stood over her, his face white with rage.

'There's more Mr Macayne.' She said meekly. 'I think you'd better come with me.'

Bob released his grip on her shoulder and followed her up the stairs. She led him along the landing, stopping outside Lucia's room. Quietly she opened the door and stepped back. Inside was a scene of total devastation. Curtains were torn down, glass smashed. The wardrobes had been turned out and ripped clothing littered the floor and the bed.

'My God!' Bob sat down heavily on the bed, his face pale. He looked up at Mrs Catt standing there nervously biting her lip. 'He'll have some explaining to do when he gets back!'

'I don't think he's coming back.' Dora Catt whispered hoarsely. 'I've been to his room. His cases and all the clothes you had sent from the Lodge are gone. The wardrobes are empty.

'What?'

He reached Andy's room in seconds. Pulled open doors and drawers. Saw the hangers dangling in the dark, empty interior of the wardrobes.

'Why?' He beat his fists against one of the wardrobe doors. 'Why?'

As he stood there pressing his face to the dark mahogany he knew Tabby was right. Andy wouldn't be back. And finding him wasn't even an option. He could be anywhere. He turned suddenly and caught his reflection in the dressing table mirror. What he saw frightened him. An aging man, grey faced and alone. A man with everything and yet with nothing. Slumping down heavily on the bed, Bob put his hands to his head and with a great heave of his shoulders, began to cry.

'Ladies and Gentlemen, please fasten your safety belts and extinguish all cigarettes, Iberia flight 902 for Alicante is about to depart.'

Nina, occupying a window seat, was busy watching the activity outside on the tarmac. At the sound of the stewardess's voice she automatically turned her attention back to the inside of the cabin, her hands immediately reaching for the two ends of her seat belt. As she reached down between the seats and grabbed the one end of the right hand strap, she suddenly found someone else had the other end. Realising she was holding onto the wrong belt, she let go.

'Sorry,' she smiled, 'thought that was mine.'

Her hand went down again, searching between the seats.

'Here.' A deeply tanned hand with well manicured nails handed her a length of grey belt. 'I think this must be yours.'

'Thank you.' She gave her fellow passenger a warm smile, her hand lingering deliberately over his as she took the belt from him.

She had been so busy looking out of the window that she hadn't noticed his arrival. But now she noticed everything about him. From his deep educated English voice to his pale well cut linen suit. And then there was the face. Wide dark brows over blue eyes, a small crescent shaped scar running across his left cheek bone giving him a hint of danger. The mouth was full, the hair thick and dark, resting on his shoulders. Thirty five she decided and drop dead gorgeous.

He smiled back, fixing his eyes on hers, then on her breasts which peeped tantalisingly through the vee in her white T-shirt.

'Rob Buchanan.' He extended a hand in greeting.

'Nina Macayne.' She smiled, placing her hand in his, enjoying the warmth and strength of his grip.

'Ooh!' She gasped as with a jolt the plane left its bay and began to taxi towards the runway.

'Are you OK?' She felt his concerned gaze on her.

'Not really. I hate flying. I get really scared, especially at takeoff.'

Her eyes were locked on his now; she widened them slightly and moistened her lips.

'Then I guess you'd better keep hold of my hand.' He smiled, tightening his grip slightly, 'There, is that better?'

'Much. Thank you.'

'So, what's taking you to Alicante?' He asked, taking his eyes off her for a moment to watch the stewardess as she approached on her routine check on passengers' seat belts. 'Business or pleasure?'

'Adventure. I wanted a completely fresh start somewhere warm, so I stuck a pin in the map and here I am! What about you?'

'Oh business. I'm a night club owner.'

'Really?'

'Yeah, you know, dinner, dancing, cabaret, that sort of thing. I've a chain of the things along the Costa Blanca. They're called *La Diversión*. It means fun in Spanish. That's what I want people to have. A good time.'

'I'm all for that.' She smiled as the plane swung around and settled itself at the end of the runway, ready for takeoff.

'If you're planning to stay in the area for a while and need a job, I might be able to help.'

The whine of the engines changed pitch, then with a sudden judder they were on their way with the world outside rushing past the window until the front of the cabin lifted and the plane rose effortlessly into the air.

'Thank you,' Nina smiled as he released her hand, 'that's very generous, but I don't need a job. I'm what they call a woman of independent means.'

'Well in that case Nina Macayne,' He smiled. 'Perhaps dinner would be more appropriate.'

'Yes.' She pitched him one of her most provocative smiles. 'Perhaps it would.'

Thursday 30th August

'Ready?'

'You bet!' Marcie's face lit up as she held tightly onto Matt's hand.

They were waiting in the wings at *The Talk of the Town,* the last venue on Marcie's eight week tour. She was clad from head to foot in glittering red lurex. Loretta Gibson her dresser had just given her hair a final dust of silver sparkle before disappearing back to the dressing room to get ready for the next costume change.

On stage, a North Country comedian who was compère for the evening was warming up the audience with slick one liners just as he had done on the previous two nights.

'I keep pinching myself.' She grinned at him. 'I can't believe Doug's news.'

'Well it's true, you're heading for Hollywood.'

'Fantastic!' She wrinkled her nose. 'Who'd have believed it? Me - a movie star!'

Doug's call had come earlier that evening with news that Marcie had been invited to fly out to Los Angeles for a screen test and discussions about playing the role of Eugené Jackson in a musical about the life of the famous forties jazz singer.'

'And you'll be coming too, of course.' She smiled confidently. 'After all, a musical needs a writer.'

'Unfortunately for me it already has one. Her son, Lennox. He's a composer and an accomplished jazz pianist. Very good I'm told.'

'Well come anyway! We'll have a fantastic time in L.A.' Her eyes lit up. 'We can go shopping on Rodeo Drive! Visit Beverley Hills!'

'Yeah, I think I'd like that.' He smiled. 'And, it'll be great to put my feet up for a while. Let someone else do all the worrying about temperamental musicians and getting the arrangement right.'

'You can still write if you want to.' she gave him an enthusiastic smile. 'After all, Doug's talking Europe once this project is finished. So I'll need a new album to launch the tour.'

'You're a hard taskmaster Marcie Maguire.' He reached out to draw a finger softly down her cheek.

She caught his wrist and held his hand against her face. 'And you Matt Benedict,' she said gently, 'are an amazing man. My friend, my mentor and my good luck charm. Without you I wouldn't be where I am today, but..' she shook her head.

'What Marcie?'

'I'm beginning to think going back to Abbotsbridge isn't such a good idea after all. There are too many memories, all the old faces, the possibility you might meet up with Ella again. I'm just scared that something will go wrong for us.'

'I have to go, I promised my father I'd drop in and I can't let my mother down. Please don't worry, nothing is going to go wrong for us. The past is just that Marcie - the past - and that includes Ella. I know now there's nothing in the UK to keep me.' he squeezed her hand. 'My future is in the States, with you.'

Seeing the comedian standing bowing to the audience, his session at an end, Matt turned his attention back to the performance 'Right! Come on, it's show time! Let's give them something to remember shall we?'

Marcie nodded, took a deep breath and closed her eyes, committing the evening's running order to memory for the last time. She walked out into the spotlight, arms extended in greeting towards the black void where the audience sat.

'Hello London!' She called and they responded with whistles and cheers. She pulled the mike from its stand and swung around to look at the band, tapping her feet to the rhythm as the first bars of *'Together Forever.'* kicked in. Matt's words swam in her head, making her smile. So, it appeared the ghost of Ella had been finally laid to rest and the torch he had spent so long carrying for her had been well and truly extinguished. She held no significance for him any more; she was a thing of the past - a memory. That meant there was nothing to stand in her way; he was free at last and she was going to do everything in her power to make sure the next person he fell in love was her. Looking towards the wings where Matt stood watching her, she blew him a kiss, raised the mike and began to sing.

Friday 31st August

'Rachel, what's the matter? You've hardly said a word all morning.'

Ella, resting her back against the low crumbling dry stone wall on the edge of the barley field, looked at her friend, sitting next to her, silently eating her sandwich.

They had ridden out this morning as they had for the last two days, to deliver the usual lunch of sandwiches, flasks of hot tea and bottles of lemon barley water to Niall and the others who were helping out with the harvest.

The weather had been hot all week. But the fresh clear blue of Monday, had by today, Friday, turned into a sticky, humid, airless day. During their ride Ella had pointed out the shimmer of heat haze which hung in the distance, distorting the landscape and muting the colours of the surrounding countryside. But now her attention turned to the strangely silent Rachel.

'Well? Are you going to tell me or not?'

'It's Mum.' Rachel made a face. We've had words again, about Niall.'

'You've actually told her he wants to marry you?'

She nodded. Ever since Niall's proposal ten days ago, she had been trying to find the appropriate time to talk to her mother about it. But Margaret always seemed to be in a crabby mood; the motor went on the ice cream freezer, melting all the stock and leaving a large pool of water over the shop floor. The washing line broke, throwing the week's wash onto the garden. There always seemed to be something happening to upset her mother and put her in a bad mood. But this morning had been different; she was off to Taunton to spend the day with her sister Ethel. Rachel heard her singing as she washed up the breakfast things. This was the moment, she decided. Sadly it wasn't. Her mother's response had been particularly vicious.

'Oh Ella, she just exploded. And before she left for Taunton she gave me an ultimatum. Niall, or her. I had to choose. And if I choose him she wants me out straight away and she's changing her will and leaving everything to Aunt Ethel.'

'Well, I know what my choice would be if I was in your shoes.' Ella said, watching Niall standing among the men drinking tea. 'Rach you can't let her do this. He loves you and you've waited all this time for him. You can't lose your chance for happiness now. Is having the shop such a big deal?'

Rachel looked at Niall, then back at Ella.

'Not really.' Her mouth set tightly. 'It's the principle. Aunt Ethel's never done Mum any favours. The old dragon's sitting on a fortune and yet when the shop went through a bad patch a few years back and Mum asked her for a small loan to help out, she refused. If the SPAR franchise hadn't come along I don't know where we'd have been. Why should mean old Ethel benefit from anything?'

'You know, I don't believe your mother has any intention of carrying out these threats,' Ella said thoughtfully, 'she's trying it on. Scared of being left on her own, and if you give in, she'll always have you where she wants you, you'll never have a life of your own.'

'So what do I do?'

'Call her bluff! Tell her you're going to marry Niall.'

'Oh dear.' Rachel gave a huge sigh.

'Rachel!'

'What?'

'Are you seriously expecting me to believe you're prepared to give *him* up for your mother?'

Rachel followed the direction of Ella's gaze. Niall was pulling off his shirt. He saw them watching and waved out.

Rachel gazed longingly at his broad shoulders and smooth bare chest before turning back to Ella.

'Of course not.' She shook her head. 'Would you?'

'No! So, you know what you have to do.'

The Ghost of You and Me

The men were finishing off their lunch now and moving back to their vehicles. This year, as always, Willowbrook's harvest was being brought in with the assistance of Eddie, Sam and Colin Robinson, two brothers and a cousin from the village who always booked holiday at this time just so they could help. Thick set Eddie Robinson climbed back into the cab of one of the combines and started the engine while his smaller wiry cousin Sam hauled himself behind the wheel of the accompanying tractor and silo. With a splutter of black smoke from its exhaust the combine resumed its journey, the tractor keeping pace, golden grain cascading into the metal depths of the silo it was pulling.

Niall and Colin Robinson, about to start up the other combine and tractor, had been intercepted by Doggie Barker who had just emerged from nearby Hundred Acre Wood with Toby. Doggie was gesturing with his right hand, pointing out towards the west. The two men walked across to the edge of the field with him and stared into the distance, shielding their eyes with their hands.

'What's that all about?' Ella frowned, watching them curiously.

'Let's go and find out, shall we?' Rachel said pushing the last morsel of sandwich into her mouth and getting to her feet.

The girls quickly picked their way across the stubble and joined the small group of men on the far side of the field.

'What is it Doggie?' Ella said, stopping beside the old man and peering in the direction they had been looking.

'See that sky. A big bugger's brewing.' He said, pointing.

Out towards the west, through the heat haze, the sky had turned a strange pinkish yellow, the sun's rays breaking out from behind the edge of clouds turned paper thin and translucent. Below this, a sliver of deep inky grey was beginning to rise up from the horizon. Ella was aware of a distant rumble, like the growl of a hungry stomach.

'Thunder?' Rachel frowned.

Niall nodded. 'How long have we got Doggie?'

The old man bent over and picked up a handful of chaff, throwing it into the air, noting the direction and force of the breeze. 'Dunno, it'll dance about in the Brendon Hills for a while afore it gets going. I guess maybe two hours at the most.' He said looking at Niall, his lips pursed.

Niall gazed at what was left of the barley. 'It's going to be tight but we might just do it.' he said then turned back to Ella and Rachel. 'Get back to Willowbrook and tell Jake to keep the herd in the parlour after milking. And make sure all the other livestock are taken inside. That includes the horses.'

'Why all this fuss?' Ella looked first at Doggie then at Niall. 'It's only a late summer storm.'

'No it's not Ella, this is different.' Rachel looked at Doggie, who realising she understood, nodded vigorously. 'What's out there is quite scary. Believe me, I know, I sheltered from a very mild one in Hundred Acre a few years ago and that was bad enough.'

'What exactly causes it Doggie?' Ella frowned.

'A freak o' the weather.' The old man said, eyes like saucers, as another muted rumble of thunder sounded in the distance. 'When three weather fronts bump into each other. The 'oly Trinity - Cold, Warm and Occluded. Bad tempered buggers they be when they get together. Of course when they come our way we usually get the edge of 'em, but I'm afraid on this occasion,' he looked solemnly at the horizon, 'it looks like it's 'eading straight for us.'

The storm arrived within minutes of Doggie's prediction. It came through the valley - first the wind, like a giant hand moving through Hundred Acre, violently shaking the trees, uprooting dead wood and loosening leaves. Thunder shook the skies above the village and sheet and forked lightning lit up the whole area, one bolt striking the conductor on the church tower. And afterwards the rain: constant and driving, drumming on roofs like massive fists. It filled the river, changing its colour to muddy brown, bringing down all sorts of debris and turning its normal steady meander into a fast flowing torrent.

At its height the wind ripped part of the corrugated roof from the Dutch barn at Willowbrook, scattering it with contemptuous ease across the paddock behind the farm and frightening the horses in their nearby stables. It whipped around the houses in the village causing mayhem; pulling television aerials from chimneys, tiles from roofs and scattering dustbin lids and flowerpots down the road like some invisible demon. Willowbrook became the place of sanctuary for those whose hard work had managed to bring in the entire contents of the barley field. Hot tea and homemade cake were handed around by Mary as everyone huddled in the front parlour listening to the wind rattling at the doors and rain lashing against the windows.

Power was lost at four, leaving the village a gloomy and desolate place with its wet roofs and darkened streets. Then, just as everyone was beginning to believe it would never end, the storm departed, rolling on down the valley towards Morden, leaving bewildered villagers to step out into an eerie wet silence to inspect the damage and begin clearing up.

Nelson Miller was feeling very pleased with himself. Today's auction had gone very well indeed. Not only had he got rid of a baler that had been cluttering up the place for far too long but he had also purchased what he considered to be one of the most important lots there, a second hand JCB.

He had been toying with the idea of getting one for some time, an absolute must he'd realised after seeing the Water Board use one to put a new main through the village. Always on the lookout for a fresh business opportunity, he could already think of a number of farmers who would be eager to make use of it for ditch digging.

And so he had left the Taunton auction at four thirty, Rowan up ahead driving the JCB while he followed behind in the Land Rover. Progress was slow as the

JCB wasn't capable of great speed and they constantly had to stop to let traffic by them. By the time they reached Wellington it had started to rain, light drops on the windscreen which eventually turned heavy and persistent keeping the Land Rover's wipers busy. Thunder and lightning followed, the sky black and angry, while a vicious wind thrashed the trees and hedgerows around them. Soon the surface of the roads became awash with a constant veneer of running water, making driving difficult. And so, finding a lay-by they had stopped, Rowan joining him in the Land Rover with a bag of corned beef rolls and a large bottle of cider. They sat eating and drinking and listening to the radio, but after an hour's wait, the sky still remained black, the rain continued to pour and the wind to rage.

'Looks like this is the tail end of one of Doggie's *Big Buggers*.' Nelson said with a loud belch before they both settled down for a cat-nap. An hour later they woke up to find although the rain was still present, the storm had all but gone. Out to the west, the sky was a little clearer and a pale sun could be seen setting slowly through a watery haze of pink and orange. Feeling it was now safe to travel, they left the lay-by, eager to get home.

And now they were nearly there, Nelson's thoughts had returned once more to his new possession and the money it could make him. He smiled as they topped Sedgewick Hill and he saw the familiar sight of the village lying in the bottom of the valley; the river brown and swollen, had burst its banks and was seeping into neighbouring fields. Not long now, just follow the road as it dropped down through Hundred Acre, he thought to himself, then turn off to the left at the bottom and head east for half a mile. The familiar sight of Saddlers End and a welcoming drink later on at the Arms drove Nelson on. He ran his tongue over his lips, almost able to taste the bitter froth from the head of a glass of Guinness. Sweet nectar, he thought and just the right accompaniment to a bit of business. For Friday night brought many of the local farmers to the pub. A captive audience for his new toy.

Ahead, Rowan in the JCB was the first to enter the dark tunnel of the wood. His progress was slow as the road was strewn with small branches which popped and cracked under its huge back tyres. Then as the road slewed to the left Nelson saw the brake lights come on and the JCB stop suddenly. He came to a halt behind it and seeing Rowan jump down from the cab, wound down in his window.

'What's up?' He called out.

'There's a tree down, right on the corner. I think we can get by but I'm just going to take a closer look.'

Nelson rubbed his stubbly chin thoughtfully as Rowan disappeared round the front of the JCB. Moments later he came into view, running back up the hill towards him.

'How bad is it?' Nelson leaned out of the Land Rover.

'We can't get through.' Rowan shook his head. 'It's right across the road. I'm going to try to push it to one side,' he said climbing back into the cab.

Nelson fetched an axe from the back of the Land Rover and followed the JCB down the hill. He could see the tree now, a large horse chestnut which had fallen diagonally across the road in a splintering heap of wood and leaves. But there was something else, something Rowan hadn't seen, hiding under the canopy of bright leafed branches. He stopped to rub his eyes, thinking the cider was making him hallucinate.

'Rowan!' He shouted and waved up at the JCB, then pointed at the tree. 'Car!'

'What?' Rowan shouted above the noise of the engine.

'There's a car.' Nelson pointed frantically towards the branches.

Rowan stopped, killed the engine and jumped down onto the road. Together they ran to the tree, pushing branches back, revealing the back end of an old green Morris Minor Estate.

'Hey up son!' Nelson looked at his son in amazement, 'I know this car. It's Margaret Sylvester's!' He pushed under the branches, feeling his way towards the driver's door. 'Margaret!' He shouted, 'Margaret, can you hear me?'

TWENTY FOUR

Saturday 1st September

Faye Benedict, responding to a knock at the front door, found a small dark haired figure on her doorstep clutching a large bunch of bronze chrysanthemums.

'Jenny! Well this is a surprise!'

'I thought I'd just call round to see how you were and give you these.' Jenny said handing them to her with a smile.

'They're beautiful, thank you.' Taking the flowers Faye looked beyond Jenny to where her car was parked. 'Have you got to rush off or can you squeeze in a quick chat and a coffee?'

'The children are with Helen this morning, I'm all yours.'

'Great. Come on through.'

'How are you feeling now?' Jenny asked, following Faye through to the large farmhouse kitchen at the rear of the house.

'Oh, fit as a flea. Went back to work last week,' Faye replied. 'Can't believe it happened to me actually. Bit like a bad dream. Have a seat,' she nodded towards the table, 'I'll just put these in water.'

Jenny pulled out a chair and settled herself at the large wooden table in the centre of the room, watching as Faye unwrapped the flowers and found a large crystal glass vase to place them in. Filling it with water she arranged them carefully then disappeared, saying they would be just right for the drawing room. Returning moments later she began setting up the percolator.

'Where's Tad this morning?' Jenny asked.

'He's gone to Taunton . Matt and Marcie are coming down from London, he's meeting them off the train.' Faye said over her shoulder as she measured out the coffee. 'Matt promised they'd call back to see me before they returned to the States.' She looked up at the kitchen clock. 'They should be here soon.'

'So the tour went well?'

'Very. They're talking about Europe later next year. And guess what? When she gets back, Marcie's flying out to Hollywood. They want her to do a musical. It's about a famous black jazz singer called Eugené Jackson.'

'Yes, I've heard of her. I think Dad's got a couple of her albums. That's great news Faye, looks as though Matt's going to be busy.'

'Not this time.' Faye drew up a chair next to Jenny. 'Eugené Jackson's son is a talented song writer and he's developed the musical score for the film. I'm not sure what Matt proposes to do.' She turned with a hopeful smile. 'Of course, you know I want more than anything for him to come home. But,' she gave a helpless shrug, 'who knows what will happen. And how are things with you? Tad mentioned there had been a bereavement in your family.'

'Yes, Nick's grandfather.'

'Was he very old?'

'In his late sixties. He had a weak heart.'

'Still a shock though, I expect.'

'Yes, we were all in Meridan Cross for the christening at the time. He went off to check his cows, and that was the last we saw of him.'

'Poor Ella and Nick, he was like a father to them wasn't he?'

Jenny nodded. 'I think its hit Ella the hardest. She was closer to him. And coming on top of everything else this year, well...' she shook her head.

'You're talking about the custody battle I take it? Bit of Macayne spite that, if you ask me! Has it been resolved yet?'

'Yes, thankfully,' Jenny nodded. 'Lucy's staying with Ella.'

'Good I'm so pleased. And how are your little ones coming along?'

'Thriving,' Jenny smiled. 'Christopher's two and a half and real handful. And as for Charlotte well she's such a good baby. That reminds me,' she reached for her bag, 'I collected Mum's photos today. There are some of the christening. Would you like to see them? I'm sure she wouldn't mind you having first peek.'

The percolator bubbled. Faye got up and poured two cups of coffee before putting on her glasses and settling down again to go through the wedge of photographs which Jenny had produced.

'Not exactly David Bailey, your Mum.' Faye said, amused as she held up one out of focus shot.

'No, she's so enthusiastic once she's got a camera in her hand that sometimes she forgets distance and light have any bearing on what she's doing.' Jenny laughed.

'This is a better one.' Faye held up another photo. 'What a beautiful house.

'That's Little Court. Nick and Ella's grandmother has devoted her life to it. I think she should open it to the public. It's an amazing place. Here,' Jenny handed her a batch of photos. 'I took these of the gardens.'

'Oh Jenny!' Faye's eyes shone as she looked at them one by one. 'The colours, and such beautiful fountains!'

'And here's a group photo.' Jenny leaned closer to Faye. 'That's Ella and Nick's grandmother Laura - the one who owns Little Court. And that's their grandfather, the one who died, with his wife Mary.'

'I've got some of the children here too.' Jenny said, opening another pack and sifting through them, 'Here.'

As Faye took another cluster of photographs from her, door chimes sounded in the hall.

'Ah they're here.' She said taking off her glasses and putting the prints down, 'I'll come back to these in a minute.'

'Looks like you have a visitor.' Matt said as Tad's BMW drew up alongside a red Escort parked to one side of the main driveway.

'Oh that's Jenny,' Tad said turning off the ignition, 'I saw her in town in the week; she said she was going to drop in to see Faye.'

Within seconds of Marcie ringing the bell, the door flew open and Faye was there, a delighted expression on her face as she looked at both of them.

'Marcie, welcome back,' she said, kissing her cheek, 'and Matt. It's so good to have you home!' She embraced her son tightly.

'It's good to see you too Mum,' Matt hugged her back, 'You gave us all a bit of a fright.'

'Not as much as I frightened myself.' She said, breaking away with a delighted smile. 'Come on through. Jenny's here. I'll make some more coffee.'

While Tad took their suitcases upstairs they followed her into the kitchen where they found Jenny sitting at a table littered with coloured photographs.

'Jenny,' Matt smiled, 'Nice to see you again. I missed you at Zeffirellis. I did manage to make Nick's acquaintance though!'

'Yes,' Jenny grinned. 'He's never been able to live down the fact he thought you were a waiter.'

'Happens all the time.' Matt joked and then turned to Marcie. 'Marcie, this is Jenny, an old friend from the Mill days.'

Marcie and Jenny acknowledged each other with polite smiles.

'Jenny, what a nice surprise,' Tad said as he joined the group and then noticed the photographs on the table. 'What's this then? Happy snaps?'

'Yes, they're Mum's. I was just showing Faye the ones taken at Charlie's christening the other week.'

'Charlie?' Faye looked at her and laughed as she refilled the percolator. 'Is that what you call her?'

Jenny nodded. 'Mum started it and now it seems we're all doing it.'

'Mind if I see them?' Marcie asked as she pulled out a chair and sat down beside Jenny.

'Of course not,' Jenny smiled, gathered up the first pile and leaned towards her ready to hand them over one by one.

'You wanna see them Matt?' Marcie twisted around to look at him.

'Actually,' He said, giving her shoulder a squeeze as he looked down at them, 'I could do with some fresh air; later maybe.'

Jenny watched him move towards the French windows, throw them open and step out onto the patio. As Marcie took the first of the shots of Little Court from Jenny, Tad pulled up a chair and settled himself beside her, peering with interest around her shoulder.

'Hey this is some place!' Marcie said, turning to share the photo with him. She stared wide eyed at Jenny. 'Who owns it?'

'Ella's grandmother. We had the christening party there.'

'Of course, I forgot, you're related to...' Her voice trailed off in mid-sentence.

'It's OK Marcie,' Pulling cups from the cupboard, Faye turned with a relaxed smile, 'You can mention her name, I don't mind. Things have changed since you were here last.'

'Yeah, Tad was telling us how she saved your life.'

'I'm glad she was there,' Faye said, gazing out of the window where Matt was crossing the lawn, head bowed, hands in his pockets, 'it gave us a chance to clear up a whole lot of misunderstanding.'

There were more enthusiastic oohs and aahs from Marcie as she looked at the gardens, followed by interested questions about the family when the group shots appeared.

'You know I think you Brits are so lucky.' She said as Jenny began to gather up all the photos into two neat piles ready to put them back into their wallets. 'You've got so much history. Mind if I see these too?' She nodded towards the pile which Faye had left.

'Of course,' Jenny pushed them towards her.

'Hey!' She picked up the first photo, 'Now this is kinda spooky!'

'What is it Marcie?' Faye frowned as she placed fresh cups of coffee in front of everyone.

'Mrs Benedict, remember when we were here before the tour.' Marcie said, tapping the print with her finger. 'And I asked you if you had any folks in town?'

'Yes.' Faye nodded, returning with the milk and sugar.

'Well that cute kid I was telling you about, the one I saw in Langleys. This is him! Except...' she frowned and then shook her head. 'At the time I thought, short curly hair and dungarees, that it was a boy! But it wasn't, it's a girl!'

Curious, Faye took the photograph from Marcie, reaching across the table for her glasses at the same time.

'Good grief.' She said with surprise, and then showed the print to Jenny.

'That's Lucy, Ella's daughter.' Jenny looked surprised. 'Surely you've seen her before?'

'Strangely no, never!'

'What's wrong Faye?' Tad frowned.

'Here,' Faye handed the photograph to Tad. 'Take a look. Tell me what you think. Excuse me, I won't be a minute.'

As Faye disappeared from the room Tad's face creased itself into a wide smile. He looked out into the garden where Matt was returning from his leisurely stroll, hands still pushed deeply into the pockets of his beige cords. 'Well I'll be damned.' he said.

Jenny looked at the photograph then at Tad. 'Like Andy isn't she? Everyone says so.'

'She's the spitting image of her father all right!' Tad replied as Faye reappeared with a small walnut photo frame and took the print from Tad.

'Here,' Faye said, holding them both out to Jenny, 'have a look at this.'

'Heavens!' Jenny stared at the two photographs, Marcie at her shoulder. The resemblance between the two children was remarkable. Then suddenly Matt walked back into the kitchen and all eyes turned to him.

'What?' He stopped at once, staring blankly at all of them.

He had gone out into the garden to stretch his legs and get some fresh air Now, on returning to the house he found them all looking at him with a rather disconcerting air of conspiracy. He turned at once to Faye.

'Mum, what is it?'

'I think you had better see for yourself.' Jenny held out the photo frame and the coloured print to him.

'Well I know this one's me!' He said setting down the frame on the table, 'but who's this?'

'It's Lucy, Ella's daughter.' Jenny said watching him intently.

'Can't you see the resemblance?' Faye said excitedly.

He looked at the photograph again and then shook his head. 'No.'

'Well I can, and so can your father!' Faye looked at Tad who nodded in agreement. 'She's just like you!'

'Mum, a camera captures an image in a split second.' He said with an indifferent shrug. 'It's just coincidence that's all.'

'But Marcie's actually seen her, when she was here, before the tour. Isn't that right?' Faye looked to Marcie for support. She nodded her head silently, biting her lip uncomfortably, her eyes fixed on Matt.

Tad picked up the photo frame and studied it again. 'You were with Ella in Meridan Cross at the right time.' He tapped the photo, 'There is a possibility this child could be yours Matt. And there's something else. I've spoken to Ella. She's...'

'Stop it will you? Just stop it!' Matt's voice seemed to fill the room as he glared first at his father, then at his mother. Only moments ago he had felt in control of his life. Now here they all were, taking charge, pushing him in a direction he didn't want to go and all because of some tenuous link with a photograph.

'I'm sorry,' He said, lowering his voice, 'but I don't want to hear any more of this...this absurdness from either of you! Everyone in Abbotsbridge knows this child is Andy Macayne's. Now if you'll excuse me, I'm going to unpack and take a shower.' He dropped the photo onto the table and turned towards the door.

'But Matt, listen!'

'No Dad!'

'Matt...please!'

'Mother that's enough!'

As he turned towards the door, Jenny, who had been sitting, a silent spectator in this family argument, got to her feet.

'OK everybody!' She said, clapping her hands loudly and causing them all to look at her in amazement. 'Please. Sit down, will you? There's something I think you all should know.'

Rachel gazed around her mother's bedroom noticing how drab it looked. It probably hadn't changed much since her grandmother's death in 1949. Of course over the years there had been the odd layer of emulsion added to the ever thickening paint crust when the existing colour began to fade or her mother, in a moment of rashness, bought a job lot of bankrupt stock paint from one of the Miller boys. But why did it have to always be cream, when it could have been yellow or blue? Don't be silly Rachel, she reprimanded herself, they are cheerful colours and your mother has never been that.

She turned her attention to the dressing table and her real reason for being in a room normally off limits to her. Night-dress, bed jacket, hair brush and a bottle of Eau De Cologne. Very specific items from a woman who when she walked into the ward had been lying in her bed convinced she was not long for this world. Still, Rachel thought, she is in a bad way; in traction with a broken leg and a smashed ankle. Which means she won't be home for a while yet. *Thank you! Thank you!* She turned grateful eyes towards heaven.

Seating herself at the dressing table, she picked up the silver backed hair brush, gazing at the intricate but worn pattern on its back, wondering how old it was. A Douglas family heirloom, no doubt. The place was full of them; grotesque ornaments, dull, worm eaten furniture. Her mother seemed to cling to the past, both physically and mentally. It had made her cynical and begrudging. It had also made her old before her time. Pushing the stool back she eased open the top drawer and took out a clean but faded pink flannelette night-dress. Placing it on the bed behind her, she reached into the drawer again searching for the knitted bed jacket; she could just make it out, tucked towards the back. She pulled at it, felt resistance and realised it was caught over the back lip of the drawer. Getting to her feet she bent forward, gently easing the drawer open a little at a time. As she pulled the garment out, a narrow strip of old newspaper which lined the bottom of the drawer came with it. Placing the bed jacket neatly on top of the night dress she turned back intending to push the strip of paper back in, but stopped. For there, protruding from underneath the edge of the rest of the drawer lining was a brown envelope.

'So that's where she hides it.' She said to herself, realising she was looking at her mother's will. The discovery made her aware that the accident had robbed her of the opportunity to talk to her about Niall again. And now, with the prospect of Margaret in hospital for several weeks and likely to be totally preoccupied with her injuries once she was out, the subject would have to be put on hold indefinitely. It was hopeless, just hopeless.

She picked up the strip of paper, ready to replace it and then stopped. She fixed her gaze on the protruding envelope again and the looped capital letter 'E' just visible. E for Ethel.

She had to take a look then. It was impossible not to. Lifting the corner of the newspaper she snatched the envelope out angrily and crossed to the window, shaking with emotion. She felt betrayed. Her mother had never intended to leave her anything at all. What she thought was hers, what she had been threatened with losing had always been destined to belong to her mean old aunt in Taunton. With trembling hands she lifted the lip of the envelope and drew out a folded sheet of paper.

As the contents lay open to her, she gave a small gasp. 'Oh Mum! What have you done?'

'Ah Miss Sylvester,' Sister Martyn gave Rachel a welcoming smile, 'Come to see your mother have you?'

'Yes,' Rachel looked along the line of beds in Maddox Ward and noticed her mother was missing. 'Where is she?'

'We decided to give her a side room.' Sister Martyn nodded towards a blue door at the end of the ward, then seeing the surprised look on Rachel's face, she said, 'Don't worry, she's fine. We just thought…well,' she hesitated, 'that she needed complete peace and quiet away from the main ward.'

'More like the main ward needed complete peace and quiet away from her.' Rachel said with a smile. 'It's OK Sister, I think we both know the kind of woman my mother is.'

As she watched Rachel walk through the ward, Sister Martyn was amazed at the change. Yesterday after half an hour with this difficult and demanding woman she had left the hospital looking quite exhausted. But today she was different – assertive, confident. As she watched her open the door of the side room she wondered what could have brought about such a dramatic change.

'Hi Mum, I've got your things.' Rachel peered around the door of her mother's room.

'Put them in the bedside locker will you?' Margaret said curtly, lying propped against the pillows with her right leg in traction.

'You're looking better.' Rachel smiled cheerfully, tucking the clothes onto the top shelf of the locker.

'Don't feel it. Did they tell you why I'm in here?'

'To give you more peace and quiet Sister said. 'Rachel replied, sitting herself down next to the bed. 'Nice isn't it?' she looked around the room, 'You've got your own TV too. I bet you're pleased.'

'Well I'm not!' Margaret protested irritably. 'I feel as if I'm in quarantine. I can't be expected to stay for two more weeks *like this*! You just go and tell that uppity Sister she had no right shoving me in here. I demand to be transferred back into the main ward at once!'

'Sorry Mum can't do that.' Rachel said, running an unsympathetic eye over her mother.

'What!' Margaret pushed herself up onto her elbow, 'Are you defying me girl?'

'Yes, I am. And there's something else,' She said lightly. 'I've decided I will marry Niall.'

'If you do madam, you know full well what the consequences will be!' Margaret spluttered.

'Do your worst, I don't care anymore!'

'Such disobedience! Whatever's brought this on?'

'This!' Rachel pulled a crumpled envelope from her jacket pocket and handed it to her.

'What is it?' Margaret peered at it. 'You know I can't see a thing without my glasses.'

'It's a letter. I found it this afternoon when I was getting your things together. I can't think what it was doing in your drawer as it's addressed to Ella!'

Margaret's expression sagged. 'I forgot it was there,' she said, turning it over in her hands, 'I was going to burn it. Suppose I just couldn't resist holding onto it.'

'Whatever for?'

'The incredible feeling of satisfaction it gave me, that's what.' Margaret said clasping it to her chest. 'Not that you would understand of course!'

'No, you're right I wouldn't!'

'She had it coming!' Margaret looked at Rachel defiantly and then she said quietly. 'That Matt, or whatever he was called, came in the shop you see. He was in a hurry to get to London.' She stared at the envelope thoughtfully. 'Of course, I knew who he was. Well, you'd talked about nothing else that week. I was very helpful, told him I'd take the keys back to Willowbrook and see that Ella got the letter. Once he'd gone I couldn't resist opening it. It was a real shock when I discovered what had been going on between them. That she was about to leave her husband to be with him.' She smiled. 'It was just the opportunity I'd been waiting for to ruin her life!' Seeing Rachel's disapproving face she said. 'Well she ruined yours! Just like her mother did mine!'

'No she didn't.' Rachel shook her head, 'Ella is nothing like her mother. She's been a fantastic friend!'

'You know your trouble?' Margaret gave a cynical smile. 'You're just too damn trusting. You don't see the danger do you? Look at you now with Niall O'Farrell, accepting his proposal. You might have his ring on your finger but he's not going to marry you! He'll take what he wants and then scarper, just like last time, you stupid girl!'

Rachel looked at her mother lying there, twisting the facts to suit her purpose. She remembered what Ella had said about her mother being scared. But she was also something else. Totally selfish.

'Niall always loved me,' she said staring at her mother coldly. 'He didn't run away, he left Meridan Cross because of you!'

'Me? Don't be ridiculous!'

'Yes it was you! You threatened to send me away to live with Aunt Ethel permanently if he stayed in the village, didn't you? He left so that wouldn't happen to me. He left because he loved me. And now he's back you're not going to rob me of my happiness again. I'd rather marry with your consent, but if you can't give me that then I'll just have to go ahead without it!'

'I did what was right at the time!' Margaret scowled at her resentfully. 'I'm not going to apologise if that's what you think. Go on! Go ahead with your plans! But hear this! I shall make sure all the village knows how you've abandoned me to be with him.'

'Fine, go ahead,' Rachel said, getting to her feet and snatching the letter from her mother's hands. 'And I'll tell them all about this!' She waved it tormentingly at her. 'Then we'll see how much sympathy you get!'

'Give that back to me at once!' Constrained by her bedclothes and the traction, Margaret twisted awkwardly towards her daughter, but Rachel stepped back, out of reach. Margaret glared at her for a moment then realising her situation was hopeless, reluctantly conceded defeat settling herself down in the bed once more with a scowl. 'Do as you like then, I don't care.' she said grudgingly, her lips setting in a thin line. 'But don't come knocking on my door if things go wrong. I want no more to do with you. Now, give me back that letter.' she held out her hand.

'I can't. I need it.'

'What for?' Margaret's face twisted unpleasantly, 'To use when you need to get your own way again? You are an evil child!'

'It's you who's behaving like the child mother!'

Margaret looked affronted. 'Well, what *are* you going to do with it?'

'I'm going to hand it over to Ella.'

'You're really enjoying making my life a misery today aren't you? Well I can tell you now Miss, if you hand that over you'll be making needless trouble!'

'Oh I don't think so,' Rachel smiled, tapping the letter in her palm, 'this letter, believe it or not, is going to make things much, much better.'

The warmth of the late afternoon sun lingered across the garden at Derwent Close; bees buzzed and flowers nodded their heads lazily in the soft breeze. Beyond the high red brick boundary wall; traffic flowed and people went about their business as Matt sat on the patio with a glass of his Father's best malt, his mind running over the amazing events which had taken place in the kitchen earlier.

He saw Jenny getting to her feet. 'Lucy is your daughter Matt,' she said, her brown eyes fixed on his, 'Andy can't father children. He's infertile.'

'Now I've heard everything!' He waved a dismissive hand at her as he moved closer to the door, ready to take refuge in his room, to get away from all their pleased expressions but Jenny stopped him.

'Before you go,' she said. 'I really think you should hear the whole story first.'

He resisted, insisting he wasn't interested, that it was all a waste of time. But

Jenny calmly pulled out an empty chair and in a very relaxed voice asked him to sit down. He looked at Jenny for a moment, then at his mother and father and knowing he was outnumbered, gave in.

And so Jenny began; intricately locking the pieces of the puzzle together. Everything; right from day one. From that first fateful meeting in the college car park. As he took a mouthful of whisky, he contemplated the irony of it all. If he had only been brave enough to tell her how he felt about her it all might have been so different. Yet there was no way of knowing the depth of her feelings for him, she had hidden them so well. The story rolled on; his mother, her mother. They too had both played their parts in reinforcing the barrier to keep them apart. And then 1971 in Meridan Cross, when he thought that happiness was within his grasp. It had been, it really had been. He saw his mother and father nod in agreement. They had spoken to Ella; it was all true they said.

On the day he left for Spain, the Macaynes had turned up in Meridan Cross and although she was desperately trying to find him, she had been forced to go with Andy to Italy. But what had become of the note? He told Jenny how he had written it and left it at the shop with the keys. The worst place possible she said, for Margaret Sylvester had always held a grudge against Ella for what had happened between Niall and Rachel. It was probably read and destroyed within minutes of his departure. And so at last he understood her anger. Saw how she thought he had abandoned her. Jenny mentioned the newspaper photographs of him and Shandy Flynn, something that had obviously reinforced Ella's belief that his intentions had been less than honourable. But of course how was she to know that Shandy, hungry for publicity and totally infatuated with him, had fallen prey to some lying journalist eager to create a celebrity headlining story for his tabloid masters.

And then Lucy; they would never have found out if Andy hadn't started his custody battle to take her away from Ella. It had been a strange twist of fate, bringing everything full circle, that Marcus Goddard's father Henry had been a GP in Abbotsbridge in the fifties and early sixties and knew that Andy's mumps had left him infertile.

As Jenny finished, he got to his feet slowly.

'I don't know what to say.' He said looking at them all. 'If you don't mind, I think I need to be on my own for a while, to get my head around all this.'

He walked out into the garden, taking refuge on a bench in the old summerhouse.

Twenty minutes later Marcie joined him, slipping in to sit beside him, her hand automatically reaching for his.

'I'm sorry Matt.'

'What for?'

'Opening up this can of worms.'

'It certainly is that.' He shook his head.

'I came to tell you that I've just spoken to Doug and he needs us back in New York immediately. The LA meeting has been brought forward to Tuesday.'

The Ghost of You and Me

'What?'

'It's for the best.' She squeezed his hand tightly. 'I've checked with the TWA desk. There's an evening flight out of London. I've reserved seats. We can make it if we leave within the hour.'

'I can't.' He shook his head, 'I have to see Ella first.'

'We don't have time Matt. We have to leave within the next half hour if we're gonna make that flight.'

He stared at her blankly.

'Matt this is my future we're talking about!' She shouted at him angrily. 'Are you telling me you're going to jeopardise everything for some small town broad and her kid. God,' she gave a bitter laugh, 'you're such a fool; she doesn't even want you!'

'That's not the point, I still have to see her.'

'Well, I say you don't! Your priority is me.' She said, pushing a finger against her chest. 'This film is going to be the start of big things. You said this place didn't hold anything for you any more and that she was nothing to you. I need you with me in LA. I'm the most important person in your life. Me.'

'Of course you are Marcie and you always will be. But I'm not involved in any of the negotiations, that's Doug's responsibility. All I plan to do is to see Ella, then catch tomorrow's flight and be with you in LA by Tuesday evening.' he squeezed her hand. 'I've never let you down before and I'm not planning to now. It is just one thing I have to do before I leave, surely that's not too much to ask.'

'Sorry Matt, I want you on that flight tonight.' Stony faced she pulled her hand away and turned to leave. 'Now I'm going up to my room to get my case and I suggest you do the same. If you still insist on staying then I'll leave without you and you can take the consequences. I can and will have you fired, you know. So it's your choice; me or her.'

Matt watched her go. This was a side of Marcie he had never seen before and it made him feel uneasy. Her whole career had taken off in a spectacular way and with Hollywood showing an interest, he sensed there was a possibility she could soon become a big international star. He didn't like what he'd been on the receiving end of just a moment ago. It reminded him of how Kendal Conway, the first singer he had worked with at Maverick Records, had treated him. There was no way he wanted that kind of working situation again. But Marcie wasn't a hard, arrogant woman like Kendal; she was a warm, affectionate girl with an unconventional way of dressing. Maybe now the big adrenaline rush of the tour was over she was worrying about the screen test and meeting all the movie moguls in Hollywood, he thought, looking for excuses for her behaviour. Well whatever it was, he'd give her a few minutes to cool down and then go and find her. There was no way he was going to allow this silly spat to sour their relationship.

Ten minutes later when he eventually returned to the house he found his mother sitting in the lounge drinking coffee and reading.

'Marcie's gone.' She said calmly, looking up from her book, 'Left five minutes ago with your father to catch the London train. And boy she was in one hell of a temper. What's happened?'

'She came to tell me that the meeting in LA had been brought forward.' Matt said sitting down beside her 'And that Doug wanted us back in New York immediately. I told her I needed to see Ella first and she just flipped. Demanded I leave with her at once. That I was jeopardising her future if I didn't. Even threatened to fire me.'

'So what are you going to do?'

'Just what I told her. I'll see Ella, then catch the flight tomorrow and join them in LA on Tuesday evening. I'm not crucial to the talks, I'm just tagging along.' he laughed. 'She's going to have some apologising to do when I arrive.'

'Matt, how did she know the LA meeting date had been changed?'

'She said she had spoken to Doug, why?'

'Not from this house she didn't.'

'Are you saying she lied?'

'It looks like it; to force you to leave without seeing Ella.' Faye said closing her book and placing it on the coffee table. 'She's desperately in love with you, did you not realise that?'

'Of course, but I always made it clear there could never be anything between us other than a working partnership. I've always been honest with her.'

'I believe you, but do you realise this whole situation has brought out a deeper, more worrying issue.' Faye shook her head. 'The prima donna thing has started already hasn't it? Tantrums: giving you ultimatums. She was one angry young woman - and it won't end there either. Seeing her like this now, the bigger the star she becomes the worse it will get. Believe me, if you go after her, you'll live to regret it. Your father's convinced this Hollywood thing is just the beginning. She's got a huge future ahead of her. Soon others will manage her career. And no matter how much she says she cares about you, she'll ditch you without a backward glance if they say that's how it has to be.' She looked at him over the top of her glasses. 'Your time with her is over Matt. Bow out gracefully. You belong here now.'

'Thanks Mum, I'll bear your wise words in mind.' Matt said as he leant over and kissed her on the cheek. 'Now I guess, I'd better go and see Ella. Can I borrow the car?'

'The keys are on the hall table.' Faye said with a smile and picked up her book again.

He drove out of Abbotsbridge to Kingsford and Ella's house, where he sat for a moment admiring its comfortable exterior and trying to work out exactly how he was going to tackle this difficult issue.

As he was thinking of getting out of the car the front door opened and a slim, brown haired woman wearing jeans and a pale lemon shirt appeared. She sported two black eyes and a plaster covered the bridge of her nose.

She walked out to the car, a friendly smile on her face and introduced herself as Helen Baxter, Ella's housekeeper. She told him that Ella was staying on in Meridan Cross to help with the harvest and wouldn't be back for another week.

'Andy gave me a black eye once.' He said, wincing as he looked at her face.

'Did you hit him back?'

'Didn't get the chance to,'

'I guess I evened the score for both of us then,' she smiled, 'concussion, six stitches and an overnight stay in hospital.'

'I'm impressed.'

She laughed. 'So, are you coming in?'

'Not much point is there, if Ella's not here.'

'Don't you want to see your daughter then?'

'My daughter,' He repeated the words slowly as he got out of the car and walked with her into the house.

Nothing had prepared him for that moment. Entering the nursery and seeing her for the first time. She was in her playpen and when she saw Helen, immediately lifted her small arms towards her, demanding to be picked up. Helen lifted her up and talked to her quietly as she brought her over to him. Thumb firmly in her mouth she gazed at Matt with a serious expression on her little face. However, when Helen handed her to him there was no protest; she went willingly, tucking herself into the crook of his arm, almost as if she knew she should be there. He held her gently, smelled her soapy smell, and kissed the soft skin of her cheek. He felt the brush of her gentle curls against his face and the pressure of her small hand against the back of his neck. This is my child, he thought. I helped create this small, perfect human being. His mother's words *'You belong here now'* echoed in his ears. And holding Lucy in his arms he knew she had been right. His life in America was indeed over.

The sun was setting beyond the trees and the shadows beginning to lengthen across the lawn as he finished off the whisky, savouring the memory of that first meeting with Lucy. Helen had said the phone lines to Meridan Cross were still down after the bad storm which had spilled off the moors into South West Somerset. So currently there was no way of contacting Ella and on reflection he decided perhaps that wasn't a bad thing. It would give him time to work out exactly what he was going to say to her.

'Hi there, Faye said I'd find you here.'

He looked up to see Jenny emerging through the French doors, a cheeky grin on her face.

'I thought you'd gone home.' He gazed at her, surprised.

'I had, but I decided to come back to see how you were.'

'I'm fine. It's been a lot to take in though.'

'I gather you've seen Lucy.'

He nodded. 'I can't believe she's mine. She's beautiful.'

'Yes she is.' Jenny smiled.

'Jen,' He looked up at her from under his heavy fringe of dark brown hair. 'About Ella.'

'Yes?' Jenny eyed him curiously.

'Well, I've had second thoughts about ringing her. I thought maybe I'd drive out to Meridan Cross tomorrow to talk to her instead.' He smiled, 'I don't expect to be welcomed with open arms, but now I'm here we've got to sort all this out, if only for Lucy's sake.'

'Tomorrow?' Jenny frowned, 'I'm not sure that's such a good idea Matt.'

'Don't you think so?' Disappointment shadowed his face.

'No. I think you should seize the moment. Go this evening.'

'This evening?' He shook his head. 'No..no, I'm not ready. I need to get my act together first. The last time I saw her she gave me a real verbal mauling.'

Jenny gave him a sympathetic smile. 'If it makes you any happier, I can come with you.'

'That's really kind Jen, but what about your family commitments?'

'It's not a problem. Nick won't mind; in fact when he realises where we are going he'll be more than happy to look after the kids.' she took a swift look at her watch. 'I'll need to get home and sort them out first, though. How about if I come back to pick you up, say, at around eight?'

'Eight?' He thought for a moment and then gave a reluctant shrug. 'Yeah, I guess that will be OK.'

Jenny turned to go then stopped, pausing for a moment to look at him. 'Come on, there's nothing to worry about.' She said seeing his uneasy expression. 'She loves you Matt, she always has done. Trust me, everything is going to be just fine.'

Marcie sat in the VIP lounge looking out of the window, watching the continuous movement of planes arriving and departing across the tarmac in the grey early evening haze which hung over Heathrow. She checked her watch. They would be boarding soon. The call when it came would be a blessing. Her greatest wish was to be airborne and home. Back to the luxury of her penthouse in Sutton Place, overlooking East River. Tomorrow there would be less pain. Tomorrow she would take control of her own destiny. Move her life on. A new life; one without Matt. Of course Doug would be angry, but she was the star now, she called the shots. She could hire and fire who she wanted to, just like Kendal had in the old days.

She raised her head at the sudden blare of the tannoy, announcing her flight, calling her to the boarding gate. A sigh escaped her lips and sadness washed over her as she got to her feet. She had tried desperately to hold onto him, to keep him away from Ella. The ultimatum had been a crazy, impulsive thing to do, but it was a risk she thought worth taking. However, it had backfired on her big time and now she had lost him. But not forever she told herself - their time would come again, of that she was sure.

TWENTY FIVE

Saturday 1st September

In Meridan Cross Village Hall trestle tables had been set out ready for the Harvest Supper. Their bare wooden frames were covered with bleached white table cloths on which cruets and small pots of bright flowers were set at regular intervals. Outside another warm September day was drawing to a close as Ella helped Mary set places with a multitude of mismatched cutlery from the hall's kitchen drawers. Around the room, Niall, the Miller boys and other helpers from the village had hung straw garlands and plaited corn dollies along with red white and blue fête bunting borrowed from Laura.

On the stage, the harvest table had been scrubbed and was piled high with the best of the villagers' produce; huge marrows, carrots, onions, runner beans, turnips, swede and beetroot, sheaves of wheat and barley decorating its base.

'I love all this, you know,' Mary said, standing back to look at the room, the last few oddments of cutlery in her hand. 'Harvest Home,' she smiled thoughtfully, 'I think traditions like this are one of the really great things about village life, don't you?'

'Mmm.' Ella looked at her and smiled. 'Bit sad though, isn't it, the end of summer? Mist in the valley, evenings drawing in, that chill in the evening air.'

'All part of the circle of the seasons,' Mary said brightly, 'Constant change. I love it. I can see you've spent far too long in the town my girl.'

'You're probably right.' Ella laughed, 'Is that it then? Are we finished?'

'Yes, I think so,' Mary nodded, 'let's go and see how Laura and the others are getting on in the kitchen.'

'The tables are laid Laura. What's next?' Mary said as they both entered the kitchen where everyone seemed to be engrossed in some sort of food preparation.

'Puddings,' Laura replied, resting her knife against the huge joint of beef she was working on, 'The glass dishes are in the cupboard and there are several giant tins of fruit salad on the worktop,' she pointed with her knife, 'Oh, and the salad cream needs to go out. Rachel left a new box of bottles under the table in the corner. And after that perhaps someone could set up the cups and saucers for the coffee on that long table next to the stage.'

'Right, let's be getting on with it then,' Mary said looking at Ella, 'If I look after the puddings can you do the rest?'

Ella nodded and went in search of the salad cream.

She was almost at the end of the second table when the main door of the hall creaked open and Rachel walked in

'Now that's what I call brilliant timing,' Ella said, smiling as Rachel approached the table, 'I've almost finished here. You can give me a hand with setting out the coffee cups and saucers.' She pointed to three large boxes sitting on the floor. 'I think they may need a wash first though.'

'Sure.' Rachel nodded, pulling off her jacket and hanging it over the back of one of the chairs, 'but first I need to talk to you about something.'

Ella looked up at the clock, aware that there was still a lot to do and less than four hours to go before most of the village would descend on the hall. 'We're a bit tight for time Rach, could we do it later?'

'Sorry it has to be now.' Rachel said firmly, taking the bottle of salad cream from Ella's hand and placing it on the table.

'Sounds important,'

'It is. I've just come from the hospital.'

'Is everything all right?'

'No. Well, yes it is actually.' Rachel replied. 'But it's not what you're thinking. You see I had to take Mum in a change of night clothes and, well to cut a long story short,' she leaned over and rummaged in her coat pocket, 'I found this tucked under the lining of her dressing table drawer,' she handed the envelope to Ella. 'I wouldn't have looked at it, but I saw the first letter - an E protruding out from a tear in the drawer lining. I thought it was her will you see and that she was leaving everything to Aunt Ethel. So I had to take a look,' she smiled, 'and it's just as well I did.'

Rachel realised she was babbling now, but she had to do something to fill the silence in the room as Ella carefully turned the envelope over stared down at her name.

'I know this handwriting,' she said as she looked up at Rachel, 'It's Matt's - this is the missing note, the one he said he'd written. Where did you say you found it?'

'It was in Mum's dressing table drawer.'

'What was she doing with it?'

'It's a long story.' Rachel reached into the box, pulled out the last two bottles of salad cream and set them on the table, 'I'll tell you while we're sorting out the coffee cups.'

Mel stood in the dining room, facing the window, watching the late afternoon sun casting shadows across the lawn. In front of her stood a half empty bottle of Famous Grouse, in her hand an empty glass. She ran her tongue over the roof of her mouth. It felt furry and unpleasant. She picked up the bottle and looked at it, frowning for a moment at the bird staring back at her from the label. Of all the disasters which currently made up her life, there was one issue which kept burning in her brain as she drank. This issue desperately needed closure but in order to achieve that she needed some answers to very specific questions first.

'So who can it be?' She asked the grouse, her voice a low, angry growl. 'Exactly who is the guilty party who has fathered Ella's brat? I guess there is only one way to find out and find out I must if I'm to get any peace.' She set the bottle and empty glass down on the sideboard and wandered a little unsteadily across the room towards the door. 'Now where are my car keys?' Reaching the hall, she grabbed them from the table. 'I'm going to get some answers out of that slut of a daughter of mine.' she said to the mirror. She studied her reflection silently for a moment convinced that the dishevelled woman she saw must be someone else. She frowned, leaning towards the apparition with its smudged make up and untidy hair, noticing the large coffee stain on the front of the blue dress it was wearing. She peered at the image for a moment then with a shake of her head left, slamming the front door behind her.

It was six o'clock. At Willowbrook, Mary sat in the back garden, chatting to Laura as they drank an early sherry and discussed final details for the forthcoming evening. Mary looked up as Ella emerged from the interior of the house, her expression serious.

'Any luck?'

'Dead as a dodo,' Ella shook her head, 'Lines must still be down.'

'I'm not surprised,' Laura said watching Mary pour another glass of sherry, 'It was an amazing storm. I've not seen anything like it in years. The damage it left. Parts of the village look as if a hurricane has passed through. Still my darling, there's always tomorrow. It won't take long to drive back to Abbotsbridge, will it?'

'I guess not,' Ella said with a disappointed shrug as she eased herself into one of the patio chairs, 'but when I put the phone down, I suddenly remembered. The last time I saw Tad, when he spoke about Matt coming home, I'm sure he said it was going to be a quick visit and they would be catching the early evening flight to New York tonight. If that's the case, it's too late, he's probably gone by now.'

'Well we'll just have to go after him!' Mary said handing Ella a glass of sherry, 'Top up?' she brandished the half empty bottle at Laura.

'Don't mind if I do Mary,' Offering her glass Laura turned her attention to Ella, 'Mary's right you know. If he's gone, well we'll just have to fly out to New York and find him.'

'What all of us?' Ella looked at them both in amazement.

'Of course, all of us!' Laura and Mary chorused, then looked at each other and laughed.

'Well isn't this cosy?'

'Mother?' Ella turned to see Mel hovering at the small side gate.

'Yes, me!' She pushed through into the garden and stood there looking at all of them.

'Have you been drinking?' Laura said noticing the high colour in Mel's cheeks and her untidy state.

'What if I have?' Mel glared indignantly at the older woman.

'Mother, if it's about the farm…' Ella said, seating herself beside the two older women.

'The farm; whatever made you think that? I have no interest in the farm!' Mel interrupted indignantly. 'No, my darling daughter,' she waved an accusing finger. 'I've come to get a few answers from you!'

'Mel, if you've come to start a row,' Mary gave a heavy sigh, 'this really is not a good time.'

'Ah yes, of course, Harvest Supper tonight isn't it? I noticed the signs as I drove through the village. Well heaven forbid I should interrupt such an important event in your pathetic little lives,' she said sarcastically, 'but this won't take long.' She focused on Ella once more. 'My life,' she said, stabbing herself in the chest with her finger, 'is now in ruins.' She looked at all three of them. 'My husband has left me, he's already in the process of divorcing me and I am now homeless and penniless. And all of this,' she glared at Ella, 'is because of you and your disgustingly depraved behaviour!'

'Mother what are you talking about?' Ella frowned.

'That child of yours,' Mel continued. 'There are rather nasty rumours circulating in Abbotsbridge that Andy is not her father.'

Ella put down her glass and got to her feet, facing her mother calmly. 'That's right, he isn't.'

'You admit it?' Mel looked horrified.

'Yes. You asked a question, I answered it truthfully. I'm sorry it's not what you want to hear.'

'So who is?'

'That, Mother,' Ella said quietly, 'is none of your business.'

'Of course it's my business!' Mel shrieked.

'Is everything all right?'

Niall pushed through the gate, Rachel beside him, the Miller boys following behind.

'Fine,' Mary said with relief as she saw her son standing there, 'Mel is just leaving.'

'No I am not!' Mel shouted. 'I will not budge from here until I get an answer!'

Laura left her seat and came to stand behind Ella, placing a hand on her shoulder.

'In that case Mel, I suggest we discuss this somewhere a little more private.' She looked at the Miller boys, 'This is family business.'

'On the contrary Laura, this is very much village business,' Mel countered, fixing the older woman with a hard stare. 'Because from the little I have learned, I gather Lucy's father comes from Meridan Cross.' She turned to look at the two young men, 'So? Which one of you is responsible? Is it you?' she said to Ash.

'Me? Are you daft or something?' He rolled his eyes as if he was dealing with a simpleton.

'Ella's a good friend.' Rowan looked steadily at Mel, 'We don't take liberties with good friends.'

'You expect me to believe that you two have behaved like monks,' she said disdainfully. 'When your father has populated half the county with his illegitimate offspring.'

'Now, just a minute!' Rowan took a step towards her.

Ignoring him, Mel turned her attention to Niall.

'Maybe it was you then, Golden Boy,'

'It was not!' Niall said indignantly.

'You're a liar!' Mel glared at him, 'Admit it; you did it to spite me because I took her away from you! I had great hopes for my daughter you know; so many plans and schemes. Not that she was ever grateful for all my hard work,' she said viciously, 'managing to disgrace me like this.'

'Stop it!' Ella shouted. 'Stop it! It wasn't him!'

'As Ella says,' Niall said calmly, looking from mother to daughter, 'It wasn't me. It couldn't have been. At the time I was twelve thousand miles away in Australia.'

'Well who *is* Lucy's father then?' Mel fixed her gaze on them one at a time. 'Mr bloody nobody?'

'If you must know its Matt Benedict.' Ella said calmly.

'What?' Mel's eyes widened with surprise, 'That thin, scrawny, odd thing?'

'He isn't odd and scrawny as you put it, he's…'

'I don't give a damn what he is!' Her mother's eyes welled up with angry tears. 'How could you do this to me? It was bad enough your brother taking that Taylor girl for a wife. But what you've done is far, far worse! Disgracing the family with your adulterous carryings on and passing your bastard child off as Andy's!'

At such a vicious outburst Laura's hand went to her mouth, Mary crossed herself and everyone else stared in silent shock. It was Ella who broke the silence, taking a step forward and bringing her hand in a stinging slap across her mother's face. With a sharp cry, Mel staggered backwards holding her cheek, shocked and surprised at such an unexpected attack.

'She hit me!' She choked, 'Did you see that? She hit me!' Seeing Ella's expression she began to back away fearfully towards the edge of the garden.

'You dare to talk to me like that,' Ella said calmly, watching Rachel step aside as Mel retreated through the gate and out of the garden, 'after what you've been guilty of yourself with Bob Macayne. If Liam no longer wants you Mother, no doubt it's because he's at last aware of what's been going on behind his back all these years. I'm glad he's gone. He deserves better. Now please leave.'

Mel stood just outside the garden, her hand at her throat, watching her hostile daughter and six unsympathetic faces staring back at her. A small whimper of fear came from her throat then she turned and fled back around the house to her car, eager to be away from Meridan Cross and this nightmare as soon as possible.

As Mel's Spitfire roared down the track from Willowbrook and turned onto the main road with a squeal of tyres, Laura turned to Ella with a smile. 'So Matt is Lucy's father. How splendid! I think we need to catch that flight to New York as soon as possible don't you?'

Lord of the Harvest, once again
We thank Thee for the ripen'd grain;
For crops safe carried, sent to cheer
Thy servants through another year

With Nelson Miller on the piano, Ella stood singing along with the other villagers as the Reverend Farr, having just blessed the harvest for the year, returned to his place at the head of one of the tables. When the hymn finished, there was a solemn moment while grace was said, then with a noisy scrape of chairs everyone sat down. From the kitchen at the rear of the hall, mill owner's wife Diana Tucker and the Meridan Cross Women's Institute appeared with bowls of salad and hot boiled potatoes which they placed down the centre of each run of tables before sitting down to join in the meal. Rolls were passed and buttered, wine was poured and the whole room erupted in to laughter and conversation.

'Well, what an eventful day.' Laura said helping herself to potatoes, 'Where do you think Mel's gone now?'

'Back to Bob I expect.' Ella said. 'They deserve each other!'

'Yes they do,' Mary agreed, passing the basket of rolls down the table to the outstretched hand of Sybil Masterson, 'Good riddance to the pair of them.'

The meal progressed. As the main course plates were cleared away, the fruit salad and jugs of cream were brought out. Next to her, Ella overheard Rowan Miller and John Tucker discussing the big storm. Two large beech trees had fallen near his mill. She smiled. Rowan, just like his father, was never one to miss an opportunity - he was negotiating a price to remove them both.

Ella felt a hand on her shoulder and looked up to see Rachel there.

'Are we still going to do the photos for the church magazine?'

'Yes - Grandma,' She looked across the table at Laura, 'Did you remember your camera?'

'Oh bother! I knew there was something!' Laura tutted, 'It's still on the hall table.'

'Don't worry.' Ella got to her feet, pulling her car keys from her bag, 'I'll go back for it; it won't take me five minutes.'

Doggie Barker came out of Sedgewick Wood, three rabbits slung over his shoulder and a brace of pheasants in his hand. Not a bad haul for an evening's work he thought. Tom at the pub would be well pleased. He stopped and held out his wrist, letting the moonlight catch the face of his watch. Eight forty five.

'I hope they've saved us some supper at the Village Hall.' He said looking down at his canine companion. Toby gave an optimistic whine, he hoped so too. 'Come on then,' He said, 'we'll be there in ten minutes if we take the short cut.'

He skirted the perimeter of the wood until he came to the spot where the footpath reached the edge of the railway embankment. Climbing over the stile he dropped silently into the grass and slithering down the bank began following the track towards the ruins of the old station.

Mel sat behind the wheel of her Spitfire staring out into the night, watching the stars. Twenty four hours ago she had inhabited a different world, one with plans and schemes. Now she was here with nothing, her life in ruins. After leaving Willowbrook she had driven back to Abbotsbridge feeling humiliated and angry, her mind full of her confrontation with Ella.

She reached Conniston Drive just after seven, calmer now and longing for her bed and a couple of sleeping pills to knock her into unconsciousness for the night. Tomorrow, she told herself I'll feel much better and can begin to sort out the mess I'm in. Turning into the driveway she drove up to the front door of the darkened house and parked in front of the pale stone porch. Slipping from behind the wheel, she searched for her house keys in her bag. Eventually finding them, she walked around the car and climbed the three graceful semi circular steps to the front door. As she raised the key to the Yale lock, she thought how strange it was that she had never noticed its brightness before. It was only when she found the key no longer fitted the lock and noticed the small scrape marks in the paintwork around its circumference that she realised why. It was new. Someone had been to the house in her absence and changed it.

'Oh bugger!' she swore loudly. What was going on? Quickly she made her way through the side gate to the rear of the house but when she inserted the back door key into the lock, it didn't fit either. Something was wrong, very wrong. Her gaze travelled upwards. A small vent in one of the guest bedroom windows was open. All she needed to do was get the ladder from the garage and she'd be inside in minutes. However, when she reached the garage door she found it had been secured with a heavy padlock.

'Oh God!' She bunched her fists into her face tightly, wanting to scream with frustration, realising that Bob had wasted no time in repossessing his house. She was locked out with everything she owned still inside. She found a phone box a mile from the house and dialled his number. Mrs Catt answered, her voice frosty when she realised who was on the end of the phone. Bob she was told, had dinner guests who had just arrived. He was busy. She was forced to explain her problem to Mrs Catt who left the phone, returning moments later. 'I'm sorry,' she said, 'Mr Macayne says there's nothing he can do this evening. He'll arrange for someone to come round in the morning.'

'Well that's not good enough!' Mel thundered. 'You just go back and tell him I want someone to sort this out immediately!'

Mrs Catt disappeared again.

'Mel!' She heard Bob's voice on the phone.

'Bob thank heavens! I'm locked out of Conniston Drive. I need to get back in now!'

'As Mrs Catt told you,' He said coolly, 'there is nothing I can do tonight. I'll get Ernie Clarke out first thing in the morning.'

'I want someone out here *now*!'

'Sorry Mel, that's not possible.'

'Bob if you don't do as I ask, I'm coming right round and I'm going to cause the biggest fuss you've ever heard, dinner guests or no dinner guests!'

'I don't think that's very wise Mel!'

'Why, what are you going to do?' She said sarcastically. 'Call the police?'

'No need, they're already here. The Assistant Chief Constable is one of my dinner guests. Now please *go away*!' He said forcefully. 'As I said someone will be round first thing tomorrow morning.'

'But what am I going to do?' She shouted down the line in angry frustration. 'Where will I sleep?'

'Simple! Book yourself into a hotel!' He said uncaringly before the line went dead.

Mel stood inside the phone box and checked her handbag. She had three pounds and thirty two pence in her purse. Her cheque book, she realised to her dismay, was sitting in the dressing table drawer back at Conniston Drive. A hotel room was therefore out of the question. Collecting all the remaining change from her purse she thumbed through her address book and started to make calls to everyone she knew.

Ten minutes later she pushed out of the phone box, tearful and tired. She had phoned all the members of her Ladies' Circle in turn, but none of them could put her up for the night. Imminent holidays, grandchildren, friends or elderly relatives stopping over, they all had plausible excuses for not having a spare bed she could occupy. Her fate, it seemed, was to spend the night in her car in the crumpled clothes she was wearing.

Anger, resentment and a desire to carry out some act of retribution against the one person she blamed for all this made her turn the car back to Meridan Cross. And now she sat in the Village Hall car park talking to herself; weighing up options, none of which she realised were sensible, not while Laura and Mary were around. She could hear the laughter and conversation coming from the hall.

If only I could get her on her own, she thought. If only… She stopped. The main door to the hall opened and she saw a familiar figure step out into the night and head across the car park.

'Yes!' She hissed.

As Ella unlocked her car and got in, Mel gave the ignition key a violent twist and heard the engine fire. With a howl of triumph she released the handbrake and slammed her foot down hard on the accelerator pedal, sending the Spitfire shooting across the rough gravel of the car park straight towards the Mercedes.

Ella settled herself behind the wheel of her car. The Reverend Farr, catching her in the corridor on the way out, had delayed her departure so now in her journey to retrieve the camera, speed was of the essence, before the tables were pulled back and dancing started. She slotted the key into the ignition, started the engine and flipped on the headlights. As she turned her head slightly to check her exit was clear before putting the car into reverse, the vehicle's interior was filled with a blinding light and there was a terrific bang as something hit the rear of her car. She felt the Mercedes shoot violently forward and screamed as she was thrown against the steering wheel and her head cracked against the windscreen. Dizzy and disorientated, she pulled herself up to see what was happening, aware of choking petrol fumes and a sticky wetness trickling down her forehead. As she hauled herself onto the steering wheel, she saw a wall looming ahead and then the front of the car seemed to explode and crumple in front of her. Moments later she was travelling upwards and outwards, wrapped around the twisted frame of the windscreen. The cool night air briefly touched her face before she was aware of a mass of red brick hurtling towards her and the whole world dissolved into blackness.

Still on the railway line, Doggie was no more than twenty yards from the Village Hall. The noise, like a small explosion, stopped him in his tracks. Then he saw the car, hurtling out into the night air from the car park above, like a wingless bird, the splinters of the perimeter fence stuck to its radiator grille. Close behind it came a second vehicle following the same aerial pathway towards the old water tower.

'Jesus, Toby!' He gasped and began to run.

Back in the Village Hall, Mary was the first to hear the noise and got to her feet.

'I didn't imagine that did I?' She said looking first at Laura, then at Rachel.

'No. I heard it too.' Laura nodded towards the jug on the table, 'And I'm sure that water rippled.'

'First hurricanes now earthquakes, whatever next?' Mary laughed.

Others had also heard the noise. People were getting to their feet - frowning, curious. Nelson Miller left his seat and went over to speak to the vicar. The Reverend Farr stood up and appealed for calm, asking the villagers to remain where they were while Nelson investigated. Nelson walked over to the main door, threw it open and walked out into the darkness. He was back in seconds.

'A car's gone down the railway embankment,' he said, 'and there's a bloody great hole in the fence!'

'Ella?' Laura shot a worried look at Mary.

'No,' Rachel shook her head, 'she went ages ago.'

'I doubt it's anything to worry about.' Nelson said in an effort to dilute the panic he could see in people's faces. 'Someone probably forgot to put their handbrake on. 'Best everyone stay put for the moment please.' He lifted his arms in a calming gesture to those present. 'Lads!' he said Rowan and Ash. 'Get the Land Rover; we'll use the spotlights on the roof rack to see what's happened. Best you come too.' he said, turning towards John Tucker and Niall.

'Hadn't we better phone for an ambulance?' Laura said. 'Someone might be hurt.'

'Nelson didn't mention anyone was in the car.' Reverend Farr said, looking at Nelson for confirmation.

'Don't think there was, Missus Kendrick.' Nelson shook his head, then seeing the expression on her face looked at his companions and said, 'We'd best go and check first. Don't want to call them out needlessly do we?'

Minutes later Ash ran back into the hall. 'I'm going to call the fire brigade.' He said. 'There are two cars down there not one and it reeks of petrol!'

'Two?' Laura frowned.

'Yes. There's this car all twisted up with a red Spitfire on top of it!'

'Red Spitfire!' Rachel gasped, remembering the one parked outside the farm earlier that afternoon when Ella's mother had been there. Without another word she got to her feet and ran from the hall.

She could see the eerie glow of the Land Rover's spotlight lighting up the trees on the other side of the railway line as she stepped out into the car park. A few villagers whose curiosity had led them to ignore the Vicar's request stood huddled on the edge of the car park looking down the embankment. As she reached them she could see clearly below the twisted metal of the cars which had both come to rest against the station's old red brick water tower, their doors wide open.

'I wouldn't think there could be anyone left alive in that,' Niall said, nodding his head towards the crumpled remains of the bottom car, 'It's so badly crushed.' He peered at it again. 'Doggie's here. He saw it happen; said one car must have rammed the other.'

Laura and Mary appeared together, both looking worried. 'Is Ella not back yet?' Mary asked.

Rachel shook her head.

'So what's it all about?' Laura said. 'Ash mentioned there were two cars.'

'Yes. And I think one's Mel's.' Rachel said looking at both women.

'Mel?' Laura looked astonished, 'Are you sure? But why would she have come back here?'

'I think.' Rachel said staring at the gaping hole in the fence and then at where they were all standing. 'She might have come back for Ella. The Mercedes,' she pointed to the spot where they stood, 'was parked right here.'

'No Rachel, that's just a coincidence.' Laura shook her head, 'She's at Little Court by now.' Seeing the anxious expression on Rachel's face she turned to Mary. 'Be a dear and drive back to the house, will you, just to make sure?'

Catching Mary's departing Land Rover in her headlights, Jenny turned her Escort into the village hall car park and stopped. 'Whatever's going on?' She said, seeing the small clusters of villagers grouped together around the parked cars.

'Beats me,' Matt leaned on the car door and pushed it open, 'There's only one way to find out.'

As they crossed the car park, Niall appeared out of the darkness, 'Jenny,' he looked taken aback. 'This is a surprise, what brings you here?'

'Hi Niall, this is Matt. We came to find Ella.' Jenny stared at the broken perimeter fencing just visible between people gathered at the top of the bank. 'What's all the fuss about?'

'Good to put a face to a name at last,' Niall gave a nod and smiled at Matt then turned his attention back to the car park. 'Oh, two cars have gone through the railings and ended up at the bottom of the embankment.'

'How did that happen?'

Niall shook his head. 'We don't know. We've done a head count. Everyone's here except Ella, but she went back to Little Court ages ago to pick up a camera.'

'But we've just come from there,' Jenny replied, 'the house is in darkness, no sign of life.'

Niall motioned them to follow him. 'Come on, we'd best find Rachel'

She was standing with Laura not far from the edge of the embankment, someone's jacket cloaking her shoulders, shivering slightly in the chill of the evening air.

'Jenny! Matt!' Laura clasped her hands and smiled as she saw them approach. 'Oh this is so wonderful! Ella will be pleased. She won't be long; she's just gone back to the house to collect something.'

'But we've just come from Little Court Mrs Kendrick,' Jenny said looking at Laura then at Rachel, 'Ella's not there.'

Laura frowned and a white faced Rachel turned immediately to look at the bottom of the embankment. Below she could see John Tucker, Rowan and Ash standing by the two cars. John was looking into the Spitfire and shaking his head. Another man who she recognised as Nelson Miller was lying on his stomach shining a torch through the side window of the crushed car beneath it.

Rowan broke away and began walking slowly back up the well trodden grass of the embankment towards them.

'Rowan?' Rachel looked at him fearfully as she reached her.

'There's a woman in the Spitfire. She's dead.' he said, shaking his head, 'I best go; Dad asked me to ring for an ambulance, just in case whoever's in the silver car is alive.'

'Silver!'

Rachel realised Matt was beside her. She felt his breath hot on her face and heard the anguish in his voice as he stared towards the tangle of metal.

'It is the Mercedes!'

He pushed past them both, desperate to get to the bottom of the slope as soon as possible. 'Ella!' He shouted. 'Ella!'

The fire began when he was half way down. Starting as a small flicker under the bonnet of the Spitfire, it gradually licked onto the spilled petrol and with a low greedy whoosh engulfed both cars within seconds. At the first sign of smoke, Nelson Miller was on his feet, grabbing his torch and joining the other men as they moved back. People in the crowd screamed, while Laura, Rachel and Jenny stood frozen with horror, watching Matt hurl himself down the slope towards the burning vehicles. As he reached the bottom he was intercepted by John and Nelson who grabbed his arms and hauled him back. He fought them like a wild animal, screaming out Ella's name, demanding they let him go, that he had to reach her. Then as the flames grew higher he seemed to realise the hopelessness of it all. His body sagged and they released him gently onto the grass where he knelt rocking backwards and forwards. Holding his head in his hands he began to sob.

Leaving Rachel to look after Laura, Jenny slithered down the bank to him. She knelt beside him, wrapping him in her arms, conscious of the fact that she too was weeping.

Around her people were running and shouting; a human chain had formed; buckets of water were being handed down the bank. Someone brought the extinguisher from the hall and handed it to Nelson, who paced backwards and forwards trying to douse the flames with it. The whole area was filled with acrid smoke, making Jenny cough. In the distance quite distinctly she could hear sirens. The fire brigade was on its way. In a world gone mad she wanted to scream you're too late! You're too late! And then suddenly she heard something; a voice carried on the night air, clear and distinct, above all the chaos.

'Over here! There's a body. Someone get Dr Beckwith!'

TWENTY SIX

Wednesday 12th September

The funeral was held in Meridan Cross. When the committal was over a small trickle of mourners gradually dispersed, moving slowly between the headstones, heads bowed, voices muted. A grey drizzle had started, lowering the sky and leaving a smoky haze of cloud through the trees on the summit of Hundred Acre Wood.

Laura and Mary, sheltering together under a large black umbrella, made their way out of the church yard and down the gravelled path towards the lych-gate and Laura's Bentley parked just beyond it.

'Has anyone been able to reach Liam yet?' Mary asked, her voice a raised whisper.

'Nick's already spoken to Mac Wilson,' Laura replied, 'he'll break the news to him when he calls in next.'

'I still can't believe it.' Mary shook her head, 'Such terrible goings on in a peaceful place like Meridan Cross. Dreadful: simply dreadful!'

'Yes.' Laura nodded. 'And then all the awful press interest afterwards. Like a pack of hyenas they were descending on us like that, wanting to pick every last piece of flesh from the bones of it all just to sell their trashy papers.'

'They were out of luck though, weren't they?' Mary replied. 'Even Margaret managed to hold her tongue. Tom Bennett told me she'd turned down a five figure sum!'

'How very out of character,' Laura raised surprised eyebrows, 'but then I hear she's done a U-turn on Rachel and Niall's wedding too.'

'Yes, very strange that, after such violent opposition to it all.' Mary answered as the rain suddenly became heavier and they paused to shelter under the lych-gate.

Laura gave a quiet smile. 'Well, I think it's wonderful that Rachel and Niall can now go ahead with their wedding plans. A little ray of warm sunshine amid all this gloom and uncertainty.'

'Yes,' Mary nodded. 'They were chatting to Reverend Farr at the end of the service. He's taken them back to the vicarage to check dates. Ah, here they are now.'

Across the road, two figures were hovering in the Rectory porch. Niall ventured into the rain first, opening out a large dark green umbrella and holding it out as Rachel tucked herself under it, holding onto his arm. Seeing them she waved, and dodging the puddles they crossed the road to where the two older women stood.

'Well?' Mary looked at them inquisitively, noting the pleased expression on both their faces. 'How did it go?'

'Fine,' Rachel smiled up at Niall. 'We've made an appointment to see Reverend Farr next week.'

'And the good news is,' Niall interrupted. 'That 22nd December is free; which means we'll be able to have our Christmas wedding!'

'That's wonderful.' Mary's expression brightened.

Laura nodded. 'I'm so happy for you both.'

'No more news from the hospital then?' Niall looked hopefully at his mother then at Laura.

'No.' Laura shook her head, her eyes blurring with tears. 'I phoned just before the funeral. Matt says there's no change. My darling girl is still in a coma I'm afraid.'

Matt looked out of the first floor window, watching the sombre grey of the day outside. The first wet slaps of rain had just touched the glass and small, thin rivulets were beginning to slowly trickle down. The sun, overcome by the sudden rush of miserable cloud, had long taken refuge. Without its warmth the world seemed a dreary, unhappy place. How long had he been here he wondered? Eight or was it ten days? He'd lost count. But stay he would. Snatching sleep in the small room he'd been allocated. Keeping his vigil. Desperate to be there when she woke up; if she woke up.

He turned to look across the room where Ella lay, eyes closed, shadows of blue and purple bruising still covering her face, a gauze pad over the four inch gash just above the hairline of her left temple. The swelling in her brain had gone down and she had come off the ventilator four days ago. At the time the balding consultant standing at her bedside had been confident that things were going in the right direction. Since then, however, all she had done was lie there, in a strange no-man's-land of life that was no life at all. He was heartbroken.

His mother arrived just before lunch with her usual delivery of sandwiches and a large thermos of coffee. 'No change then?' She said one eye on Ella.

'I'm afraid not.' He shook his head sadly.

She stayed with him for two hours. He was glad of her company. A comforting hand in his; her conversation a distraction from the silence within this room with its white walls and clinical smell.

When she left he drank the coffee but found he could only manage one sandwich. He left the bag in a corner ready to hand it to her when she looked in again. Turning back from the window, he took up his place again in the chair beside Ella. Taking her hand gently he kissed her finger tips.

'Ella!' He said fiercely. 'Please! Wake up!'

He looked at her again. It was hopeless. She looked like a Tussaud's waxwork.

'No improvement then?'

He looked up to see Katie, the little red headed nurse who made regular checks on Ella standing at the other side of the bed. She gave him a sympathetic smile.

Watching her as she went through her usual routine, he shook his head feeling defeated. When she had finished she left, giving him a comforting smile. The door creaked behind her and there was silence; he was alone once more.

Gazing at Ella, he remembered things he'd read in the paper about victims of accidents just like hers. People who had been in comas for years, only to have their life support systems switched off eventually, when grieving relatives realised there was no hope. The thought of such a decision having to be made was more than he could bear. He leaned his head into the palm of her outstretched hand, feeling a heavy weariness envelope him. He rested there for a moment, his eyes closed. Then all of a sudden he opened them again, frowned and lifted his head slowly. He stared down at her hand. There was movement in her fingers; he had felt movement in her fingers!

'Ella!' He rubbed his eyes and looked at her face. 'Ella.' he whispered softly. Was there movement there? He was sure he'd seen a brief flutter under the paleness of her lids. He gazed down at her hand again. It was motionless against the sheets, the fingers tilted slightly upwards as if holding some invisible object. He reached out and held it in his for a moment, but there was no resistance - no movement at all.

This is all my imagination, he thought. I've been here for over a week with no proper rest. My mind is in overdrive. He looked at her hand again, porcelain stillness against the pale blue of the bedding. Nothing was going to happen, nothing at all. I'm so tired, he thought, so desperately tired. Leaning forward, he rested his head gently against the softness of the bed and closed his eyes again.

'Ella I need you.' He said, burying his face in the bedclothes. 'Please come back to me.'

His voice trailed off as he felt something soft touch his head and begin to move gently through the thickness of his hair. It reached his face; the cool, soft touch of fingers tracing their way slowly over his cheekbone, lingering for a moment on the rough stubble of his chin. He raised his head slightly to find Ella's grey eyes were open and fixed on him. She withdrew her hand and lay there staring at him silently.

He sat up but his heart sank as he saw only blankness in her face. The doctors had warned that on regaining consciousness there was a possibility of memory loss. Then quite unexpectedly she smiled at him, heavy-lidded and drowsy like a child who had just woken from sleep.

'Matt? Is it really you?'

The Ghost of You and Me

He nodded.

She gazed around the room. 'Where am I?'

'In hospital, you've been very ill.' He replied, reaching up to punch the red emergency button above her bed.

'What happened?'

'You had a very bad accident.'

She raised a hand to her head and frowned. 'Did I? I don't remember...'

Just at that moment the doors parted and the red headed nurse appeared. Seeing Ella lying there awake she smiled and left, returning moments later with a couple of white coated doctors.

Matt patted Ella's hand as he got to his feet aware he was in the way now the doctors had arrived. 'I've a few people to call; they'll want to hear the good news that you've woken up. I won't be long.'

Ella watched him leave. She turned to the nurse who was adjusting the blinds at the window.

'What day is it?'

'Wednesday 12th September.' The nurse turned and smiled at her. 'You've been asleep for ten days.'

'Ten days?'

'Yes,' the smile was there again. 'And that boyfriend of yours, well he must love you so much.' She said with just a hint of envy, 'Do you know, he's been here by your bedside ever since they brought you in? He told me he'd even given up his job in America so he could stay here to be with you...'

Later, when Matt returned, he came to sit by Ella's bed and took her hand in his.

'Laura and Mary are on their way and Mum will be here later.' He said. 'Everyone's over the moon at the news that their Sleeping Beauty has woken up.'

'I'm not much of a Sleeping Beauty at the moment.' She said with a tired smile as she relaxed back on her pillows. 'I insisted they gave me a mirror. How silly was that? I look as if I've gone ten rounds with Jo Frazier.'

'Don't worry, the bruising's only temporary, it won't stay long.' He said running a soft finger down her cheek.

'I was also told I've been in a coma for ten days.' She looked at him thoughtfully, 'You know what that means don't you?'

'No?' He frowned.

'I've missed my twenty fourth birthday.'

'Never mind,' Matt laughed, 'we can throw a big party to celebrate when you come out of hospital.'

'We?' She gave him a curious smile. 'Are you planning to stay then?'

'Only if you want me to.'

She considered his words for a moment. 'Well since you've been here ten days already...' she hesitated, 'I guess you might as well stay a while longer.'

Matt smiled to himself, realising someone had been talking. Probably Nurse Katie, chatty little thing that she was. 'Did you have any specific length of time in mind?' he asked.

'Well I was wondering…' She gazed up at him, her grey eyes filled with love. 'Would forever be asking too much?'

'No,' He said as he leaned over and kissed her. 'I think forever sounds just about right.'

On 22nd December 1973 Meridan Cross village celebrated the marriage of Rachel Sylvester to Niall O'Farrell. Following the service, the Reverend Farr blessed the civil marriage of Ella Macayne to Matt Benedict. Both events took place at All Hallows Church and Laura Kendrick opened the doors of Little Court Manor to host a joint reception for both couples. Family, friends and villagers were invited to join the celebrations. Issy Llewellyn took charge of the catering and Nelson Miller and his sons the music. A good time was had by all, especially Margaret Sylvester who totally out of character, cried during her daughter's wedding ceremony and later at the reception danced with Doggie Barker and got very drunk.

The End? Not quite
Joanna Lambert will be back with her new novel
Between Today and Yesterday
in 2011

Lightning Source UK Ltd.
Milton Keynes UK
21 October 2010

161668UK00004B/32/P